THE TATTOOED HEART

JEZRA KAYE

3Ring Press
New York

Library of Congress Control Number: 2012932776
ISBN: 978-0-9793527-8-2
eBook ISBN: 978-0-9793527-9-9

Published by 3Ring Press
191 St. Marks Avenue
Brooklyn, NY 11238

Printed in the United States of America

First Edition: April, 2012
10 9 8 7 6 5 4 3 2

Book and Cover Design by Jonathan Fulton
Cover Photo © 2006 Eva Serrabassa
Author Photo by Ben Strothmann

**Visit www.thetattooedheart.com
and www.3ringpress.com**

Without my friends and family, this book, and perhaps I, would not exist.
My love and thanks go to Jerome Harris and Laurika Harris-Kaye.
To my writer's group, Rose Rubin Rivera, Anne Lopatto, and Mary Moreno.
To Maggie Kydd, for holding down the fort.
And to Heather Lewis—author, alchemist, teacher, rest in peace.

My deepest thanks go to Lucy Osborne and Cindy deStefano for
generously guiding me through your worlds. You made Gracie's journey
rich and resonant.

one

It must have been the panther.

There's no other reason I would have let a big, dumb, good-looking frat boy hang out after hours at Stacy G's, except that I liked his tattoo.

Normally, nobody stayed past closing time. I'd kick the last few customers out, and then I'd wash down my bar and put away the bottles, straighten the place up a little, lock the doors, pull the grate down and sprint three blocks to my rented room with a can of Mace tucked into my hand in case I ran into some kind of trouble.

But the trouble I ran into that night wasn't on the street; he was right there with me in the bar at four o'clock in the A.M. Sexy, sloe-eyed, too tall, way too young and sixty pounds bigger than I am. I don't know why I bothered with him, but I was tired and bored and maybe I thought Frat Boy was just what I needed to shake up my routine. I must have thought he'd be sleek and polished like the panther tattooed on his arm.

Talk about false advertising!

I was straightening up the room when he put the move on me, so I laughed, and ducked it. "I'm cleaning," I said, half-flirting. "Don't distract me."

The point, which any halfway intelligent person would have got, was *hold your water, we'll get to that.* But this guy apparently didn't get the message. Instead, he grabbed me by my neck and crotch, and hoisted me up, slamming me on top of the bar. I can tell you, that killed the mood.

I tried to scream, but that's hard to do with someone's hands around your throat. So when he started in on my clothes, I dropped my arm behind the bar and went for the first thing I could reach, which turned out to be a bottle of Johnny Walker Red I'd left in the well for one of my regulars. Time stopped moving long enough for me to swing it at his temple, and the wild girl gods must have been out that night 'cause the bottle broke clean on his stupid head and the glass fell away and smashed on the floor and nothing rained down on me but scotch.

By the time Frat Boy was finished screaming, I'd twisted away and was on my feet; and just before I reached the door, feeling grateful that I hadn't locked it yet, it slammed wide open and in came a man I'd never seen before. A big, hard-looking man, gleaming with righteous anger and seemingly bent on saving my ass.

He took in the scene—Frat Boy was now lurching toward us, his face streaked with blood—and then my Good Samaritan did the thing that cracked my heart into a thousand pieces. He grabbed my wrist and pulled me behind him, out of harm's way.

When he dropped my would-be attacker to the floor, it was almost an afterthought.

"Thank you," I said, fervently.

He blew on the knuckles of his right hand. "No problem. You got a bandage around here?"

"Maybe. Let me check the back. You want a drink?"

"Sure." His smile had a warm glow. I felt like I'd spent my whole life sleeping inside a block of ice, and now that smile was going to melt the ice and leave me naked in a world I didn't know.

I went and found the first aid kit and wrapped his hand, and then I called the police. When they showed up twenty minutes later, Frat Boy was mumbling in his sleep and Marcus and I were sitting at the bar drinking Patrón.

First thing they tried to do was arrest Marcus. I had to stamp my foot to get their attention. "Not him," I yelled. "The white guy!"

Finally they heard me. They mopped up the perp, stood around while I locked up the bar, offered to drive me to the hospital—an offer that I declined—glared at Marcus and drove off.

After that, I took him home so I could thank him properly.

It seemed to be a big night for tattoos. Among the many impressive things that were revealed when Marcus took off his clothes was a big dragon that wrapped around one very large, very hard bicep. Its tail swept gracefully down Marcus's left arm. Its body wrapped around his back and its head curled up over his shoulder. Its stark, cunning eyes looked straight into mine when, after we'd made love, I lay with my head on Marcus's chest. I felt like the dragon was checking me out, trying to decide if I was good enough to be with his owner.

"Where'd you get that thing?" I asked, tracing it with an appreciative finger.

"Back east," he said. "New Bedford, Mass."

"Army?" The guys I knew with tattoos had all picked them up at some base or other.

"Nah. I don't believe in killing people."

"Did it hurt?"

"Sure."

I cuddled closer. "So why'd you do it, if it hurt?"

He smiled. I could feel it in his chest, and when I looked up, the smile was a little sad. "Well, I didn't have much of anything, growing up. I wanted something they couldn't take off me."

"Who?" It wasn't like me to ask all these questions. I usually didn't want to get involved.

"Cops. Gangbangers. Anybody. You know."

His hand was warm on the back of my head, and I found that I was nuzzling against it, or maybe I was nodding my head to say *yeah, I know just what you're talking about.*

"It's pretty," I said. "The dragon. Like you."

That made him laugh, and he pulled me up on top of him so we were looking eye to eye. I wondered if the dragon was jealous.

"You're the one who's pretty," he said, which wasn't something I was used to hearing. Usually men said I was hot, but Marcus looked like he meant "pretty." Then he kissed me, slow and tender, as if he was drinking the secret of life. As if we had all the time in the world.

I didn't realize until that first night with Marcus how sick I was of the SRO where I'd been living the past few years. The Gendarme—a fancy name for what was basically a flophouse—was dingy and drafty and usually smelled of booze and piss. Marcus took one look at the lobby, at the vinyl chairs with knife rips in them, the cage where the night clerk locked himself in, and said, "You deserve way better than this."

I didn't know what he was talking about. But the next day, when I woke up to find that I was still wrapped tight in his strong arms, I started thinking that, if this lasted more than a week—if this didn't turn out to be drive-by sex—it would be nice to entertain Marcus in a place where he could take a leak without going down the hallway.

Of course, I didn't really think he'd stick around for even a week. But when a month went by and I was still looking at that dragon tattoo in bed each night, we started talking about a real place to live. And lucky for us, there were places in the Mission. We settled on a two-room walk-up that was painted white and had high ceilings.

The Mission was low-key in those days. It was still mostly Mexican, with some white old-timers and students and hustlers, people who liked paying cheap rent in a half-decent neighborhood no one had ever heard of. Every block had a restaurant with a Mariachi band, and a sidewalk stand where, for a dollar, you could buy a burrito the size of your head. People were mostly friendly, and the ones who weren't gave you fair warning—though truthfully, since I didn't speak Spanish, it may have been a lot rougher than I knew.

Our landlady was happy to have what she took for a respectable couple on the premises. We paid on time and stayed out of trouble. We even did a little maintenance for a few bucks off the rent each month, taking out the trash and sweeping the sidewalks on Tuesday and Thursday when they cleaned the streets.

By that time, I was working in the Mission, too. I'd been sick of Stacy G's, even before getting slammed around by Frat Boy; sick of the yuppie clientele, those spoiled brat kids who ordered blender drinks and wanted to tell you how great they were. Eventually I found work at a small neighborhood bar called the Tijuana. I opened up at six each morning, brushed off the felt pool table, cashed people's VA checks, served them a liquid breakfast and otherwise left them pretty much alone. It probably would have gotten old real fast—particularly getting up that early—but after two weeks Miguel, the owner, moved me up to managing nights.

Even at night, the Tijuana crowd was no-frills: Hookers and bikers; working men and waitresses; locals trudging home from the swing shift, dragging their groceries and sometimes their kids. The money wasn't what I was used to—unlike the manicured crowd at Stacy G's, nobody at Tijuana tipped me for putting extra cherries in their drink—but the place was lively. It kept me awake. I hired Marcus to do some maintenance and act like a bouncer when someone needed bouncing.

With both of us working, there was enough money to furnish our apartment after a fashion. I bought some throw pillows for the bed, and we got a 26-inch TV. We even paid Rosita, at the fabric store, to sew some bright blue curtains for us.

It was the most settled I'd ever been. And I was just starting to believe it might last when that first Carnivale came around.

Carnivale isn't really a carnival, and it certainly isn't a holiday. It's more like a yearly ritual—an excuse for everybody in the Mission to let down their hair and get sloppy drunk. The beat cops all take their guns off. The bar owners pour double shots on the house, and put people's drinks into plastic cups so they can take them out on the street.

That night, my boss Miguel, who wasn't usually on the premises, let a guy ride into the Tijuana on a horse. It was a friend of his, or else Miguel was just impressed with the guy's nerve, so when the man and his horse bellied up to the bar, Miguel served them each a Seven-and-Seven. I can't stand those, personally—they're too sweet; I don't drink anything sweeter than Johnny Walker Red—but the horse liked that Seven-and-Seven just fine.

Of course, when Sanitation showed up, Miguel wanted to claim that I was the one who'd let the horse in. Probably I should have kept my mouth shut, but I never could stand to be the fall guy. I told them it wasn't me, that I knew a horse's ass when I saw one; and then I smiled at my boss.

Well, Miguel didn't like that smile one bit. Tension had been brewing between us over the little matter of my never getting a raise, and this was his chance to act tough, with an audience, plus get rid of too-expensive me.

He opened the register and took a bunch of bills out and threw them in my face. He called me *puta*, a prostitute. So then I had to scoop up the coins in my pocket—my night's tips, a pitiful pile of change—and throw them at him. One slapped Miguel in the eye. He screamed, and I figured that was fair, since I was now unemployed and Miguel was just embarrassed.

The next day was Decoration Day. It was cold and dreary gray, even for spring in San Francisco, and I was teary, unfocused and desolate until Marcus offered to take me to my baby sister's grave. We bought a little peony plant, its pink, blowsy blossoms tippling in the wind, and we took the bus to South San Francisco, past the blue and pale green and honey-colored wood frame houses leaning out towards the sea, to the cemetery. I bought a little plastic trowel— not very strong, but strong enough—and we planted the peony at the head of Rosie's grave, and I cried and Marcus asked if, when we got home, I wanted to go to São Sebastãio and light a candle for her.

By then, we'd been together for months, but I'd never gone to church with Marcus. Growing up with a mother who liked to praise Jesus while she was swinging a belt had turned me off to the whole idea. Plus Marcus's church did their thing in Portuguese, a language he'd grown up around that sounded like gibberish to me. So instead of going to church, we went home and lit a memorial candle we bought at the corner bodega. We pulled the shades down and smoked some weed and danced to Dinah Washington and I cried some more. I felt pretty sorry for myself, and I thought *once a year, why not?*

The next morning, Marcus woke up early and said, "One of us has to get a job."

I said, "You have a job, what are you worried about?" And he said, "No, I don't. I went back to the bar after you fell asleep last night and punched Miguel in honor of your sister."

All I could do was hug him and whisper *thank you,* I was so moved.

I was sorry to see the job at Tijuana go; and not just because we needed the money. I liked being a barmaid. I liked drinking my meals, breaking up fights, feeling superior and compassionate at the same time, stealing from the boss (though not very much) and playing those endless free games of pool. I liked smashing an occasional glass to make a dramatic point, and having an excuse for anything I wanted to disown later.

Marcus didn't care for it much. I don't think he'd ever had a job he liked; he was more of a drifter at heart than me. So I offered to go job hunting. It's easier for a white girl, that's the simple truth.

But there was some kind of recession going on, and the long and frightening short of it was, there weren't any jobs—not for anybody. Every day I spent pounding the pavement just made that all the more clear.

I tried the temp agencies. The newspaper ads. The government jobs office. I even tried other bars in the Tenderloin, though I knew that, after the way I'd quit Miguel, no one would hire me.

By now, Marcus was looking as hard as I was. We were hurting for money, and when he heard through the Mission grapevine that Miguel was willing to take me back, he said, "Go talk to him."

"You go," I said, not too helpfully since Miguel hadn't offered to take Marcus back.

"Naw," he said, "we'll starve together."

We started trying to hustle small change. We tried delivering circulars, which paid about thirty cents an hour. We tried doing odd jobs, which paid better but there were none.

Marcus hired on as a day laborer, the only one in the crew who wasn't Mexican. By then it was summer, and they trucked him inland to lay cement; it was ninety-four degrees in the shade and he spent the money on Gatorade, trying not to faint from the heat.

I knew I'd hit bottom when I started wondering what the sweatshops in Chinatown paid, and that's when I decided on the strip club.

"Over my dead body," Marcus said.

"I'm not gonna touch anything. I'm just gonna shake a little tail feather."

"That's what they all say, at first."

I said, "How the hell would you know?" and Marcus had to shut his mouth.

Girl-O-Rama had started out tongue-in-cheek—a '50s, car-hop-style café where girls happened to take their clothes off—but by now the fun was gone and nothing but the sleaze remained. They always needed more girls there, probably because the owner didn't pay shit and people didn't stay. I knew they would hire me.

Once he saw that I was serious, Marcus took me over to Teddy Morris for my costume. Teddy made everything that got stripped off in the Tenderloin. She was a thousand years old, but you could see she'd once been pretty in a push-up bra kind of way.

"College girl," she said squinting at me.

"Watch your mouth," I answered.

She said, "I'm not talking about your *life*, I'm talking about the *part* you're going to play onstage."

"*Part?* The only parts they want to see are tits and ass."

"You got it all wrong," she said. "People want romance. Mystery. Illusion." Then she sighed heavily. "No one cares any more. It's all gone downhill to horse shit."

I was about to tell her she was crazy when Marcus opened his mouth and said, "What was it like when you were dancing, Miss Morris?"

It was such a smooth move that I gaped at him. But I shouldn't have been surprised, 'cause I already knew that Marcus could melt any woman's heart—deaf, blind or lesbian included. Hadn't he won me over from the first? Marcus had a way of making you feel special that wasn't about trying to hustle you. Who else would have massaged my feet when I was dead tired from bartending? Who else would have cooked me paella, even though it took hours in the kitchen? No one else had always made sure that I got off like a rocket each time we had sex.

So by the time he was finished paying attention to Teddy, she had spilled her whole life story. And while she was talking she forgot about that college girl nonsense and made me a good serviceable pair of pasties and a g-string.

I planned to wear a short robe over them. That was fine with Marcus, who knew that the less I was wearing to begin with the less sexy my striptease would be. And Teddy, though she was scandalized, was so in love with Marcus by that time that she wasn't going to criticize his girlfriend. He kissed her hand when we left, and she giggled.

Don, who managed Girl-O-Rama, was another story. He wasn't going to be soft-touched by Marcus, and he certainly wasn't going to be charmed by me. Not that I was trying.

"Get the fuck off my stage," he yelled, when I was two minutes into my debut number. The place was filled with customers—and it was four in the afternoon, so I'll leave it to you to imagine what class of people I was entertaining.

"What's a matter with her?" one of them yelled. "What's a matter, Don, you blind?"

The others started chanting, "Stay, stay, stay, stay." So Don threw up his hands and I stayed.

"I'm paying you to *strip*," he told me after I came down off the platform, "not walk around in your underwear."

"I did strip," I said calmly, trying not to show how cold I was in three square inches of clothing, total. Trying not to show how desperately I needed that job.

"Where's the sex? Where's the mystery?"

Where the hell did they get these lines? "You must know Teddy," I wise-assed, hoping to get him turned in another direction.

"Everyone knows Teddy," he scoffed, "the old bag. I'm talking about *you*. You get two layers of clothes on tomorrow night, and you take 'em off like you mean it, or you're outta here with no pay."

I sighed wearily, but there was no argument to be made. The man clearly had his standards to uphold. The next day I went back to Teddy and bought her version of a co-ed ensemble, with a tight sweater that was hell to take off and one of those short, awful pleated skirts and real goddamn saddle shoes, like it was 1950 instead of 1982. I was almost more embarrassed about the clothes than about stripping them.

Not that I was crazy about doing that, either. My main problem was the clientele. The men that gathered round the narrow stage at Girl-O-Rama glistened with sweat. They stunk of it; they thought it was excitement.

I thought it was fear. They knew what they were looking for wasn't there—they knew that Don was milking their wallets, and the dancers and waitresses thought they were trash—but if they drank enough they didn't *remember* that they knew.

Imagine all the "love" in your life coming from a skinny, shivering crack-head who can't stand to look at you when she's not high, crawling under the table on naked knees to give you a half-hearted blow job. That's how pitiful the whole thing was.

We were playing those men like crazy, and damned proud of it. Don made us hustle drinks between our sets, and while we were laughing and cooing and leaning in close enough to rub against the men (those of us who let them touch the goodies) or pretend that we might (those of us who usually didn't), we were thinking about food and shoes and our kids, if we had them, and the bills we were going to pay with their tips.

I would sooner have died than let one of them touch me. When their hands extended in my direction, I bent my knees and twisted out of the way, throwing out some line—"Hey, Sweetie," or "Ease up, Lover Boy"—to soothe what I imagined was the sting of my rejection.

But maybe the rejection didn't sting them. Maybe it was all part of the game.

Truthfully, I didn't know who was in the worst shape at Girl-O-Rama—us or them. All I knew was that we were the ones pulling in the money.

Marcus wasn't thrilled with my new job, but he didn't hate it either. Not when he had all those long, luxurious hours at home alone. Plus, he was a damned good wife. While I was dancing at Girl-O-Rama—my body prancing around the stage while my mind went as far away as it could go—he dusted the furniture and pruned the ficus plant he'd bought with the last of his Tijuana money and took our clothes to the laundromat and worked up recipes for black bean soup and Cajun spareribs and sweet-and-sour chicken and broccoli. I'd get home about five a.m. and find the place clean, the bed turned down and something tasty on the stove. I'd eat my dinner, take a long, long shower that was hot enough to wash off most of the night, and then climb into bed, where 180 pounds of solid celebration was waiting for me. Marcus was so warm and strong, it was pretty easy to shut out the job—and I was good at shutting things out.

Mostly, I felt like a hunter, coming home late and victorious each night, my body soaked with perspiration, my g-string stuffed with animal cash. I teased Marcus that, except for a couple of obvious things, he should have been the woman and me the man. That would have bothered some women, but the truth is, I was bone-deep happy.

We both were.

two

I didn't have the dream as often, once I started living with Marcus. Some nights I could tell it was coming—that dead-weight, dull-edged sense of despair was usually a pretty good clue—and I'd pretend to fall asleep and then get out of bed and spend the night sitting up on the bathroom floor, reading a book or just watching time pass.

But some nights, I couldn't help myself. Some nights I'd be so wrung out that even though I could feel the dream hovering, I couldn't resist tumbling into sleep. Tumbling straight into hell-to-pay.

Marcus would wake me, his strong hand on my shoulder. "You're having that dream again," he would say, carefully wrapping me in his arms.

The dream was hellish, but familiar. It always took me time to come out of it. Sometimes when he woke me, I'd snarl at him. Sometimes I would try to hit him. Sometimes he'd wake up to find me flopped half off the bed, asleep, unbalanced, sobbing my guts out. Someone about to step off a bridge. I never told him why I was crying, though he asked me every time.

One night the dream got so bad that I threw up on the floor beside the bed. Marcus sat up, turned on the light and dragged me into the bathroom to wash up.

"We're going to the beach tomorrow," he said, running water into the tub.

"The beach? You know I gotta work!"

He pulled off the little muscle shirt I slept in. I had to raise my arms so he could get it over my head.

"We're going to the beach," he said. "You need sunshine."

Well it's true that, working nights in a bar, you get pretty short on Vitamin D. It's supposed to be good for depression. Maybe he thought I needed a dose. But generally speaking, I wasn't depressed. Generally speaking, I was just haunted.

After my bath, we went back to bed and had mind-numbing sex until I finally fell asleep. When I woke up again it was ten in the morning and Marcus had rustled a car from someone.

We drove to Bolinas, a place I'd heard of in hippie rock songs but never thought I'd ever see. Just miles out of the city, it was like crossing into another world. We drove along cliffs that were high enough, you knew if you screwed up you were going to die real quick. I'd never known that Marcus could drive, but he handled that car, a 1973 Camaro, like he'd spent his whole life on a race track. All I could do was hang out the window looking at the trees and rocks. The ocean sparkled far below us, cut into diamond patterns by the sun.

How had he known I needed this?

Bolinas was a sleepy town. I'd thought it would be loaded with tourists, but either it was past their season or they didn't want to drive along those cliffs. Most of the people we saw were white, but they were harmless-looking, left-over hippies, folks that might have been artists or musicians or gardeners or something else I didn't even know about. We walked along the town's main street, taking our time, looking into store windows, our hands laced together, talking about the things we wished we could buy. We stopped at a little café and ate hamburgers, washing them down with ice cream cones. I felt like I was 10 years old—the kind of 10 years old I'd never been—sneaking off for a special day with somebody who cared about me.

Finally, we walked down to the ocean. I could see this was a pilgrimage for Marcus. As soon as his sneakers touched the sand he bent down to take them off, tying the laces together and hanging them across his shoulder. "You, too," he said, pointing at my clogs.

I was a little skeptical. How the hell did I know what was hidden in that harmless-looking sand?

"Come on," Marcus said, "take your shoes off. I'll carry them."

Sighing, I stepped out of them. I never got the hang of refusing Marcus, except when it was for his own protection, or something near to life-and-death.

I squished my toes in the stuff, gingerly.

"Isn't that better?" he asked, smiling.

Was it? I closed my eyes and felt the warm grains of sand tickling my feet.

"Yeah," I told him. "It's not bad."

We strolled along the water's edge, past rich-looking houses on the cliffs above. "Are you sure this is OK?" I asked, not knowing if I was more worried about the houses falling down on our heads or about the rich people having us arrested.

"Hush," Marcus said, pulling me close and putting his arm around my shoulder. "Just check it out. Don't think about it."

We walked in silence for a long time, waves tickling our toes, wind ruffling my hair, sunshine burning the skin on our faces. The waves made a sound that was soothing and rich, like I always imagined a lullaby would be. The sky, when I looked up, was heartbreak blue—so clean and pure you thought you must have made a mistake about what it was like to live on earth.

"I grew up by the ocean," Marcus said. "New Bedford used to be a fishing town."

"You came up in a place like this?"

"Not like this," he smiled gently. "There are no other places like this. But I grew up pretty near the ocean."

An image popped into my mind: Filthy alleys, seedy bars, men on the prowl for little boys. I knew he hadn't had a fairy tale life. It wasn't even the same ocean.

"Can we take a shell home?" I wanted to have the beach shell, but what I wanted more was to change the subject. When I bent down to pick it up, it was rough and mottled, gritty with sand. It wasn't going to win any beauty prizes, but it smelled like freedom, like today.

"Don't see why we can't," he said. "The clam is done with it, that's for sure."

I loved that Marcus knew things like that. To me, it could have been a lobster shell. But Marcus knew all kinds of stuff. He knew how to cook, how to tie knots, how to make love. He knew how to iron shirts and dance the merengue.

Eventually the sun went down, in a rush of color you could almost feel. After that, it started getting cold, and soon, with the breeze coming off the ocean, I was shivering in my shorts and tank top. But neither one of us wanted to leave, so we sat huddled behind a big rock, listening to the waves and watching the stars come out. Marcus kept me warm by wrapping me up in a bear hug that was better than any coat.

There was only one moment when the cold seeped inside me. That was when he asked about my dreams. "I try not to bug you about it," he said. "But last night…"

"I was just scared." I shrugged. "It passed."

"You're sure you don't want to tell me what you're dreaming?" He breathed a kiss into my hair. "Maybe it would help to talk it out."

Poor Marcus, he couldn't stay out of my head, though it wasn't a good place for him. But I wasn't going to make up some lie, tell him some bullshit just to shut him up. And I sure wasn't going to tell him the truth. My heart wasn't big enough for that kind of pain.

"Yeah, I'm sure." Could he feel how I'd tensed up? It wasn't so much that I *didn't want to* tell him, it was more like totally unthinkable. So I just shook my head and waited until he got that I really meant it.

We stayed on the beach for a long time more, but finally we were both ready to leave. We got up and stretched out the kinks—it was cold as soon as he wasn't holding me—and walked gingerly across the sand that was wet now, heavy with the night air.

At the beach's edge, we put on our shoes. And then we walked to the borrowed car, and got in it and this time I got behind the wheel and drove with me still navigating.

I did that because Marcus couldn't.

Marcus didn't tell me at first that he had never learned how to read. At first it was, "My eyes hurt." "I'm too tired." "I hate maps." "Have a look at this for me, would you?"

I knew something was wrong, but I didn't know what. Maybe I didn't want to know. One day I got mad and blew up at him: "Read it your goddamn self, I'm not your servant."

That's when he explained to me.

Marcus was smart, informed, well-spoken. He could talk to people from any walk of life. He listened to the news on National Public Radio. People who can read just squander it; he knew more than most of them.

I didn't care if he could read or not, but he did. It bothered him when I read a street sign, or brought home a magazine or peeked at my horoscope over someone's shoulder on the bus. I think it made him feel left out.

That's why I started trying to teach him—and "try" was the operative word. I was good at reading; I'd always taken to it, since the first time Lucille, my second foster mother, opened *Babar's Circus* and pulled me onto her lap. Nobody else had ever done that, and nobody ever would again, but Lucille was enough. She got me hooked for life. The problem was, I'd learned so easily that I didn't know how to pull reading apart and put it back together in a way someone else could understand.

Not that it would have mattered if I'd been a better teacher. I gradually came to realize that something you need for reading was scrambled inside Marcus's brain. We would lie in bed and I would take his hand and make him trace letters on my stomach, the way I liked to trace his tattoo.

The difference was, he couldn't do it. He couldn't form the shapes and the sounds at the same time, no matter how often he tried. After a while, and him being nearly in tears once or twice, I stopped trying to teach him, and we fell back into doing the usual things with his hands. I couldn't keep pushing it, knowing how badly failure was making him doubt himself, and pretty soon we went back to acting like his not being able to read was a secret.

All this time, I had a little secret, too. It was called benzedrine. I started taking bennies when I began stripping at Girl-O-Rama. They were better than coffee, and they were cheap—five bucks would get you a hundred pills, each one good for hours without sleep. I liked the buzz. I liked how you could mellow them out with alcohol, or top them off with marijuana and feel like you'd just blown some coke. They were a poor man's high, just right for me and my lifestyle.

Most of the time, I liked how Bennie felt. But once in a while I'd get the shakes so bad I couldn't dance. Couldn't sleep. Did stupid things, like putting my fist through a glass door instead of pushing it open because there was so much energy vibrating through me I didn't know where my hand stopped and the door began. That one cost me eight stitches, and afterwards I tried to be more careful. I tried not to drop a bennie if I was angry, or depressed. I tried to not take more than five or six or seven or eight a day. I didn't want Marcus to find out; I didn't want him worrying about me. And he would have, he hated seeing people he loved in danger. But at least, I figured, it wasn't meth.

My best friend, Blondell, was hooked on crystal methedrine. Her example was what kept me off of meth, because when I met her she'd already been dancing at Girl-O-Rama for five years and I figured *this is where you end up when you take that shit*. Plus, I tried it once.

That was during my second week at Girl-O-Rama, and I was tired. You'd think that being a bartender, being on my feet all night, would have prepared me for fifteen minutes dancing on stage, fifteen minutes off, but it didn't. The stress was worse, being a dancer. Unlike with bartending, you had no control over the attitude you got. You couldn't cut people off or bounce them out. You couldn't take their drink away or smack them on the head with something, like I did one time when this big Polynesian kid tried to strangle his brother. As a dancer, you just had to stand there naked and take it, no matter how mean or vile or in your face they got.

The other thing that made being a dancer stressful was the schedule. If you think fifteen minutes off-stage is a rest, I have to tell you it isn't. It's a quick piss break, and just enough time to start a conversation before the two girls on before you get off, and then you're on again.

Don liked his girls to work in twos—one black, one white; one fat, one thin, stuff like that—and he paired me with Blondell because, between us, we fit all the categories. She was a short, black, skinny lesbian with dyed yellow hair, and I'm a straight, white, curvy brunette. That was the reason he stuck us together, for contrast. It wasn't because he thought we'd be friends.

We'd trudge onto the stage, strip and shake our butts for fifteen minutes, hurry off the stage, hang out for a few, bitch and moan a little and next thing you knew we'd be back up again. Four hours of that and I was ready to kill myself. I'd have traded it for a twelve-hour bartending shift in a heartbeat.

Finally, Blondell said, "I can help you."

"Shit," I said, "I'll take whatever you've got." I didn't ask her what it was.

We had to find a quiet place to hide backstage, cause Blondell wasn't sharing with anyone but me. She chopped the stuff up, we snorted it, and then we waited a minute or two and hit some more, which took up our whole break so that neither one of us got to pee.

Halfway through our next act, the stuff finally worked its way up through my congested nose and hit my brain like a fuel tank explosion. I thought sparks were going to shoot off my fingernails; when I looked at my hands

I could see the molecules of blood pulsing through the swollen blue veins. Funny how I'd never watched blood moving in my hands before.

"Dance!" Blondell hissed. She didn't want me to get fired. She didn't want me telling on her, either.

When the set was over, walking down the stairs that led off stage took the most extreme caution I'd ever used in my life. I knew that if I put one foot wrong, I'd go crashing down and it was hundreds and hundreds of feet to the floor.

I felt Blondell's hand clamp around my elbow.

"What the hell *was* that stuff?" I whispered.

"Shut up, Gracie!"

"What?" I asked her again when we got backstage.

She grinned. "Crystal methedrine, baby. You like it?"

I tilted my head and looked crossways at Blondell. I could see inside her skull. I could see little globs of yellow dye, shimmied up with her natural black hair. I could see below her gums, count the layers of spongy flesh before you hit the bone beneath her smile. Some pure, vengeful power was alive in me. I was never going to sleep again as long as I lived.

"Yeah," I said. "It's OK."

"That's good," she replied, 'cause you're gonna be high for about five days."

The first two nights, I paced the floor, unable to sleep, unable to calm down. I didn't hate it, but it wasn't a trip I'd have chosen to take.

Marcus kept shaking his head at me. "That's a white trash drug," he said.

I said, "I got it from a Black girl, don't give me that crap." I could talk like that to Marcus because he knew I didn't mean any disrespect. The fact was, we were in what you'd call a rough milieu. The people I knew spoke their minds, and squeezed in the cuss words for good measure.

Three days later he was still shaking his head. Blondell hadn't lied about how long it would take. By that time, we were both pretty grumpy, with me stalking the apartment all night, clattering in the kitchen and making up songs, and Marcus half trying to sleep through it the best he could, and half trying to talk me down a little bit.

On day four, Marcus said, "If you come home all fucked up again, I'm going to have a little chat with your new friend."

"Don't worry, I'm not going near that stuff again," I told him, and I meant it.

Day five, I came down. My body felt like it had been thrown off a roof. My soul felt shattered. A massive wave of despair rolled over me, and I knew it would keep on rolling till I hit it with another drug.

I grabbed Blondell when she walked in the door at work and shook her, hard. "You gotta give me something to come off this. Something up but gentler, huh?"

Blondell had just the thing, and that's how I got hooked on benzedrine.

Technically, I kept my word about not going near the meth again. Bennies and meth are kissing cousins, but methedrine runs you crazy, and bennies just help you run. Still, I didn't tell Marcus because I knew how he would feel about it. "It's still speed," was what I figured he would say, and I didn't want to argue about it because I didn't want to quit. I didn't want him throwing my pills in the toilet. I didn't want him lecturing me. But mostly, I just didn't want to face him. I didn't want him knowing how weak I was. I was afraid of seeing myself through his eyes.

I hid the pills in a box of tampax, the one place I figured no man would ever go, and I stayed as high as I could stand. At night, long after he'd fallen asleep, I would lie in our bed watching my hands vibrate and listening to the voice in my head. They had an urgency that I liked.

Maybe Marcus knew, deep down, but he kidded himself, or played along. Confrontation wasn't his style, and I'd set it up so he would have had to call me a liar to get the truth. I told him I was pre-menstrual, nervous. I told him I had allergies. I told him I was stressed, and I *was* stressed. It's stressful lying to your lover. It's stressful only sleeping four hours a night.

The summer of the second year we were together, my hair started to fall out. Not in big clumps—that would have woken me up right away—but gradually. I'd find long brown strands of the stuff all around me. On the bathroom sink, on the kitchen floor, on the sheets.

"Take some vitamins," Blondell said. "Take that super protein stuff. Have you been eating like I told you?"

"I don't know." I couldn't remember. Marcus had a job now—security guard for a bank, doing the graveyard shift—and he'd stopped cooking. He grabbed a sandwich on the way to work, and I always told him I was eating with Blondell. After saying it so often, I must have convinced myself, but the truth was I never thought about food.

"Eat something," she said. "That's how you die from it, you starve."

Food didn't taste like much, but I forced it down. I bought those big, horse pill vitamins and took one every day. I drank some water. I didn't want to kick the bennies, but I didn't want to die either. Not yet.

♥

Bennies made the dream more random. I never knew what form it would take: One night I'd be foaming at the mouth, lying on the floor like a rabid dog, my body twisted up, distorted. One night, I'd be drowning in a vat of something caustic and industrial. One night, I'd be standing naked in a snow storm, the skin blistering off me, stripped away by the cold. The dream had many variations, but my attitude was always the same. I'd be out of my body, hovering up by the ceiling, looking down on all that torment and thinking *yeah, that's about right.*

♥

One night, I cut work to go dancing with Marcus at his church. We took a bus out on Presidio and walked until we came to a small brick building.

"This is São Sebastão?" I stopped short on the sidewalk, looking at it.

I don't know what I'd expected. Some big, wealthy edifice? Some hollow place with Cathedral ceilings, stuffed with loot from its parishioners?

São Sebastão was nothing like that. A small stone building, going to seed, with a little garden in the front. Uneven steps leading down to the basement. Music blaring through the open door.

I don't know why, but I suddenly felt like maybe I didn't know Marcus at all. I knew some things—that he liked to cook and keep house and watch old movies on TV. I knew he liked kids, and despised it when people were needlessly cruel to each other. I knew he couldn't read and I knew he loved me, though I couldn't imagine why.

I thought about the candle he'd lit for my sister's soul on Decoration Day. Someplace in this building, he'd prayed for Rosie.

All of sudden, I wanted no part of it. I said, "I can't go in there with you."

Marcus patted my arm, the way you'd pat a horse who suddenly refused to jump a creek. "Sure you can," he said, as if my comment had been reasonable. "We're dressed fine. They know me."

It was true that we were dressed right—him in a white satin shirt and black pants that were just tight enough, me in a red dress Marcus had picked, that swirled around my knees and wasn't see-through. "What kind of music are they going to play?"

"Salsa and swing and Cape Verdean." He smiled. "It's hot. You'll like it, Gracie."

Walking into that church was like walking into a secret world. It was strange to realize that Marcus had a whole life I'd never pictured, with lots of friends I'd never heard of. He knew Blondell, who was my only friend besides him. I didn't know anything about the people that welcomed him to São Sebastãio, slapped him on the back, hugged him, hugged me just because I was there with him. "You're Gracie," one man said, with a big-toothed smile. "You're just as pretty as Marcus said." And a woman told me, "You sure are lucky that a fine man like Marcus be so true to you."

It was strange at first, being the only white person in the room, and strange being the object of all this attention, but after a while I got used to it. Marcus danced the way he did everything—calmly, deliberately, gracefully. I envied how he took in the music and let himself become one with it, not riding on its surface like I did at work. And I envied how easily he laughed and smiled and talked to people without seeming to lose himself in who they were and what they wanted.

After the dance, which was fun—the kind of fun I hadn't had in a long time—we walked out with my hand through his arm. "They're like your family," I said, trying not to sound hurt. "You never told me how important this is to you."

He patted my fingertips. "There are things you don't tell me, Gracie."

I looked up into his eyes. They were gentle and kind, not even ironic like mine would have been if I'd said that to him. "All right," I said, "that's true. But I can't dance without the stuff I take. I can't face it."

He shook his head. "I'm not pushing you. I know you're gonna quit when you're ready. I'm just saying, you're a private person. I don't hide any more than you do."

"Me?" It shocked me to feel tears stinging my eyes. "You read me like a book. You know everything that counts."

Then I stopped, remembering Rosie.

"Nobody knows everything," Marcus said, and this time I didn't argue.

♥

After that, I cut down on the speed. Way down. It wasn't really a decision. It was more like driving down the highway and watching a new town fade up on the horizon. I hadn't been looking for that place, but I knew it when I got there.

Now that I was eating again, Marcus went back to cooking. He got his security guard boss to put him on swing shift at the bank so that he'd get home first; and when I showed up, he fed me.

One night, he made black bean soup and cornbread. I sat up on the kitchen counter, my feet tucked beneath me, watching the muscles ripple in his arms as he took the cornbread from the oven, watching the way he skinned an orange, the way his fingers held the paring knife. His every motion was clean and smooth; it was like watching water flow.

I said, "I love you."

He said, "Grace, I want us to make a baby."

I shuddered.

He put the knife down. "Why do you do that when I talk about children? Act like I'm walking on your grave?"

"Marcus." I shuddered again; I couldn't help it. "I can't have kids. I just can't."

"Why not? You love me. I'll take care of you. I'm not gonna up and walk away when it gets tough, you know that. You *know* me!"

"It isn't you, Babe. It's me. I just can't do that for you. I absolutely. Totally. Can't."

He stared at me for a minute. Then he picked up the paring knife. He finished the orange he'd been peeling, tore it into little sections and threw them into the soup pot simmering on the stove. The soup, the cornbread smelled delicious. I knew it would all taste like dirt in my mouth.

He said, "You're not even going to talk about it?"

I wanted to cry, I felt so distraught, but that didn't change the truth of things. "There's nothing to talk about; I'm not going to change. Ask me for something else," I begged him. "Anything!"

But he didn't.

It was true that the problem was all in me. I'd always known I'd never have kids; I knew I couldn't trust myself around them. But it tore at my heart to say no to Marcus, to fail him after everything he'd done for me. For days after that conversation, I argued with myself and brooded. Sometimes I even pictured the children we would have—sassy hips, dark eyes, cocoa skin, a girl today, a boy tomorrow. But then I would remember, and the picture would fade.

For days, we slept on opposite sides of the bed, separated by a valley of hurt. But Marcus didn't bring it up again, and after a while, the question seemed to fade from in between us. We settled back into each other's arms, settled back into keeping house. We didn't exactly forget about the children that would never be. We just buried them, each of us in our separate ways, and tried to live for what we had.

♥

Before I met Marcus, I'd never thought about black and white. I didn't really have to, being white myself.

Of course, I knew how things were stacked between white and black folk. White people like to say they don't know, but deep down you can bet they understand who gets hassled by the police and who doesn't; who gets a slap on the wrist and who rots in state prison; who has the good jobs, who lives longer.

They know. Maybe they think it's a damn shame, but it's not their shame. They know about it from a distance, like I did.

Now it had come a little closer. I couldn't look at how fine Marcus was, or how much I liked the shape of his butt, or how we looked rubbing together and not think about the social side of it, stuff like which of us would have gotten lynched and which one run out of town for doing what we were doing fifty years ago.

We didn't talk about it a whole lot. The one time I said that I felt guilty for having it easier than him, Marcus laughed at me. "Sure," he said, "life's a walk in the park for you!" I'd never heard him be sarcastic before. I almost didn't recognize it.

I said, "I'm not talking about me personally, I'm talking about me as a white person."

He said, "If you're not talking about you personally, what are we even talking about?"

I couldn't let it go, though. I'd never really understood before, and it hurt me now to think how close he'd come to being somebody's property—bought, sold, whipped, chained, bred, beaten, worked to death. He'd only missed it by a hundred years.

But Marcus didn't want to hear it. "Gracie," he said, when I tried to explain what I was upset about, "don't make me a symbol. I don't stand for anything but myself."

three

After the crystal meth episode, I never thought Blondell and Marcus would be friends. But he was a live-and-let-live kind of person, and particularly once I'd kicked the bennies, he didn't really hold a grudge.

Plus he and Blondell were tattoo buddies. She had five or six of them, and even though they were small tattoos compared to Marcus's dragon, she never got tired of telling him that he must be some kind of wuss to quit getting tattooed after just one time.

Marcus would say that he hadn't quit, exactly. There just wasn't anything else he needed to wear on his skin.

I'd never had a best friend before, and now I suddenly had two of them. It was nice that they got along, nice to hear them teasing each other.

Most nights, Marcus was home when I got in from work. But sometimes he waited outside Girl O'Rama, and we'd go out when I got off. Lots of times when we did that, Blondell joined us. The three of us would head for an all-night diner, or a rib shack or after-hours club. Blondell would occasionally bring a girl with her, but I never bothered to get to know them. They never lasted more than a few days. Blondell was a head case about love.

"Here's how I see it," she told me and Marcus once. "You can love somebody, or you can fuck somebody, or you can fuck somebody that you love, but if you do that you're losing twice as much when its over."

"How do you figure that?" Marcus asked her, reaching across the table for ketchup. We were at the Dew Drop Inn Diner—the name was corny but the burgers were good.

Blondell rolled her eyes at Marcus. She had pretty eyes, almost black, with long, thick lashes. Come to think of it, they both had pretty eyes. "Add it up, Einstein. When you're fucking someone you love and they leave you, you lose the sex plus you lose the love. That's twice as bad as losing one or the other. That's why I never do sex and love together."

Marcus flashed me a secret smile, the kind that said *I'm doing both together.* "Why does it always have to be about losing? We can't you just hang on to what you've got?"

Blondell made a disgusted face. "I don't know, Champ. I think it's called 'life'?"

"Would you two cut it out for a change?" My food was gone, so I snagged a French fry off Marcus's plate. It was still hot enough to burn my tongue a little. "You sound like an old married couple."

Blondell giggled. Marcus grinned. "All right," I said, "maybe not an old married couple. Maybe a broken-down brother and sister. You're always bickering about some bullshit."

"I used to have a brother," Blondell suddenly offered. Her voice had that jumping-off-a-cliff quality that people get when they finally blurt something out.

"What happened?" Marcus asked, suddenly gentle.

"The usual." She shrugged, but the shrug looked phony as a three-dollar bill. "He died. He made it all the way to twenty-three, and then he had to go and get his ass wasted by these gang types he was hanging out with."

We were all silent for a moment.

"Well, what about you?" Blondell asked. "You got any brothers, Gracie?"

I guess it had never come up between us. I'd never told anyone but Marcus. "I used to have a sister," I said.

"Oh, yeah?" Blondell looked at me funny. "What happened?"

"The usual," I said. "She died."

Blondell knew a *KEEP OUT* sign when she saw one. She turned her attention on Marcus. "What about you, you ever have a brother or sister?"

"My big sister, down in Bakersfield." It sounded like he was almost apologizing for actually having a sibling who'd lived.

Well, he didn't have to apologize on my account. I'd met Marcus's sister once, and the truth was, I thought she was as good as nothing.

Our meeting hadn't been too pleasant. Mary Jo was an LPN and had been in town for some kind of convention. She came over early one morning, and Marcus made a killer breakfast—sausage and pancakes and a big fruit salad. He did his best to get the two of us talking, but there hadn't been much point to it. I'm not my best at eight in the morning, and Mary Jo was proud and superior. She sure didn't look happy when she heard that I was dancing in a strip club, and for that matter, she didn't seem too impressed with Marcus being a bank rent-a-cop.

I think she blamed me for the whole situation. You could see that I wasn't what she'd had in mind for her baby brother.

"His sister's a tough broad," I told Blondell now.

"That's right." Marcus was humoring me. "Mary Jo could kick my butt to Christmas."

Blondell just grinned at him.

♥

Christmas came around before I knew it, and Marcus wanted to buy a tree.

"What's with the tree thing all of a sudden? You didn't want to buy a tree last year."

"Last year I was still humoring you. Now that we been together forever, I can be my own true self."

I grinned and punched him in the arm—not the arm with the dragon tattoo, that would have felt like cruelty to animals—his right arm, which was hard as steel.

The truth was, I loved Marcus's sentimental streak. Christmas trees weren't a big thing in San Francisco, we were more about redwoods and eucalyptus. Being from the east, though, Marcus wanted one.

I couldn't say no; he never asked for much.

The week before Christmas, we went to buy ornaments. I wanted things like skeleton death heads and miniature handcuffs and cackling dwarfs. Marcus just rolled his eyes at me and bought tinsel and sparkling balls and a black angel with her wings spread wide.

I said, "Where did you ever see a black angel? That's already not traditional. If you're going to do that, we might as well get the freaky dwarfs."

"First of all," he said, "I never saw any kind of angel, so as far as I'm concerned, she's just as good as a white one. And second of all, you never saw some butt-scratching dwarf sitting up on a Christmas tree."

"I've barely seen a Christmas tree, period. I don't know where you get all this Christmas stuff."

"It's OK," he said. "It isn't going to hurt you." So we bought the tinsel and hung it on the four-foot pine tree Marcus brought home on the bus one day, and truthfully, it didn't hurt much. It was like picking at a scab, this idea that we were regular people, that we could do such a normal thing; I felt raw, like I was oozing something, but I wouldn't actually say it hurt.

The other holiday Marcus kept was Decoration Day. Memorial Day. We went back to Rosie's grave, and then we went out to Cielito's Mexican Palace and ate a big meal and danced some cumbias to celebrate one whole year of being together.

"I want you to see something," Marcus said. And right there in Cielito's, he lifted his shirt up and showed me his new tattoo.

For weeks he'd been wearing a gauze bandage on his chest. He wouldn't answer any questions, and wouldn't let me watch him change it, but I knew that whole area was tender to the touch. He didn't even want me to mention it to Blondell, which is why I figured it was probably a tattoo. Of course, I'd been curious about it, but Marcus did things in his own time. I figured there was no point in pushing him.

Now, when it was revealed, I gasped. My hands started shaking, I was so rocked back.

Marcus had tattooed my name over his heart. *Gracie* it said, in bright blue script, with a big black flourish underneath and small red hearts sprinkled around it.

"Damn!" I said. "Marcus, that's permanent."

"So are you," he said, and he took my hand.

♥

Five months later, Marcus threw up blood.

He was bent over the toilet bowl, retching his guts out. I stood beside him, holding his head, feeling the chill of fear run up my arms and down through my chest to my gut.

He didn't want to go to San Francisco General. Men don't like hospitals, and who can blame them? But he was just as scared as me, and eventually I got his coat on and tugged him out the front door.

A cab took us there. We got the cab in the usual way, me standing in the street, Marcus hanging back until I had the door open and my body half inside. By that time, when he stepped forward, the cabbie couldn't bolt without throwing me and getting sued, so he stayed put and let Marcus get in. He dropped us at the emergency entrance and we trudged inside like refugees. I was leaning on Marcus as hard as he was leaning on me.

We sat there for a long time. Four, maybe five hours. The TV was blasting out bad sit-coms, the laugh tracks loud and creepy over the sounds of people arguing, moaning, crying. A man's broken wrist stuck out through his skin. An old woman lolled in her wheelchair, looking like she'd either just had a heart attack or was working up to one. A young woman in a blood-stained blouse with bruises on her face huddled in the corner. Every so often, Marcus would be taken with another fit of coughing, and would go to the men's room to throw up more blood. The fourth time, I wouldn't let him go. I clamped my leg over his so that he would have had to push me off to stand up, and Marcus would never do that. So he sat there vomiting blood on the floor, and then they said he could see a doctor.

The examining room was small and smelled rancid, but the doctor was kind. She ordered a chest x-ray, and hours later, when it came back, she ordered a room for Marcus.

They did a lot of tests on him, but he wouldn't tell me how they came out. He wouldn't tell me anything, and after a week they sent him home.

"What'd they say is wrong with you?" I asked, when he came back from his follow-up appointment.

"They still don't know. But they got the bleeding stopped, so I don't care."

I did. "What do you mean, they don't know? How can they not know?"

Marcus just shrugged. "Not everything has a name," he said. "And I feel better, so what's the difference?"

Marcus went back to his security job. He still had what sounded like a cold in his chest, and it made me nervous to hear him cough; but it didn't seem to slow him down much and I tried to put it out of my mind.

Then, gradually, the other symptoms started. Strange, disconnected stuff; swelling that came and went in his throat, a rash here, a sore there, a fever that spiked and then disappeared. There didn't seem to be a pattern, or any way to make sense of it.

He went to the hospital clinic every week. After the first few visits, he didn't want me going with him. He said I made him tense, which I could understand; I was angry, I would pace around the waiting room and scowl at people. Usually we had a big row of seats to ourselves, because people didn't want to sit close to me.

Marcus was tiring easily by then. All my emotion was a drain on him, at least in public, which was mostly where I let it out.

I had to let it out someplace. I was scared out of my mind by now, and I was hating Girl-O-Rama more each day. Since I'd given up benzedrine, I was dancing in a sober state and it was a harrowing experience. I wanted to quit the place, but I couldn't. Marcus couldn't work anymore, and the clinic was cheap but it wasn't free.

He wasn't cooking anymore, either; he didn't have the energy. Blondell and I started passing by an all-night deli on the way home from work. She would sit in the cab and make the driver wait while I ran in and bought some soup and sandwich meat, and then the cab would leave me at home and she would go and score some drugs.

Blondell had ramped down from crystal meth when I got off the benzedrine. Now she only blew coke, and she seemed a lot better for it. But still, with her scoring and me not, a gap was opening up between us.

"You might feel better if you got high," she said, but I just shook my head.

"I'll feel better when Marcus does."

"That'll be soon," Blondell replied. "You got a strong man there, you'll see."

"Yeah," I said. "It's just a matter of days."

We both knew we were lying, and maybe that's where the real gap came from. Before, I felt like I could tell Blondell when I was feeling angry or frightened or sad or lost. Now I was feeling all of those things, and I couldn't say a word to her about it.

♥

We didn't know until ten weeks before he died that what Marcus had was AIDS. By then, he'd been sick for months. The weakness, the fevers, the rashes, the sores—it didn't add up until the hospital sent him to a new clinic in the Castro, and that's what they said it was.

He told me on a Thursday afternoon, as I was getting dressed for work. Suddenly my legs wouldn't hold me, and I sank down onto the bed.

"How can you have AIDS!?" I gasped. "You're not gay!"

That's how we thought then. They'd only just stopped calling it GRID, gay-related immune deficiency, and people just knew you couldn't get it if you were straight. Which is just like knowing that you can't get pregnant if the guy doesn't come; ignorant stuff you grow out of the hard way.

He said, "I just do, Grace. I have AIDS." His voice was soft but implacable. I knew he was trying to convince himself.

The cold that ripped through me was so sharp, so fast, I felt like it was pouring from every cell in my body. My heart was beginning to freeze up. "You're telling me this *now*?" I shrieked, trying to put some heat in my veins. "You know I have to go to work!"

"I thought maybe work would distract you."

"Distract me? From you *dying*?" And then the ice cracked and I jumped up and punched him hard in the chest, right on the tattoo of my name.

His arms came up and wrapped a loose circle round me, holding me safe while I hit him, blindly, over and over, sobbing my brains out. "It's OK," he kept saying, just like I wasn't trying my best to hurt him. "It's OK, Grace."

I started choking. Choking on something I was never going to be able to swallow. My body heaved and struggled briefly. Then I doubled over and puked my guts out on the floor.

Marcus picked me up and put me on the bed. I rolled into a tight ball, turning my face away from him, and sobbed and sobbed while he went and got some wet paper towels. He wiped my face with some of them, and used the rest to clean the floor.

I was still crying when he finished, and he tried to pull me into his arms, but I wouldn't budge. I wrapped my arms around my knees and held tight, all my muscles tensed against him, keening like an old village woman. I didn't know my name, or what century it was; I was swimming in a vast, ancient pool of grief and I would gladly have drowned there.

But after a long time I felt his hand on my shoulder, pulling me back just like Marcus always did. And finally I could feel him, stretched out on the bed beside me, and I turned into his arms and held him and the two of us sobbed; and oh the words of love we cried.

We lay there for a long time. Hours must have ticked by. I knew I wouldn't be going back to work. I wouldn't be leaving him again, until the last time.

Finally he said, "This doctor at the new clinic told me they have a test now. I want you to find out if you have it."

I hoped I did, but I wasn't going to tell him that. Poor Marcus, he'd worked so hard to make me happy.

He said, "I want you to call this guy, Dr. Weiss, and I want you to get tested, and if you come up clean, there's something I want you to do for me after I'm gone."

"What?" I couldn't look at him; my eyes were swollen almost shut. My voice sounded like something squeezed from hell.

"I want you to have a baby."

I groaned; I felt a terrible empty space open up, a space of wasted possibility. I'd known how badly he wanted kids; why had I said no to him? Why hadn't I put the past aside? Why hadn't I given him the one thing he'd asked for?

But he said, "It's not for me. I'll be dead long before that."

"Don't!" I started crying again.

"It's all right," he said, stroking my neck. "You're going to die, too, someday, and I'll be waiting for you."

I thought, *you won't have to wait long.*

"Naw, you're not going to do that, Gracie."

I hated it when he reached inside my mind. "Why not?" I snarled.

"Because you're going to be pregnant." I could feel him smiling against my hair. "Pretty clever, huh?"

Too damned clever. "I won't do it."

"Yeah, you will." He pulled back a little and lifted my chin so that I could see his wan and serious face up close. "It's my last wish. Promise me."

The chill went through me again. I clamped my mouth shut.

"Promise."

"Marcus, anything but…"

"Promise!"

I'd never seen him look like that. It frightened me, and I said what I had to say to chase the anguish from his eyes. "All right, I promise."

Marcus smiled to himself, and closed his eyes. He said, "Thank you, Grace. I know you don't mean it. But you will."

four

Dozens of people came to the Requiem Mass at São Sebastãio.
Father deSouza talked about how Marcus had brought warmth and
hope to everyone he knew, and people lit candles and sang a lot of mournful-
sounding hymns that were still beautiful—so beautiful they made me cry,
although I tried to hide it.

When it was over, an altar boy folded the clean white cloth that had
draped Marcus's coffin, and six men carried it out to the hearse. I had asked
Father deSouza to make an announcement, and there was a quick, collective
gasp when he told the congregation that I wanted to go to the cemetery alone.
But I think people understood that I needed to keep Marcus for myself one
last time, because every last person who'd been in that church filed by to hug
me or kiss my cheek or press my hand and murmur a well wish, or a hope that
I would find peace. I was moved and chastened by the time the last of them
was gone and I climbed into Father deSouza's battered Volvo.

On our way to the cemetery, it started to rain. It was a gentle early spring
rain, but steady and relentless; I knew it would be cold against my skin. The
priest didn't try to make me talk. He just drove for what seemed like days,
following the slow-moving hearse. I sat and watched its mournful tail lights,
too tired to think, too numb to feel.

There were three workmen waiting for us at the cemetery. The rain had
begun to soften the ground, and even though there was a canopy at graveside,
one of the men almost slipped under the coffin's weight. Finally they got it

balanced on the metal frame that stood above the open grave; and that's when the feelings rushed in on me. The raindrops pattering against the hardwood casket, the terrible quiet, that gaping wound in the ground were suddenly all too much to bear. Father deSouza took my arm just as I began to sway, and somehow I steadied myself. He opened his prayer book, faced the grave, and murmured, "Into Your hands, Oh Lord, we commend the body of your servant, our brother Marcus..." Tears and rain sluiced down my face and puddled in the gathering cold. I didn't make a sound, though. Somehow it mattered that I not interrupt the priest's words. They were dim and sounded far away but Marcus would have found them comforting.

"Ashes to ashes, dust to dust, in clear and certain hope of the Resurrection."

If only he was right, then Marcus would live again, his spirit released. He wouldn't lie forever in this hole in the ground. I wanted so badly to believe that, just like I wanted to feel that nothing of Marcus was in that box, nothing that mattered, but of course I didn't believe that either. I had loved his body along with everything else about him. I couldn't separate his soul from it now.

"May the angels take you into Paradise. May the martyrs meet you at the gate."

"Gracie!" Father deSouza's voice was loud in my ear. I glanced around, disoriented.

The three workmen had come forward. At a nod from the Father, one of them released a winch, and the coffin began to slowly lower.

"Do you want to throw a flower on the casket?" he asked me. I couldn't answer, so we stood there in silence and watched until it was deep in the ground.

Then he turned to me. "We should go now," he said. "I'll drive you home."

I just shook my head. I wasn't leaving.

"I'll take you wherever you need to go."

Where I needed to go was into the ground, beside Marcus, but I couldn't repay the priest's kindness by saying so. Still, what he saw in my eyes must have troubled him. He said, "If you don't want to leave yet, I'll stay with you."

"I need..." I shuddered, trying to get the words out. "I need to be alone here for a while."

Suddenly he looked tired and old. "I can't leave you out here by yourself. It will be dark soon."

"I'll be all right." The words sounded thick, almost foreign on my tongue.

"Excuse me, Father." We both turned. One of the workmen was standing at my shoulder. "Beg your pardon, will you be leaving soon? We need to start…"

I said, "You can go ahead. I'm going to stay for a little while."

"But…"

I couldn't argue anymore. I turned to Father deSouza. "Please," I whispered fiercely. "And thank you for loving Marcus."

He didn't want to go, but he knew I wasn't going to leave; and finally he patted my shoulder and walked away. I watched his car drive slowly down the rain-soaked hill. I watched the three men work, their shovels rising and falling with terrible regularity, the mound of dirt at graveside shrinking, shrinking, until it was all gone.

"We have to take down the canopy, Miss." It was the man who'd spoken before. I think I nodded once.

"It's going to be dark soon; you'll catch your death of cold staying out here. Why don't you let us drive you down in the truck?"

"No." I shook my head. "But thank you. I'll come down soon."

He looked as doubtful as the priest had. I said, "I'm OK. I'm not gonna get you in trouble." And then I closed my eyes, and when I opened them they were loading their shovels onto the back of their truck.

If the silence had been terrible before, it was frightening now. It felt like anything could jump out at me from inside the night: ghosts or demons or memories. It felt like I'd given myself to the darkness, like I was giving myself up for dead.

You'll catch your death of cold, the man had said.

God, I hoped so. I stumbled over to Marcus's grave. My legs folded out from under me, and I sank down onto the rain-soaked ground.

The temperature was dropping steadily lower, the earth pulling heat from wherever my body touched it. It was cold there, cold and unforgiving. My joints locked, and my muscles ached from trying to fight off the chill. But after a while the thoroughness of it shocked me into submission, and my body gave up struggling. I rolled onto my back and lay there, waiting motionless, watching the few bright, tedious stars that came out until even that was too much work and my eyes drifted back in my head and closed.

That's when I knew that I wasn't alone. Now I could feel the spirits that were poised inside the thick, cold night. I could feel them like a thousand hands, pulling me, trying to suck me into Marcus's arms. And as much as I knew that's where I belonged, as much as part of me wanted to die, I didn't want to be dragged into it. I didn't want to be bested by ghosts. My eyes flew open and I stared at the night, feeling empty and angry, disconnected from my soul. No one was going to kill me while I slept! *You try it,* I thought viciously. *You fucking try it!*

Silence.

And then my mother appeared, looking so real I forgot that I'd conjured her. She wasn't her true self—high on heroin, or wanting to be, looking at a point just past me for something she never found. Instead, she looked like *mother.* Clean, and smiling gently. Wearing (I would have laughed, if it wasn't so gruesome) an apron.

Gracie! Time for dinner!

Far away, something smelled good. Something warm and nourishing. I understood that this mother took care of us. She cooked, she cuddled, she watched over her children.

Rosie appeared, lightly touching my elbow, a child whose voice held the adult that she would never become.

You know that's not how it was, she said.

I didn't want to argue with a three-year-old, but I didn't want her to chase our mother away. *She loves us,* I shouted inside my mind. *She comes when we call her. She doesn't want us to be lonely!*

Rosie's smile was filled with pity. She read my thoughts, and the longing on my face.

It wasn't like that, she whispered in her angel's voice. But I couldn't turn away from how things should have been.

And then I saw Marcus. The ground shifted beneath me. In my mind, I was the one who was buried there. He was the one who was left to grieve.

I watched him from beyond death. There was no rain, there were no stars, but the wind howled through the graveyard as he dropped to his knees on the mound above where my body lay buried. Tears were streaking down his face, acid tears that left small grooves in his soft skin.

I went to him in the wind. I touched his mouth, his hands, his hair, his eyes. I whispered. But he wouldn't listen to me, he didn't really know I was there. He sobbed wildly, calling my name. At that, something inside me broke. I felt ready to die now, ready to follow Marcus's soul. I felt life beginning to slip from me.

But Rosie was there again. Her pudgy little hands pulled me back from the darkness. *No,* she said gently.

I slapped her hands away, but she grabbed me with the strength of the dead. *Let me go,* I screamed, desperately. *Let me go and comfort him!*

She said, *There is no comfort, Gracie. Don't you understand by now?* I woke up shivering violently, the night dissolving around me like a dream. I was lying outside, on Marcus's grave. My legs were so tense I thought the bones were going to shatter. I was panting hard, from long exertion. My hands were clawed into the ground, great fistfuls of cold, damp earth clutched inside gnarled, old fingers. My nails were broken off at the quick, my arms were bruised, my shoulders aching.

To the east, light was seeping over the horizon. I tried to move and found that I couldn't. But as the sun rose, my muscles and joints began to warm. Soon I could stretch my fingers, then my forearms, then my legs. I tried to take a deep breath; it dissolved into a wracking cough. I turned my face and spit out phlegm that was thick and lightly tinged with blood.

I sat up slowly. My head was pounding. It didn't feel like I was ever going to stand or stretch or walk again. But people would be coming soon— people going about their business, people I didn't want to see — and that was finally enough to drag me slowly to my feet, to make me stumble blindly off that hillside.

I don't remember how I got home. I must have been soaked and filthy and wild-eyed. Maybe I was delirious. Maybe I walked across town. Maybe somebody gave me a lift. Somehow I ended up in the Mission, standing outside our apartment door.

My hand was shaking so bad I dropped the key twice. But finally the door opened and I stepped into that emptiness.

It was quiet, lonelier than the hillside. Clearly no one lived here anymore. I stumbled into the bedroom and fell across a bed that smelled of death and tears.

There wasn't a part of me that didn't hurt. I kicked my shoes off, curled up on my side, pulled my legs up and wrapped my arms around them.

Something loud was hitting my head.

I lay on my stomach, my eyes too heavy to open, and felt the sound slap against my eardrums. It had a rhythmic pulse, like being rocked on a wave. If I sunk below it, I could probably fall asleep again.

"Gracie! Goddamn it!"

A muffled voice. I was probably dreaming.

I yawned deeply, reluctantly. That cleared my head just enough for a fuzzy thought to trickle in, the thought that someone was kicking my apartment door.

"Gracie, you goddamn cunt, open up!"

The voice was familiar; it was someone I knew. Her name was on the edge of my mind, far away but getting closer.

My eyes creaked open. I rolled stiffly onto my back, surprised to find that I was fully dressed. The clothes felt damp and stuck to my body.

"I'll kill you, bitch! You're scaring the goddamn shit outta me!"

Oh, God, it was Blondell! I gasped, and a mouthful of air sobbed into me. She didn't even know that Marcus had died!

I opened my mouth to call out to her, but no sound came except a thin, hurt moan.

I would have to get up and open the door. Blondell would kick until she broke it down, or someone called the police or shot her.

My feet touched the floor. It was cold, and it shocked my memory awake. Marcus, the rain, the grave, the night. I remembered opening the apartment door, and then there was nothing. It might have been an hour, a day or a week since I'd staggered down from that hillside.

I shuffled to the front door, unlocked it, cracked it slightly open. Blondell stood there with her foot poised in the air. Her foot looked unnaturally large to me, in thick, dark brown boots with heavy laces. I didn't understand why Blondell had boots like that.

She said, "Thank you, Jesus." Then to me, "Your phone's not working."

I hadn't known. I said, "I'm OK."

"Yeah," she said, "I can see that." She slipped through the door as if she thought I was going to close it on her, and walked right past me into the kitchen. She was carrying a plastic bag, which she put down on the table. Then she walked into the bathroom. A moment later, I heard water running.

When she came back, I was sitting at the kitchen table, my head resting on my hands, reading the writing on the plastic bag. Wu Fat Chinese Take-Out. Wu Fat Chinese Take-Out. Wu Fat Chinese...

Blondell's hand squeezed my shoulder. "Come on," she said. Her voice was gentle, which normally would have frightened me. "Come and get in the bathtub."

I wanted to ask what was the use, but there wasn't even any use in asking.

She came around and crouched beside me. The way my head was facing, I'd have had to shut my eyes to not see her.

"When did he die?"

"Tuesday." I half-wondered what day it was now, and then hated myself for wanting to know.

"Ummm." She looked sad, but she didn't say anything else, except, "Get your clothes off. You smell like a bum."

I went into the bathroom and undressed, knowing she could probably make me. I'm bigger than her, and Blondell's built stringy, but she's tough as hell and mean in a fight. That's one of the things I loved about her, knowing she could take care of herself. No one was going to catch her off guard and slam her sorry ass up on some bar.

The bath was warm and fragrant. It was comforting, which was a terrible shock. I had no right to be comforted, but I couldn't stop my body from melting into the water's warm embrace, or my mind from noticing how good it felt. All I could do was bite back the guilt and the pain. I didn't want to make a sound that would bring Blondell running. I didn't want her to feel sorry for me.

After a while, she knocked on the door.

"Get out," she called. "Food's getting cold."

I didn't care, but it was the same story. If I didn't eat, she would shove it down my throat.

We sat there for a long time, me in a white jumpsuit she'd found in the bedroom, her in a t-shirt and jeans and those stupid shit-kicker boots. I wanted a drink, but there was nothing in the house. Marcus had made me throw it all away the last week. Maybe he was afraid I'd mix it with his pain pills.

"You going back to work?" Blondell said.

"No."

"Then how're you gonna eat?"

I didn't bother to answer. She knew I didn't care.

"Oh, Gracie." She reached across the table and took my hand. "You never had a goddamn chance, did you?"

It was true; from the moment I'd met Marcus, it was all over for me. Thinking about that, I couldn't hold back anymore; I dropped my fork and started to cry. Blondell got out of her seat and came around the table and wrapped her arms awkwardly around me. "It's OK," she said.

She moved the plate of Chinese food away, and I put my head down on the table and cried my heart out. Blondell stood there patting my shoulder, saying, "It's gonna be OK, Grace. It'll be OK." And the funny thing was, I believed her. Someday it *was* going to be OK, but that didn't matter.

After a while, I stopped crying and Blondell sat down and gestured to the plate she'd moved aside. "Eat something," she said. "It tastes better than it looks."

I picked at the chicken fried rice, chewing slowly, feeling the muscles on my face. All the tone had gone out of them. If they had to hold up a smile, they wouldn't know how to do it.

"OK, let's go," Blondell said, when it was clear that I'd eaten all I was going to.

I looked at her blankly.

She said, "You need to pack a bag. I'm taking you home to live with me."

At Blondell's, I mostly dreamed memories. Dreamed that I was fourteen again, just after I ran away — too proud to go back, too angry to grieve, eating from garbage cans and screwing men who had nothing to offer but a dry bed. Those dreams were cold, like falling off a cliff in slow motion.

But sometimes I dreamed about my sister. Rosie came in the middle of the night. She was wearing a nightgown and she got in bed with me, into the empty space that was waiting for her.

"Grathe," she lisped. She didn't have her teeth around my name yet. Probably she would have outgrown the lisp if I hadn't killed her first. And just the way she said it, like I would say "ice cream" or "sunshine" or "Marcus" made me realize how much she loved me. I was all she had, and look how it had ended.

I felt the tears burning my skin. I felt the streaks they would leave. I thought, *you're sleeping, you could wake up now*. But I didn't want to wake up; there was nothing for me in the real world. In my dreams, I had Rosie for company. Even after what I'd done, she didn't have it in her three-year-old heart to hate me.

♥

Rosie trusted me, that was the horror of it. She was too young to know better, but still. When the child welfare people came, they cursed my mother. *A five-year-old minding a toddler...!* They didn't seem to blame me, even a little bit. But I did.

♥

I missed so much about being with Marcus. The sex, the cuddling, the nights wrapped around his solid back, listening to him breathe, breathing his scent. It was terrible not having him to touch, but it was worse, much worse, not having him to talk to.

I don't think I'd ever had a real conversation before I met him. I was used to people saying things like, "How you doin'?" "How much, Foxy?" "Hey baby, you wanna get high?"

Marcus said, "Are you all right now?"

It was back at my place, that first night, after he'd come to my rescue at Stacy G's. We were lying in my bed, or rather, I was splayed across his chest, watching that dragon peek up over his shoulder.

I lifted my head and looked him in the eye. "What?"

"Are you all right?"

"Sure." I couldn't figure out what he was asking. After what he'd just done to my body, why wouldn't I be all right?

"You had to fight off that guy in the bar. You almost got hurt. It seems like you might have had some reaction."

That's when I realized that Marcus was asking about my feelings. "I'm OK," I said, and then I shocked myself by adding, "The only time I felt a little shaky was right after the police came and we left the bar."

He nodded like he knew just what I meant. He said, "You ever notice how one minute you're solid as a rock, got everything covered, and then when you let your guard down, *that's* when the feelings hit you?"

"No. I never noticed that."

"Well," he said, wrapping me tighter in the safety of his arms, "maybe you never let your guard down."

♥

One night at Blondell's, I dreamed that I was five years old again, handing Rosie the bottle of bleach.

Drink this, I said, in my little girl's voice. So innocent. So curious. I wanted to see what would happen if she did it. *Good Rosie, drink this*.

I woke up convulsing with dry heaves.

♥

Even then, I knew why I was doing it, knew why my mind was dredging up those memories. The pain of losing Marcus was so sharp I had to blunt it with the strongest stone I could find.

It turned out there was something worse than losing him. It was the darkness he'd kept away.

"I don't understand why you lock everything inside," Marcus said once.

"You sound like I made some kind of choice about who to be!" I snapped. I was annoyed and hurt and shocked to find myself pushing back tears.

But Marcus wasn't put off by my feelings. "You did," he said. "You are. Right now. Each minute, you're choosing who to be and then you're being it."

I stamped my foot. "You stop that shit right now, Marcus! You think you're a goddamn mind reader..."

But he just laughed and gave me a hug. You couldn't make Marcus mad for trying, and I tried plenty of times. The only thing that made him angry was someone innocent getting hurt.

That's why I never told him about Rosie.

Later, I was so sorry I hadn't spoken. After he was gone, I could see that Marcus would have understood. Not just the words, if I'd been able to say them; Marcus would have understood that there are times when I close my eyes and feel the acid burning down my throat, the skin bubbling and peeling away, the foam coming out of my mouth, the gagging and retching as my eyes tilt back into my head and darkness comes down in one long scream.

Maybe if I'd been better with words, I would have told him; but the words only came to me after he was gone. It was like he'd willed his words to me. At night, after Blondell went to work, I sat on her couch with my arms wrapped round my knees, crying and rocking and talking and talking, explaining everything to Marcus. I told him about killing Rosie, and how I didn't dare have children. I told him about how desperately I loved him, how he was the only good thing in my life and how guilty I felt for every time I'd hurt him.

I told him things I'd never dared think, and things I would have died before admitting. The words were like tiny charges of dynamite, blasting down the walls around my heart 'till it was standing open, for him to walk in.

But it was too late then. He was dead.

SIX

One night, Blondell came home crying.

"What?!" I grabbed her and held on tight.

She clung to me, her small body shaking. "Granny B. had a stroke."

"Oh, my God!" I felt the world shift into slow motion, like it does when something important is about to change. Granny B. had raised Blondell from a baby. She was supposed to be retired now, back in Washington D.C.. She was supposed to be growing tomatoes.

"I called during break and they said…" she broke off, sobbing. "They said she was in the hospital, she might not even live through the night."

I held her while she cried. Then, abruptly, Blondell moved out of my arms and starting prowling the bedroom, mechanically gathering things into a pile. Her blue jeans. A sweater. A few extra g-strings. She put on those god-awful boots. I hadn't seen them since the day she almost kicked my door down.

I went to the closet and pulled out the suitcase I'd brought with me that night. I opened it up on the bed and put in her things as she found them. When she stopped, I closed the suitcase, zipped it shut, handed it to her. "How are you going to get there?"

"I'm going to the airport. First goddamn thing they put me on, that's what I'll take."

That was a big deal. Blondell had never been on a plane. She'd told me once she was scared to death of them.

"I'll go to the airport with you."

"No. You don't wanna be seen with me."

"The hell I don't!"

"You don't." She flashed me a grim, self-satisfied smile. "I grabbed some bills from ol' Don's office on my way out the back door."

Thank God he didn't know where we lived! He'd have had the shit kicked out of us both by now, had his crooked cop friends do it. "I guess you're not coming back, then, huh?"

"Guess not."

"Oh, Blondell!" We hugged each other for a long time. Both of us were crying now.

"Keep the place," she said, digging in her pocket and handing me her front door key. "And call me at Granny's."

"I don't have your number."

She wrote it down on the inside of a matchbook. Then she hugged me again and said, "You'll be OK, Grace. You'll find something to live for."

♥

Days passed without my noticing. Days and nights of pacing the apartment in cold shock.

Rosie. Marcus. Blondell. It didn't take much to lose someone. You blinked your eyes and they were gone.

One night, tired of pacing, I dozed off on the couch and was jolted awake just before dawn. It wasn't a dream that woke me up — this time it was a memory, the memory of what I'd promised Marcus.

"Oh, God!" I rolled onto my stomach, screwed my eyes shut and pulled a pillow over my head.

I waited an hour for the thought to go away, but it didn't.

I'd promised Marcus to have a baby.

And he'd said, *I know you don't mean it, Grace. But you will.*

♥

Marcus had said I should see Dr. Weiss. Joel Weiss, they told me when I called the clinic.

Two hours later I was sitting in his office.

Dr. Joel Weiss was young and serious. He wore thick glasses and a big, sad expression. He must have been pretty close to my age, but he looked at least a hundred years older. I wondered how many of his patients had died, how many of his friends and lovers.

Too many; it was clear on his face.

We talked about nothing for a few minutes. I knew a lot of people were waiting, but he made me feel like he had time. Finally he said, "Did you know that Marcus wanted us to find an experiment he could be in? Something that would maybe help other people."

I hadn't known that. "Did you find one?"

"No," he said. "There aren't any. We don't even know where to start."

It seemed like all I did these days was cry. "I didn't even know how sick he was till near the end." And then I heard myself blurting out, "How do you think he got it?"

"As far as we know, it's carried in blood and semen. It could have been sex, or a transfusion, or a needle."

But Marcus didn't shoot drugs, and I knew there hadn't been a transfusion. I didn't want to think about what that left. I didn't want to think about a young, pretty Marcus on the street, on his own, how it must have been the same for him as it had been for me.

"Whatever happened," Dr. Weiss said, "it was a long time before he met you."

We were both silent for a moment. Then I said, "Marcus wanted me to get pregnant. I mean, now; not when he was alive." Dr. Weiss looked almost as surprised as I'd been. "Kind of in his honor," I explained. "If I have AIDS, would I give it to the baby?"

"You probably would."

My heart contracted, which surprised me. Five minutes ago I hadn't planned to get pregnant. But when he asked me did I want to take the test and find out, I said yes.

♥

Two weeks later, Dr. Weiss called. Two weeks of shuffling around Blondell's apartment, or staring at the alley outside her kitchen window. He said, "You're negative for the antibodies. You should take the test again in six months, but as far as we can tell right now, you don't have the HIV virus."

Something drained out of me—fear, or maybe it was hope. "Why not?"

"I don't know," he said. "There's a lot we don't know about it yet. Did Marcus use a condom when you made love?"

"Sometimes. I didn't want to get pregnant."

There was a long pause, during which I wondered if Dr. Weiss remembered our last conversation. "Are you sure you want to now?" he asked, finally.

"No," I said. "I'm not sure of anything."

I could hear him nodding across the phone line. He must have been an expert on human confusion. "This isn't really scientific, but it seems to me that if you're going to get pregnant, you might want to get out of town. Almost every reported AIDS case in the United States is in San Francisco or New York City."

I thought about that. "You recommend any place in particular?"

"No," he said. "It's a pretty big country."

After we got off the phone, I shut my eyes and pictured the big country. Miles and miles of corn fields and shopping malls and churches and Dairy Queens, untouched by people like Marcus and me. And I knew what I was going to do.

I'd lived my whole life around San Francisco, but now there was nothing to hold me here. I got out the canvas shoulder bag I'd brought with me all those weeks ago, and threw in a spare t-shirt, a sweater, a lipstick, a toothbrush, a book, some underwear and my only picture of Marcus. I tucked twenty dollars—all that I had, which Blondell had insisted on giving me—into the back pocket of my blue jeans, and slung the bag over my shoulder.

It wasn't even heavy. It should have had more heft to it, filled with everything I was carrying away from the life I'd lived for 27 years. But it wasn't the first time I'd traveled light.

It wasn't the first time I'd run away, either.

I wanted to feel sad or sober, to feel like this was a big moment, but in truth I didn't feel anything except relief that I was going to get away. *Get away clean,* I thought to myself. No obligations, no relationships. The people who cared about me were gone. My leaving was just a formality.

It was late May—mild in the daytime, but still cold when the sun went down. I put my keys on the kitchen table, grabbed my heavy, lined denim jacket and walked out of Blondell's place, pulling the door shut behind me.

seven

By noon, I was standing at the on-ramp to I-280 with my thumb stuck out. It hadn't occurred to me to do anything but hitch. Hitch-hiking was the fastest way to get to an unknown destination, and I certainly wasn't going to pay for transportation I could get for free.

But I hadn't hitched for a while, and I was rusty. When a beat-up blue Chevy squealed to a stop at the curb, I got into the back seat and closed the door without even bothering to look at who was up front.

Fortunately for me, it was just two young kids. Jake was driving—he was friendly, introduced himself right away. His buddy Sammy grunted hello and went right back to being a nervous jerk with the radio. He would listen to the first verse of a song, then get tired of it and change channels. It didn't matter if the song was good or bad, rock or pop, jazz or country, thirty seconds was his limit. I didn't say anything, even though it drove me crazy. First off, I was riding in their car. But more to the point, Sammy reminded me of myself on speed, and the last thing you want to hear when you're high on speed is what someone else thinks.

After a few minutes Jake glanced back over his shoulder. "Where you going?" he asked, casually. I could have told him anything.

What came out of my mouth was, "Bakersfield."

Damn! I thought. Where had that come from?

But of course, I knew exactly where. Mary Jo lived in Bakersfield. Marcus's high-and-mighty sister.

Though Marcus had almost never brought up her name after our disastrous first meeting, I knew that he and Mary Jo spoke. I'd see a Bakersfield number on the phone bill now and then, and he'd spoken to her near the end, just before he started getting delirious. But I hadn't called her about the funeral. Partly, it had just slipped my mind.

Well, apparently she was on my mind now. There wasn't any other reason I would have named that particular location.

The drive to Bakersfield was pretty painless, if you didn't count the stone sitting in my chest. Sammy finally settled down with a heavy metal radio station. I was used to music you could strip to—Madonna, Stevie Wonder, Michael Jackson, Marvin Gaye—and could barely stomach Twisted Sister and Motley Crue, but it didn't really matter. Once we headed inland, it was all a blur anyway; a blur that got steadily more flat and dry and dusty the further we left San Francisco behind. Sometimes, Sammy would "sing" along with a particularly grisly song on the radio, mumbling in a cracked, dull voice. Sometimes, Jake would yawn, or stretch, or swerve too close to one of the countless trucks we passed. Twice, they stopped to piss and buy beer, and I thought about getting a different ride, but I didn't care enough to move. I was on automatic, watching their Chevy grind up the miles.

The names of towns sounded different down here — Earlimart, Delano, Famoso, where Jake said they had NASCAR races. Then we passed a sign that said *WELCOME TO BAKERSFIELD*. By that time, the sun was dropping below the horizon. The road had leveled to a straight, unbroken line of asphalt, telephone poles and RV lots. My neck hurt from holding my head up and my legs hurt from sitting still.

Jake pulled into La Corona Truck Stop. Well, not quite *into* it. He stopped on the access road, which was lined on both sides with empty trucks, their giant engines still running. "Everybody out," he said.

Everybody meant me. I picked up my shoulder bag and my jacket, which already felt like a dead weight, slung them over my shoulder, mumbled some kind of thanks and stepped out into a furnace. Heat was pouring off the idling trucks--even with night about to fall, it must have been 90 degrees out there.

I trudged through the gauntlet of trucks, looking around warily. In front of me was a big parking lot, and beyond it, past the gas pumps and benches, was a low-slung building with a bright neon sign that read, "Coffee—Restaurant—Showers—Sundries." Above it was a giant billboard:

THAT 'LOVE THY NEIGHBOR' THING?
I MEANT IT!

–GOD

Around me, on a dozen speakers, Tammy Wynette was singing her new hit single—at least, that's what the DJ said—and a loudspeaker voice kept cutting in, saying, "Shower Number 65 is ready. Shower Number 73 is ready."
The building I stepped into was really three different places: A store where they sold motor oil and maps and air freshener and shirts and books on Christianity; an area, down a corridor, marked *DRIVER'S LOUNGE. PROFESSIONAL DRIVERS ONLY!* and a restaurant. My mouth watered at the picture of a steak on the menu they'd posted out front. But with only fifteen bucks in my pocket — Jake and Sammy had wanted gas money — I bought a baked potato, slathered it with sour cream and washed it down with a cup of lukewarm coffee.

Then I went looking for a pay phone.
It was near the women's bathroom, which was labeled *FILLIES* and, in case you didn't get it, the door had a picture of a flirty girl horse with long eyelashes. The phone was in an old-fashioned booth. I shut the glass door, picked up the yellowed phone book that was dangling from a rusted chain, and forced myself to turn to G.

There were lots of Grahams in Bakersfield, and none of them was Mary Jo, but two had just the initial "M." I called the first one and a man answered.

"Can I speak to Mary Jo?" I asked, pretty sure that he was white and wouldn't know her.

He hung up without answering me.

I made a face at the phone, and called the second number. It rang once, twice, three times. Then a tired-sounding woman's voice said, "Yeah?"

"Mary Jo?" I asked, quietly.

"Who is this?"

"Gracie."

There was silence while she looked for me in her mental file. I could hear the second when it clicked in. Gracie, white girl, messin' with my brother.

I said, "Don't hang up. I gotta talk to you."

"Why? Where's Marcus?"

My stomach dropped a few floors. *She didn't know!* I hadn't thought about that possibility.

I couldn't speak. The silence stretched out way too long. A short white woman in khaki shorts and a polo shirt walked past the phone booth into the ladies' room. And then I heard Mary Jo's voice, trying to sound hard and just sounding terrified. "Where *is* he? What's going on! You better tell me, fast!"

I started shaking, and turned to face the wall. "He's dead."

"Dead?!" She was yelling now. "How can he be dead?!"

I couldn't yell back, not in such a public place; it came out as a broken hiss. "He called you! Didn't he *tell you?!*"

"What are you talking about?"

"He called you in March. I saw the phone bill!"

"He called me on my birthday!" I heard the breath shudder out of her body. "God damn you, I knew you'd kill him!"

I slammed the receiver down, and somehow managed to get outside and halfway to the far end of the parking lot before I started sobbing violently. Two men passed me, headed toward the building. One of them looked like he wanted to come over, but I waved him away with an angry hand and started pacing a small, tight circle, biting my lip and thinking *fuck you, fuck you, fuck you, fuck you!*

But after a while, the passion went out of it. The tears tapered off, and the noise died down in my head. I went back inside and put another dime in the phone.

"I thought you knew," I said, when she picked up.

"How would I know?" She sounded like she hated my guts, but I could hear from her voice that she'd been crying, too. "Nobody told me anything."

I said, "He didn't tell me, either, 'till it got so bad he couldn't hide it anymore."

There was a long, grim pause at the end of the line. She didn't want to talk to me, but I was the only one she could ask. "What was it?"

"They said it was that new thing. AIDS."

"Damn," she said, and some of the fight had gone out of her voice. Being a nurse, she knew about AIDS. "*Goddamn*. Poor Marcus!"

"Well, that's it. I just wanted you to know."

"Wait!" She must have heard that I was going to hang up. "Where are you?"

"What do you give a shit?"

"Look, I didn't mean that about you killing him."

I said, "It doesn't matter. He's gone. You don't have to talk to me again."

"Yeah, I do," she said, sounding bitter about it. "You're the only one knows what happened. Where are you?"

Fuck you, I thought. *You fucking bitch!* My hand was on the phone to disconnect her, but I couldn't do it. Whatever she thought of me, she was still Marcus's sister. She'd all but raised him. I couldn't cut her off like that.

"La Corona truck stop. Right off 99."

"In *town?!*"

"Yeah."

I wasn't going to explain, but apparently I didn't have to. She said, "Are you driving?"

"No."

"Well, stay put. I'll come over."

"But…"

I was talking to myself. She had already hung up.

I went back in the café, got a booth, ordered more coffee and sat there not drinking it, running my hand along the back of the red vinyl seat.

Finally, Mary Jo walked in. Without a word, she slid into the opposite bench and put her purse up on the table.

The sight of her jolted me. I'd forgotten how much like Marcus she looked. She had his wide, full mouth, and his eyes – swollen now from crying but still looking like if you jumped into them you could dive down for miles and meet yourself at the bottom. She was tall like him, too, but where Marcus had been solid as a tree trunk, Mary Jo was slim. I was willing to bet she was strong, though. Stronger than she looked, unless you were looking hard.

I was looking hard, and so was she. I knew what she saw on my side of the table: the burnt-out wreck of what used to be a person, held together by nothing but habit.

She said, "Back when we met, in San Francisco, I wasn't very nice to you."

I shrugged, truly not caring.

"I didn't like you being a speed freak."

That got my attention. I stared back into her red-rimmed eyes. "How'd you know?"

Her mouth quirked up a little, with that arrogance I remembered. "You're kidding, right?"

I tried to sneer right back at her, but it probably looked feeble. "I quit that stuff. Marcus made me quit." Hearing the words, I realized they weren't quite right. "Well, he didn't make me. He made me want to."

She nodded, her lips pressed tight together.

The waitress came and poured more coffee. I rubbed the back of my neck, where an ache had settled in for the long haul. I didn't know if it was guilt or grief or the stress of being on the road that made every muscle in my body hurt. Maybe it was all three of them. I said, "Even if I wasn't a bargain, I did my best to make him happy."

She nodded again. You could see this was killing her. "He looked happy enough that time I saw you."

I nodded, too, to let her know I appreciated that. And then we both sat there, smelling stale coffee and feeling real sad.

"Where you gonna stay tonight?" she asked, suddenly.

I shrugged. *Under a bush somewhere*, I was thinking.

"Hmph," she said, just like I'd spoken. "I'll bet Marcus would just love that!"

Damned if she didn't have his intuition! I thought *don't you talk to me about what Marcus would feel.* And then I wanted to squirm, 'cause she was right about what he would have felt.

Mary Jo hadn't taken her eyes off me. I was the one who finally had to look away. When I looked back, she was reaching into her purse. Her hand came back out with a few dollars bills that she put under the salt shaker.

"Come on," she said, standing up slowly. She moved like she'd aged twenty years in that many minutes. "I've got something to show you."

eight

Mary Jo lived in a pretty stucco house in what looked like a nice section of town. Even in the dark, I could see that her front yard was neatly kept, with plants and cactus in little pots, and a tree that was smooth and gnarled like driftwood.

Inside was pretty, too. Her living room had more plants, and was painted beige and salmon pink. There were shawls draped over two cozy-looking chairs, and a long, wide, over-stuffed couch with beige and white pillows. The room was soft and neat and homey; if anyone but Mary Jo had lived here, I would have called it feminine.

"Nice," I said.

"It's close to the hospital." She pointed to the couch, in a way that wasn't unfriendly but told me she didn't have much slack left. "Sit down."

I did. Mary Jo went into what looked like a bathroom and shut the door. A moment later I heard water running, and when she came out I could see she had splashed some on her eyes.

She walked straight to the bookcase and reached for the top shelf. I'd known it would be something like this, but still, my stomach started to clutch as she took down a leather-covered album.

When she held it out to me, I thought *this woman doesn't like me, but she's trying to be nice.* What was I going to do, throw that in her face?

My hand shook as I opened the album.

And there was Marcus, little and sweet and about the same age Rosie was when she died, staring up at me from the same face he would have when he was thirty. He was wearing a red plastic fireman's helmet, and sitting on a beat-up plastic fire truck.

My eyes rolled shut. I think I moaned.

"Put your head down." Mary Jo took the book from my hands. "Open your mouth and let the air in."

I did what she said, lowering my head between my knees. I tried to breathe deep and slow, tried to not pass out or throw up on her beige carpet.

"Damn," she said, sitting down beside me. She didn't sound like a nurse anymore. She sounded like a woman who was truly sorry.

I sat up slowly. "I'm OK," I said, but I really wasn't.

We sat there for a little more, but neither of us had the heart to make conversation. After a while, Mary Jo said, "You might as well sleep on the couch, it's too late for you to go anywhere." She went to the closet and took out a pillow and sheets and a towel and blanket, and I thanked her and we said good night. I turned the light off and curled up under the blanket, not bothering with anything more, and lay there and tried not to listen to the muffled sobs from Mary Jo's room.

The next morning I told her about the first time Marcus threw up blood, and the emergency room at the hospital. About how he started going to the clinic and wouldn't talk to me about it, just kept getting weaker and weaker, but then there were times when it seemed to have passed and he would be himself again, laughing and dancing and making love, although I didn't say that part to her. And then about how he started to fail, his body like a battleground with the sores and rashes and the fungus in his mouth. I told her how he melted away 'till, at the end, he was just half his weight. We both cried, talking about that part. Women always say we don't want to be loved for our bodies, but when you get right down to it, we love our men the same way. And Marcus was so fine, so beautiful, losing him was bad enough without watching his body turn to dust.

Then I told her about the funeral and all the people at São Sebastãio, how much they loved him. And that's where I ran out of steam and stopped talking.

Mary Jo got up. "Poor Marcus," she said again. Her lips were clamped together, tight.

She went in the kitchen to make breakfast. She made bacon and eggs and cut up some bread and heaped it on a plate. I wasn't hungry, but I made myself eat it; who knew when the next meal would come. When I was finished, she said, "Where are you going now?"

"I don't know. Back east, maybe."

Saying it made me wonder how Blondell was doing, and whether her Granny B. had pulled through. I thought about calling her in the next town; thought about getting some change, finding a pay phone. But I couldn't picture what I would say to her, particularly if the worst had happened, so I thought maybe I would wait a few days.

Blondell wasn't much for telephones, and I wasn't ready to face more death.

Mary Jo was watching me as if she could look into my mind. For a second, it made me curious about her, curious about what kind of person she was; but the feeling passed as fast as it had come up. I was too worn out to maintain it.

"You want a ride to the bus station?" she asked.

"No, thanks. But you can point me toward the highway."

"You're *hitching?*" Mary Jo gave me a real hard look. "Are you trying to get killed so you can be with him?"

I started to tell her it didn't work like that, but what did I really know about how it worked?

When I didn't answer, she stood up sharply. "All right," she said, "I'll take you to the highway. You can kill yourself if you want to. And if you don't, give me a call someday."

♥

Heading east on Route 58, the heat was fierce. I'd only stood for ten minutes in the spot where Mary Jo left me before sweat was trickling down my shirt front and plastering my blue jeans to my legs. Ten minutes after that, my eyes were tired of squinting off the sun, and the arm that was holding up my thumb had begun to ache. Every car, every truck that sped past me kicked more heat into my face, and pretty soon I was pacing angrily, growling at passing cars like a surly dog. By then, I wondered if *I* would have stopped to pick me up.

Someone finally did, though; a middle-aged, thick-set white man with a buzz cut. I got into his Ford, half-grunted my thanks and hunkered down, careful not to look at him. In my experience, it was good to stay away from people with those haircuts. A few drinks and they got unpredictable – angry and self-righteous, a bad combination.

It took him five minutes to ask my name. "Susan," I said. By that time, he'd switched on the radio *("CUZZ—Bakersfield's Best Country Music Station")* and I was pretending to listen so I didn't have to talk.

"Where are you going, Susan?"

The true answer was *damned if I know,* but what I said was, "Vegas." I liked the sound of the word in my mouth. *Vegas* didn't sound like the places I'd been.

He said, "I'm not going that far, but I'll take you to North Edwards." And then we went back to not talking.

I was grateful that Buzz had the air conditioning on. Outside his car, it was flat, brown, barren and so hot the air shimmered up in a haze from the road; but inside it felt just fine.

After a while, we passed a long row of scrubby mountains.

"Tehachapi Range," Buzz said, waving his head in their general direction. I hadn't asked, and he didn't sound like he expected me to answer, but the sound of his voice was somehow reassuring.

A little further on, we drove by some hills that had row after row of what looked like white, wooden, three-armed storks on top of them. I turned around to stare at the gawky structures as we drove past. They looked lonely, stuck on that hillside just past arm's reach of each other, like lovers who were doomed to spend their lives not touching.

"Wind turbines." He sounded proud, and I snuck another look at him, the first real one since I got in his car. It surprised me to see steel grey in his hair.

A little ways past the scrubby mountains and the foothills with their windmill storks, the land flattened out. Most of what had passed for trees was gone, except for an occasional squat, gnarled stump rising out of what looked like scrub brush.

We drove through a tiny town called Mojave.

Flight Test School, said a sign by the road.

"Why is there a flight test school in a little place like that?" I asked, the words out of my mouth before I remembered I wasn't talking to Buzz.

He threw me a *where have you been?* type glance and said, "That's because of Edwards. Edwards Air Force Base."

Flight test school. Air Force Base. NASA landings. This guy's hair cut. The light finally went on in my head. "You're going to leave me on a military base?"

"Hell, no! I'm going to leave you on the road outside of it."

That didn't sound much better to me. "Are you sure that's legal? My being so near a place like that?"

"Sure it is. Just stay off government ground and nobody'll shoot at you." He was grinning, but I couldn't tell if that was a joke or not. "We don't take well to trespassing," he explained.

Yes, sir, I wanted to say.

Finally, he spoke. "You're not carrying water, are you."

"No." *Sir.*

"I'll give you some. It's hot out here."

Hell, what was it back there? I thought, but I didn't say it. Apparently we were coming up on my destination, and I was grateful for any help I could get. More grateful than I wanted to admit.

Ten minutes later, he pulled off the road at a sign for *EDWARDS AFB*. We both got out, and he walked around to open up his car trunk.

Inside was a big red cooler. He reached in and handed me a screw-top jar. "Drink it slowly or you might get cramps," he said.

The water was cold. That first long, shuddering gulp made me feel almost alive, and suddenly I was desperate with thirst. I took another drink, trying to slow down, then pried my mouth reluctantly off the jar lip.

"Here." I held it out, but Buzz shook his head.

"You'd better keep it. People die out here without water."

They *die?* "Thank you," I said, touched in spite of myself.

"You're welcome. You be careful, now."

I nodded. He got in his car and drove away and I stood there clutching the jar of water. My bag felt heavy on my shoulder.

How long does it take to get used to the heat? How do they stand it without any trees? Why would anybody want to—BOOM!

The sound came out of nowhere, and startled me so bad I almost jumped into the road. It was like hearing the world crack in half.

I looked around frantically. Nothing behind me. Nothing overhead. Then I saw what looked like a plane, far off to the right and moving fast, literally streaking toward the horizon.

That's what had made that noise?

I opened the jar and took a steadying drink of water. Screwed it shut, and felt the sun burning my arms. And suddenly, I wanted out of there, bad. Whatever they were doing in this place, I didn't want to see it, hear it or know about it.

I stuck my thumb out, determined to be a model hitchhiker. Last time, it had taken forever to get a ride. This time I wouldn't pace, I wouldn't glare, I would try my best to look pleasant.

An hour later, I was done with that approach. All it had got me was some gravel kicked up by trucks that were going too fast to stop, and a few snotty looks from old people in big cars. I'd finished the jar of water, and would have smashed it in frustration, but knowing that I was six inches off U.S. Government property cooled me out. A little bit.

What cooled me out more was the total strangeness of my surroundings. Bustling, temperate, hip San Francisco—the place where I'd spent most of my life—already seemed like a waking dream. If I'd stepped off the edge of the earth, I couldn't have felt any more uprooted. Who'd known that, just outside the boundary of my world, there was heat like this? Sky like this? Emptiness that so perfectly matched the gaping emptiness inside me?

I was hypnotized by the bizarre landscape.

It's a pretty big country, Dr. Weiss had said. I hadn't understood him then. I'd thought he meant that it covered lots of ground. Now I saw that it was also big in variety.

Maybe out here I could elude myself.

Finally a pick-up truck drove by. It was red and rusty, but moving fast. I thought I saw a woman driver, thought I saw her head swivel toward me as she sped past.

Just when I'd given up hope of her stopping, the truck jerked roughly off the road and squealed to a halt. I picked up my bag and was about to jog over when her engine revved, her wheels spun gravel and the truck came careening backwards toward me on the road's narrow shoulder.

I jumped onto government land. Maybe I'd get blown up for it, but I wasn't staying on that shoulder while some lunatic came barreling down on me. Good thing I did it, too; the truck screeched to a halt in the place where my toes had been ten seconds before.

I walked over, cautiously. The passenger side window was rolled down, and a voice like sand paper came out of it, saying, "What are you waitin' for? Get in!"

Well, I would have, but I was too busy staring. She gave me another few seconds. Then she said, "The ride's free, Honey. The peep show's twenty bucks."

I scrambled into the truck.

She burned rubber squealing back onto the road, and gunned the engine unmercifully. I couldn't tell if she was pissed at me for staring, or if that was just how she always drove. "What's the matter, you never saw a tattoo before?" she growled.

Hot pain suddenly lanced through me, pain that was bad enough to blur reality. I could feel Marcus's arm under my fingertips, feel the motion of my hand tracing dragon scales up his arm, feel my tongue form the letters of my name on his chest. I shook my head, trying to clear it. "Yeah, I've seen tattoos before." What I'd never seen was a sixty-year-old broad with bright red hair and hot pink lipstick and tattoos splashed on her arms and legs, and covering what I could see of her chest.

"This is nothing," she said. "I've got Franklin Roosevelt on my thigh. I've got the Virgin Mary on my back. I've got birds of paradise on my tits. I'm a walking work of art, and don't you forget it."

Maybe I was hallucinating. Maybe Buzz had put something in that water. My mind seized on a small detail; something solid, to steady me. "What does that thing on your wrist mean?" I asked.

"*That thing* on my wrist is a snake eating its own tail." She glanced down at the picture, fondly. "Ancient symbol for eternity. Winston Churchill's mother had one."

"Winston Churchill's mother had a tattoo?"

"Lots of fancy women had tattoos back in the day. You just think it's a biker chick thing 'cause you grew up in the '50s and don't know any better."

I thought of Blondell, who had a butterfly on her left breast, a blood red rose on one ass cheek, an African woman in leg chains on the side of her right thigh and two or three geometric patterns. I had looked at those damned tattoos for months on end, and never thought to ask what they meant to Blondell.

If I ever saw her again, I would ask.

I said, "I don't think it's a biker chick thing."

"Well, good," the illustrated woman replied. "I guess you're smarter than you look."

I didn't have anything to say to that, so we rode a fair distance in silence. I entertained myself by sneaking looks at her skin pictures, and she passed the time chain smoking and cursing other drivers.

Finally, she glanced at me again. "By the way, where are you going?"

"Probably straight to hell," I murmured, before I'd had a chance to think.

The woman threw back her head and laughed. She had a nice laugh— scratched up, like her voice, but generous. "That's in the other direction, Honey."

I could feel the corners of my mouth edge up. It surprised me to be half-smiling so soon after losing Marcus. I looked out the window, ashamed about it.

When I looked back, she had a fresh Camel in her mouth and was touching the dashboard lighter to it, driving seventy miles an hour with the steering wheel held in three fingers of her left hand.

All right, I admitted, the old broad had style. In fact, she reminded me of someone, and I had to think for several minutes before I realized that someone was Blondell. Aside from race and the difference in their ages and the fact that Blondell didn't know how to drive, they could have been twins, they seemed so similar. I thought *if Blondell lives long enough, this is how she's gonna be.*

"You smoke reefer?" the woman asked suddenly.

I looked at her sideways, and she laughed again. "You think I'm too old to get high."

I did, which was silly and I wasn't going to say so.

She shook her head. "I would've made that same face at your age. Let me tell you something, Honey. Old people are just young people whose bodies have crapped out on 'em."

"You're not that old," I said, lying through my teeth.

She shot me a look that shut me up quick, and said, "Reach back over the seat for my purse and get me the joint that's in there, would you?"

Now I really was shocked. "You want me to go into your *purse?*"

"Why not?" She grinned. "Not much in it, plus I got a gun up here under my leg."

I couldn't help it; I chuckled.

I found the joint and gave it to her. She lit it off her cigarette and tossed the cigarette out the window. Then she took a long, noisy haul and held the joint out toward me.

I tried not to stare too hard at the arm she was waving in my direction. It was solidly tattooed down to that wrist-snake—a hodge-podge of unmatched pictures and patterns that seemed to meld together, even as they stood apart. My eye picked out a butterfly, an American flag, the word *MOTHER*, blindfolded Justice holding her scales, a Hula girl, a baby eagle—and that was just one arm.

For all that they made a bold statement, though, the tattoos themselves were strangely muted. They weren't the vibrant greens and reds and blues that had sparkled on Marcus's dark skin. Hers were mostly a dull slate gray. Their black outlines were strong and clean, but they looked like they'd been around for a while.

Well, that was enough art criticism. I took the joint she was holding out, and dragged the familiar, comforting smoke as deep into my lungs as I could. Holding it there, I thought about how long it had been since I'd smoked any grass.

I hoped it wouldn't make me paranoid or weepy. But instead, it made me grandiose, the way marijuana often does.

I'm never going back, I thought after two puffs. *I'll just keep traveling, living on air, until I come to someplace I can...*

"You gonna hold that thing all day?" a droll voice asked.

"Shit! I'm sorry." I held the joint out to her.

"No problem. You got a name?"

"Yeah." I thought about telling her I was Susan. It seemed like a silly thing to do. "Grace."

She inhaled slowly. Exhaled. Passed the joint back. She said, "I'm Blanche."

I must have been even higher than I thought, 'cause the next thing I heard myself saying was, "Where are *you* heading, Blanche?"

"A little town called Wagon Wheel, over in Nevada."

The grass was making me more inclined to talk than I'd been before. "What kind of a town is that?"

She said, "A one-horse town. Used to have a gold mine. Then it was a ghost town. Now it's two stores, a casino, couple of trailer parks for the old folks. Tattoo joint. Nice, though. Nice people. Nice to look at, if you like the desert. Do you?"

By now she'd completely lost me. "Do I what?"

"Do you like the desert?"

"Don't know," I said. "What does it look like?"

She laughed so hard I thought she was going to fall off her seat. "It looks like what you're seeing out the window," she said. "That's the Mojave."

"But it's got… " I didn't know what to call them. "Bushes."

"Shit," she said, sputtering out more laughter, "that's just mesquite."

"Where's the sand dunes?"

"In Arabia, you fool!" she said. "This is high desert, American-style."

The desert! No wonder I'd been thirsty. No wonder it was quiet.

"And hot," she said, with a cute little grin. Apparently I'd spoken out loud.

"Is your town—Wagon Wheel— is that in the desert, too?"

"Honey," she said, "don't let 'em fool you, it's all damn desert around here. They just poured water on top of some of it."

Half an hour and six Camels later, she pulled off the road. A big sign said we were about to hit the junction of I-15 and I-40. "Here's where you get to choose," Blanche informed me. I didn't know what she meant, so she added, "I-15 goes to Las Vegas. I-40 goes to Flagstaff, Phoenix, Albuquerque…"

Her voice trailed off and left those place names hanging in the car. None of them seemed right anymore, not even Vegas.

"You're going home?" I tried to sound casual.

"I'm going home," she said, all friendly like.

"To Wagon Wheel?" I was vamping for time.

She didn't point out how stupid I sounded, just gave me a little smile and said, "That's right."

Her smile made it even harder to think about facing the road again with no water, no plan, no clue how to survive out here.

I took a big breath and said, "OK," as if she'd asked a question, and I'd just figured out the answer.

"OK what?" She lit another cigarette.

"OK." Mentally, I crossed my fingers. "I'll go to Wagon Wheel with you."

nine

Crossing from Southern California into Nevada was like crossing through Alice's Looking Glass.

SLOTS! a billboard screamed.

NICKEL SLOTS!

We were two feet over the state line. The billboard was bigger than a good-sized truck. Same desert, same scrubby brush, same sunlight burning the back of my arm where it rested on the window ledge. But different, all of it.

FILL YOUR TANK! JAKE'S HOUSE OF SLOTS!

I turned around in my seat to see the billboard again, but I needn't have bothered; another one came up in half a mile.

JAKE'S HOUSE OF SLOTS! FREE TANK OF GAS WITH EVERY WIN!

A mile later, it was, *ONLY SIX MILES TO JAKE'S HOUSE OF SLOTS! HOME OF THE ENDLESS CUP OF COFFEE.*

"They stole that," Blanche harumphed.

"Stole what?" I pushed some damp hair back off my face. Was it my imagination or was it hotter here than in California?

"Home of the Endless Cup of Coffee. That's the slogan for Finer Diner."

"Finer Diner?"

She nodded. "In Wagon Wheel. Home of the Endless Cup of Coffee, until that dumb bastard Jake stole it."

THREE MILES TO JAKE'S WORLD-FAMOUS HOUSE OF SLOTS!

"He stole the endless cup of coffee?"

"He stole the *name*," she growled.

It was strange, wanting to play her straight man. "Why'd he do a dumb bastard thing like that?"

"Cause he's a dumb *bastard*," Blanche crowed, and when she laughed, I laughed with her.

The rusty sound was still echoing in my ears when, a minute later, Jake's World-Famous Home of the Nickel Slots whizzed by. It was a broken-down gas station with one pump and three slot machines under a sagging portico.

"That's Jake's House of Slots?!"

Blanche nodded.

"That's a fucking rip-off!" I sulked.

"Most things are," she said. "Relax, we'll be home in half an hour."

And she fell silent, leaving me to wonder why that word, *home,* sounded so damned good.

♥

Wagon Wheel was just what Blanche had said it would be: A one-horse town with two stores, three trailer parks and one seedy-looking, low-slung casino, The Gaslight. I didn't see the tattoo parlor, but judging by Blanche, it would be close by.

She pulled into The Gaslight's parking lot, squeezing past three tour buses and into a space between a sports car and a silver Coupe de Ville.

"Don't be fooled by the cars," she said. "This place is a rat bag, and always will be. But if I don't play some slots, I'm not home." She got out of the truck and gave me a look that made it clear I could either follow her or sit there and get heat prostration.

I don't like gambling and I don't like crowds, but I liked the idea of sweltering to death less, so I opened the door and got out slowly, uncoiling muscles that were plenty stiff.

"Where do you live?" I asked, catching up with her.

She pointed at a billboard just across the road: *PARADISE MOBILE HOMES. TEN MINUTES TO SCENIC COTTONWOOD LAKE.* An arrow pointed the way to Paradise, and a big handmade sign, stuck in the ground below the billboard, added *PARADISE TATTOOS, FIRST TRAILER ON THE LEFT.* "You coming?" she asked, walking briskly toward the sound of one-arm bandits and an old jukebox.

I trotted behind her, through a door that squeaked, into my first taste of desert air conditioning.

It was cold. Cold enough that the hairs on my arms stood up and I sneezed six times in a row. Cold enough that objects suddenly had an edge instead of a fuzzy outline. Cold enough that I didn't ever want to go outside again.

The Gaslight was basically two medium-sized rooms. To the right was a diner—Finer Diner, was my educated guess—with half a dozen tables and a long, old-fashioned countertop. In the room on the left, nickel and quarter slot machines fanned out in rows around a bar with a blaring TV suspended over it.

The diner was full, and every slot machine was taken. If half the people in there weren't over 70, I would eat the front door.

Blanche made a bee-line for a slot machine that had an official picture of Ronald Reagan hanging over it. I wasn't in the mood for Ronnie myself, so I wandered into the diner and sat down at the counter. Behind it was a pass-through window to the kitchen and an old, hand lettered sign that said, *COFFEE SERVED BY A WAITRESS IN THE CAFÉ WILL BE WRITTEN UP ON A TICKET AND PAID FOR.*

There were two waitresses working the room—one middle-aged and sturdy, the other one looking barely out of her teens—and the older one put a menu in front of me. "What'll it be, Kiddo?" she asked.

I opened the menu cautiously. "Don't know," I said. "How much is coffee?"

"Fifteen cents, but don't you mind, it's worth every penny. I make it myself. And this is the Home of the Endless Cup of Coffee."

I glanced up at her, feeling a still-unfamiliar sensation at the edges of my mouth: it was a grin. "You cook, too?" I asked.

"No," she said. "Homer does that. He's not too bad, though. Try the eggs—they're cheap and it's hard to ruin them."

I handed the menu back to her, wondering if Nevada had a program to breed these tough, straight-talking old broads. "Eggs over easy and coffee."

"That comes with toast. You want whole wheat or regular?"

"Regular." I paused, took a breath, jumped off the ledge. "You got any work around here?"

"Homer! Over easy, don't burn 'em." She was pouring my coffee while she called through the pass-through, so I wasn't sure she'd heard me 'till she turned back and said, "Not much. What kind of work you looking for?"

I glanced into the other room— loud, dim, smoky and small— and decided not to mention bartending. "I can waitress."

"We don't need anybody right now. Val is helping out with the rush, and people don't eat like they used to."

"How come?"

"Beats me. Too busy at the slots, is my guess, or maybe it's Homer's cooking. Do you cook?"

I saw Marcus, standing over a pot of soup, his big hands tearing orange sections into little pieces. It was just an image, a flash, but it went through me like a bullet. If I hadn't been sitting, it would have brought me to my knees.

The waitress was looking at me funny, and I gave my head a little shake. I didn't cook. I'd never had to learn. Marcus had taken care of me.

My arms felt almost numb with cold, and I wrapped my hands around the Endless Cup of Coffee she'd put in front of me. That *Helen* had put in front of me. That was her name, it said so on her name tag. I could feel the cup's warmth against my fingertips, but it wasn't spreading further, so I dragged the cup to my mouth and drank. Maybe Endless Coffee would melt the block of ice that was moving toward my chest.

"Helen!" I heard Blanche's gravelly voice, felt her slip into the empty stool to my right. "Get this girl a double orange juice. She needs the sugar."

"You gonna pay?" With my head bowed, all I could see was Helen's hand as she slid a plate of eggs and toast in front of me. "What'd you get rich poking fly boys down at Edwards?"

Blanche didn't sound offended by that. "No, I got rich playing your damned slot machines." I looked up to see her lift both hands and pour a pile of quarters onto the counter. Everyone in eye shot stopped what they were doing to watch her—or else, they were looking at the faded tattoos jiggling on her bare arms.

Blanche didn't even notice the attention. "Make that two double O.J.'s," she said.

❤

By the time Blanche got tired of playing her slots and we drove over to Paradise Mobile Homes, the sun had long since dropped below the horizon. Paradise was a handful of rundown trailers, placed at a fair distance from each other in a scraggly parking lot.

"It's not much," Blanche said, opening the door to the first one on the left, "but I got air conditioning and a spare couch."

"I'm not the Queen of England," I said. "Without you, I'd be sleeping in a ditch tonight."

She nodded and I stood there, taking in my strange surroundings.

We were in what would have been the living room, if it hadn't been covered with tattoo art. The walls were plastered almost floor-to-ceiling with sheet after sheet of cartoon-like pictures—eagles and skulls and naked hula girls were jostling up next to pictures of Jesus, the stars and stripes, the Confederate flag, some biker insignia, some World War II stuff...

In addition to the drawings all over her living room, Blanche had a tattoo parlor in her kitchen. Or rather, her kitchen had cabinets, a stove, a sink and a formica countertop, but instead of a refrigerator, a big lounge chair was pushed close to the sink. And instead of the kind of table you'd eat at, she had a big wooden work desk covered with papers and cans of utensils, and jars of colored stuff the texture of paint, and a small black electric apparatus that looked like something from a torture chamber.

Come to think of it, the place was a little dungeon-like, with a heavy layer of grime on the windows, a blue shag carpet that looked none too fresh, and cigarette ash lying around everywhere.

It all seemed to call for some reaction. "You drew all these tattoos yourself?" I asked, gesturing to the walls around us.

"Those are called flash," she said. "The artwork. The tattoo's what goes on your body."

"So did you do all those tattoos on your arms?"

"Don't forget the rest of me."

"There's more?"

"Honey, I've got a body suit! And no, once I was done practicing on myself, like everybody does, I didn't do any of my own tats." She grinned. "That would be like fucking yourself."

I wasn't sure which thought was more unsavory: My new friend trying to fuck herself, or picturing her without any clothes on.

She smiled as if she knew what I was thinking, and I made a strategic retreat. "Blanche, you got a telephone?" It was long past time for me to call Blondell. So far I'd been too scared to do it.

But Blanche was shaking her head. "A phone makes it too easy for people to find you."

I gave her a half-smile. I knew the feeling.

"Bathroom's right here, if you want to wash up," she said, pointing to a narrow door. Behind it was a four foot bathtub, a toilet and the tiniest sink I'd ever seen. It looked like if you washed a shirt in it, the water would slop all over the sides. In the mirror above it, I looked like a zombie. And since the mirror was dull and wavy, I figured I probably looked much worse than that. But at least Marcus wasn't staring back from behind my eyes, the way he had been every day at Blondell's. Maybe the mirror wasn't good enough to catch his image, or maybe he didn't know where to find me, out here in the desert.

I splashed some lukewarm water on my face, but I didn't see anything to use for soap, so I gave up on washing and just dug through my shoulder bag for a toothbrush. I used that to scrape the film off my teeth and tongue. Then I brushed my hair as hard as I could, but it still felt like two weeks of oil was matted in. When was the last time I'd washed it, anyway?

When I went back out to Blanche's living room, I felt marginally more human. She had a pan of water boiling on the stove, and had set two mismatched china plates on the counter.

"You must be about ready for dinner," she said, digging around in the overhead cupboard and pulling out a half-crushed box of Red Rose tea bags, a jar of peanut butter and a twelve-pack of stale-looking Little Debbie brownies.

I sat in the lounge chair while she brewed strong tea, laced it with lumpy sugar, tore the plastic off two brownies, and put one on a plate for me. "Those are pretty good with peanut butter," she said, waving the jar of Skippy at me.

"How long have these been sitting around?" I asked—ungraciously, considering that I was hungry.

But, as usual, nothing seemed to phase Blanche much. "Long enough to grow hair," she said, biting off half her brownie and chewing it hard.

Since that one wasn't killing her, I took a cautious bite of mine. It tasted like chocolate soap and had the texture of a moldy sponge.

I put it down and started nursing the tea. That at least was drinkable. But if I was going to eat any real food the next day, I'd obviously have to come up with the cash to buy it. "Blanche, you think there's any work around here?"

"What are you looking for?" she asked.

Not stripping; I'd had my fill of that. "I can waitress. I've been a bartender."

"There's just Finer Diner and they're staffed up right now. You don't cook, do you?" she added hopefully.

This time, at least I'd seen the question coming. "No," I said. "I never had much need for it."

"I don't suppose you want to learn tattooing..."

Was that a note of hope in her voice?

I shuddered, sorry to disappoint her. "I don't like needles," I explained. It was true. When I was little, I'd seen too many of them—around my mother, around her friends....

"Well, I don't bet any customers will come by tonight anyway."

"Why not?" I had to stifle a yawn.

"It's Monday night." I hadn't known that. "It's not pay day, it's not a holiday and not too many people are on the road."

"Then how do you make a living?" I asked.

"Like Helen said, tattooing fly boys down at Edwards."

The base. She must have worked there over the weekend. "Well, I'm strong, and I don't mind working hard," I said. "Aren't there any odd jobs in town?"

"Not too often, and when there are, we got all these old retired people to do them. They don't even want to get paid, they just want to get out of the house for a few hours."

Reluctantly picking the brownie back up, I dipped a piece of it in the tea. It wasn't too bad when you'd softened it up—and faced that no second course was coming.

"There has to be *something* old folks can't do," I whined. Then I winced at how desperate I sounded. Well, I didn't want to go back to stealing; I'd never been good at it, and now I was too old.

Blanche shrugged. "Stick around a day or two, I'll see if I can think of something."

For some reason, I believed that she would try. Believing it dropped my guard down a little; and just that fast, all the exhaustion of the last two days— the heat, the road, the grass we'd smoked, the emotion last night with Mary Jo—rose up in my mind and crashed down on me in one bruising weight. I could feel it from my eyebrows to my big toes.

"Better lie down before you faint. You look like a ghost," my hostess said.

I could easily imagine that was true. I put down my brownie, walked to the couch and dropped my body heavily onto it.

"Take your shoes off," Blanche admonished.

I kicked them off, swung my legs up, curled into a ball.

Blanche went and pulled a pillow and a thin blanket out of her back room and handed them to me. "It's safe here," she said with surprising insight. "There's only one key to this place, and I keep it close."

I blinked at her. She was actually starting to blur around the edges. "You sound just like the girls I used to dance with at this shit hole back home," I mumbled, burrowing down under the blanket.

"Do I, now." Blanche sounded matter-of-fact, but the last thing I saw before I nodded off was her wicked little grin.

♥

For the first time in what seemed like months, I fell into a dreamless sleep. I woke up feeling profoundly lost. It took a minute for me to remember I was lying on the couch in Blanche's trailer.

The light was funny, that was part of my problem. I stared at the window. It seemed to be streaked with a mixture of cigarette smoke and grease.

"Why's the window so dirty?" I yawned, still too asleep to realize I was being rude.

"I don't do windows," Blanche cackled, pleased with her joke—whatever it was.

That woke me up; thank God I hadn't offended her!

"What time is it?" I stretched my arms out.

"Tuesday."

"Morning?"

"Afternoon, Honey."

"Damn." I sat up gingerly. My head hurt like the day after a bender, though I hadn't had anything to drink.

"You need some food," Blanche diagnosed. "It's just about time for the Early Bird Special."

"Look, I've only got about ten bucks and that's got to last me…"

"Don't be insulting, Miss Thing," she said. "I've got a business. I can stand you for one meal."

She put a *GONE TO THE GASLIGHT* sign in the front window, then drove us back to Finer Diner.

Helen served us again, but this time we sat at a real table. Blanche got chicken-fried steak and gravy and I set my jaws to work on Homer's pork chops—so grateful I wasn't going to have to pay the bill that I didn't even care they were dry and rubbery.

Halfway through the meal, Blanche suddenly put her fork down. "Emily Pearson," she said, just like I would know what she was talking about.

"Emily Pearson?"

"She might need a little help with her house."

"I don't do windows." I personally thought it was a mildly amusing thing to say.

But Blanche didn't laugh, she just gaped at me.

"What're *you* looking at?" I growled.

"You," she said. "You made a joke."

Yeah, and I was sorry about it. "Who's this Emily Pearson person?"

Which sounded funny, too, though Blanche had the good sense to ignore it this time. "She lives out past the end of town. Got a real house, kind of pretty, but it's overgrown. She might need someone to clear out the scrub brush. She's old and sort of bent over—she shouldn't be doing that kind of thing herself."

"Fine," I said. "But what's scrub brush?"

"Dead weeds, dry scrub pine. Stuff that fires up like kindling if you touch a match to it."

"Why would you touch a match to it?"

"You wouldn't, that's the point. But some sorry ass neighbor might drop a cigarette or maybe there's a lightning storm, the next thing you know your place is gone, poof!" She paused. "You ever use an axe?"

"Do I look like I ever used an axe?"

She gave me a quick once-over. "Well, you look strong enough, and you're not dumb."

"What's dumb got to do with using an axe?"

She shook her head like I was a damned shame. "Real city girl, aren't you? Dumb is when you don't know to get your leg out of the way in time."

"Jesus!"

She smiled, as if I'd passed some test. "I'll take you to see Emily tomorrow."

♥

"I brought someone over to meet you," Blanche said, when Emily Pearson opened her front door.

Emily was Blanche's opposite. They were both old and white, but Emily was small and mousy in a drab, faded housedress and Blanche was wearing tons of make-up, a yellow shirt that showed off her heavily tattooed cleavage, white pedal pushers that showed off her heavily tattooed calves and bright red high-top sneakers.

"Her name's Grace," Blanche continued, filling Emily's front steps with her personality. "I figured she could help you move some of that brush back from around the house."

"Come in, then." Emily turned without waiting for our reply and hobbled slowly back to her living room. I could see why Blanche didn't want her chopping things; she moved like someone whose bones were fused into funny positions.

"I can't pay you much." Emily motioned me into a chair. "Twenty dollars a day is all."

I managed to choke back a disgusted groan. At Girl-O-Rama, I'd made that in an hour. On the other hand, Emily Pearson didn't make me want to puke or take drugs, and twenty dollars probably went a lot further in Nevada than it did in California.

"How many days you think it'll take?"

"That depends on how hard you work. Two or three, I figure."

Sixty dollars, tops. "OK. But somebody's got to show me what to do."

♥

Eight hours later, I was curled up in Blanche's bathtub, cursing her, cursing Emily Pearson and cursing whoever invented scrub brush.

It didn't even help that Emily had fed me homemade vegetable soup, given me the twenty bucks in cash and thrown in a loaf of banana bread.

On the other side of the bathroom door, Blanche was belting out *Mind Your Own Business* with Hank Williams. The sound—kind of like a duet between a country angel and a drunken jay bird—would have made me smile if I hadn't been so tired and discouraged and sore. Muscles that were totally unfamiliar ached. If I never moved my shoulders again it was going to be too goddamn soon.

The song ended. "You drowning in there?" Blanche called out cheerfully.

Why is everyone so goddamn cheerful? I thought. *Why is everyone being so goddamn nice to me?*

A single, fat, self-pitying tear dripped down my cheek into the tepid bath water. Blondell, Blanche, Emily... even Mary Jo had been nice, in her own way.

Being nice to me was Marcus's job, a position that was supposed to remain empty. All these idiots trying to fill it were just pissing me off.

"You want to eat that banana bread for dinner?" Blanche called out, through the still-closed door. Behind her, I could hear another country song. This one was about driving down a lonesome highway. Blanche had sounded a little worried.

"Sure," I called back indifferently.

As if there was anything else to eat at Blanche's.

As if I gave a shit what we ate.

But that vegetable soup at Emily's had been good. Tomorrow, she'd said, she would show me how to make it.

ten

Blanche got up the next morning and toasted what was left of the banana bread for breakfast.

While we were eating it, she said, "How come you're not with anyone?"

I said, "None of your goddamn business."

"Yeah." She nodded. "That's my reason, too."

Then we finished our toast and she drove me over to Emily's.

Eight back-breaking hours later, she came back to get me. Blanche and Emily chatted for a minute and then we got into Blanche's truck.

"You want to go out and eat?" I asked. I wasn't up for brownies for dinner. "My treat."

"Why, you got a hole in your pocket?"

"Emily paid me extra."

Blanche snorted. "Extra nothin' still ain't much. But if you want to be a fool and get parted from your money, who am I to argue?"

"Damn, you're gracious."

"That's me," she said. "A bundle of charm."

But all she ordered for dinner was eggs, which was Blanche's way of being protective of me. I didn't have too much to protect, and I was too tired to care anyway, so I ordered a steak and gave her half.

We were splitting a cup of rice pudding for desert when a man walked in and Blanche waved and called out, "Francisco!"

He waved back at her, and walked over to our table. A stocky, good-looking Chicano—forty, maybe a little more—with dark skin, sable hair that fell in waves to his shoulders and big, sad eyes. Blanche scooted over and he sat down beside her.

"Hi, beautiful Blanche." He kissed her delicately on the cheek.

She smiled that secret smile that women of any age get when they think a man is attractive. "Hi, yourself. This is my friend Gracie."

We shook hands across the table. "I heard you were in here with a pretty *gringa*," he told Blanche.

My eyes narrowed. "How'd you hear that?"

It sounded harsh, and I was surprised when he merely said, "Haven't you ever lived in a small town?"

"No."

"Well, trust me, you're big news. You were over clearing Emily Pearson's land today, right?"

"That's right. Yesterday, too."

"Well, there you go." To him, that settled it.

Our waitress came over with more coffee. It wasn't Helen tonight, it was a young girl with dirty hair whose name badge said *Valerie.* "Evening, Francisco."

"Hi, Val." He gave her a gentle, sad-looking smile that seemed to have been specially matched with his eyes. "How's your little girl doing?"

Val smiled back at him. "She took three steps in a row last night. Then she fell smack on her little butt."

"Well, they do that. Next year she'll be running you ragged."

Val finished pouring the coffee and went off, looking happy at the thought.

"Where are you from, Miss Grace?" Francisco asked.

"No place." I didn't like his attitude, and I sure didn't like him getting in my business.

"Gracie!" Blanche looked like she wanted to take a swat at me. "He's just making conversation."

I gave her a hard look. "Well, you two go right ahead and converse. I'll be outside."

"That's OK. I'll let you ladies enjoy your coffee in peace." He stood up, tipped the hat he wasn't wearing in my direction. "Nice to meet you. And you stay sweet, Blanche."

Then he walked away, saying something to Val as he squeezed by her in the narrow aisle.

"Are you crazy?" Blanche hissed, when he was out the door.

"Not the last time I checked."

Val came by and said, "Francisco paid for your supper, girls." She gave me a smug smile, like she'd stuck it to me personally. "You have a nice evening."

I stood up, walked around Val and didn't stop till I was outside. I'd have walked straight to the curb and stuck my thumb out, too, but I remembered just in time that my picture of Marcus was back at Blanche's house.

She came out a moment later, opened her car door and got in without looking at me.

She didn't speak to me the whole way back to her trailer. She didn't speak to me while she was making tea. And she didn't speak to me when I lay down on her couch and spread her blanket from my toes to my chin.

Then she came over and pulled up a chair across from me and said, "What the hell is eating *you* up?"

"Nothing."

"You don't like Mexicans?" she pressed.

I said, "I don't like people asking questions."

"Why? 'Cause he said you were pretty?"

I glared at her. "It's none of his damned business where I come from, who I'm working for, what I look like or any of it."

"Hmph." She said it like now she understood something. She lit a cigarette, inhaled deeply and stared right at me while she blew out the smoke. "You want a brownie?"

"No, I don't want a goddamn brownie." Even to me, that sounded ridiculous. "But thanks anyway."

"Let me tell you a little story," she said. She was looking at me so intently that I sat up on the couch and wrapped the blanket around my legs, prepared to listen even though I couldn't have cared less.

"Francisco's people been in this town more than a hundred years. You know we took this place from the Mexicans, right?"

I hadn't known or cared, but I nodded so that she would go on. Hell, I owed her at least that much.

"I've known him since he was a boy. He up and grew into a fine young man—smart, well-educated, not like most people around here. And he brought this pretty little wife back from where he went to college. Cute little white girl like you, soft-spoken, seemed to be pretty smart in her own way."

"Where is she?"

"Over in the local graveyard. She had a lump in her stomach the size of your fist. They couldn't cut it out without killing her, so they sewed her up and sent her home to die."

I didn't want to hear this. "Nice deal," I said.

"Yeah. Francisco sure thought so." She took a long, deep drag off her cigarette and pounced. "You oughta cut people some slack, Gracie."

Just like that, my eyes filled with angry tears. "Let me tell you something," I snarled, "you don't get slack just for burying someone."

She didn't even blink, and I saw too late how she'd set me up to say that. Not that it mattered, now that I'd unleashed the memories. "You *bitch*," I growled, plenty loud enough for her to hear, and then I put my head down and wrapped my arms around my knees and let the tidal wave of anger and grief slam into me.

I felt Blanche's hand touch my head. "You gonna throw up?"

I gave my head a little shake, as much to knock off her hand as to answer. Tears were puddling on the blanket that covered my legs. I felt the hair beside my face curling into damp clumps. The muscles in my mouth ached from holding back the sound of raw despair.

"I'll make some tea," Blanche murmured, hurrying from the scene of her crime.

When she came back, I'd stopped crying. I felt calm, though I probably looked a wreck. She handed me a hot mug of tea, stiff with sugar, and I sipped it slowly, staring at her, daring her to make something of it.

"You're going to finish up at Emily's tomorrow," she said.

I nodded.

"You looking for some more work around here?"

I shrugged.

"Hmph. I'll see what I can do, then." She stood up and tossed her thin, yellow hair just like she was twenty and the hottest thing in three states. "Get your sorry ass to sleep. I'll wake you in the morning."

After she'd gone, I lay on her couch and stared at the streaky, moonlit sky through her living room window, and thought about Marcus. Thought about how safe I'd felt lying next to him, how my arms would wrap around his big, warm chest while he lay with his back pressed against me, sleeping. I played it over and over in my mind, passing the time, putting salt on the wound so I wouldn't ever forget the terrible pain that was the only thing I could give him now.

"Wake up, Grace." Confused, I pried my eyes open and looked up at Blanche. It was morning; I was lying on her couch. I didn't remember falling asleep. "You want a ride to Emily's?"

I felt exhausted. My muscles ached. I pushed my legs out from under the blanket and set my feet carefully on the floor.

"Yeah," I whispered. "Thanks."

Another day. What was the goddamn point of this?

Blanche dropped me off at Emily Pearson's, and sure enough, I had the rest of her yard cleared out by the end of the morning.

"How would you feel about cleaning inside?" Emily asked me over lunch. I'd stacked all the brush in a neat pile along the side of her house, and now we were sitting in her yard eating tuna fish and cheese melt sandwiches with pickles. She poured me some water from a jar with lemon slices in it. "I can't get down on my knees anymore, and that would give you the rest of the day's work."

I wasn't clear what she expected me to do on my knees, so I just said, "I don't really know how to clean. You'd just be throwing your money away."

"I can tell you what to do," she said hopefully. So hopefully that I was tempted, even though I knew she didn't really have the money and her place wasn't really what you'd call dirty.

Now Blondell's place, back when I'd been staying there with her, *that* was dirty! I thought about how I'd laid around her apartment for weeks on end and never washed a dish, never made a bed, never picked up a towel or brushed crumbs off the table. I'd been so messed up I hadn't even noticed, and Blondell had never mentioned it.

Damn, now I was putting salt on that wound, too. I hadn't even called Blondell. The only friend I had left in the world, and apparently I was just going to blow her off while her grandmother was dead or dying.

"It's not that hard," Emily said, misinterpreting my frown. "And I could really use the help. Why don't you try it?"

"All right," I agreed. Which is why I was on my knees two hours later when I heard a car drive up outside, and someone honked.

I went out, figuring it was Blanche, but it was her friend Francisco driving a Ford that had seen better days.

I wiped my hands on my jeans and turned to go back into the house.

"Hey! Grace!"

All right, so he wanted to talk to me.

"Not much of a car," I said, walking up to the driver's side window.

"Not much point in driving something fancy around the desert."

I said, "Emily went to town to get ammonia. You just missed her."

"I'm not looking for Emily." He didn't smile, which I appreciated. He'd already got the point that I wasn't interested in being his friend. "Blanche asked me to bring you home. I just dropped by to say I'll pick you up on my way back from Kingman."

Don't any of these people have phones? I wondered. *And where is Kingman, anyway?* But what I said to him was, "Why?"

"Why did she ask me to pick you up? She said you'd appreciate it."

"Then why didn't she come out herself, like she did yesterday and the day before?"

"She said her back hurt."

I scowled. "You buy that?"

"No." Then he added, "Ammonia?"

I scowled again. "She's teaching me to clean house."

He shook his head. "They make housecleaning products that don't take the skin off your hands."

"She's teaching me to wear those little yellow gloves." Which was way more than he needed to know. "How come you're doing Blanche a favor, anyway?"

He gave me a complicated look. "I thought you were into privacy."

"I am."

"Then it's none of your business."

He had a point, but I made a face anyway. "I don't mind walking back," I said.

"Suit yourself." He paused. "It's three miles."

Damn, three miles! After a full day of chopping wood and scrubbing Emily's floors?

He said, "I'll see you around five-thirty."

♥

"What'd you and Francisco talk about?" Blanche asked, when I got back to the trailer.

"Nothing."

"Nothing?"

I went in the kitchen and started rattling cabinets. They were just as empty as yesterday, which was really a shame 'cause I was hungry.

"Nothing?" she asked again.

I let go of the cabinet door I was holding and turned to her. "Gee, and here I thought I was speaking English."

"What's gotten into you?" she snapped. "Three days ago you were a nice person."

"Three days ago you weren't trying to mess with me!"

"That's what you call *messing with you*? Getting you work? Feeding you? Helping you find a nice guy?"

"I don't want to find a nice guy!" I yelled.

Which was true. I wanted to screw some miserable shit and get pregnant and get this over with.

Or did I? My hand stilled on the cabinet door as I realized that my actions weren't matching my words. After all, miserable shits weren't hard to find. I could go out and find one right now.

Damn you, Marcus! I thought, seeing the trap. Of course, Marcus knew me better than I knew myself. He'd probably known I wouldn't go out and pick some sorry bastard to be the father of his baby.

Blanche was looking at me funny. "What's wrong? Somebody just walk over your grave?"

"No." I shook my head. Then I shivered. "Not mine."

She nodded, more gently. "That guy you were crying about last night?"

I sat down heavily on the nearest chair.

"You want some tea?" Last night, she'd sounded concerned about me. Right now she sounded positively anxious.

"No. Thanks," I added, mildly ashamed of how I was treating her.

"You want some food?"

I managed a feeble smile. "You don't have any."

"You want to smack me in the head?"

Poor Blanche. I wasn't being fair to her. I said, "Naw. You mean well, for a meddling old broad with more tattoos than a bar full of sailors."

"Watch who you call old, Little Miss. And keep your foul mouth off my tats."

"Yes, Ma'am." We smiled at each other, sadly. Then I said, "Why didn't he have kids? Your friend. Francisco."

"His wife died. I told you. Why are you asking?"

"Just curious."

She gave me a thoughtful look.

I said, "There's no law against being curious, is there?"

"No." She had the good sense not to grin at me, though I could see she wanted to. "There isn't."

♥

It took almost a week for my curiosity to build to the point of doing something about it. In the meantime, I kept busy—sort of.

I spent one day cleaning Blanche's trailer. I wanted to thank her for putting me up all that time, and I figured, after cleaning Emily's house, how hard could the trailer be? But unlike the gentle schooling I'd got at Emily's, cleaning for Blanche was a grueling crash course in how to scrape grease off the windows and scrub ground-in cigarette ash out of her cheap shag carpet. When it was done, I smelled like the town dump and Blanche had the biggest grin I'd ever seen on her; I guessed my thank you had been delivered.

Two different afternoons, I did a little noon-time waitressing at Finer Diner when Val's kid got sick. As I'd imagined, waitressing was just like bartending except the trays were bigger and heavier and you had to walk farther to deliver them. I didn't make much in tips, but I got a little exercise and met a few more of the people from town.

Aside from that, my main entertainment was spending money on meals for me and Blanche, and sitting around basically moping.

Three times, Blanche's doorbell rang and she opened it to some guy wanting a tattoo. One of them, she sent away for being drunk and probably under age. One of them, she sent away for wanting a swastika on his chest. "I don't do that sorry-ass shit," she told him, shoving him back out the door.

"Blanche," I said, "you're running a business. Why you want to be so high and mighty?"

She just rolled her eyes at me. "They don't teach young people crap," she said. "That swastika stuff is from the Nazis, those rotten bastards that killed all the Jews and anyone else they thought was inferior—gypsies, homos, freaks, retarded people. Babies, old geezers without any teeth…"

"All right," I said. "I get your point."

"If that little sick punk wants to turn himself into a Nazi billboard, he'll have to find someone else to sling the ink."

Well, you couldn't disagree with her reasoning, but by then I was wondering if I would *ever* see Blanche do a tattoo. She'd already made plain that she didn't need the work. Apparently two weekends a month at her friend's shop in North Edwards did the trick for her.

Not that I was interested in tattooing, particularly; she'd already asked me three times if I wanted to learn the business, which I didn't. But I needed something to distract me—something harmless and reasonably compelling to chase the other thoughts from my mind. Guilty thoughts about Marcus's promise. How neatly he'd trapped me into having to get pregnant!

Finally, I got my wish. On Saturday night, the doorbell rang and in came an honest-to-God customer. He was about 25, a short, stocky white guy wearing shorts and a t-shirt who walked around self-consciously looking at all the pictures on the walls.

Turned out that new art wasn't really his interest, though.

"How much to cover something up?" he finally asked Blanche.

"That depends on how big it is."

He looked pointedly at where I was sitting on the couch.

I stood up. "Blanche, I'm going in the back," I said. No point in my scaring her business away.

But Blanche wasn't having it. "Listen, Buddy," she told the guy. "Gracie's my apprentice. She can see whatever you plan to show me."

He wanted to argue, you could tell, but he wanted that tattoo covered up more. So he dropped his drawers and there it was: A naked girl with great big tits was scrawled across his right thigh, over a big gold banner that said *LUCY*.

It hit me like a Mack truck: The thought of my name scrawled across Marcus's chest, of his ruined body being lowered into the ground.

When was I going to stop getting blind-sided? Queasy with grief, I turned away quickly and went in the bathroom, vomit rising in my throat. Inside, I hovered over the toilet bowl, waiting for my guts to either spill or settle down. But thanks to Blanche's habit of not feeding us, there wasn't enough in my stomach to throw up.

Through the door, I heard her saying, "Kid, you don't ever want to use names."

"Well, it's too late to think of that now," he replied. "Can you make it go away or not?"

When I came out, feeling unnaturally calm and chastened, Blanche had pulled up a chair and was giving the problem close scrutiny. I felt sorry for the poor guy, standing there in his briefs while she studied him, and I pretended not to notice that he was getting hard from the attention. Talk about embarrassing!

Finally Blanche gave him the verdict. "There's a couple of ways to go," she said. "I could black out the whole thing, but that would be ugly. Or I could just black out the name, but that would be weird; it'll look like the girl's sitting on a slab of granite. Or we could make it into something else."

He looked interested. "Like what?"

"A bike would work," she said. By now I was craning my head around to try and see what she was seeing. "She could be lying on a hog chopper."

"Damn," he said. "You can really do that?"

"Sure, you want to see how?"

He nodded, and Blanche sat down at her work table. A few quick lines, a little shading and five minutes later she'd drawn a picture that was good enough to make both our jaws drop.

I couldn't even imagine having that kind of talent.

"Wow," the kid said. Then his brow furrowed. "What's that gonna cost me?"

"Hundred bucks."

He looked stricken. "Hundred bucks?"

"That's a lot of work, young man, in addition to it being original art."

"I'm not arguing." He threw his hands up. "I just don't have it."

Blanche shrugged. "What have you got?"

"Sixty," he said. You could tell he hadn't even thought about lying to her.

"You give me fifty-five, we're straight."

"Don't you want the other five?"

Blanche shook her head. Her smile was gentle. "Put the other five in your gas tank. That way you're sure to get where you're going."

The kid bent down, pulled up his pants, took out his wallet and handed over three $20 bills. While Blanche went into her cookie jar for his change, I thought about standing by the side of the road in the sun-drenched desert, waiting to be rescued. If it wasn't for Blanche, I might still be standing there. It shouldn't have surprised me that she wouldn't take his last dollar.

"OK," she said. "Get in the chair."

And suddenly I realized that I didn't want to watch this after all. Sure, it would probably be a trip, and who could argue with the value of art. But I wasn't into watching people get tortured, and even if it didn't hurt him, it might hurt me. My stomach was already clenched.

Plus I had a personal matter to see to.

"Hey, Blanche, can I borrow your truck?"

She flashed me a knowing smile.

"Going anyplace in particular?"

"Out," I said, "on a social call." I was damned if she was going to make me tell her what I had in mind, not when she'd sent Francisco chasing after me at Emily's house.

I wouldn't give her the satisfaction.

"Well, you won't find it without a map," she said. "He lives a little out of the way."

Wise-ass bitch! I almost gave up the idea then and there. But if I didn't make a move now, I wouldn't, and the guilt was starting to feel real heavy.

Marcus hadn't ever asked much from me. Just that one irrevocable promise. "Fine," I snapped at her. "Draw me a map!"

♥

I almost turned back half a dozen times. It was hard to keep my hands on the steering wheel, and that made me even angrier. Why was I making a big deal out of this? It wasn't like I'd never screwed anyone!

It wasn't like he was too good for me.

I turned off the road just where Blanche had said to, and bounced her rattletrap pick-up down a winding, pock-marked dirt lane to a two-story, weather-beaten cabin.

I rolled down the window, killed the engine and sat there waiting for my stomach to calm down—or maybe waiting for Francisco to show.

A minute later, he stepped outside. The way he stood and looked at me, you could imagine him holding a rifle, though he wasn't.

Then he walked right up to my window, leaned over and looked me in the eye. "Not much of a truck," he said pointedly.

Good! I was glad he had a little bite in him.

I said, "No point in driving something fancy in the desert."

He nodded. I was starting to feel like we understood each other. He didn't like being interested in me any more than I liked needing him.

"So what are you doing here?" he asked.

I thought about calling Mary Jo from that phone booth—about how angry and awkward we'd both been. There was no good way to kick somebody off a ledge, even when the someone you were kicking was yourself.

"I need to get me pregnant," I said. "You interested in the idea?"

He did a double-take, and then he threw back his head and laughed so hard it almost scared me. "God, that's good," he said, trying to catch his breath. "That's really, *really* good."

"It's not funny!"

"No? You haven't said three civil words to me since we met, but you want me to get you *pregnant*? Do you want to fall in love and get married, too?"

I shook my head. "I've been in love. Now I'm looking for a business deal."

That calmed him down right away. He looked in my eyes, and I guess he could tell that I meant it. He said, "You're an unusual woman."

"I'm just doing what I have to do."

"Well, a business deal is usually two-sided. What do I get out of it?"

I liked him better for calling me out.

"Me," I said. "For a little while."

eleven

Francisco invited me into his home, but only because he was too much of a gentleman to laugh in my face and send me packing.

"Make yourself at home," he said. "I'll get us some coffee."

The cabin was bigger than it looked from outside, with a large living room and what looked like a sleeping loft upstairs. The living room had a stone fireplace, a couch that was covered in bright, woven fabric, two deeply cushioned wooden chairs and a coffee table with antlers wrapped around its base. While Francisco was occupied in his modern-looking, roomy kitchen, I sat down on the couch and quietly bounced up and down on it, testing it for the throw-down I was pretty sure we'd get to later.

It was good and sturdy.

Of course, there was always the sleeping loft. He probably had a comfortable bed up there. In fact, I thought, the whole place looked comfortable with its throw rugs and pictures and pottery and nice furniture—the things a college degree could buy.

Francisco came in, carrying two mugs of coffee. "You take sugar? Milk?"

"No." I stuck my nose in the cup and inhaled the thick, dark smell. Blanche didn't even try to make coffee; I hadn't had any since our last trip to Finer Diner.

When I looked up, he'd sat down on the edge of the coffee table and was studying me from closer than I liked. "So," he said, "why do you 'need' to get pregnant?"

I didn't see any point to lying. "I promised a friend who died."

"I see." He looked at me so hard that I thought maybe he did see. He probably knew what was owed to the dead just as well as I did. "My wife died, too."

I took a sip of coffee. "Blanche told me about the cancer."

"Um." It was more a grunt of pain than a comment.

He drank from his own cup, taking his time about it. Finally, he said, "What's your plan? We have sex from now until you get pregnant, and then you leave?"

I winced at how that made me sound, but truth is truth: That *was* my plan.

I said, "I don't mean any disrespect. You seem like a pretty nice person."

He nodded solemnly. "Thank you. I appreciate your frankness. And since we're being frank, Grace…" He stopped, and now his eyes were amused again. "You don't mind if I call you Grace? That doesn't seem too intimate, does it?"

The clever bastard, using manners to try and intimidate me. It was a good thing I didn't scare easily.

I said, "You can call me anything you want."

"Well, since we're being frank, Grace, it would probably be a pleasure to have sex with you, but I can't get you pregnant."

"Why not?" And I thought, *OK, gloves off.* "You mean to tell me you're shooting blanks?"

There's not a man on earth who wouldn't get pissed at that, and Francisco was no exception. He ran one hand angrily through his thick hair. "Is that how you get what you want from people? By making them so mad they give in to get rid of you?"

Surprisingly, that hurt. But I kept my gaze level and stuck to the point. "*Why* can't you get me pregnant?"

"Because there's nothing as ugly as a man who walks away from his own children."

"You're not walking away. I am."

He said, "It's the same thing, if I agree to it."

"Maybe we could work something out." God, was I *that* desperate to get this over with as quickly as possible?

Of course I was.

"Just what are you suggesting we work out?"

I said, "You could have it some of the time."

"*It?*" I'd only seen Francisco looking stoically polite; he didn't look that way now. "Babies are usually male or female. And for me to take *him* or *her* some of the time, we'd have to have an ongoing relationship. And for that, we'd have to trust each other."

I shrugged. It was better than growling at him. "Stranger things have happened."

He said, "Not lately. And—not that any of this is my problem, but—how are you going to support a child?"

"I'll work."

"Doing what?"

I was angry enough to tell him: "Bartending. Dancing. Stripping."

He grimaced.

"Don't look at me like that!" I said. "What do *you* do that's so high and mighty?"

"I'm a consulting engineer." He paused to see if I knew what that meant, which I did—just barely. "Mostly I work on mine operations."

"Oh. Then I guess you *do* get to look down on me."

"I don't look down on you. But you can't raise a kid doing that kind of work."

"Why not? You think it's catching?" He was really getting to me, mostly because he was right; none of the strippers I knew had managed to hold onto their kids for long and the ones who had their kids had mostly screwed them up good. "Not that it's any of your damn business, since you're not gonna be the father."

He looked at me for a long, shrewd moment. "You're right," he finally said. "I'm not going to be the father. And since we agree on that, if you're interested you're welcome to stay for dinner."

I had started to stand up, but I sat back down on the couch again.

Bingo! I thought. *Got you now.*

♥

Francisco was a good cook. He browned some beef and then cooked it with beans that had been soaking, and vegetables and garlic. I hung out in the kitchen and watched him. I felt incredibly sad that he wasn't Marcus, but I tried to keep that to myself. I wasn't here to feel sorry for people, including Francisco and me. I was here because I'd promised Marcus.

Around the time the sun went down, he opened two Mexican beers and we drank them and talked a bit, and then we each drank a few more beers, waiting for the stew to thicken.

At some point, just making conversation, I told him about cleaning Blanche's trailer, and the way she'd smiled at me when I was done.

He said, "She must have liked that. I'm sure no one cleaned up after her when she was traveling with the circus."

"Circus?" It made sense now that he'd said it, though it bugged me to not have guessed it for myself. You never saw a woman on the street tattooed from head to toe. It would have been hard for Blanche to hold down any kind of regular job, but working for a circus, she would fit right in. I wondered if she'd tattooed people, or if she'd been a sideshow freak.

"She never told me she'd been with a circus."

"You probably didn't ask," he said.

Well, that shut me up right away. It was true that I hadn't asked Blanche much about herself. I hadn't been what you'd call wildly interested in other people for a long time now.

The minutes stretched on while I mulled that over. Francisco didn't seem to mind the silence. He just went about his business, making dinner, taking an occasional swig of beer.

Me, I was more swilling the stuff. Four beers later, my head was swimming. I went into the living room and lay down on the couch for a while.

I must have dozed off because I woke up to find Francisco leaning over me. I blinked hard, getting him into focus. Then I looked past him. Outside his window, the night was an inky, opaque black.

I shivered.

"It's late. You should eat something." He held out his hand, and I took it to steady myself as I sat up.

I was cold; he must have seen it in how I moved. "Why don't you go and dish up some food for us, and I'll make a fire."

I went into the kitchen to serve the stew. When I got back, he was piling sticks into a kind of teepee formation in the fireplace.

I set the two bowls of stew on the coffee table and sat down on the couch to watch him. He laid some heavier pieces of wood against the sticks and then balled up some newspaper and shoved it underneath them. When he lit the paper, small flames shot up, sparking and sizzling where they touched the wood structure.

There was something strangely hypnotic about it, watching that fire look for something to catch onto.

Francisco seemed a bit hypnotized, too. He stood up, stretched his neck, then came and crouched in front of me.

"Grace…"

It was halfway between a question and a plea. I answered by threading my fingers through the soft, thick black cloud of his hair. I pulled him toward me.

I won't pretend that trying to kiss him was an impulse; it was calculated, but I did feel a hazy sense of desire. I was much more aware of being hungry, tired, tense and buzzed from the beer, but still, that hazy desire was real.

I couldn't do it, though. My lips were almost touching his when I suddenly started to shiver all over. My hands fell back away from his face.

Francisco didn't freak out or get mad. He just picked up a bowl of stew and handed it to me. "Eat this," he said, and his voice was surprisingly gentle, given how I'd treated him. "I promise you'll feel better."

I took a cautious bite; it was wonderful. *Of course it was,* I thought, feeling bitter. Of course he would be a good cook, like Marcus. Marcus was gone and here I was, about to screw a stranger like he'd planned.

We ate in silence, but Francisco kept glancing at me. At the precise moment that I finished my stew he took the bowl out of my hands and set it back on the table. "I'm putting you to bed upstairs. You're too tired and upset to drive."

"What are you, now, a mind reader?"

"God," he said, but he didn't seem angry. "You have that defensive thing down cold."

"I don't like being pushed around."

"Is that what you think I'm doing?"

I gave him a hard look, hating the whole situation. "All right," I said. "You're right. I'm tired. I appreciate being able to stay."

"You can have the loft. I'll sleep down here."

I followed him carefully up the steep staircase. The loft was cozy and warm and almost empty, with nothing but a wooden bed table and a double bed piled high with quilts. There was barely room for the two of us to stand there side-by-side looking at it.

"Make yourself at home," he said, turning to go back toward the stairs.

"No, wait!" I grabbed his arm and held on hard.

Francisco gave me a searching look. "I'm sorry." He sounded equal parts stern and sad. "I'm not going to let you use me to make a baby."

It was time to go for broke. "That doesn't have to be part of it."

"But…"

I put my finger over his lips, to hush him. They felt soft and full and warm. I tugged him over to the bed, pulled back the covers and started taking my clothes off.

He didn't watch. In fact, he turned away, which was nice because then I could pretend that I was alone. I got my clothes off quickly, slid under the quilts, pulled them up to my chin and closed my eyes.

When I opened them, Francisco was lying in the bed beside me—arm's length away, staring at my face.

He said, "You are one mixed-up woman."

"Well, I guess if you got a problem with that, you could go downstairs."

"Yeah, I guess I could," he said. "But there's something about you that I don't want to leave alone."

"It's my sparkling personality."

He smiled. "There's something *alive* about you. Tough and alive and ornery and interesting. It's more than just killer sex appeal."

"Look," I said, "don't strain yourself to figure it out. We're both adults, that's good enough."

"Well, it's good enough to start with," he said, turning on his side to face me.

The two of us moved cautiously together. I pressed carefully into his warm flesh and tried to adjust to the shock of a body that was shorter (than Marcus's) and thicker (than Marcus's). I stuck my hand out and cautiously touched his bottom lip, and then I leaned over and kissed him. Just a little kiss, sort of an apology.

He tasted good, like roasted walnuts. I pulled him closer, and just like that all the loneliness we both felt kicked in and he was on top of me and my arms were wrapped around him and his hands were plowed deep into my hair and I was drinking his taste and feeling his muscle and heat against me, feeling his swollen penis press my leg and telling myself *shut up, don't think, just do this!*

"Hold on," he said. I didn't know I'd closed my eyes again, but that got them open. He sat up, opened the night table drawer and took out a small, unopened box of condoms.

I couldn't resist a little dig. "What, were you expecting company?"

"Stop it, Grace! I already bought your act." He picked up a foil packet and angrily tore it open, but he was careful when he put it on. He put the box and the foil and the plastic on the night table. And then he was on top of me again, muttering to himself, his teeth on my throat, his hands on my breasts, his knees pushing my legs apart.

I yelled when he surged inside me. It hurt, like I'd expected. What I hadn't expected was that, after the first few awkward thrusts, after I began moving with him, just as we melted into a groove, Francisco started crying.

I knew about men's tears from Marcus, knew they ran hot and bitter. I wasn't surprised that Francisco's tears burned my cheeks or that my body felt cold and brittle underneath his. But neither of us stopped moving. We were in it now, there was no way to go back.

Afterwards we lay there in each other's arms and I thought *now there doesn't have to be a first time.* And then I looked at Francisco and realized that he was thinking the exact same thing.

After a while he reached over and turned off the bedside light. With it out, the room was in total darkness. "Whoa!" I wasn't about to admit that scared me, so I just said, "How'm I gonna find my way to the bathroom?"

"There's a flashlight in the drawer." He yawned deeply. "I'm sorry, I don't think I can stay awake."

"That's OK." I didn't want to talk.

I closed my eyes and listened to his measured, even breathing. To the slow thud of his heart inside his chest, beating sixty times a minute, more or less. And then I started counting.

I counted sixty beats ten times, and then I did it again, and then again.

Half an hour had passed, and his breathing hadn't varied. The man was stone cold asleep.

I moved the covers off my legs and slid my feet carefully to the floor. I opened the bed table drawer and felt around carefully for the flashlight he had told me would be there, then waited a minute to see if he moved. When he didn't, I took the top two condoms out of the box he'd put on the nightstand, and crept downstairs to the kitchen.

It was deeply quiet here, in a way that not even Blanche's place had been. At Blanche's you could feel that the other trailer park residents were close by, even when you didn't see or hear them. Here there was nothing but the cabin and the quiet that surrounded it. It the midst of all that silence, I was amazed that the guilty pounding of my heart wasn't loud enough to wake Francisco.

Shielding the flashlight, I opened drawers until I found the one he used as a catch-all. In the city, his catch-all would have held take-out menus and books of matches and maybe a pair of extra sneaker laces. Here, it held 3-in-1 oil, assorted nails, extra car keys and, down at the bottom, the thing I was looking for.

What would have happened if I hadn't found it? Would I have gone quietly back to bed and wrapped around Francisco, or pretended that he wasn't there? Would I have come back another night, bringing my own secret weapon for wreaking hell with his plans?

It didn't matter, because there it was, tucked in the jumble at the bottom on his junk drawer. A safety pin. A sharp instrument. The means to my end of disabling his condoms.

I took one to the bathroom and locked myself in. First, I took a piss. Then I opened the pin and bent the business end back, forming a pretty decent tool. I used it to poke what I hoped were tiny holes through the two foil packages I'd brought downstairs with me.

It was delicate work, and of course I didn't *know* that I'd pricked through the latex of the condom itself. But my hands were steady with cold determination. I thought there was a good chance that I had succeeded.

I ditched the safety pin deep in the trash and went back upstairs. Francisco had rolled onto his side, facing away from the bed table. I put the condoms back in their box and the flashlight in the drawer, not bothering to be too quiet about it. Then I crawled back into the bed, sidled near to his warm, broad back and fell asleep.

The next thing I knew, Francisco was on his knees in the bed, bending over me, looking worried.

"Wha'?" I squinted up at him. Beyond him, through the window, I could see that it was barely dawn.

"You're sweating all over. You screamed someone's name."

Sleep was dragging me back down. "'Snothing," I mumbled, closing my eyes. I opened my arms without knowing why. "Nightmare."

"Nightmare! How often do you...?" Then I heard him sigh loudly. He moved into my drowsy embrace. Already, after one time, his smell, his texture were pleasantly familiar. God, what a miserable, unfaithful little bitch I was!

I felt his lips brush over my forehead. Then he settled himself against me and we both fell back asleep again.

When I woke up, he was lying on his side next to me and we were kissing. It was sweet. I had the impression that I was the one who'd started it.

Francisco propped himself up on one elbow and looked down at me. "I'm sorry to be in such a hurry last night."

I said, "Don't be sorry. You're a man."

He winced; but some people just don't know when to run. He said, "I want to *really* make love to you."

He was serious and, strangely, I found myself giving him a serious reply. It seemed like the least I could do, under the circumstances. "I don't want to feel anything."

"Of course not." He gave me a piercing smile. "Why should you get any pleasure, when you had the bad taste to survive?"

I thought of Marcus, holding me while I pounded his chest and screamed that I hated him for dying. And I thought of the terrible, cruel trick that I was about to pull on Francisco. "You do whatever you want," I said. "I'll just pretend to be someplace else."

He was smiling for real now. Any man would have taken that dare. "Go ahead and try it."

He waited a second, to see if I would bolt, I guess; and when I didn't, he slid one hand up over my stomach and ribs, and cupped my breast with it, squeezing. Then he dipped his head and snared my nipple with his teeth and bit it lightly. When he started to suck, I tried to pull away, but his mouth suddenly gentled and he stroked my neck with his other hand. "Shhh," he murmured into my breast, his hands moving over me. I moaned—it had a strangled sound—and he raised his head and said, "Breathe. Don't panic."

It had been so easy the night before, but now he was really touching me, his hands and mouth coaxing an answer from my skin. I wanted the answer to be no, and I started to push him away; but then I remembered why I was doing this and my hands ended up resting on his shoulders, half-consenting as he licked and nuzzled his way down my body.

I didn't want him sucking me, it seemed way too private, but I didn't know how to tell him to stop. I thought it would be quicker to just endure, but he was gentle and clever and soon my body was ebbing and flowing to the rhythm he set, and then he pushed two fingers inside me, his mouth hot on my clit, and my insides just exploded.

I screamed; and then it was my turn to rain hot tears. He slid up beside me on the bed and held me while I rode out the tidal wave of anger and grief.

I don't know how long the two of us lay there. After a while, I sniffed away the last of my tears and spread my legs. "You didn't get yours yet," I said, tugging him on top of me.

"Can't do it without a condom," he murmured.

Those goddamn condoms! I almost told him right then and there, almost opened my mouth and said *throw the top ones away*. But I hadn't come this far to not go through with it. I couldn't fail Marcus and go on living. "Then put a goddamn condom on," I growled, stretching out my body while I waited. I wanted to jump outside my skin; the stretching helped relieve a little tension.

What followed was like the night before but with kissing, stroking, murmured sounds that might have been endearments. I didn't want to come again, didn't want to feel anything except the shudder that ran through him when he poured himself into that first condom, and then, half an hour later, the second one. I didn't want to enjoy this, but I couldn't help how he made me feel, even though I hated both of us for it.

Afterwards, he lay beside me, tracing my cheek with his fingertip. "Will you stay here for a while?"

"I can't. I need to get back on the road."

He was shocked; you could see it in his face. Shocked and more than a little betrayed, because he never would have had sex with me if he'd known I was going to leave the same day.

Well, I hadn't known it myself 'till just that moment.

"You're not going to stay in town at all?"

I shook my head, clamping my lips together. This was the hard part, trying not to explain myself. The more I said, the more I would regret later.

"But why?" He was still trying to take it in. "You're leaving today?"

"I'm meeting a friend who lives back East." *I need to leave before you guess what I've done!* "Her grandmother's dying, she's all broken up."

His hand stilled briefly on my face. "Gracie…"

I touched his bottom lip with my finger. It was like a closed circuit, each of our hands on the other one's face. I said, "Trust me, Francisco, it's better this way. You wouldn't like me if I stayed. I'm actually not a very nice person."

"Do you think I like you better for going?"

I kissed him, feeling a little sad. He didn't know I was already gone. "What I think is, you deserve something better. You're a good guy. Let's just leave it at that."

And then I got out of the bed and started putting my clothes on.

He watched me 'till I was almost finished. Then he reached for his own shirt and chinos. "Well." He looked and sounded shell-shocked, but one thing about people with good manners, they always go back to the safety of politeness. Some other guy would have hit me, or thrown things. Francisco just said, "Please give my best to Blanche."

"Sure thing." My voice sounded like gravel. My skin felt hollow. My soul was bruised, and I didn't know why. I didn't even know this guy.

Reluctantly, he followed me downstairs. "Do you want some coffee, Grace?" he asked with that same dazed politeness.

I did, but I didn't want the conversation that would go with it. I turned away so that he couldn't see how tempted I was. "Naw, but thanks."

He wrote something on a piece of paper. "Here," he said. "This is my address and phone number."

I took the paper. "You've got a phone?"

"Yeah." He looked sad. "I have a phone."

"Oh." I wish I'd thought to ask the night before. It was too late now to call Blondell, when I was on my way out the door. "Well. Maybe I'll call you someday."

"You do that," he said. It would have been ironic if it hadn't sounded weak.

I tried to smile at him, but I couldn't. I had to get out of there *now*, before I changed my mind.

"Goodbye, Francisco."

"Goodbye, Grace." He opened the front door, letting the warmth we'd shared out of his cabin.

I scraped my foot across the floor. Hell, I wasn't going to explain, but maybe I could apologize. "Listen, I, uhm…"

"Grace," he said, "just go."

So I did.

♥

Blanche didn't take it as well as Francisco. "You're gonna *what?*" she yelled in my face. I guess I was lucky she didn't spit at me.

I didn't give an inch of ground. "I'm gonna go. I'm getting back on the road today."

"Just like that? You just pick up and leave?"

"Yeah. Just like I came. What did you think?"

"I thought maybe you were looking to get something real into your sorry life."

"I am," I told her. "It's on the road. You gonna say goodbye to me?"

"No," she yelled, "I'm not gonna fucking say goodbye to you!"

"Look, I know you're pissed at me…"

"Good guess!" She pulled out a Camel, lit it and blew the smoke in my face.

I took a step back. I don't like cigarette smoke, and now I didn't have to breathe it anymore. How had I stood it for over a week? Thank God I was getting out of here!

"Look, Blanche, you been good to me, but…"

Blanche gave me a disgusted glare. Then she tossed her cigarette to the floor and put the heel of one red sneaker daintily on top of it. The death's head tattoo on her calf flexed as she ground and ground that Camel butt into the blue shag carpet that I'd scrubbed on my hands and knees just days before.

"Have a good life," she sneered at me. "And don't let the door hit you on your way out."

It was a lonely day of travel. Pissed off though I was at Blanche, I had to admit that I missed her company. All that pushy energy of hers had dragged me a little out of myself. When Blondell had left to go back east, it hadn't mattered tremendously because I'd been totally sunk in despair. Yes, I'd missed her bitterly, but what was a little more loneliness against that gray backdrop of grief?

But recently, I'd started to notice things more—well, with Blanche, you couldn't help noticing—and what I noticed now was how quiet it was out on the road, in those long empty spaces between rides.

The day would probably have felt different if I'd liked the people who picked me up. There was nothing wrong with any of them, but there was nothing particularly right about them, either. The best thing I could say about the lot was that nobody seemed to want to talk to me. They all floated by in a broken stream: The twelve mile ride, the station wagon ride, the really slow driver. None of them really caught my attention, and fortunately I didn't catch theirs.

Well, it wasn't surprising that people seemed dull after tattooed Blanche and bird-like Emily. But even the normal Wagon Wheel people like Helen and Val at Finer Diner seemed to have more vitality than the folks I met traveling north on I-15 that day.

Of course, this entire line of thought wasn't exactly comforting. *Damn,* I thought, *you're getting sentimental over people you only knew for a minute.*

Was I that hard up for human companionship? I had to remind myself that, interesting as Blanche might have been for a while, she sure hadn't turned out to be a real friend. Friends don't throw a fit when you leave them. Friends know better than to ask for too much.

All day, my thoughts ran around that circle; while my body rampaged on a different track. My body still felt stretched and pampered, the muscles loose from this morning's release. At home with Marcus, that had been a good feeling; but now, I just wanted to take a shower, to wash the guilt and the smell of sex and the novelty of having been touched off my skin. I tried to shut out the physical impressions: Francisco's taste. Francisco's hurt expression. Francisco's hands stirring the stew like Marcus's hands on a million nights. Sense memories, skin memories are harder to block out than thoughts. Each one was like a little knife cut, an acid taste of my body's betrayal.

No wonder I didn't want to talk to anyone! This was better handled in silence. I gritted my teeth and let it wash through me—loneliness, boredom, and cringe-making memories.

All in all, a pretty bad day. And that was *before* I got to Las Vegas.

You could see the town rise up in the distance, like a shimmering neon code that people spent their whole lives trying to crack. I didn't understand the allure of gambling, but I knew that, in a place filled with clubs, there'd be dancers and strippers and waitresses and hustlers and hostesses and bartenders. There'd be something I could do in this town—or at least, that's what I thought when I first got there.

I'd never seen so many big hotels before. Bright and tawdry, pulsing with energy, they were lined up like cheap hookers along the neon Strip. I started at one end and spent about twelve hours working my way to the other, stopping in each hotel I passed to sip a glass of water in the bar and check out what the dancers looked like.

From the Dunes Hotel to the Golden Nugget, from Caesar's Palace to the Las Vegas Hilton, with the Riviera, the Sahara, the Frontier and the MGM Grand thrown in for good measure, the competition was impossible. Las Vegas seemed to have an endless supply of long, tall girls with custom-tanned skin and silicone tits and curvy legs and flat stomachs and sickeningly white teeth. No one was hiring dancers or strippers, and if they were, they sure wouldn't have hired me.

Next to those girls, I looked like a peasant from some village where the people lived on potatoes.

Plus, they had *stuff*—beautiful stripper stuff that put my Teddy Morris schoolgirl outfit to shame. They had wigs and eyelashes, gloves and boas, silk and satin peek-a-boo gowns with rhinestones in strategic places, six-inch heels with hot pink fluff around the straps and glitter that stuck to their bodies when everything else was long since gone.

They were the real thing, those Vegas girls—the real eat-your-heart-out, 1000-watt, big money, wouldn't-have-been-caught-dead-in-a-place-like-Girl-O-Rama professional strippers. After just one night going from hotel to hotel and peeking into all the floor shows, I was pretty clear that I wouldn't be dancing in this town without plastic surgery, four more inches of height and hundreds of bucks worth of costuming.

And dancing wasn't the only kind of work I wasn't going to find in Las Vegas. All the bartenders were men, and even though some of the croupiers were women, I didn't play cards worth a damn and this wasn't an on-the-job-training kind of place.

Since I'd hitched into town that afternoon, Francisco's disappointment and Blanche's anger still ringing in my ears, I'd spent twelve hours working my way from one end of the Strip to the other, asking everybody I passed if they knew where I could find work. In the lounges, bars, arcades, even on the street, the answer was the same—no work, no way—though I did get eight or ten lewd propositions, three invitations to dinner and more dirty looks than I wanted to count.

"Try the Mustang Ranch," said the twenty-fourth person I asked where the jobs were. Maybe he was trying to be funny. Or maybe he thought I wouldn't know that the Mustang Ranch was a whorehouse.

"They don't need me, they've got your mother," I replied, sweetly. For one pleasant minute it felt like the old days, trading insults with Don at Girl-O-Rama, and then I thought *God, if I'm nostalgic for that, I'm in way more trouble than I thought.*

Well, clearly I *was* in trouble. It was past midnight, and when I reached the end of the Strip, where the big hotels were abruptly replaced by porn shops, pawn shops and liquor stores, I didn't need a map to tell me that I'd hit the five-dollar-blow-job part of town. Any work I found here would be a short slide into oblivion, so I went into the first clean-looking diner I passed, ordered some thin coffee and sat there thinking about my options.

They all sucked. I didn't have the money to get a room so I was either going to sleep under a bush tonight or start hitching out of town at a very un-advantageous hour. And since I could only afford one good meal, I was either going to go hungry tonight and eat tomorrow, or do it the other way around.

The fact that I'd left lots of people I liked and not one but two warm beds back in Wagon Wheel didn't make this any easier. I'd done the right thing by leaving—as angry as Blanche and Francisco had been, I knew they would thank me for it someday—but right now I was too hungry and discouraged to think clearly about what my next move should be.

All right, at least that was something I could fix. I beckoned to the waitress and ordered steak and eggs with fried potatoes, an English muffin, a fruit cup, juice, coffee, and a piece of cherry pie. If this was my last supper— or at least, my last one 'till I made some cash—I was going to make it good.

I was sitting there waiting for it to arrive when someone in the booth behind me cleared his throat and said, "How's a little girl like you going to put away a big dinner like that?"

I turned around, and looked at the would-be smooth guy who'd spoken to me. If he was a day more than fifteen years old, I was the Virgin Mary.

I said, "Fuck off, Junior. It's past your bedtime."

But instead of backing down, he got up, walked over and sat across the table from me.

Too thin, I thought. Too young. He even smelled young. Marcus would have been like that. "Get out of that seat if you want to keep your butt in one piece!" I growled.

He didn't move. "I thought we were having a conversation."

"You must be a sorry piece of shit if you think *fuck off* is conversation."

I wasn't disturbing him in the slightest. This child had obviously been well-trained, though I couldn't approve of what he'd been trained for. "You're really beautiful," he said.

"You're really transparent. And you're probably really hungry. But I don't have enough to share and I don't give a shit, so you're wasting your time. Go find some rich woman who likes dark meat and run your little game on her."

He looked so hurt, I dropped a year off my estimate of his age. Blondell sure could have taught him something about how to hustle white people.

"Come on," I said, "you better toughen up if you want to play Junior Gigolo. That's not the worst thing you're gonna hear!"

"Women *love* being called beautiful," he protested.

"Is that a fact!"

I could see him switching gears. "Damn," he said, as if he'd just made a big discovery. "You're not like the other women I meet!"

I leaned across the table. "Sorry, Kid. That one isn't going to work either."

"My name's Rory," he offered—not that I believed him.

"You need to stop with the clichés, Rory. And you need to stop trying to pass yourself off as a man of the world when we both know you don't shave yet and you probably fucked ten girls, tops, your whole life."

"Well, how the hell many have *you* fucked?" he asked, his voice rising.

"None," I said, leaning back in my seat with a little "got-cha" smile.

It was true, I'd never gone lesbian. Most of the women I knew swung both ways, but I had this strange idea that I was better off sticking with men.

Rory laughed at that like he meant it. That's what softened me up to him—that, and feeling guilty about taunting him for being black. Marcus would have had my head on a platter if he'd heard that stuff.

But the kid wasn't through with his would-be hustle. "I'm not *that* hungry," he announced disdainfully, looking like he'd just one-upped me.

"You're not?"

"No, ma'am. I just came over 'cause you looked interesting."

Just then the waitress brought my food.

I said, "If you're not hungry, then you won't mind watchin' me eat this, right?"

He gave me the surliest look I'd seen since Blanche threw me out of her trailer the night before. In his case, it just made me laugh.

I said, "See? You walked right into that one, letting your damn pride tell you how to act instead of thinking it through."

"I was doing fine," he snarled. Finally, he'd given up taking me for a mark.

"If you were doing so fine, how come I got the food and you don't even have a damn breadstick in front of you?"

"Cause you're a tough bitch," he said.

"Thanks." I didn't bat an eye, just kept on eating.

"Fuck you!" He stood up to leave.

"*Sit down.*"

It surprised me a little that he did, but then he was apparently more desperate than I'd realized. I pushed the rest of my steak and eggs over to his side of the table and handed him my fork. "When you're trying to get over on someone, start with the truth," I said. "Start with something true that you can embellish."

He gave me a doubtful look and then dug into the food like a starving bear cub. "Why the hell should I do that?"

I said, "'Cause you don't lie worth a damn."

"There's nothing wrong with how I lie."

"Look, Kid, I'm just telling you what I know. You can take it or leave it, I don't care."

"Yeah? Why do you want to bother with me?"

I sighed heavily, which was dangerous. Breathing deeply made me feel the empty space in my chest. "You remind me of somebody," I said, pushing half the pie across the table at him. "A guy who learned the hard way, just like you will."

♥

In the end, I didn't have to sleep in the bushes. It turned out that Rory had a mother, who couldn't have been much older than me from the picture I saw when I went home with him at about 4AM. She worked overnight as a chambermaid, which left the shabby apartment they rented just beyond the strip empty.

Once I'd made it clear to Rory that I wasn't going to play Mrs. Robinson to his under-age self, he offered me the use of her bed and didn't even hassle me to change my mind during the night. So I ended up sleeping well, if briefly. It turned out that steak and eggs I ordered was the best investment I'd made in a while.

I got up early the next morning, took a shower, got dressed, said goodbye to Rory or whatever his name was, and walked two miles to I-15. The heat didn't feel as bad as Wagon Wheel, or maybe it was just too early in the morning, but either way I was grateful when I caught a ride in the first ten minutes with an old white guy who said his name was Al.

Al was sixty-ish, like Blanche, and like Blanche he looked tougher than any young person. His biceps were as big as my head.

"Where are you going?" he asked, when we'd introduced ourselves.

I liked him, so I said, "I don't know. Got any place to recommend?"

He kind of glanced at me, but mostly kept his eyes on the road, which I appreciated. Trucks—big ones, with wheels that were half as tall as his car—were whipping around us, and his little ride wasn't much of a match for the tail wind they stirred up.

He said, "I recommend Wyoming. The mountains are real beautiful up there."

I tried to bring up a map in my head. "Where is it?"

"Go on up to Salt Lake City and then head east on Route 80."

It sounded like a very long way. "Sorry," I mumbled, covering a yawn.

Just then we rounded a curve and drove into some heavy sunlight. Al was wearing dark glasses, but he pulled his windshield visor down. "Sun's pretty strong up here," he said. "It makes a lot of people sleepy."

So did only sleeping four hours, but I didn't bother to tell him that. We talked a little more—I found out he'd worked a road crew, got the biceps from a jackhammer—but neither of us had a whole lot to say and after a while I closed my eyes and leaned my head against the door jamb. I was just going to rest for a while—I wasn't even planning to let my guard down, let alone fall asleep—but the metal was cool on my forehead, the sun was like a blanket, and pretty soon I dozed off.

When I woke up, the light was different. "Sorry," Al said, "but this is where I turn off." I looked around, trying to get my bearings. It was late afternoon. We were parked in one of those little off-road rest stops.

"Where are we?"

"Just north of Provo." I must have looked blank. "Utah," he added.

"We didn't get to Salt Lake City yet, did we?"

"Not yet. It's about forty miles."

I thanked him and opened the door, reaching for my shoulder bag. But it wasn't beside me where I'd left it, it was sitting on the back seat.

Al must have moved it while I slept. *Dumb!* I thought, leaning over to grab it. What if Al had been an asshole, what if I'd had to jump out of his car without it? I'd have lost Marcus's picture and what little else I owned.

Next time I slept, my arms would be wrapped around that bag.

"You try what I said, young lady. Head up to Wyoming, it'll straighten you right out."

"Okay," I answered, wondering what Al thought he knew about me. For a second, I felt a little off balance. I got out of the car and he drove away, kicking up a prim little cloud of dust.

I stuck out my thumb again, and another car drove up almost immediately. I was so happy to not have to wait for a ride that I got right in, literally without looking.

You always know just a minute too late when you've done something fatally stupid. As soon as I pulled the car door shut behind me, I knew it.

I'd told Francisco that you get a feel for things, working the kind of places I had, and it's true. The straight world, that's all about illusion, appearances; my world was about what's underneath the mask.

But the driver of this car wasn't even wearing a mask His ugly little state of mind was right there to see, if I'd bothered to look. And now there was going to be hell to pay because, this being the Interstate, I couldn't just get out at the next stop light.

My fault for getting careless.

My fault for getting lazy.

My fault for thinking the roll I was on would just keep rolling. They never do.

OK, I would tough it out.

"How you doing?" I asked the driver.

"Doing great," he leered. "What's your name?"

"Jane. What's yours?"

"Timothy. You sure got some nice tits, Jane."

I said, "Thank you."

"Bet you like having those tits sucked, don't you?"

"Timothy, I'm just looking for a ride."

He leered again. His repertoire of expressions was obviously pretty limited. "Well, I'm gonna ride you, and suck those pretty tits you got, too."

My fingers tightened around the door handle, as if we weren't going 70 miles an hour. "Pull over, Timothy. I'm gonna get out now."

"You cunt!" he shrilled. No more Mr. Nice Guy. "I'll smack you silly and *then* chew your tits up!"

Big, mean, violent, stupid; great, the perfect combination! I knew this wasn't going to work, but I had to give it one more try.

"Timothy, pull over NOW!"

Without warning, the car lurched sharply to the right, throwing me against the door. For a second, I thought he was going to stop; but no, he was only swerving onto an access road that paralleled the highway.

A second later, he jerked the car through another sharp right-hand turn, this time onto a small dirt road that was all but hidden by thick trees. We careened down it, ricocheting over ruts and potholes, getting slammed around and scraped by branches as Timothy's car sped maniacally into the woods.

You had to be crazy to drive like this; it was bone-jarring, frightening. And how the hell had he known there was a road there?

"Stop it!" I screamed at him, but of course he ignored me and just kept going. I was now more scared of bleeding to death in a twisted pile of smashed-up metal than I was of getting raped and maimed.

And then I felt the unnatural calm that sometimes takes over when it's life or death. It descended on me like a cool nightfall. I could hear Marcus in my mind, Marcus teaching me self-defense: *Take a nice, deep breath and get centered, Grace...*

That's how Marcus fought—from his center. He'd studied two or three martial arts, and listening to him now I felt his knowledge sinking into me. I felt myself fill with what he called *intention*.

I looked at the side of Timothy's face, at the hollow just beside his right eye. I put a big red "X" there, in my mind. And then I pulled my arm back and—with a war cry that wrenched out of my throat—slammed the bone at the base of my palm straight into that spot, with all my power.

It hurt like hell, but it worked. Timothy's head smashed into the doorframe so hard I thought it was gonna explode. Blood spurted out from his face. He slumped back in his seat as the car jerked violently to the left.

I grabbed for the steering wheel and tugged it back just in time to keep us out of the trees. We hadn't stopped moving, though. I brought my leg up and kicked his foot off the gas pedal, trying desperately to control the car.

His body flopped toward me. I screamed and shoved at his dead weight, accidentally pushing him onto the steering wheel. The horn started blaring, loud and steady, but the car rolled to a blessed stop.

I was shaking so hard I thought I would throw up, but this was no time to get all squeamish. I reached around Timothy, shut off the car, grabbed the keys and my bag and ran like hell toward what looked, just barely, like an overgrown path.

Ten steps, twenty, forty, a hundred, my sneakers crunching on dead leaves and roots and plants and small stones. I was winded already, but I didn't even dare to think about stopping. Two hundred, three hundred, four hundred, five… My legs were cramping, I could barely see, but I ran until I couldn't hear that horn blaring in the distance, just the sound of my hard, shallow breaths.

That's when it sank in that I was running *away* from the highway, not toward it. Running deeper into the woods. I stopped short at the biggest tree in sight and fell to the ground, massaging the shooting pain in my calves and shaking with anger and exertion.

Damn, damn, damn, damn, damn, damn, damn! I wasn't going to make it to Salt Lake tonight. I might not even make it back to the road. I'd be lucky if I didn't freeze to death—it was going to be cold when the sun went down, my jacket was probably no match for these mountains—and *what the hell was I doing running in the wrong direction?* I thought of Rory's mother's nice, warm bed; the third I'd walked away from in the last two days. There wouldn't be a nice warm bed for me tonight, you could make book on that.

A deep sense of weariness came over me. What was I, some kind of nutcase? Some kind of masochist? Some kind of magnet for bone-deep trouble?

Well, it didn't really matter. At least I'd had a good meal last night. At least I hadn't gotten hurt. At least it wasn't raining, not like the last time I'd slept outdoors, which I wasn't going to think about right now. That time hadn't killed me and, if worse came to worse and I had to spend tonight in these woods, that wasn't going to kill me either. I thought about Marcus saying *what doesn't kill you makes you strong.* Black folks are always saying things like that, and I guess they ought to know. I *was* strong, or I had been until his dying wore me down. I was probably going to live forever, even though I didn't want to.

By the time I'd thought all that through, it was pitch dark. I got to my feet, dusted the leaves off my clothes and looked uneasily around me for the best way out of those woods.

That's when I noticed a light flickering between the trees.

thirteen

The light was coming from the smudged window of a rundown shack.

Home sweet home.

I circled the place carefully. It looked terrible but it smelled damn good.

Someone was cooking, and singing while they worked. A child, if the thin, high-pitched song that floated out was any clue.

I'm a little teapot, short and stout.
Here is my handle, here is my spout.
When I get all steamed up, hear me shout
Just tip me over and pour me out.

That song, as much as the light, as much as the smell of what might have been soup, drew me up the three crumbling brick steps that led to the back door.

I crouched there, listening. I could hear someone moving inside. I could hear what sounded like the brief whistle of a tea kettle before it was lifted off a fire. From here, I was enveloped in the warm, thick smell of home-cooked food.

It was irresistible. Before I'd had a chance to reconsider, I opened the door and stepped inside.

Someone screamed. Something shattered. A thin, pitiful-looking girl with stringy, shoulder-length brown hair and pale eyes was standing in the middle of the room, shaking. A dish had broken at her feet, and thick green liquid oozed over her shoes.

"I'm really, really sorry," I said. "I didn't mean to scare you. I'm not dangerous, I'm just hungry and I smelled the food and heard the singing and…"

I must not have been too convincing; her eyes were still wide with terror. "You have to go," she said, her voice trembling. It was the childlike voice I'd heard through the door, though she looked to be about seventeen. "You have to go before he comes."

Ignoring that, I walked over to the sink, picked up a sponge and wet it. "Here, let me clean that up for you."

She was still rooted to the spot, but she swatted feebly at me as I scraped the goo, which was pea soup, from around her feet. Her shoes were filthy and had holes in them; her clothes were basically rags. I picked up the broken pieces of her dish and put them in the sink.

"Sit down," I said, firmly. "I'll get you some more."

To my surprise, she shuffled over to the scarred wooden table and sat down heavily. Apparently she was used to following orders. I took two bowls from a cabinet with a missing glass front and ladled soup from a cast iron pot on the stove. "Where do you keep spoons?" I asked, setting the bowls down on the table.

She didn't answer. Instead, she put her head down in her hands and moaned.

The spoons were in the fourth place I looked. I brought two to the table and sat down opposite her.

"Might as well eat," I told her. "I'm not gonna leave until you do."

The soup was delicious, and not just because I was hungry. I ate greedily, then pushed the bowl away. She was still hunched over, her hands wrapped around her head, making this low, frightened, keening sound.

"Come on," I said, kinder now that my stomach was full. I reached out and touched her hands. Her head shot up, and she recoiled back so hard I thought her chair was going to tip over.

"Hey, I'm not gonna hurt you!" I tried to make it sound convincing. "What's your name?"

Rosie, is what I thought she said.

Rosie. My sister's name.

For a second, my stomach clutched with fear, as if one of my ghosts was sitting there in front of me. But I didn't *really* believe that this beat-down, backwoods 16- or 17-year old was the ghost of my chubby three-year-old sister.

The only ghosts I believed in were the ones that talk to you in dreams.

I took a desperate, steadying breath and tried again. *"What's* your name?"

"Annie. Anna May."

The world snapped back into place around me. I realized I'd been holding onto it by a thread. "That's what people call you? Anna May?"

"Timothy calls me Little Cunt," she whispered in her child's voice. "And Gregory calls me Stupid Bitch…"

Ah, Timothy! The piece of shit cretin I'd KO'd and left bleeding and unconscious had obviously been headed home. That's how he'd known about the dirt road turn-off. He was the *he* Anna May was afraid of.

As for the other person she'd mentioned, I didn't even want to know who that was; he would obviously only make things worse. "Anna May, eat! I don't know how much time we've got before Timothy or that other guy shows up."

"He'll hurt us!"

"I'll protect you. I promise."

I'd spoken the words before I knew it. I was promising to *protect* her against a Neanderthal? I hadn't made a promise since the one I'd made Marcus, and look where that was taking me.

Still, didn't I owe her a little protection? I'd scared her, made her break a dish, helped myself to her food without being asked. And she was so horribly vulnerable, alone out here in the middle of nowhere. She was more alone than I had ever been.

"Eat!" I said again. "I mean it."

She didn't want to, but her spoon dipped into the soup, rose mechanically to her mouth, dipped in again.

"You're a good cook," I said, trying to distract her. "How'd you learn?"

She didn't look up at me, but tilted her head so that her hair fell forward like a curtain, a practiced move that blocked my view of her face.

"My mama showed me," she mumbled.

"She taught you to put all that stuff in there? The carrots and potatoes and that green stuff?"

"Leeks," she said, as if I'd dragged the word out of her.

"What?"

"Leeks. It's like an onion you chop up."

I poked at the wide bits floating in my bowl. "That's what this is?"

She nodded.

"Is it hard to learn to cook like that?" I asked her.

"No," she said, "it's easy. My mama showed me when I was a little girl."

I said, "You were singing like a little girl just now. You know, that teapot song?"

She looked embarrassed. "I don't know any grown-up songs," she said. "Do you?"

"Yeah." I thought about what they played at Girl-O-Rama. "I know some stuff by Michael Jackson and Tina Turner and Hall & Oates and..."

"Who are they?" she asked.

"They're singers. Famous singers. Don't you have a radio?"

She shook her head. And that's when we heard footsteps on the path outside the cabin.

Anna May jumped to her feet, wild with panic. "Please, please go," she begged, sounding like someone who begged a lot. "He'll hurt you. *Please!*"

But it was too late. The door opened and Timothy walked in.

I grabbed Anna May's wrist and pulled her behind me, out of his path. "Get in that corner, GO!" She scurried to where I pointed.

Timothy and I just stared at each other. He didn't look any more surprised than I was. I guess we'd both known, right from the start, that one of us was going to get hurt. I'd been lucky the first time, taking him off guard, but now we were going to fight on his turf and he was six feet tall, twice my weight and angrier than he'd been in the car. *Of course he's angry*, I thought, *there's blood caked down the whole side of his face.* If I'd wanted to live more, I would have been terrified.

"Look..." I started to say.

But then, amazingly, Anna May moved. "Timothy..." She started forward, and for a second her body was brave and purposeful.

"Get back," I yelled, at the same time Timothy snarled, "Stay out of it, cunt!"

She seemed to shrivel at the sound of his voice, a hundred and ten pounds of scared girl again.

I had to get her out of this. I pointed to Timothy's bloody face. "Loser!" I taunted. "You look like some girl beat you to shit."

Good, he'd forgotten about Anna May. He lumbered toward me, slowly, like a locomotive gathering steam.

I backed up, felt the kitchen counter at my waist. *Breathe!* I heard Marcus tell me. God, I wished he was here right now!

"No!" Anna May screamed, rushing forward. "Don't! I'll do whatever you want!"

I wanted to puke. I wanted to kill him. Why hadn't I taken a knife from the drawer?

Offhandedly, Timothy knocked her to the ground.

OK, maybe I was better off without the knife; my hand strength was no match for his. *Use your legs!* I heard Marcus saying. *Use your center of gravity!*

I boosted my backside up on the counter, clutching the edge to keep my balance. Then I pulled my legs up high and kicked out, just as Timothy rushed me.

Both feet landed square in his gut, with plenty of thigh muscle behind them, but it wasn't hard enough to stop him. The weight of his body pressed my legs back. I screamed and flailed and pushed them out again, feeling the ache from that run in the woods. I didn't have the strength to knock him down, but I got him off me, got him off balance long enough to rally and kick him in the chest—another direct hit with both feet flat on target. This time he actually staggered back.

I jumped off the counter, ducked around him, grabbed a chair and smashed it on his head. "Stupid fuck," I yelled, as he went down. "You stupid fucking piece of shit!"

And then I heard Anna May scream.

It was more a scream of pain than fear and, when I looked, I saw the reason why: She'd grabbed the hot, cast iron soup pot in her bare hands and was carrying it toward me, struggling with its weight.

"Put that down," I yelled. "You're gonna burn your…"

She put it down, all right. With the ultra calm of someone in shock, she held the pot up level with her chest and dropped it straight down onto Timothy's crotch. It landed with a sickening crunch, and soup splashed out in every direction.

Stepping carefully through the mess, I grabbed Anna May, dragged her to the sink and turned on the cold water. Her hands were an angry red; she made a gurgling sound when I shoved them under the tap, but she looked strangely peaceful. "Is he hurt?" she asked dreamily, and I was willing to bet that she didn't really know. I wasn't sure how smart she was, and she seemed to be in a kind of trance.

"Oh, yeah. He's hurt."

"Good," she said, matter-of-factly. "Am I gonna have to go to jail?"

"No," I said. *Over my dead body.* The water was so cold my hands were going numb, but I kept holding her reddened palms under it. "Did you ever call the cops on him?"

Her eyes widened, as if this was a horrifying idea. "Call *Gregory?*"

That was the other man she'd mentioned. Suddenly it was clear as glass that I couldn't leave her anywhere near him.

"I'm taking you with me," I said, turning the water off. Stepping around Timothy and the mess on the floor, I started opening cupboards, grabbing things to eat. Crackers, peanut butter, cheese from the refrigerator, a few apples — I threw them all into my shoulder bag and then turned back to Anna May. "Do you have a flashlight?"

"No."

"Do you have any money?"

"He puts it in that jar." She nodded toward it.

There was eighty-three dollars inside. Thank God I wouldn't have to go through his pockets.

"You got a jacket?"

"No."

He'd sure kept her on a short leash, the bastard. "Then I guess you're packed. We need to go *now,* Anna May, come on."

If it had been slow going *to* the shack, it was torture walking back to the car. Anna May was cold and scared, and her hands were hurting her badly now. I put my jacket over her shoulders, but I didn't want to risk putting her burned hands through the arms. There was no moon, and the stars weren't strong enough to light our way, through the thick canopy of trees.

The two of us half-stumbled down the trail I found, me shivering and holding her elbow through the jacket to keep us together.

Finally, we reached the Buick. My stomach heaved when we got into it, but I managed to keep from vomiting. Timothy's blood was smeared on the door, and dribbled on the steering wheel. His smell was soaked into the upholstery.

I put the key I'd been carrying in the ignition, but I wasn't ready to touch that steering wheel. Anna May sat straight in the passenger seat, her hands resting palm-up on her knees. The skin was angry red and blistered.

"Here," I told her, stalling for time, "I'll do your seatbelt."

She shrank back as I reached across her, but she let me snap the belt into place. Then she surprised me by whispering, "Tear off my skirt."

"What?"

"To clean that." She nodded at the steering wheel.

"I'm not tearing up your clothes!"

She said, "It's already teared. Don't make yourself touch him again."

She was right; I didn't want to touch his blood. "Thanks." I leaned over and ripped a piece of cloth from the hem of her skirt. The fabric was so thin it was like tearing paper, but it was thick enough to do the job.

I tossed the bloody rag out the window and turned on the ignition.

"You put on your seatbelt, too," she said in that childish wisp of a voice,

Startled, I looked at her. She had a little half-smile on her face. It was the first time she'd met my eye, and probably the first time she'd ever given an order.

I snapped my seatbelt on. Then I put the car into gear and backed carefully down the rutted road. Part of me wanted to floor it and get the hell out of there fast, but I didn't want to make a mistake, and I didn't want to jostle Anna May around.

It seemed to take a year before we reached the highway. There weren't many other cars out; it was strangely quiet in the starry night. I pulled onto the road, gunned the Buick and hit 70 in what seemed like seconds.

Anna May let out a hard breath. Her whole body relaxed into a slump. "What's your name?" she asked, twisting in her seat to face me.

75. 80. This thing couldn't go too fast for me. "Gracie," I said, driving with one hand so that I could scratch my dirty scalp with the other. "Grace."

"Thank you, Gracie-Grace."

"You're welcome." I glanced over and saw that little smile again. She looked proud of herself, and for my money she had every right to be. Truth was, I felt proud of springing her from Timothy's clutches.

Of course, there was always the question of what happened next. I said, "Anna May, is there anybody who can protect you from those guys?"

"You," she said.

"Anybody else but me?"

She thought about that for a long enough while that I knew the answer was going to be no.

"Well, never mind," I said. And then I couldn't help asking, "Anna May, what happened to your Mom?"

"She died."

"How old were you?"

Her brow furrowed. "Eight?"

I remembered how precisely she'd aimed that pot, and felt another wave of nausea. "Timothy's been raping you since you were eight?"

She said, "What's *raping?*"

My jaw was clenched; I had to make an effort to loosen it. "It means when somebody makes you have sex with him. You know, touches you. Sticks things in you…"

"On, no," she said, her tongue suddenly loosened. "My mom died and then his dad died and *then* Timothy started and sometimes Gregory …"

Her voice trailed off. I didn't know what to say. *I'm sorry* didn't seem to cover it. Lots of girls I knew had stories like hers; that's how they ended up working the Tenderloin. Compared to them, I'd gotten off easy. I couldn't even begin to imagine the grinding horror of Anna May's life.

We were quiet for a while. So quiet that I almost didn't hear her when she whispered, "I wanted to make him stop."

"Well, you did. He's never gonna mess with you again." *Please let it be true,* I thought desperately, aware that it was a prayer of sorts. "How're your hands feeling?"

She thought about that. "Hot and crinkly."

"Crinkly? Do they hurt bad?"

"Not too bad."

I nodded, hoping that was true, too. "In a little while, I'm going to stop and get some aspirin and bandages. Meantime, if I made you a pillow from my jacket, do you think you could maybe get some sleep?"

"I can try," she said.

Brave girl. "Why don't you close your eyes and try right now?"

Five minutes later, she was dozing with her head against the door frame.

I turned up the heat so she wouldn't get chilled, and when I hit Salt Lake City I turned east on Route 80, toward Wyoming.

fourteen

I'd forgotten that I like to drive.

I was desperately tired, but sleep didn't stand a chance, so I turned on the radio, opened my window and drove fast, letting the miles blow by.

Anna May hadn't woken up yet. I would have thought, with her past, that she'd be ruined for anything as normal as sleep, but I was glad she could escape for a little while.

When we crossed into Wyoming, I got off the highway and followed a smaller road heading north toward Grand Teton-Bridger National Park. I stopped once to fill the gas tank and buy aspirin, gauze and ointment for when Anna May woke up. And once, at about midnight, on top of a mountain that took half an hour to climb, I stopped, got out and just stood there, looking at trees that were taller than the buildings back home and ravines that were deep enough to swallow a nightmare.

Summer or no, it was cold up here. The wind was stiff, but I didn't mind. I was hypnotized by how big and raw and beautiful it all was. Millions of stars were spread across an endless, 3-D, blue-black sky. The air was shimmery, crisp and quiet, except for the sing-song wind and sometimes, far off, the fading sound of another car.

In spite of everything that had happened, it made me feel a little hope.

But that didn't last long. When I got back in the Buick, which was technically a stolen car, and looked at Anna May, who was technically a kidnapped minor, and thought about Timothy—technically, we could be charged with aggravated assault, and that was if the bastard *lived* – I knew that all the perfect nights in Wyoming didn't change the fact that I was in big trouble.

Much worse trouble than before.

Alone, without food or money or shelter, I'd still had options. Now I was literally boxed into the Buick. But I couldn't bring myself to regret it, not if there was a chance for Anna May. I thought about how Marcus had showed up to rescue me from a would-be rapist that long-ago night at Stacy G's.

This time, it had been my turn to rescue someone I didn't know.

Coming down the other side of that mountain, the winding road was impossibly steep. I passed a sign that said *6% GRADE*. Two brutally sharp turns later, the Buick breezed past a jack-knifed tractor-trailer that had overturned and gone off the road. It was sprawled on its side like a monstrous dead animal, a massive load of uncut logs still strapped to its flatbed.

"Jesus!" I hit the brakes, then remembered just in time to feather them instead of stomping. Already I was skidding; I steered into the skid and threw the car into low gear.

If it was this hard to stop a puny Buick on this long descent, no wonder that hulking thing had flipped over!

Anna May slept through it all. I brought us to a halt 500 yards or so past the truck and sat there for a minute, collecting myself. Then I got out, shut the door quietly, and walked back up the hill to look at the wreck.

I don't know what I expected to find but, to my relief, the big cab was empty. The only thing showing signs of life was a radio handset, twisting slowly on its short black cord.

On the road nearby was a jumbled pile of stuff: Cigarettes, papers, a half-crushed Coke can, a large men's denim jacket, well-worn. I didn't know if the truck driver was dead or alive, but either way, he wasn't coming back for that jacket. I picked it up and walked back downhill on legs that felt weak from too much adrenalin.

Inside the car, my hands shook so bad that I couldn't fumble the key into the ignition. I was tired, that was my problem. Tired and overstimulated from fighting Timothy, that dash through the woods, the long night's drive and everything that had come before it: Losing Marcus. Meeting Mary Jo. Leaving Blanche. Lying to Francisco.

What the hell did I think I was doing, playing with people's lives like this? What if Francisco *had* got me pregnant? What if Anna May went to jail? What if *I* went to jail for my part in it? How the hell would anything ever come out right again?

And just like that, it was all too much for me. Too much pain, too much danger, too much responsibility. For the first time since leaving San Francisco, I covered my face with my hands and started crying, trying to keep as quiet as possible so I didn't wake Anna May.

Then I heard a shimmery whisper. "Hey!"

So much for not waking her. Anna May's face looked hazy through my tears. "Don't cry," she said. "You saved me."

"Not yet," I sniffed, feeling suddenly foolish—and worse, like I'd screwed up my responsibilities. I was supposed to be taking care of her, and here she was, trying to reassure me. "You're not saved, you're just on the run." My voice was a weird blend of gruff and sulky.

She shrugged, like it was no big deal that we were on the road with no place to go. "You helped me hurt Timothy. You took me away. You're my hero, Gracie-Grace."

I wiped my face on the sleeve of my jacket. If I was Anna May's idea of a hero, she was even more naïve than I'd thought. But I couldn't stand to disillusion her—that would happen soon enough anyway—so I just sniffed back the rest of my tears and tried to pull myself together.

"Let me see your hands," I said. The self-pity and the tears were over. Somebody had to be in charge.

She held them out for me to examine. The redness was down and the blisters had popped, which was good for healing though it probably hurt like hell. I spread some ointment on her hands and bandaged them with the roll of gauze, tearing it off and tucking the end piece under the rest to hold it in place. Then I put two coated aspirin in her mouth and held a bottle of orange juice to her lips so that she could wash them down.

"That's good," she said, when she was finished drinking. "Thank you."

"You want something to eat?" I asked. "Cheese? An apple? Peanut butter?"

"No." She yawned. "I just want to go back to sleep."

She laid her head against the door and I covered her with the trucker's jacket. "You gonna rest?" she murmured, already drifting away.

"Soon as I can," I promised both of us.

♥

Two hours later, I pulled up beside a little sign that read:

RIDGE, WYOMING
POPULATION 106

That wasn't a town, it was a bar party. But Ridge, Wyoming had to be tonight's last stop because I literally couldn't go any farther. My head hurt, my legs were stiff, my eyes were crossed from squinting at the road and trying to ignore the sheer drop beside it—and that didn't even count the bruises from fighting Timothy.

From what I could see, driving through at 15 miles an hour, Ridge had one store and one gas station (both closed), one row of mailboxes, lots of farmland and a few houses. I didn't want to park right in front of a house, but I didn't want to stop on the main road either. Finally, I pulled into a dirt lane that was overhung with big trees. I cut the engine, climbed into the back seat, stretched my legs and was out cold before I'd put my head down.

Cold was the operative word, too. It was just as chilly in the mountains as I'd feared. But I couldn't afford to run the engine just to keep us warm, and I couldn't bring myself to roll up the windows, not with Timothy's smell still in the car.

Anna May seemed to sleep through the chill, but after that first brief bout of slumber, I tossed and turned for the rest of the night—drifting off, then waking up to change positions and drift off again, only to wake up shivering from head to toe and rub my arms and legs to make friction until finally, at the start of dawn, I warmed up enough to drop into a deep sleep.

The next thing I knew it was full daylight, and something was pulling hard at my scalp.

I bolted upright, and the "something" shrieked and let go of me. We both froze, staring at each other in horror. God knows what kind of nightmare she saw; I saw a little girl, about five years old, with brown eyes and ultra-straight white-gold hair.

Then she moved and broke the spell. "Mommy, Mommy!" she screamed, dashing down the dirt road toward a house I hadn't seen the night before—a small clapboard house tucked in among a dense row of trees.

Oh, shit! I thought, groggily. I was parked in somebody's driveway.

Anna May groaned and struggled to sit up in the front seat. I kept watching the little girl. She reached the house just as the front door banged open and a middle-aged woman strode out carrying a rifle.

That woke me up! I opened the door, stepped out and stepped away from the car, holding both my hands up in the traditional gesture. I didn't want this woman, whoever she was, to think I was dangerous. I didn't want her to see that the car I was driving was smeared with blood.

The woman stopped just outside arm's reach, her feet planted comfortably apart, the rifle pointing down. She looked like she knew how to use it, and I stayed right where I was, dead still.

"You're parked on my property," she said with what I privately thought was the perfect tone: Hostile, but not aggressively so.

"Sorry." I meant it. "I swear I didn't see your house last night. We were just looking for a quiet place to sleep."

The woman spared a glance at Anna May and then, rightly figuring she wasn't a danger, turned her eyes back to me. She was staring so hard that she didn't hear her daughter sneak up behind her, but I kept a corner of my eye on the child. By now it had occurred to me that she was about the same age I'd been when I killed Rosie. I knew it was crazy, but I was more scared of her than I was of the rifle.

I said, "We'll get out of here right away."

And we would have, but the girl ran around her mother and started jumping up and down, saying, "Touch her hair, Mommy. Touch her hair!"

"Stacy, you stop that! Don't be rude!"

"But Mommy, it feels like little wires!"

God, when was the last time I'd washed my hair? Or brushed it, come to think of that. I'd always been proud of my long, thick curls, but the last few months were another story.

Meanwhile, the mother looked mortified. "We never see anyone with hair like yours," she explained. "Are you Spanish or something?"

"I don't think so." Of course, what did I know about it, really? I look white, and people have always treated me that way, but I didn't look as white as these two. The little girl's skin was almost translucent, and Mom's gray-blond hair was as straight and fine as her daughter's.

"Her hair's not real," the girl insisted, tugging on the skirt of her mother's housedress.

"Yes, it is," I interrupted firmly. I crouched down, level with her little face. Sure, she spooked me, but enough was enough; being eye-to-eye with her somehow made me feel less like she might suddenly start chewing on my ankle.

"You pulled my hair," I reminded her. "You know it doesn't come off."

"You *pulled* her hair?!" Her mother sounded horrified. "You tell the lady you're sorry, right now."

"Sorry," she mumbled, looking at her dusty Keds.

Mom said, "She didn't mean any harm."

"I know that."

Meanwhile, the little girl was pouting. "I still wanna touch, Mommy."

Still crouching, I said, "I'll let you if you tell me your name."

"Stacy." She gave me a shrewd look. "You know I'm Stacy. Mommy said so!"

"You're right." I grinned reluctantly. "You're a very smart little girl, and you can touch my hair if you don't yank it."

I took a breath and tilted my head forward. "Be GEN-tle," Mom warned, as both grubby hands reached for me.

Stacy touched. Then she patted. She gave a little furtive tug and let go.

"It's real!" She sounded awestruck.

I stood up. "Told you!"

"Why's it feel like that?"

"*Stacy!*"

"It's OK," I told her Mom. Stacy's curiosity was refreshing. I almost envied her ability to care. "It feels like that 'cause I'm traveling and I haven't been able to wash it for a while. Plus it gets all tangled up when I sleep."

Stacy considered that deeply. "Why is it brown?" she asked, suspiciously.

"I guess from my mother. Why's your hair yellow?"

She looked at her mother. She looked at me. She giggled happily. We both smiled.

"I'm Linda," her Mom said, shifting the rifle to her left hand and holding out her right.

I shook it solemnly. "I'm Grace, and that's Anna May in the car."

Anna May gave a little wave. Linda's eyes widened when she saw her bandaged hands. "Is she OK?" she asked me, keeping her voice down.

"Just a little burn," I murmured. "Guess I ought to change those bandages."

Linda weighed that carefully, considering what kind of threat we posed. Through all of this, I'd kept my hands in plain sight, and anyone could tell that Anna May was harmless in the normal course of things. "You can do that inside," Linda finally offered, cautiously, but with an easy warmth that must have meant she was used to being generous.

"Thanks." The word sounded rusty, but I meant it. I went around to Anna May's door and opened it, helping her out. "We appreciate your kindness."

♥

We stayed at Linda's place all morning, what with one thing leading to another.

At first, Anna May looked scared to even go inside. But as soon as Linda opened the front door and we caught the smell of baking bread, both of us relaxed a lot.

Marcus used to say there was nothing like hot bread to take your guard down, and as usual, he was right.

"You girls can use that bathroom." Linda pointed to a door off the small, cozy-looking living room. Later, I would learn that she and her husband George, who was off working a two-week stint at the sawmill, had raised six kids besides Stacy in this tiny house. And those kids had really been *in* the house most of the time, 'cause Linda said it snowed nine months a year.

"I want to help fix her hands!" Stacy was still bouncing up and down. It didn't seem likely that Linda ever got to rest.

"Now, Stacy…"

"We'll put her to work," I offered quickly. I owed Stacy for getting us inside the house, even if she hadn't done it on purpose. And by now I'd figured out that she didn't scare me if I thought of her as a short adult without much self-control who wanted to help but didn't know how.

To my surprise, though, she really *did* help. She held the strip of gauze I'd cut while I daubed ointment onto Anna May's hands, and when I was done wrapping them, Stacy put her finger down so I could knot the ends around it.

"Good job," I told her. I felt like I was doing a pretty good job myself, of staying calm and communicating with her.

"Can you help me get the eggs?" she asked, proudly.

"Sure," I offered, more from tiredness and ignorance than generosity. I thought we were going to get a cartoon of eggs from the refrigerator, but it turned out that Stacy meant *get* the eggs, as in *get them from underneath the chickens*.

First thing those chickens did when we walked into their coop was dive bomb straight for Stacy's and my feet. It was like being in that Hitchcock movie; I yelped and jumped back out of the way. "What'd they do *that* for!" I shrilled, forgetting for a minute that I was the grownup.

"They like sneakers," Stacy explained patiently. "And they like green things. If your sneakers are green, they try to eat your toes."

"Yuck." Fortunately mine were blue, but still…

Meanwhile, Stacy had walked over to a giant chicken that was still sitting on its nest and calmly poked her hand under it. When she pulled it out, seconds later, she still had five fingers—they were holding an egg.

"I'm not doing that," I told her.

Stacy looked puzzled. "Who does it at your house?"

"I don't have a house." The sad truth of that washed through me. "And I don't have any chickens, so I'll just watch you."

"You can hold the eggs," she offered, graciously.

"OK." I took the bucket she'd been carrying, and the egg, and set it carefully on the bottom, wondering what it would taste like.

Seven eggs later, we went back to the house. "Just in time," Linda said, opening the oven door. The smell, which had been good before, was now heavenly. My mouth started watering.

Linda put the bread on the counter, closed the oven door and turned to me.

"You want to get cleaned up before breakfast?"

I hadn't known we were invited; hadn't realized I was holding my breath. "I'd like to wash my hands," I said.

"You can take a shower if you want."

It was tempting, but I said, "Not much point. I'd just be putting the same clothes back on." Actually, I had another T-shirt, but that was pretty dirty, too.

Linda looked me over, weighing whatever she hadn't weighed outside. "I have to do some laundry after breakfast," she said, finally. "I probably have some old clothes you can wear for an hour if you want to wash yours, too."

I did want to, desperately; but for some reason I couldn't just say yes. "Why?" I asked, tilting my head as if that would help me look inside her. "Why are you being so nice to us?"

"I don't know." Linda sounded as mystified as I felt. "You were nice to Stacy, and there's something about that girl you're with that…" She shook her head sadly. "You're taking care of her?"

"For now."

She didn't reply, and for a second I thought about asking if Anna May could stay with her. Linda was good enough to do it, and *normal* in some way I couldn't define. But then I thought about the trouble that might be following Anna May and me. What if Timothy hadn't died? What if Gregory was on our trail? What if, the next time Stacy went outside…? My mind played the scene before I could stop it: Stacy, Timothy, Linda, the rifle…

"Are you all right?" Her voice, her hand on my arm, jerked me back.

"I guess I'm worried about Anna May." That was true, as far as it went. "Linda," I suddenly blurted out, "I gotta find a cop to talk to. Somebody decent. Somebody who can…" I spread my hands, sighing, helpless to explain without telling Anna May's secrets.

Linda seemed to understand, though. She thought for a long moment, then said, "There's a man who was elected sheriff last year, over in Foster, halfway cross the state. He's young, and they said in the paper that he doesn't like putting people in jail, he'd rather get them into rehab or help them find a new job, that kind of thing."

He sounded too good to be true. But cops can be as good as anyone else, when they want to be. A slow motion image flashed through my mind: A young white cop carrying me out to the squad car the night Rosie died, while his partner subdued my mother.

I forced the memory away. "Is it hard to get to Foster?"

"Not if you don't mind a lot of driving." Linda's voice was too gentle, her eyes were a little bit too astute. I hated to think what she saw on my face, but the only thing she said after that was, "Well, do you want to wash those clothes?"

♥

For hours after we left their house, Anna May talked about Linda and Stacy. It was strange, in a wonderful way, to hear her speak so many words. One time, she said how sweet they were; one time, how nice they were; one time, how smart Stacy was; and once she said how good her dress felt now that it was clean (even if, I noted silently, it was still just a rag, missing the piece I'd torn from the hem, and damp from only two hours on Linda's outdoor clothesline).

In between those passionate comments, Anna May listened to the radio, like someone inhaling big, greedy gulps. She liked all the singers that we heard: George Jones, Kenny Rogers, Merle Haggard, Dolly Parton. All of them were new to her, and would have been new to me, too, if it hadn't been for that station in Bakersfield. All of it put a look on her face that I could only describe as bliss.

One song in particular seemed to move her. It was dusk, the third time we heard Dolly Parton's high, pure Southern voice singing *Calm On the Water.* Anna May joined in, whispering every third word of the chorus. Her light, childlike tones seemed to shimmer in the twilight air:

> *There's a calm on the water, a hush in the crowd*
> *There's peace in the valley, there's a stillness about*
> *There's a light in the darkness, there's joy in His love*
> *There is life everlasting, let us lift Him up.*

When the song ended, I turned the radio off. I wasn't tired of listening, but there was something perfect in what had just happened—almost like watching a prayer get answered. I wanted to let it echo for a while.

After a long silence, Anna May asked, "Do you like God, Gracie?"

I wasn't going near that one. "Do you?"

"Course I do." She raised one bandaged hand to the windshield, her fingertips touching the glass, and beyond it the sky, the emerging stars, the music, freedom. I was thinking that, if God got credit for this perfect moment, shouldn't He also take some blame for the hell she'd gone through to get here? But then again, maybe that was just my failure to understand what God meant to Anna May. I hadn't understood that with Marcus, either; faith just didn't seem to fit my nature.

Fortunately, though, I didn't need to have faith. All I had to do was get us to Foster. I drove through the dark for hours, sometimes with the radio on, sometimes with all the windows down, sometimes—after Anna May finally fell asleep, her head pillowed on the trucker's jacket—with nothing but memories for company.

I thought again about the two cops who'd come the night Rosie died and stopped my mother from beating me. I don't know who called them; some neighbor must have thought the screams and curses, the sounds of breaking glass and crashing objects were over the top, even for us. I just remember being carried to the squad car, and the young cop wiping blood off my mouth and holding my hand all the way to Child Services.

"Rosie's sick," I remember whispering, desperate to make him understand that she was in worse shape than me. "She drank bad stuff and screamed and her eyes got funny and things came out of her mouth and now she won't talk to me." That's when he said that it was going to be OK; or maybe he said that *I* would be OK, someday. He said it so gently, he made me cry 'cause I didn't know grown-ups could sound that way, and when I looked up, he was crying, too.

Was it possible I remembered that? Remembered sitting in the back seat, watching tears slide quietly down that young cop's face? Tears were slipping down my face, too, as I drove us through the Wyoming night.

I don't know how I stayed on the road, but sometime after midnight I pulled into Foster. Signs led me to the big stone building that served as the courthouse, sheriff's office and jail. It was dark, the streets were rolled up tight. They clearly didn't keep San Francisco hours here.

I followed another sign to the deserted parking lot in back. Deserted places usually aren't safe, but it was hard to imagine Foster being dangerous.

I parked as close as I could to the building, hoping it would block most of the hollow, cold wind that had come up. By the time I turned the car off, went round to the side, unbuckled Anna May's seatbelt and lowered her to a lying-down position in the front, it was close to four in the morning. I got into the back seat, locked the car and closed all the windows except a crack to let out the rest of Timothy's scent.

I expected to toss and turn until dawn, just like I had the night before outside Linda's, but the last two days and nights had taken more out of me than I knew I had. I curled up into a tight, chilly ball and—almost before I'd had time to close my eyes—was lost in a mercifully dreamless sleep.

Tap, tap. Tap, tap. Tap, tap. Tap, tap.

I struggled to wake up, groggy and confused.

A cop—sheriff—was tapping on the window above my head with his nightstick. *Good thing I closed it*, I thought, sitting up stiffly. I yawned and looked him over. Thinning hair. Puffy eyes. A shirt that strained to cover middle-aged paunch. This couldn't be the man Linda had meant.

I ran my fingers roughly through my hair, trying to comb out the new tangles. Then I rolled down the window and said, "Good morning, Sheriff."

"Deputy," he informed me. "Deputy Fred Coombs. You mind coming out of there with your hands up?"

With a strange feeling of déjà vu—hadn't I just done this yesterday?—I opened the car door and stepped outside. "Her hands are burned," I said, nodding toward Anna May so I wouldn't have to move my own hands. "She can't get out of the car by herself."

Deputy Fred Coombs gave me a suspicious look, but when Anna May held up her bandaged hands, he went over and opened the door for her. "What brings you two ladies to town?"

The food, I wanted to say, but didn't. I hadn't gotten off one good wisecrack since leaving Blanche in Wagon Wheel.

"We came to see your boss," I told him, wanting to keep things vague for now.

He didn't look particularly surprised. Maybe there were women in the parking lot waiting for his boss every morning. "In that case," he said, "why don't we step inside."

♥

Linda had forgotten to mention that Joe Rollins, the recently elected sheriff of Foster, Wyoming, was a very attractive man. About my age, a little over my height, slim—what you'd call wiry—with brown hair and dark brown eyes, he wouldn't have been anything special except for his crooked, high-beam smile, the dimple on his left cheek, that one curl that flopped over his forehead and the absolute attention he gave Anna May and me as we sat around his desk and talked.

Not that I was impressed by all of that. I was too busy telling our story, and trying to keep Anna May from confessing. I'd just finished describing the fight, and he said, "Let me see if I'm following you. This man, Timothy, comes in the kitchen door."

"That's right."

"And he knocks Anna May aside, and then he lunges at you."

"That's right."

"And you manage to push him back, and then you hit him over the head with a chair."

"That's right."

Sheriff Joe Rollins steepled his fingers. "And then *how* did he get the broken pelvis?"

This was the tricky part. Anna May and I had talked about it in the car last night, but I wasn't sure she was going to stick with the program. "I dropped a big pot on him."

"No, you didn't!" Anna May said, in a voice that was surprisingly loud, for her. "*I* did that!"

So much for my strategy.

"Anna May, be quiet!" My own voice was as calm as I could make it. "She *did* try to help me, Sheriff, but she doesn't know jack shit about fighting."

"I do too know how to fight!" Anna May shrilled. "I threw the pot on his thing and broke it!"

"No, you didn't, Anna May. You just…"

"Excuse me," Sheriff Rollins said. It was the nicest way anyone had ever told me to shut up. "Why did you do that?" he asked Anna May gently.

"He was trying to hurt Gracie. And I broke his thing so he couldn't stick it in me anymore."

At that, I felt a desperate chill. If I'd been a praying woman, I would have prayed that Joe Rollins was the wisest, kindest man on earth.

We sat there in silence for a minute. Then he reached for the phone on his desk.

"Who are you calling?" I heard myself ask. Some of the possibilities were bad.

"My grandmother," he said, dialing the number.

"Your *grandmother?*"

He gave me a smile that whispered across the hair on my arms. "She's a retired lawyer," he explained. "She's worked with lots of battered women."

♥

Lillian Rollins was a dynamo. Seventy years old and five foot two, she was dainty as a bird, with small, blue-veined hands and white hair twisted up into a bun, yet she still managed to look like she could knock a building down. She was wearing pressed blue jeans and clean white sneakers and a tailored business shirt and a tweed jacket. She looked like a short Katherine Hepburn playing a cowgirl.

She looked like salvation.

There was no other place to talk at the jail, so Sheriff Rollins left the room while Lillian, Anna May and I sat around his desk and spoke. Lillian took notes on a big yellow pad, in round, perfect writing that made me think of hoop skirts. But there was nothing old-fashioned about her mind.

"Did this Timothy hurt your hands?"

Anna May said, "No, I did that when I dropped the pot."

"How about that bruise on your face?"

I must have looked as confused as Anna May; we'd both forgotten the purple welt that was half-hidden by her hair. "I think that's from when he knocked me down, just before he tried to kill Grace."

Lillian nodded and wrote it down. "And do you have other marks on your body that go along with what you've told us?"

I expected Anna May to blush, but she was deeply innocent, in her own way, and eager, once she started talking, to tell us the entire story. "I have marks and other burns and things. They're really ugly. They're not pretty at all."

"What did you get burned with?"

"Mostly Timothy's cigarettes."

My stomach twisted into a hard knot. Lillian was taking this well, but she didn't know Timothy, hadn't seen his vicious leer, couldn't imagine how frighteningly overmatched Anna May had been. I could picture it all too clearly—the house, the man, the way she'd cowered in the kitchen. I felt the air going out of the room, felt like I was going to throw up or faint or both if I didn't....

Suddenly, the sheriff was there, setting a wastebasket in front of me. "Here, use this," he said, laying his hand on the back of my neck, a place that hadn't been touched for a while. I hadn't heard him come back in the room, and his voice still sounded far away. "Put your head way down," he told me. "Open your mouth and try to breathe."

Why did that sound so familiar? Had Mary Jo said that to me, in Nevada? No, Mary Jo was in Bakersfield. Blanche and Emily were in Nevada. I wasn't in Nevada, was I? I was in—I felt so weak, so tired, so sick, so...

When I came to, I was lying flat on my back, which isn't a way that I ever sleep. A single light bulb hung from the ceiling. Past my feet, I could see steel bars; I was lying on a thin mattress, over what felt like a wooden plank. But my head was on a pillow and a light cotton blanket was spread over me, and tucked in. Did they cover you with a blanket in jail?

"Good, you're awake," said a man's voice. Joe Rollins walked into the cell and sat down beside me on the narrow cot, in the curve defined by my waist. "Are you feeling better?"

"I don't know. I'd have to think about that." I could feel the heat coming off his body. It confused me tremendously. No man sits that close unless he wants to touch, but I couldn't for the life of me figure out why. I was halfway to being a hobo by now.

He gave me a dimpled smile. "Anna May said you've been up for days."

He had the earthy, soap-and-sweat aroma of a healthy, sexual man. I tried not to inhale too deeply, tried to think about what he'd asked me. I hadn't slept more than a few hours last night, after leaving Linda, or the night before, when we fought Timothy. Or the night before that, at Rory's mom's place in Las Vegas, or the night before, in Wagon Wheel…

No wonder I was confused. "What time is it?" I stifled a yawn.

"Nine-thirty. At night."

Why was this man still sitting here? It was intimate and scary, alone in a cell with him, only the light from that one naked bulb to keep out the night, the dreams, the mountains, the monsters like Timothy running wild in them…

I pulled myself to a sitting position. I was stiff, and still sore in places, and now I was level with those deep brown eyes, but I still felt less vulnerable sitting up. "Thanks for letting me sleep," I said. "I'm sorry you didn't get to go home yet."

"No problem." He looked right into my eyes. "There's no one to go home to."

He was definitely interested. And, of course, I had that promise to Marcus to fulfill. What if I hadn't gotten pregnant with Francisco? It was still roughly the right time of month; it still made sense to try again. And you could do worse than getting knocked up by a good-looking guy with a steady job who loved his grandmother and was kind to strays.

I should have been grateful for how easy he was making it. I *would* have been grateful, or at least not freaked out, if I hadn't been so attracted to him.

Being attracted wasn't in the program. It seemed too close to being alive.

"How'd you know I wasn't dead?" I asked.

He smiled again; it *was* a nice dimple. "Fred's an Emergency Medical Technician. He said you were sleeping very deeply—sort of like being in hibernation—so we thought the best thing would be to just leave you alone."

I was mostly surprised by his first point. "Fred your deputy's an EMT?"

"Don't be fooled by looks," he said. "Fred's the smartest man I know."

Fair enough; but I don't like being chided, even gently. "Then how come you're the sheriff, not him?"

"I'm more electable," he said with a shrug, as if being smart and sexy, popular and successful was nice, but essentially no big deal. And then he said, "Off the record, how bad was it, back there in Utah?"

Interesting—a man who could change the subject when the subject was himself. It made me like him even better, which made me even more uncomfortable.

I said, "Off the record, I don't know how come she's alive. They talk about people being animals, but he…" I shuddered. "He really was one."

Joe's mouth flattened into a grim line. "Some people give animals a bad name."

We both thought about that for a minute.

"So where is she?" I asked him.

"Anna May? She went to Lillian's. Lillian said you can both stay with her until we get to the bottom of this whole thing."

I could feel my mouth tightening around the edges. What did he mean, *the bottom of this thing?* If he didn't think our story was true, Anna May and I were in really big trouble. "Don't you believe us?"

He said, "I just collect the evidence. But I don't think there's any doubt about what we're going to learn when Lillian takes her to the clinic tomorrow."

I struggled to hide both relief and embarrassment. "You have a *clinic* here in Foster?"

He gave me the kind of teasing grin I hadn't seen since Marcus died; the lighthearted smile of a man who knows women like him, but is too nice a person to use it against them. "You think we're a bunch of hicks," he murmured, leaning in close enough for me to feel his breath on my face.

My heart slammed sideways into my ribs. This went way beyond *attracted.* The modesty, the dimple, that teasing smile were pushing my disoriented brain, my grief-stricken body over into hunger.

Joe Rollins was way too much temptation for a girl who had things to forget.

"I don't think you're hicks," I said, trying to cover my reaction.

"Oh, yeah, you do." And then he reached up and ruffled my hair.

"Don't do that!" I snapped, furious at him. I was filled with desire and confusion, and now he was treating me like his kid sister.

"Don't do what?"

"Don't touch me like I'm a pet." Anger, disappointment made me talk fast and recklessly. "Don't touch me at all, if you don't mean it."

"Oh, I mean it," he said, his tone very different.

We stared at each other for a long time. And what I liked was that, even though he looked dead serious now, the laughter didn't go out of his eyes.

sixteen

If you've never had sex in a jail before, I highly recommend it. Sex is always partly about power, and since jail is about nothing but power, all those images play in your mind, adding an edge of breathlessness.

Not that Joe and I needed the setting to add spice to what went on between us. We both were excitement enough for each other. I was used to Marcus, who was taller and heavier and more deliberate than me. Joe and I were close in size, but he was faster, harder, stronger than I was. He knew his way around a woman, and it was quickly clear that, even without the gun, the handcuffs, the badge, the keys, I would have been utterly in his power. He was wise enough to play that down, and brave enough to put himself in my power, too.

All night, I waited for guilt to come, as it had just days before with Francisco, and shatter the relief, the passion. I waited for Rosie's taunting whisper, for Marcus's lonely accusations, for the cutting voice of my own self-hatred; but none of that came into my mind. The space was filled with Joe and me.

Eventually, we got hungry for food. Joe went over to the half-sized fridge that was sitting in the corner near a hot plate and an ancient Mr. Coffee machine, and got out some giant roast beef sandwiches. Fred had apparently bought them that afternoon, while I was sleeping like the dead. Between us, we ate three of them, sitting on the cot, half-wrapped in blankets, talking and touching.

Joe was easy to talk to. I gave Lillian the credit, since he said she'd raised him from the age of eight. We talked about snow, which I'd rarely seen and which he saw from October to May. ("Sometimes you just finish shoveling and another ten feet falls on you.") We talked about San Francisco, where I told him I'd worked as a bartender. We talked about what music we liked.

All those normal, first-date topics seemed surreal after what my life had been the last year, but I was too drugged by sex, too lulled by safety, to care. And with all the things we talked about, we didn't talk about what our bodies had just done.

It was past two in the morning by the time we left the jail. By then, we'd made love three or four times, depending on just what you counted. Walking out the back door, we came into clear, moonlit quiet. The air was brisk, the moon bright, the sky washed with almost as many stars as I'd seen on that mountaintop with Anna May. By wordless agreement, we ignored Timothy's Buick, parked in the lot behind the jail—Joe had the keys, which I guess meant that he'd impounded it—and walked over to his county car. I hadn't been in a cop car since that night when I was five, but exhaustion and Joe's body had disconnected me from those memories. Neither of us had spoken a word since leaving the jailhouse. I felt strangely weightless, riding through the night beside him.

Minutes later, he pulled up outside a small house. It had a white picket fence and two window boxes with flowers that bobbed happily in the moonlight.

Joe killed the engine, turned and pulled me into his arms.

"Thank you," he said, nuzzling my cheek.

"You, too." I freed myself as gently as I could. I didn't want to start up again in the car in front of his grandmother's house. "How do I get in there?"

"Door's open," he said, looking as disoriented as I felt. "Out here, we don't lock them."

Crazy, I thought. *These people are crazy.*

"I'll walk you in," he offered.

"No." I kissed him lightly on the mouth. "Not if you want to come out in one piece."

"OK." He ruffled my hair again. This time it didn't feel condescending. It felt hot. "I'll see you soon."

He sounded like he meant that, and I thought about it all the way up Lillian's walk. Joe sat in the car and waited till I'd opened the front door and waved goodnight before he drove away. It was sweet and totally unnecessary, since we were probably the only two people awake for a hundred miles, but it made me feel warm and protected just the same.

A small light was burning in the living room. The couch was piled with blankets and pillows, and next to it, on the coffee table, was a stack of fluffy towels and a note that said *Welcome, Grace. The couch is fairly comfortable, and I've left a plate of food in the refrigerator if you're hungry. The shower is upstairs. Feel free to use it at any hour; I'm a heavy sleeper. And of course, wake me if you need anything. Lillian.*

Touched by her thoughtfulness, I turned the lamp off, slid out of my clothes, wrapped up in a blanket and lay down. The couch was more than *pretty comfortable*, it was paradise after two nights in Timothy's car—firm and clean, it smelled like cotton fresh from the dryer. I closed my eyes and thought about Joe, remembering the feel of him on my skin; and then I must have drifted off because the next thing I knew, I was looking at Marcus.

He was lying on a hardwood floor, flat on his back and as still as death. Little Rosie sat cross-legged beside him. Her face, her hands were three years old, but her arms were spindly, long enough to reach all of him, and her eyes looked to be about a thousand. She was pouring a liquid over him, and wherever that cold, clear substance touched—his arm, his hand, his stomach, his chest—Marcus's skin dissolved into gray smoke, leaving a weathered skeleton behind.

I bolted upright, choking down a scream, my eyes wide open, arms wrapped around my chest to keep me from unraveling. My whole body was damp with sweat; I was panting hard, chilled to the bone.

"*Why?*" I hissed at Rosie, clutching my knees up to my chest, but of course she didn't answer me, she never did when I was awake. "*Why are you doing this to me now?*"

Silence. I threw off the blanket that was tangled round my legs, got up and put my clothes on. Then I made my way by moonlight into Lillian's kitchen—a cozy place, but cold now, in the pre-dawn air.

The clock said it was almost five. I could walk out now, be at the highway when the sun came up. I could head for D.C., find Blondell and get a job and…

No, I couldn't. I sat down heavily on a kitchen chair, remembering Anna May, upstairs. Until she was settled, I couldn't move on. There was no logic to it, nothing I could explain to anyone else, but it had to do with paying back the universe for everything Marcus had given me. I didn't know why Anna May was the one holding my I.O.U., but I knew I couldn't leave until she was okay.

Defeated, I went back to the living room. This time, I didn't undress. I just wrapped the blanket around my clothes and got back on the couch, half-sitting so that nothing could sneak up on me in the sleep I wasn't strong enough to resist.

I woke to the smell of dark roast heaven. Unless I was still dreaming, someone was making real coffee, the kind I hadn't had since leaving San Francisco. With my clothes on, all I had to do was kick the blankets off and stagger into the kitchen to see.

Lillian was standing at the table, her small hands putting things in a bowl. Anna May sat on a stool, nearby. Her hands looked smaller, too, and after a second I realized it was because my clumsy bandages were gone, replaced by some kind of adhesive pad that covered her palms and nothing more.

The coffee hadn't been a dream. Lillian wiped her hands and poured a tall mug for me.

"Thank you." I stuck my nose over the edge and inhaled gratefully.

"You're welcome." She looked amused by something. Maybe it was my coffee jones; or maybe—here was an unsettling thought—she guessed that I'd spent half of last night wrapped around her grandson.

I hoped to hell I wasn't blushing, but just in case, I ducked my head and took a long, slow sip of coffee. "This is good," I said, feeling it rush straight to my veins. "Where'd you get it?"

Lillian said, "I go over to Jackson Hole twice a year and stock up." I thought she was kidding 'till she opened her freezer door to show me rows and rows of neatly stacked brown coffee bags. "Jackson Hole is really changing," she said with a sad little shake of her head. "Used to be, people went there to see that arch made of elk antlers. Now they go to watch the tourists."

We observed a few seconds of silence at that thought. Anna May finally broke it to ask, "Did you sleep well, Gracie-Grace?"

Now I *knew* that I was blushing, but I gave Anna May a happy smile. "I slept great. How about you?"

"I slept the best in my whole life," she said.

Lillian's solemn eyes met mine over Anna May's head and, for a second, I could feel the pledge that united us. I wasn't the only person bound and determined to set this right. Then Lillian gave herself a little shake, and when she spoke her voice was bright. "Anna May's giving me her recipe for biscuits."

I shrugged. "I don't know how to cook."

Lillian seized on this safe topic. "Anyone can cook," she said. "You just haven't had a chance to learn yet." She glanced down at the contents of the bowl. "For instance, baking is like chemistry. Did you take chemistry in high school?"

"No," I said, and then, for some strange reason added, "I dropped out when I was fourteen."

She looked startled. "I would never have guessed that. You seem to be well-educated."

I shrugged again. "I like to read. I wish I had a book now."

Lillian smiled. "Feel free to borrow whatever you want."

I nodded my thanks and leaned over, looking into the mixing bowl. It didn't look like chemistry to me, it just looked like a bunch of flour with a big glob of white stuff sitting on top.

I said so to Lillian.

She laughed. "The flour isn't just flour. It's flour, salt, baking powder and baking soda, with a touch of sugar. The 'white glob' is shortening." She pushed the bowl across the table to me. "Do me a favor and cut it in, would you?"

I had no idea what she was talking about, but Lillian produced a wide, blunt blade with a wooden handle from one of her drawers and held it out to me. "Use this to chop that ball of fat into pea-sized pieces. Don't worry about making them uniform."

I hadn't been worried about any such thing, but it struck me that it might be a relaxing kind of worry to have. I pressed the thin blade straight into the white goo, and when I lifted it up again, the whole ball lifted up with me.

Lillian and Anna May both laughed. Anna May's laugh was tentative, but the two of them together had a nice ring. "Here," Lillian said, handing me a regular knife. "You can use this to scrape it off. It'll stop sticking when the flour gets mixed in."

I didn't know how *that* was going to happen, but I started to carefully chop, then scrape, then chop, then scrape, and pretty soon I could see that the flour, which clung to the smaller balls of fat, was keeping them from sticking to the blade as much. I privately thought it was pretty cool.

As I worked, Lillian tried to teach me chemistry. "See the proportions in the bowl?" she asked. I half-nodded to show that I half-understood.

"Those are the proportions for biscuits."

Hmph. I looked more carefully. A handful of fat, a small stack of flour.

"Most everything else you want to bake has eggs in it, too. If you want muffins, you add more sugar. If you want cookies, you add more fat. If you want a cake, you add more liquid and flavoring. That's about all there is to baking."

"You're kidding."

"You'll see, when you start reading recipes."

Anna May looked into the bowl. "You're almost done," she said happily. "Just give it a few more chops."

Mystified – *how did they both know this stuff?* – I chopped twice more, then stood back to look. The flour was crumbly now, and had little, pea-sized balls of fat spread through it.

Maybe I was drunk on Lillian's coffee, but this was fun. "What do I do next?"

Lillian handed me a measuring cup that was filled to the top with milky sludge. "Pour in the buttermilk, then stir it a few times with this fork."

I did as she said, while they watched me proudly.

"That's enough," Lillian stopped me. "Flour gets tough if you work it too hard."

I looked up at Anna May. "This is your recipe?"

She nodded solemnly. "Lillian doesn't use buttermilk, but I do."

"That's why we put in the baking soda," Lillian explained. "You need it to react with an acidic liquid like buttermilk, or else the biscuits won't rise."

I stared at her.

"You should write that down," Lillian told me. "You never know when it might come in handy."

♥

After breakfast, which was delicious, I asked Lillian a favor. "Do you mind if I call Washington, D.C.? I can pay you for it."

She said, "You don't need to pay me anything. Do you want us to leave the room?"

Did I? If Blondell answered, it would be nice to talk to her alone. But what was the real chance of that?

"I don't know," I said, truthfully, because part of me was just as scared that I'd get Blondell as that I wouldn't—scared that her voice would remind me of the full-body grief I'd been feeling the last time we saw each other.

Lillian pushed away from the table. "Anna May and I are going to the clinic," she said, carrying her plate to the sink, "and then I want to take you girls shopping."

I couldn't think about that now, not when I was already digging in my shoulder bag for my wallet, where I'd put the matchbook cover with Blondell's number. I barely heard Lillian and Anna May leave the room.

Lillian had one of those thin, white telephones that hangs on the kitchen wall. My hand shook as I dialed it. One ring. Two. Three, four, and then a phone company voice came on and said, "The number you have dialed in area code 2-0-2 is not in service. Please check the number and try again."

OK, maybe I *had* dialed wrong. But part of me knew that I hadn't, even as I pressed the numbers again. And heard that message. And hung up, trying hard not to slam the receiver down. My lower lip was shaking as if I wanted to cry, which was stupid, since I'd known she probably wouldn't be there. It must have been six weeks since she'd left San Francisco; anything could have happened in that kind of time.

When Lillian and Anna May came back downstairs, I was sitting at the table with another cup of coffee. Lillian looked at my face and didn't ask about the call. Anna May said, "I'm going to see the nurse."

"That's good." I hoped it would be.

"She's going to give Anna May a check-up and take some X-rays," Lillian said, matter-of-factly. "And then we're going to go buy some clothes. Should we pick you up on our way to the store?"

"No, that's OK." The truth was, I needed some time alone, and I wasn't much for window shopping. What was the point of looking at things I couldn't have anyway? "I'll stay here and read, if you don't mind."

"I don't mind." Lillian picked up a pencil. "Call Joe if you need anything," she said, writing down the number. "And pull the door shut behind you if you leave. And let me know if you're not coming home for dinner." She smiled. "No point in wasting food."

♥

After they were gone, I topped off my coffee and walked upstairs to look at Lillian's study.

It was my idea of a fantasy room. It had one of those big, reclining leather chairs in a sturdy dark brown color that looked comforting. Next to it, was a long-necked floor lamp and a little table, and tucked in one corner was a desk that you could tell she didn't use for much. Bookcases covered three of the walls. Floor to ceiling, they were jammed full of hardbacks, paperbacks, big and small books, thick and thin books, hundreds of them sitting there just waiting to be sampled.

It was way too much for me to take in. I went back to the hall and poked around the rest of the house, into Lillian's room, which was soft, but mostly serviceable, not a girly kind of room at all, and the room where Anna May was staying, that must have been Joe's when he was a boy.

His room had a low bookcase against one wall, with baseball trophies on the top shelf—Joe had apparently been the pitcher on a winning Little League team—and a neat row of yellowing Hardy Boys books on the shelf below. I crouched down to look at the Hardy Boys, and sure enough, each of their spines was numbered and the numbers were lined up in a row, from 1 to 27, the point at which he'd either gotten too old for them or just lost interest.

Over the bookcase hung a framed certificate. Joe had a bachelor's degree in criminology, with honors, from the University of Minnesota; which meant that he was just about as smart as I'd thought, even if he didn't have the brains to go to college in a place where it didn't snow. The honors part seemed like a big deal to me, but maybe since his grandmother was a lawyer he didn't feel the same.

Turning, I stared suspiciously at the closet, afraid, for some reason, that the door might suddenly pop open and the ghost of Joe's childhood self come dancing out. It wouldn't have surprised me, with the way Marcus and Rosie's ghosts were always dancing out of my mind. But maybe they only did that 'cause they had to. It struck me that, while Joe's past lived on in this room, Marcus and Rosie had totally vanished from the world of *things*. Except for my picture, and the ones at Mary Jo's, there was nothing to prove that Marcus had ever lived; and Rosie hadn't left even that much. No wonder they were trying to stay alive in my dreams.

And if I thought about it head-on, I *did* understand why they'd both come back now. The sight of me and Joe rolling around in that cell last night had literally been enough to wake the dead.

Still, it didn't pay to sympathize too much with ghosts. *The hell with you,* I groused at Marcus. *This was your goddamn idea in the first place!*

Nobody answered, and I was glad. I didn't want him talking back to me—didn't want him pointing out that, while *he'd* thought up the part about me getting pregnant, the part about enjoying it had totally been my own idea.

No, I wasn't ready for that. I closed the door to Joe's room behind me, and took my topped-off, now-tepid coffee back to Lillian's study to find a book.

♥

They came back in the late afternoon with a shopping bag and a bucket of fried chicken. "She's tired," Lillian explained, nodding toward Anna May. "We just didn't feel like cooking tonight."

But Lillian looked like the tired one to me. Anna May seemed really different, and it took me a minute to realize that it was because she was wearing new clothes.

"You look beautiful," I told her truthfully. Well, her face still looked gaunt, and her hair was the same, but dressed in a long skirt and pretty top, she seemed younger. She even moved differently.

"Tomorrow we're going for a haircut," Lillian said.

"Wait'll you see what we bought for you, Gracie!" Anna May reached gingerly into the shopping bag.

"But…"

She pulled out a white cowboy shirt and Wrangler jeans, holding them by her fingertips. "Try them on, Gracie. See if we guessed you right."

I was really moved, but I tucked my hands firmly behind me. "I can't pay for them," I told Lillian.

"I can." She looked pleased with herself. "Do you know what I went through to get my law degree?"

"No, ma'am."

"Wyoming's the Equality State. It was first to give women the vote." She grinned, a little ironically. "It's not like we could afford to waste *anybody's* brains or talent out here. Still, if it hadn't been World War II, if all the men hadn't been overseas, I might not have gotten into law school. I was almost 30 by then; trying to raise my daughter, working nights, studying like a fool all day, and I still made the top of my class. And, even then, when I started practicing, the judges used to ask me who I'd slept with to pass the bar."

I could picture it. "What'd you tell 'em?"

"Same person you did."

We all laughed at that. Lillian took the clothes from Anna May's fingertips and held them out to me. "I went through all of that to make some good money so I could afford to buy you these jeans."

I couldn't refuse them after that. The clothes fit great, and they felt so good that I realized it was over a year since I'd had something new.

"Thank you," I told both of them, thinking that I'd probably said *thank you* more times in the last few weeks than the whole rest of my life put together.

If I wasn't careful, it could get to be a habit.

♥

Lillian was preoccupied at dinner. Afterwards, we threw out the paper plates and went in the living room and watched TV. We watched a sitcom and the news, and then we watched a show about two women cops called *Cagney and Lacey* that was really good.

"That's what you're like," Anna May said afterwards.

"Me? I could never be a cop!"

"You're like that one with the blond hair. You're tough but you're nice, and nobody can hurt you."

Boy, did I wish that was true.

Anna May went up to bed. I could easily have done the same, but since we were in the living room, I waited to see what Lillian would do.

What she did was ask, "Would you like a drink?"

I said yes, gratefully. I didn't miss drinking beer for breakfast, but I didn't like having no alcohol at all. Sometimes you need to fuzz things up, and I hadn't had much chance to do that lately.

She poured us something dark and rich-looking. "Sherry," she said, handing me a short glass. "That's what nice women of my generation drink."

I'd drunk some sherry at Stacy G's, when I was getting to know what was in the bar, but it sure hadn't tasted like this: Thick and warm, mellow and soothing. Lillian still looked pretty sad. "Are you OK?" I had to ask, even knowing it wasn't my business.

She put her drink down and rubbed both sides of her forehead, hard. "You never get used to it," is what she said.

I waited, figuring she would go on.

"I represented a woman whose boyfriend busted her jaw so bad she lost five teeth. A woman whose husband kicked a hole in her stomach. A woman who was gang raped and left on the highway to bleed to death."

Poor Lillian. You could see how it hurt her to always get there after the fact.

I said, "But she didn't die, right?"

She looked at me like I'd spoken in Chinese.

"That woman," I explained. "The one they raped and left on the highway. You knew her *after* that happened, right?"

Lillian nodded, very slowly.

"So she didn't die. They wanted her to, but she didn't die. Anna May didn't die, either."

"No. Thank God."

Somehow this seemed very important. "And you helped all of them, didn't you? Just like you're helping Anna May now. You helped them all start over again."

Lillian made a shivering motion, as if she was shaking something off her skin. "I didn't do a very good job with Joe's mother," she said, and if I hadn't known first-hand how guilt worked I might have thought she'd changed the subject.

Instead, I nodded. "Then *you* get to start over, too."

After a second, Lillian gave a tiny nod of her own. We both sipped slowly on our drinks.

"Did Joe call today?" she asked, too casually.

I figured that she guessed he hadn't. I was disappointed, but I didn't want Lillian to see that. "Nobody called today," I said, sounding a little too casual myself.

"Hmph." Her head bobbed up and down, as if she was working out a math problem in her mind. "Joe's a good boy," is the answer she came up with.

I had to smile at that, even if the smile was a little sad. Of course, she'd raised him from a child; but did he still seem that young to her? "If he's a good boy, what the hell do you think *I* am?"

She raised her glass, saluting me. "I think you're a good girl."

seventeen

I slouched into the kitchen early the next morning, grateful for a light but undisturbed sleep. Apparently not seeing Joe Rollins helped keep Rosie's ghost at bay.

Anna May poured me a cup of coffee, and two minutes later the phone rang.

Lillian picked it up, said hello, then listened for a while. "I'm ready," she said, and her mouth was set in a hard enough line that you could well believe she *was* ready—for anything. Then she listened some more and, in a very different tone of voice, said, "You can ask her yourself, she's sitting right here."

She handed me the phone with such a straight face that I knew it was Joe.

"Hello?" I didn't like how tentative I sounded.

"Hi. I just wanted to see how things are going." There was an awkward pause—at least, *I* felt awkward—and then he said, "Actually, I wanted to see if you're free tonight."

I felt like I'd suddenly spiked a fever. "Hold on, I'll check with my social secretary." I put a hand over the receiver and asked Lillian, "Am I free tonight?"

"Your calendar's clear." Her eyes were sparkling. "Ask him if he wants to come for dinner." Then she turned to Anna May, who looked confused, and whispered, "It's Joe. For Gracie."

I glared at both of them. You could still hear me glaring when I told Joe, "Yeah, I'm free tonight. What about it?"

He chuckled. Apparently I didn't scare him. "Do you want to do something?"

"That sounds all right. Lillian wants to know if you want to come for dinner."

"Sure," he said. "We'll go out afterwards."

Go out where, I almost asked, *the Dairy Queen?* But he probably would have just laughed again. Apparently I didn't intimidate him, which made me feel even surlier.

"Okay," I snarled.

He *did* laugh, and then he hung up.

"Idiot," I mumbled into the receiver.

When I looked up, Anna May and Lillian were both grinning.

"You got a problem?" I snapped.

"Not a one," Lillian replied cheerfully. "Wash your hands and put on an apron. We're going to teach you to make an omelet."

♥

After breakfast, while Anna May was showering, I cornered Lillian. "What were you and Joe talking about?"

She poured herself another cup of coffee, black and thick as sin. "He's been on the teletype to Utah."

My stomach, which had been comfortably full of pretty good eggs, did an ugly somersault. "How's Timothy?"

"Alive, with a shattered pelvis and lots of burns on his lower body."

"That's all? Damn, what a shame!"

"No, it's not," she said sternly. "If he'd died, it would have been hell to keep you two out of jail. As it is..."

"As it is, what?"

Lillian drained her coffee mug in one long gulp. It made a thudding sound when she set it down on the table. "As it is, we're going to have to handle Gregory."

"I'd like to handle him," I muttered.

She threw me a complicated look. "While that would certainly be fun to watch, I need to advise you—as your lawyer—to stay far away from him."

"My lawyer?" I squinted at her. "What do I need a lawyer for?"

Lillian sighed deeply. It loosened the muscles on her face, and for a moment she looked startlingly old, and vulnerable. Then her control snapped back into place.

She said, "You need a lawyer because you're the one that Gregory's threatening."

"What?!" My skin felt clammy. "Threatening *how?*"

She laced her fingers together, resting her strong, wrinkled hands on the table. "Anna May's under 18, and Gregory's claiming that, when you took her over state lines, you did it for 'immoral purposes.' That violates the Mann Act; it's worse than kidnapping."

Images of our trip across the Tetons—of bandaging Anna May's hands, which were all but healed now, and the jack-knifed semi and the blanket of stars—flashed through my mind. "Well, I figured it would violate *something*."

"You were brave to do it anyway," Lillian said.

"No, I wasn't." And then the rest of it sank in. "He's trying to get me for *kidnapping?*"

"Kidnapping, grand larceny and aggravated assault."

For once, I was speechless.

"He says," Lillian continued, "that you broke into the house looking for something to steal, and when Timothy tried to stop you, you attacked him and took Anna May hostage."

"*Shit!*" It was ludicrous—but it was also easy to imagine people believing that version of events.

"He's technically a sheriff," Lillian noted. "And he's not a total fool."

No, apparently he wasn't. "I *did* steal a bowl of soup," I confessed, fighting a vague but serious sense of panic.

"And the car," Lillian observed dryly.

"And the car." I could feel my mouth twisting. "Why am I supposed to have done all of that?"

"For money. You're supposed to be a drug addict."

Well, that part was convincing. Even though it wasn't true now, it had been; and even without that clever embellishment, what jury on earth would take the word of an ex-stripper with no family, no job, no last known address over some guy who had the title *sheriff?*

No, I was guilty until proven innocent.

"Well… I guess it's time for me to move on." I sounded gruff and stilted, but what I felt was pure regret. I liked Anna May, I liked Lillian and I probably could have liked Joe way more than I should.

But Lillian had jumped to her feet. "That's not what time it is!" she said, shaking a finger down at me, just as if we were in a courtroom. "It's not time to run away! It's time to stay put and let us take care of this. You don't want it hanging over you, for the rest of your life, do you?"

"Of course not. But…."

"But nothing, Young Lady!" She swatted my words away. "I thought you trusted Joe and me."

"That's a damned sneaky thing to say!"

"Tough!" she spat out. She seemed about to rail at me, but then she abruptly checked herself and sat down again.

"Gregory doesn't want to arrest you," she explained with elaborate patience. "That's just how he thinks he'll get what he wants."

"Which is…?"

She grimaced. "I think he wants Anna May."

"Jesus!"

"Yeah. He'll probably offer to not bring charges against you if we let him walk away with her."

My stomach did another nauseated flip.

"So you see," she said, grimly matter-of-fact, "we're actually in a stronger position if you stay."

I didn't like it, but I could feel the pull of conscience, as she wanted me to.

"If Gregory thinks he's got an easy win, he won't be looking for a trap. And then, when he gets here, we'll be the ones driving the bargain."

For a second, I thought she meant that they were going to give me up.

Lillian must have seen it on my face. "Not you," she said quickly. "We're going to tell *Sheriff Gregory* that we won't charge him with statutory rape if he stays out of both your lives, for good."

"But you can't make that stick," I protested. "It would just be Anna May's word against his."

"Well," Lillian looked pleased with herself, "that would have been true until recently. But apparently there's some new research in England that says it may be possible to identify a rapist from the DNA in his semen."

"Are you serious?" I hadn't heard anything like that; not that I'd been following the scientific press, exactly. "How?"

Lillian shrugged. "According to what I read, it's something about how gene sequences repeat themselves." She met my incredulous look with a Cheshire cat smile. "I don't understand it either," she said, "and I don't think more than a few people do. Which means that, if we tell Gregory it works… it works."

I stared at her with open admiration. Then I saw the flaw in her reasoning. "But you said they can tell from the DNA in semen. That would mean you'd have to have…"

"A sample," she finished. "I know. We do." When I looked at her questioningly, she added, "Anna May was ashamed to give you her underpants when you did the laundry."

"What!?"

"She hid them in the pocket of that jacket you gave her. They have some organic material on them."

It took a second for that to register; then I shuddered through my whole body. "What did you find at the clinic yesterday?"

Lillian said, "Old cigarette burns. X-ray evidence of old fractures that healed by themselves. There's some hearing loss in her right ear, probably from being punched in the head. Her left eye is weak. You've noticed that she limps a little. She had two different venereal diseases…" Lillian's voice trailed off. For all I knew, the list went on for hours.

You never get used to it, she'd said last night. I cradled my bent head in my hands and waited for my stomach to settle. When it did, I looked up to find her studying me.

"You really did save Anna May's life," Lillian said. "So you might as well stick around and see how things turn out."

♥

I spent the day upstairs in Lillian's study reading *Deadlock*, by Sara Paretsky. Paretsky's detective heroine was tough and smart; she knew how to fight and she didn't mind fighting against big odds to get justice for her cousin, who was murdered because he knew too much.

It wasn't hard to see why Lillian owned that book, and diving into it helped me forget our conversation. It also helped me forget that Lillian's grandson Joe was joining us for dinner. There was no reason to think that he'd been anything more than a particularly satisfying one-night stand, but I couldn't shake off a dangerous little thrill of pleasure at knowing I would see him again.

Late in the afternoon, Anna May called me down to help her and Lillian whip up a chicken and rice casserole. They seemed to have decided I would make a good apprentice cook, and I was glad for the distraction and the company. Of course they gave me the worst job—chopping onions—but they were so happy when I did it half-right that I felt good about the effort. Afterwards, I went upstairs to take a shower, and by the time I came back down, the kitchen smelled great.

The doorbell rang just as Lillian was taking the casserole out of the oven.

"Go let Joe in," she said, without looking at me.

Walking to the door, I got ready to be disillusioned. The Joe Rollins I thought I'd met was probably a trick of my imagination. But Joe looked better than I remembered, manly and touchable in well-worn jeans and a flannel shirt.

I had changed into the clothes Lillian bought me. My hair was clean and tied back with a ribbon. I didn't look as good as Joe, but I looked good enough that he smiled when he checked me out.

Then he kissed me, casually, as if we did this every night.

Well, two people could play that game. I said, "How'd you manage to show up just as dinner was coming out of the oven?"

"I smelled it from the car." He grinned. "Plus, Lillian's very punctual."

In the kitchen, his punctual grandmother gave him a fierce hug and asked, "Who won today, Joe? Good or Evil?" You could tell this was a routine they had.

"It's a little too early to say," Joe replied, "but Good's looking pretty good so far." He picked up two bowls that were waiting on the counter—green beans topped with canned fried onions, and a garden salad with vinegar and oil—and carried them over to the table. Then he filled four glasses with water and took them over in one trip, wedged between his hands. Watching him made me sad for what I'd lost when Marcus died, and sorry for what I'd done to Francisco.

When we were all sitting down, and Lillian was piling big heaps of casserole onto everyone's plate, Joe asked Anna May how she was doing.

"Good, thank you." Her eyes were lowered, her voice was soft, but she wasn't too shy to suddenly look up at him and say, "Gracie made the salad."

Joe gave me a big smile.

"Don't get too excited," I told him. "A trained bear could make the salad with these two telling him what to do."

"She made the eggs for breakfast, too!"

Damn, was Anna May trying to sell me to Joe? I felt like I was on the auction block. "They're trying to teach me how to cook," I explained, keeping it matter-of-fact.

Was that amusement in his eyes? "Nice thing to know, if you like to eat."

"Joe's a good cook," Lillian said. "I made sure he wouldn't have to get married just to get a decent meal." Then she tossed him a challenging look. "I'll bet he can name every ingredient in this dish."

This was clearly a routine of theirs, too. I envied Joe the comfort of home as he ran down the ingredients: Chicken, mushrooms, chicken broth, white rice, red wine, garlic, onions, salt and pepper.

"You missed one." Lillian winked at me. "Good thing I didn't bet money on him."

"Good thing," I agreed on cue.

"What did he leave out?" she asked me.

Well, I'd known there would be a test. There always is, eventually. Fortunately, I'd watched her carefully. "Oregano," I said, smirking at Joe.

Lillian smiled. Joe smiled. Anna May clapped her hands together. You'd have thought I just won Jeopardy.

"I guess there's hope for me yet," I murmured.

"I guess there is," Lillian murmured back.

♥

In fairness to Joe, he did offer to take me out. Apparently there was a movie theater in town, and a cowboy bar that played live music and had some pool tables. There were also a few coffee shops where we could get some desert and talk.

Another time, any of those would have sounded good. Tonight I just wanted to crawl into his arms and stay there for at least a month. So we drove ten minutes across town to the house where he'd been living for the past five years.

I liked the place as soon as we walked in. It was cozy, masculine and solid. Downstairs was an eat-in kitchen, a living room that didn't look used and a screened-in porch where Joe kept snow and rain gear and a parka that looked like it would do an Eskimo proud. Upstairs was a guest room filled with boxes, a bathroom that was clean in spite of its yellowed wallpaper, and his bedroom.

We stood on the threshold, eyeing his bed—a King-size number with big, fluffy pillows, flannel sheets and a down comforter. It was obviously going to compare favorably with the wooden jail cot we'd shared two days before.

"Do you want a beer, or something?" He sounded just a little unsure.

"No," I said. "I'm fine."

"Do you want to go down to the living room?"

"Not unless you want to."

"Do you want me to make a fire?"

"Not really."

"Damn, Grace." He cracked a boyish grin. "What *do* you want?"

"Damn, Joe." I touched the dimple in his cheek with my fingertip. "Why don't you see if you can guess."

There was nothing wrong with his guessing ability. But I did notice, as we tumbled to the bed in a hot, untidy heap, that once again we'd gone straight into having sex without stopping to talk about it.

That was fine with me. If we didn't talk about birth control, I wouldn't have to lie to him. He probably figured I was on the pill, as fast as I'd come on to him. But since he wasn't using a condom, it struck me that, smart as Joe Rollins seemed to be, he was either way too trusting or secretly out to get himself screwed.

Fortunately those thoughts didn't last past the moment when our clothes came off. And when Joe started kissing from my toes up to my mouth, pretty much *any* kind of thinking stopped. He took his time about it, hitting all the classic spots and some other places—like behind my knees and the center of my palms—that I hadn't realized were dry and lonely until he kissed them. By the time he pushed deep inside me, every cell of my body was screaming with pleasure. I screamed, too, when I came. It was that good.

Afterwards, he kissed my eyes and gently wiped between my legs with some tissues. Then he pulled me tight against the length of his body and drew the comforter up to our chins.

It was luscious under that clean, warm weight, his damp legs tangled up with mine, his arms wrapped around me, his breath on my cheek. I didn't care what this was going to cost, in guilt or dreams or plain bad faith. I could have died happily, right then and there.

After a while, Joe got out of bed. I lay on my stomach, watching him through lazy eyes as he put on a robe and walked over to his bureau.

"I've got something you might like to try," he said.

I squirmed over to the side of the bed and scooped his flannel shirt off the floor where it had fallen. His back was still turned and I pressed it quickly to my face and took a deep breath of his smell. Then I slid into it, rolled the sleeves to below my elbow and buttoned the middle button.

Joe sat down on the bed beside me, holding a cigar box in his hand.

I should have guessed right away what was in it, but I felt so lazy and disconnected that he'd set a flat mirror on the bed and was carefully unrolling a plastic bag before it clicked in my groggy brain what he was up to.

He took a small white lump from the bag and set it on a mirror. "Do you like coke?"

Did I? It seemed like forever since I'd snorted, though I knew it must have only been a year or so, back at Girl-O-Rama with Blondell, before Marcus got sick.

"Where'd you get it?" I asked, ignoring his question. I sat up, plumped two pillows and settled them behind my back.

"Cheyenne." He peered into my eyes. "And it's not from a drug bust, if that's what you're thinking."

I didn't care one way or the other. "I was just curious, that's all."

But this must have been a sore point with him. He said, "I bought it with cash, same as everyone else."

You're not everyone else, I thought, *you're the Law.* And then I thought, *Damn, aren't we getting prissy.* "I would have taken it off some dealer," I told him, my lip curled in disdain.

"Maybe." He gave me a look. "Or maybe, if you'd been elected to the public trust, you'd feel differently."

Well, that was way too pious for me. I've always hated being lectured to, and even if he didn't mean to lecture, his voice had that instructional tone. "They didn't elect you to blow coke," I snapped.

He winced; I must have hit the mark. "I don't *blow coke* on the job," he said. "I just do a little on my own time."

"That's bullshit." For some reason, I was angry. "You pop people who're doing drugs *on their own time*, right?"

"Not if I can help it. Not unless they're dealing, or cooking up meth in the basement or slipping angel dust to kids."

I suddenly remembered what Linda had said about the sheriff in Foster, that he tried to get people into rehab instead of throwing them in jail. No wonder. But that still didn't explain why I was so upset. What did I care if Joe Rollins was a cokehead? Why did it look so wrong to see him chopping up that small white lump with a razor he took from the box?

"Do you want some of this or not?" he asked, more embarrassed than impatient.

"I don't know. Is it any good?"

For answer, he licked the tip of his right index finger. Then he touched it to the pile of white powder. A thin coating of it stuck to his skin.

"Open your mouth," he ordered.

I did, and he swabbed his finger gently but thoroughly along my gums.

Oh, it was good, all right. A cold, abstracted sense of calm whooshed straight up to my head. It was like standing outside my body, hovering above the ground. Such a nice rush from such a small taste.

"All right," I said. "I'll have a little."

Joe looked pleased, but he didn't say *I told you so*, like some men would have. "How do you want it?" he asked politely.

I felt so guilty for giving him hell. "In a hundred dollar bill," I said.

He grinned at me, sloe-eyed and sexy. "You must run with a pretty fast crowd. The largest bill I've got is a twenty."

"Sold," I told him. "Sold American."

The cocaine was good, but having sex with Joe was better. Afterward, we lay in each other's arms and I thought about how exotic he seemed after all those years with Marcus. Joe was a strange color, a strange texture; there was something almost hypnotic about touching him. I couldn't stop swirling the light brown hair that was dusted across his chest. I couldn't get over how soft it was, how it tickled the edge of my fingertips.

"Where were you going when you met Anna May?" he asked, catching me in a moment of weakness.

I yawned, too drowsy to think about what I was saying. "As far away as I could get."

He threaded his fingers through my hair, cupped the back of my head and kissed me lightly. "Why?" His lips were still teasing mine.

Oh, shit, I thought.

He must have felt me stiffen.

"Shhhh," he murmured against my mouth. His hand moved down to stroke my back. "I'm just making conversation. Don't tell me anything you don't want to."

When he said that, so sweet and gentle, it was hard to not blurt out my whole life story. I made a mental note to look out for this guy. He obviously knew how to make people confess.

"Did you ever think about getting a tattoo?" I asked instead.

"Sure, but somehow it just never happened." He raised his head and grinned at me. "On the other hand, if it turns you on…"

"It's not that." I gave him a lazy smile that was half relief at having changed the subject. "I met this woman tattooer in Nevada. She offered to teach me how to do it, but I'm not great with blood and needles."

He smiled. "Then it doesn't sound like your thing. Still…"

"Still, it might have been a good living."

"Not if you don't like it. But that isn't what I was going to say. I was just thinking I might need one someday."

"A tattoo? Nobody *needs* a tattoo," I told him.

"I don't know about that," he replied. "Sometimes there's things you've just got to tell the world."

❤

It was after four a.m. when I got back to Lillian's, and I didn't wake up until 10:30 the next morning.

Or the next.

Or the morning after that.

I'd spent most of three whole nights with Joe, and I wasn't tired of him yet.

If the hours—or the company—I was keeping bothered my housemates, neither of them let on about it. Instead, they greeted me each morning with gigantic grins and a big mug of coffee. Then they told me what was for breakfast. Then they taught me how to make it.

That first day, it was little link sausages.

The next day, it was hashed brown potatoes.

By that night, Joe was running low on cocaine, and I begged him not to buy more on my account. I didn't want him breaking the law for my benefit, plus I figured we'd get more sleep without it. We stretched out the last of what he had left by dabbing it in strategic places and licking it off each other's bodies. The rush was good, the sex was good, the sleep was good once the blow ran out; and the next morning, at Lillian's, I made blueberry pancakes for breakfast.

The blueberries were from a little store that sold them fresh-picked locally. I mixed the batter up from scratch, then folded the berries carefully in, with Anna May and Lillian giving me tips.

Those pancakes were the best thing ever. Anna May ate as much as me, smothering them in real maple syrup; but Lillian cut hers into pieces and mostly pushed them around her plate.

As soon as Anna May went upstairs to shower, Lillian got the coffee pot from the stove. When she topped off our mugs, I noticed that her hand was trembling. I'd seen Lillian pretty damned upset, but I'd never seen her show a sign of nerves.

"Gregory's here, isn't he?" I guessed.

She sat down across from me. "He's supposed to arrive this afternoon."

I clutched my mug between two hands, glancing toward the staircase. We could hear the shower running upstairs, and Anna May singing that Dolly Parton song about calm on the water and God's everlasting love.

"Are you going to tell her?"

Lillian looked troubled. "I hadn't planned to," she said, still wrestling with it.

I understood the impulse to protect Anna May, but I also understood its limits. "Fighting with Timothy was good for her. She was proud of herself. It made her strong."

That didn't ease the worried look on Lillian's face. "I'm sure it did," she said. "But think about how likely it is that she'll say something to incriminate herself."

"Damn!" I couldn't argue with that, given how vehemently she'd insisted that *she* was the one who'd hurt Timothy. "What do you think we oughtta do?"

But Lillian was way ahead of me. "Would you take her to the library?" she asked. "The two of you can work on her reading."

♥

The main library in Foster was a dusty, one-room affair. The librarian was a middle-aged matron who—like everyone else I'd met out here—looked like she doubled as a ranch hand. She set us up in the Kiddie Korner, and we spent the day reading our way up from brightly colored picture books to Louis Sachar's *Someday Angeline,* about an eight-year-old girl who's so smart that everyone in school makes fun of her. Reading it made me think about how Anna May's education had stopped when she was just eight and her mother died. Mine would have stopped, too, if it hadn't been for Lucille, my one good foster mom who read to me.

Finally, we'd read every children's book they had. It was just after 3:00 pm; too soon to make dinner, too late to start much of anything else. "What do you want to do now?" I asked.

Anna May said, "I want to see Gregory."

I sat down hard on a Kiddie Korner chair. "How do you know about that?"

"From Lillian."

"Lillian *told* you?"

Anna May shook her head.

Of course Lillian hadn't told her. "Then how did you…?"

"She didn't eat your pancakes, and they were really, really good."

I had to smile at that, but it was a sad smile. "Anna May, you're way smarter than people give you credit for."

Anna May considered that. "I don't think I'm smart," she said. "But I don't think I'm too dumb, either."

"I can't take you around Gregory."

"But you'll protect me, Gracie-Grace! You and Lillian and Joe can protect me!"

"It's not that." I ran a hand through my hair, resisting the temptation to pull out a clump. How did you explain *incriminate* to someone who thought like a child? "It's more that you might say something that gets you into trouble later on."

"Like what?"

"Remember the day we met Joe? Remember how you told him that you dropped the pot on Timothy, even though I was trying to get you to shut up?"

"But Joe's our friend!" she said, aggrieved that I couldn't tell the difference between him and Gregory.

"You didn't know that when you first met him."

Anna May stamped her foot. "I did too know he was our friend! I knew it right away, and so did you!"

After that, I couldn't say no.

♥

Gregory looked enough like his brother that when we walked in and saw him hovering over Joe's desk, I went dizzy with nausea.

Joe didn't seem bothered, though. Sitting behind the desk, his chair tilted back at a casual angle, he might have been dealing with a minor break in his day's routine. He looked past Gregory and met my eyes. "Grace," he said, "good afternoon. And to you, too, Miss Anna May."

For a big man, Gregory moved quickly. He spun around and fixed Anna May with a look that should have shriveled her.

Lillian was at Anna May's side before I'd fully registered her presence. "Don't talk," she hissed at her client, and for all that she was the oldest person in the room and weighed about a hundred pounds, her voice was the most powerful one there. "Don't say a word without my permission."

"OK," Anna May whispered back. But it wasn't a timid whisper; it was like the two of them were sharing a secret.

"Now, where were we...?" Joe mused, loud and clear.

With a last ugly glare at Anna May, Gregory turned back to him. "You were talking some bullshit about..."

"Oh, yeah," Joe said, as if he'd just remembered. "Statutory rape. Aggravated assault. Abuse of a minor. Sexual slavery. Kidnapping. Trafficking in persons." He looked at Lillian. "What did I leave out?"

Her eyes narrowed. "Torture."

"That's right," Joe said. "The badly mended bones. The scars from cigarette burns. The organ damage. The VD." He shook his head sadly. "Of course, even with the forensic doctor's report and the hospital photographs and X-rays, we can't prove how much of that *you* did, and how much was Timothy. We *can* prove rape, though, since you left bodily fluids behind."

"I'll leave *your* bodily fluids behind," Gregory snarled, proving that he was Timothy's brother, because how else could he be that dumb?

Behind us, the jail door opened and Fred Coombs walked in with three other men who wore khaki uniforms and guns. Fred was tapping a nightstick impatiently against his leg.

Funny, I hadn't noticed before how beautiful Fred Coombs was.

He and one of the other deputies planted themselves behind Joe, while the other two men flanked the front door.

"You're certainly welcome to try," Joe said, finally rising to his feet. The look on his face was one part contempt, two parts mayhem. "But I should warn you, there's a blank line on this warrant for your arrest"—he waved an official-looking paper—"just in case we need to add anything about you assaulting a peace officer."

Gregory started to speak, then paused. He knew a trap when it was sprung.

"Now, look..." he started, trying to sound reasonable.

But Lillian interrupted him. "Joe, would you excuse us," she said quietly. "I think my client's finished here."

I looked at Anna May and—with one of those flashes of insight you have sometimes—I could see that it was true. She was through with this scene, with Gregory, with her past which was about to unravel.

She'd already walked away from it all.

"We'll talk later," Joe replied, without taking his eyes off his prey.

Lillian took Anna May's arm and the two of them stepped past the deputies and out the front door, with me close behind.

In the parking lot, we piled into Lillian's beat-up car. Anna May was in the passenger seat. I was in the back, behind her.

"Is Joe going to hurt him?" Anna May asked as the three of us buckled ourselves in, on Lillian's order.

"No." Lillian permitted herself a small sigh of regret. "Nobody's going to touch him."

More's the pity, I thought, mentally filling in what she'd left unsaid. I could see Lillian's eyes in the rear view mirror; they looked remarkably like Joe's and I knew that—although he would walk away unscathed today—if Gregory ever came back to Foster, Wyoming, he was literally a dead man.

But Anna May had missed that angle. "Are you sure he'll go away?" she asked, sounding nervous for the first time.

Lillian said, "I'm positive."

"That's good," Anna May said, and she actually yawned. "Lillian, can we make fried chicken for dinner?"

I thought then that her childlike mind was the greatest blessing she could have. Maybe with that, and Lillian's care, Anna May was going to have some kind of life.

"I don't really feel like cooking," Lillian answered with a smile. "Why don't we all go out for dinner, and you can have whatever you want."

Anna May was the center of attention at dinner that night. Our party—Joe and Lillian, Fred Coombs and his wife Maida, Anna May and me—had a big round table in a corner of Cassie's Cafe, and though we didn't drink much because Joe and Fred were on call, and Anna May was under-age, we made up for it by eating our way through giant platters of steak, fried chicken, green beans, mashed potatoes, and rice.

"We got a book from the library," Anna May announced at one point to Maida Coombs. "It's about a boy named Max who lives in the jungle."

"That sounds like *Where the Wild Things Are*," Fred's wife replied, with so much warmth that it made me glad she and Fred had six kids.

"I can read it all by myself!"

Lillian, who'd been having a sidebar with her good-looking grandson the sheriff, glanced up and smiled. "You can do a lot of things by yourself, Anna May," she said. "We're all very proud of you."

♥

After dinner, Joe suggested that we all catch a movie. But Fred and Maida had to get home to let their high school babysitter go, and Lillian and Anna May said they were too tired to do anything but roll into bed.

I said yes, though. What the hell. Joe had asked me to go out somewhere with him almost every night I'd known him, and I didn't want him thinking I had some problem with us being seen together in public.

There was just one movie theater in town, and just one film playing: *Flashdance*, a Hollywood tale about a strip club where all the girls are gorgeous, all the customers are nice and no one gets naked except one bad girl who's having a breakdown. In the real world, clubs were going nudie faster than you could say *lose the g-string and pasties*—Girl-O-Rama was an exception, which was the main reason I'd chosen to work there—but the star of *Flashdance* ended her set wearing more clothes than a swimsuit model. And in the daytime, she worked as a union welder, which was a joke. The film was sexy and fun, which I guess was the desired effect, and I held Joe's hand and we kissed a lot. But the rest of the time I was biting my tongue so I wouldn't say anything too sarcastic.

It wasn't until we left the theater that I realized Joe seemed to be biting his tongue, too.

"Are you OK?" I asked him, shivering a little as we walked down the windy street. Even in mid-June, Wyoming's night air had a bite to it that I wasn't used to.

He put his arm around my shoulder. "What'd you think of the movie?" he asked, ducking my question.

"It was basically bullshit," I said.

"How do you know that?" He pulled me closer without breaking stride. He was warm and solid—a nice windbreaker.

Good question. How was I supposed to know that? "Common sense would tell you that it's just somebody's fantasy." And my fantasy didn't include telling respectable Joe Rollins too much about my previous life.

By then, we'd reached his car, which I'd been delighted to learn was a red Mustang.

"You ever been to Las Vegas?" he asked, opening the passenger door for me.

Boy, had Lillian done a great job with him!

"Just for a day." I slid into the car. The night I'd spent in Las Vegas with Rory didn't count, so I wasn't going to mention it.

Joe closed my door and walked around the car, getting in on the driver's side. "My mother lives there," he said casually.

If I hadn't seen him face down Gregory, I might have thought that casualness was for real.

"Your mother's in Vegas?"

"Yeah." He turned his key in the ignition.

"Doing what?" I asked.

"I don't know. She used to dance."

He gunned the engine, pulled out from the curb and had the Mustang up to sixty in about ten seconds.

"Really," I said, trying to match his tone and make it sound as if I couldn't have cared less. "When did all of that happen?"

"Right about the time I turned eight."

"So that's how come Lillian raised you?"

"That's right."

For a minute, I watched Joe negotiate the streets of his home town, deserted now except for us. I said, "I wouldn't have thought Lillian's daughter would be tall enough to be a showgirl."

"She's five-nine," Joe said. "Or so I'm told."

"Does she like it?"

He glanced over at me, a blank look on his face.

"Your mother. Does she like dancing in Vegas?"

"I don't know." He sounded like the question had never occurred to him. "I haven't seen her since she left."

My mouth dropped open. So much for pretending I wasn't interested. "How old are you, Joe?"

"Thirty-two."

I did the math. "You haven't seen your mother for twenty-four years?"

He glanced at me. "She wrote me some letters when I was in high school. I never wrote back."

"Then what makes you think she's still alive?"

He said, "Lillian talks to her sometimes."

"Wait a second!" I couldn't wrap my mind around it. "You know she's alive, you know where she is, you know she speaks to Lillian, and you don't even *talk* to her?"

"And say what?" Joe kept his eyes on the road. "I barely even know the woman."

Smart, sexy, confident Joe; I guess everyone's got something that hurts.

"How often do you speak to *your* mother?" he snapped, in that way men do when you've got them cornered.

"My mother was a junkie," I said. "They took me away when I was five, and she OD'd two years later."

That took the wind right out of his sails. "Whoa! I'm really sorry, Grace."

I was sorry, too; damned sorry that I'd blurted all that out. At least I hadn't told him about Rosie, but I was going to have to be more careful.

"There's nothing for you to feel sorry about. I made it OK. I'm here, aren't I?"

"Yeah." Joe reached over and took my hand. "I'm glad," he said.

♥

Joe had said he bought cocaine in Cheyenne, but I knew he hadn't driven halfway across the state yesterday. So where had this new stuff come from?

I didn't ask him about it, though. The coke was good, I was happy to share it. We sprawled on the sensual world of his bed, ignoring what we'd learned in the car, and busied ourselves with drug ritual until, finally, he pushed the paraphernalia away and we slid into each other's arms.

The tastes and textures of Joe's body were like home after just four nights. His touch was exciting, but comforting, too; a warm, smooth balm that made me feel safe. No wonder I was so strung out on him. As much as I told myself it was just sex, I could feel my body soaking up his smell, imprinting the suppleness of his skin. Banking memories against what was about to come.

Today had changed things; tonight even more so. Anna May was free. Gregory was gone. If I wasn't pregnant, it wasn't for lack of trying. We both had lives to get back to—or rather, Joe had a life and I had a promise.

I hadn't missed noticing that Marcus and Rosie had both been silent since my first night with Joe. They were obviously giving me room to maneuver, but it was only a matter of time 'till they came back with a vengeance and I didn't want to be in his bed when they did.

Plus from now on, things were just going to get stickier between Joe and me. We'd both said too much tonight in the car. We'd let ourselves get too close, and tomorrow we were going to regret it.

I didn't want to see regret in Joe's eyes. And I sure as hell didn't want to see his reaction if I eventually turned up pregnant.

Then there was that little business with his mother. Another dancer, another bad girl. Wild and weighed down with some guy's baby; a constant disappointment to her bright, ambitious, law school-going mother. It wasn't hard to imagine the relief Joe's mother must have felt when she finally stepped onto the highway, leaving everything behind.

But I didn't want to leave Joe like that, and I sure didn't want to leave him like that after we'd both gotten even more attached. It was better to go now, while I was still just a convenience to him, before it felt like a real betrayal.

That was what I told myself, lying there for hours staring at the ceiling. And once I'd let the truth of it sink in, I could see that there was no excuse for lingering even another day. It was all downhill from here anyway—one of those damned-if-you-do, damned-if-you-don't situations where it gets harder to go and harder to stay and harder to make up your mind which to do.

I snuck a guilty peek at Joe. His eyes were shut tight, and that damned curl was falling over his forehead, asking to be stroked back. One of his legs was wrapped around mine. It would be hard to disengage, and harder to gather my things and sneak downstairs. But what was the alternative: Stay so that I could hurt both of us even worse when the time came?

I slid my leg out from under his, thinking *don't hate me when you wake up, Joe.*

But it was too late. Somehow, I'd woken him.

"Don't go yet." He pulled me close.

I'd never left him in the middle of the night, but I knew that wasn't what he was talking about. "How do you know I'm going?" I whispered.

He made a bittersweet sound. His eyes were open now, drilling deep into me. "You must think I'm a real idiot."

"No." I kissed him desperately. "I think you're way more than I deserve."

And then I had to have him again, hard enough to make me forget. I wasn't trying to hurt him, but I wasn't trying to soften things. My hands were greedy, my teeth sharp on his neck. I rolled on top of him and tried to make a rough memory that we could both take out and enjoy now and then.

When it was over and he'd drifted back to sleep, I felt like crying. *Not now,* I ordered myself. *Not 'till you're out of here.* I kissed both his eyelids, his forehead, his nose and his sweet mouth, lingering way too long. I wrapped myself around him and held on like a drowning woman. And then I pried myself loose and got off the bed.

What the hell had Joe done with the keys to Timothy's car? If they were at the jail, they were out of my reach. But if he'd put them on his ring, the way part of me thought I remembered...

Joe didn't stir when I pulled my clothes on. He didn't move when I tiptoed to the bureau where his key ring and gun and badge and wallet were all lying in plain sight. I glanced back, but he was still breathing slowly, his chest rising and falling in a deep, hypnotic rhythm.

If he was awake, I didn't want to know it. The Buick key was on his ring; I took it off and shoved it deep into the front pocket of my blue jeans. Then I rifled Joe's wallet and took the three $20 bills I found there. I thought about leaving a note that said *I'm sorry*, but sorry didn't begin to cover it and, anyway, I didn't have anything to write on. So I stuffed the money in my pocket with the car key and tiptoed out of Joe Rollins' life.

I went to the jail first, to get the car. It took me twenty minutes to walk there—it was cold, but not unpleasantly so now that I was moving fast. It felt good to walk, good to be in the clean night air again.

The Buick turned over nicely. I spared a thought for that piece of shit Gregory who'd been too intimidated by Joe and Lillian to think about collecting his brother's car. Then I put it into gear and drove over to Lillian's to get the rest of my stuff.

As usual, she'd left the front door unlocked for me.

It wasn't usual, though, for me to find her up, sitting in the kitchen drinking a cup of hot tea. I waved hello and walked past her, upstairs to where I'd stashed my shoulder bag in the corner of Joe's room, where Anna May slept. Anna May didn't wake up, and I was careful not to look at her—or at Joe's things—as I packed up my extra set of clothes, my toothbrush and my picture of Marcus.

Then I went down to the kitchen and sat in the chair opposite Lillian.

"You're leaving," she said. It wasn't a question.

I nodded. "I stole some money from Joe."

"You're planning to pay it back, right?"

"Yeah."

"Then it's called borrowing."

I shrugged. "Whatever you say."

She smiled a little. "Do you have his address?"

Damn, I didn't. She went and got her purse, some paper and a pen, and she wrote down her address and Joe's. Then she took some bills from her purse, wrapped them in the paper and handed it to me.

"Didn't you hear me?" I took out the cash and held it back out to her. "I already have Joe's money."

"Well, now you have mine, too."

"What if I don't pay it back?"

She said, "I don't remember asking you to. But I *am* going to ask you this, Grace. When you get someplace, write to Anna May and me. Let us know you're OK, so we don't have to worry about you."

"Why would you...?"

"Just do it. All right?"

I frowned at her. "I might never get *someplace*." And if I did, how the hell would I recognize it?

But Lillian didn't look put off by that. "You will." She gave me a gentle smile. "I know you will, Grace. Eventually."

nineteen

I turned onto Interstate 80 and drove east until my legs were numb, my hands were cramped and my head felt like someone was trying to crack it open with a sledgehammer. You could say *what was my hurry?* since I didn't have a schedule or even much of a destination. I guess I was trying to outrun the sadness I felt about leaving Joe and Lillian and Anna May, the sense of weariness and futility that I knew would swamp me if I let it.

Back when I was still working at Stacy G's, the yuppie fern bar I'd tended before I met Marcus, someone had once quoted me the line *wherever I go, there I am*. At the time, I thought the guy was nuts—a leftover hippie in corporate clothes. But somewhere into my sixth straight hour of driving east on I-80, I began to understand what he might have meant.

I could run from lots of things, but it was hard to outrun myself.

It was hard to outrun my guilt about Joe, too. I told myself it was better that he hate me; better for him to find someone he could be proud of, someone with a future. That was true, but it didn't keep me from missing him, or feeling guilty and disloyal to Marcus.

Still, there was a numbing comfort in driving alone through the endless darkness. When dawn began to play at the edges of the horizon, I was sorry to see it come. The only good thing was, I wouldn't have to face it. I was too exhausted to keep my eyes open.

I pulled off the road at the next gas station.

"You know a place that's safe to sleep in the car?" I asked the scruffy-looking man who filled the Buick's tank.

"Three exits up, that's where all the truckers put in. You can't miss it."

I kept myself awake those last miles by calculating how long I could live on Joe and Lillian's money. That got me to the truck stop, which was huge even compared to the one I'd seen back in Bakersfield. I drove straight to the back of the lot and parked behind two gigantic tankers, figuring that out of sight was out of mind.

After that, all I had the strength to do was kill the engine, tip my seat back, half-sprawl out and fall asleep. I wasn't even worried about dreams. They never seemed to come in daylight.

The next thing I knew, the sledgehammer I'd felt for half the ride was back again, pounding rhythmically on my skull.

Or was it? I lay still for a minute, noticing that I didn't actually have a headache. The morning sun was warm on my still-closed eyelids. In the near-distance, I could hear idling truck engines and the muffled sound of loud-speaker announcements.

Gradually it occurred to me that the sledgehammer wasn't *inside* my head. It was *above* my head, outside the Buick.

I opened one eye cautiously. What I saw through the window looked so bizarre that it took a minute for my groggy brain to register it: A man's hairy balls and penis, clutched in their owner's hands, were being pressed rhythmically against the glass.

Some damn fool was humping my car!

The sight, less than four inches from my face, was completely disgusting. And the worst of it was, I had to pee and I didn't much feel like going through him to do it.

Well, there didn't seem to be much help for that. I couldn't imagine just sitting there 'till he finished his act and slunk away—plus I really didn't want to have to clean his stinking cum off the window. So my choices seemed to be: Open the door hard and knock him down; or get out the other side and ignore him.

Disgusted, I opened the passenger door.

"You fucked-up creep," I screamed as soon as my feet hit the ground. "I guess ignoring wasn't quite my thing. "Get your sleazy-ass self away from my car!"

"And if you don't," added a deep female voice, "we're gonna cut off your dick and shove it down your throat."

Well, well, well, I thought. And then she moved around from behind the guy, and I saw her for the first time. She was short and strong-looking, maybe forty-five, with graying hair. She was holding a baseball bat in her right hand and she looked like she knew how to use it. She was white, but not in that homogenized, West Coast way where everyone looks the same. She looked Polish or Russian or something.

"Are you deaf?" she snarled at the guy, who hadn't even let go of his cock yet. "Zip it up and get outta here!"

She raised the bat, and started toward him, and he took off like a scared little rabbit. His penis was still flapping when he ducked around the nearest truck. We could hear his pounding feet for seconds after we couldn't see him anymore.

I walked over and stuck out my hand. "I like your style." I grinned at her.

She had the kind of handshake I'd expected—firm and confident. What surprised me was the gentle sound of her voice, now that she was done yelling. "You'd have been fine without me," she said.

"Yeah, but it wouldn't have been as much fun. Can I buy you breakfast?" I asked, with reckless gratitude.

She gave me a generous smile. It made her look young, and almost pretty. "It's nine in the morning," she replied. "I had breakfast four hours ago. But you can buy me a cup of Joe before I get back on the road."

I winced a little at the word—I never wanted to hear the name *Joe* again—but coffee sounded good to me. "Hang on a second." I grabbed my shoulder bag from the back seat, then locked the car. "I'm Grace," I told her as we walked toward the café.

"Dena," she said. "Dena Korzinowski."

♥

"You can't totally blame the guy for what happened out there. Parking in the back like that!" She rolled her eyes. "He thought you were a lot lizard."

I took a sip of good hot coffee and washed down a mouthful of ham and eggs. "A what?"

Dena had broken down and ordered toast. She sat across from me, the baseball bat propped against her seat. "Lot lizard. You know. A hooker."

Lot lizard. I had to smile to myself. "I never owned a car before," I explained, forking up more breakfast. Of course, I didn't really own one now, either, but I wasn't going into *that* story. "I guess I don't know how to act."

She was suddenly very serious. "The road's tough on women. You gotta be nice, but not soft. Walk with your head up. Don't flirt. Don't tease. Anyone tries to stare you down, you make damn sure you're not the first one to look away."

"How do you know all that?"

"'Cause I'm out here alone, too." She gave me a big, proud smile. "I drive the black Western Star that was parked near you."

I put my fork down. "You drive a truck?"

"Hell, yeah," she said, "What'd you think?"

What I thought was that it was pretty damned cool. I'd come two-thirds across the country and hadn't seen a woman *in* a truck, much less driving one.

"Korzinowski Trucking, out of Valley Stream, Long Island. That's New York," she added helpfully.

"You *own* the truck?"

"My husband did." Her eyes clouded over, but the cloud passed quickly. "We drove team for two years before he died."

The waitress—a young, curvy girl whose uniform was about to pop off—came over and poured more coffee. Every man in the room watched her flounce back to the kitchen.

"When Frank taught me to drive, people thought he was crazy. But women are better drivers than men." Dena glanced at the specimens around us. "We don't get all wound up like they do, showing off and acting wild just 'cause some girl in a convertible flashes her tits."

I choked; the coffee'd gone down the wrong way. She handed me a glass of water and I drank it, sputtering 'till my windpipe cleared.

When it did, I said, "You're joking."

"Hell, no! You get up there, high off the ground, you wouldn't believe what people wanna show you."

"You mean, like that guy outside?"

"Not the men," she clarified. "They see a woman riding all that steel, they're too busy peeing themselves to flash you."

I grinned at her. We both drank our coffee. Dena was tough, but for all that mouth, you could see she was a lady, too. Her hands were clean, her nails were buffed, her salt-and-pepper hair had a nice curl. She wasn't trying to be a man, just trying to get over in their world.

Finally she said, "You ever think about hitting the road?"

I couldn't read her expression. "I'm on the road now," I hedged.

She snorted. "In *that* thing? No offense, but you got lousy taste in transportation."

Dena didn't know the half of it! I shrugged, as if that car wasn't loaded with enough memories to make a movie. "The price was right."

Dena picked up the crust of bread that was left on her plate and chewed it thoughtfully. "You ever want to take up trucking, just give me a call. I'll be glad to show you the ropes."

"Why?" I was asking that a lot these days. I couldn't figure out why anyone would want to help me when I so clearly didn't deserve it.

"I don't know." It was her turn to shrug. "Maybe I'm tired of being a freak. Maybe I want another partner. You get lonely on the road, and the hours are long."

"I'm sorry," I mumbled awkwardly.

"No need. Frank and I were more like friends than like some big romance. He was a good guy, but he used to piss me off with all that complaining. You never could've told me how quiet it would be without him."

"Well, I appreciate your help with that pervert." I pushed my plate away.

"Sure." She gave me a piercing look. It wasn't like I'd been subtle about trying to change the subject. "But remember what I said: You call me if you ever want to learn. I bet you'd be a good team driver."

"You don't even know me."

"Sure I do. You're smart. Tough. You don't complain, you don't scare easy. You can sleep in a car. You've got what it takes to be a lady trucker."

I had to grin at her. She took it as encouragement.

"I wouldn't even suggest it if you weren't tough. You got to be tough to face bad weather, bad roads, accidents, traffic jams, shit loads, paperwork, bears, D.O.T. trying to bust your ass..."

"What's D.O.T.?" I asked, forgetting that I wasn't interested.

"Death on Truckers." She saw that I didn't get it. "You know, Department of Transportation. And 'bears' are cops. Like the bear that shits in the forest."

"You're not making it sound real good," I pointed out.

"It's not." She smiled, like she'd just scored a point. "It sucks big time."

"So why don't you sell the truck and get out?" Not that it was any of my business.

"I'm hooked," she said. "I like being my own boss. I like the road. I like the money. I like my privacy."

I thought about dancing at Girl-O-Rama. There hadn't been one thing I'd really *liked* about it. "You're a lucky woman."

She said, "I make my own luck. You could, too." Then she dug in her pocket and pulled out a dog-eared piece of paper. "I'm going to give you my broker's number. You ever want to get your motor running, call him. He'll find me."

I smiled at her quote from Steppenwolf's *Born To Be Wild*. It was a good tune; I'd danced to it at Girl-O-Rama.

Dena chugged down the last of her coffee. "Don't forget what I said." She stood up and hefted the baseball bat. "Park in plain sight, and don't screw around."

"I'll remember." I gave her a big smile and a fake salute. I liked Dena, even if she was trying to hustle me.

She raised the bat, saluting me back. I watched her walk out the café's front door, and then I paid the bill, bought a candy bar and went to the bathroom.

I walked back to the car singing,

> *I like smoke and lightning*
> *Heavy metal thunder*
> *Racin' with the wind*
> *And the feelin' that I'm under*
> *Yeah, Darlin', gonna make it happen*
> *Take the world in a love embrace*
> *Fire all of your guns at once, and*
> *Explode into space.*

Like a true nature's child,
You were born to be wild.
You can fly so high,
And never touch the sky.
Born to be wild...
Born to be wild...

♥

Two long, tedious, lonely days later I pulled into Washington D.C. so late at night that it was basically morning and went looking for a place to park the car.

That scene at the truck stop several days before had made me wary about parking off the beaten path. I didn't want any surprises, so I drove around until I found the seedy part of town and drove around *that* until I found a Greyhound bus station. It was closed, but I figured it would open before dawn, and when it did, it would have coffee and people and telephones and a bathroom.

I parked the car across the street from the station and made myself comfortable in the back seat. I didn't much like the way I smelled, but knowing I could wash up in the morning made it easier to take.

One thing I'd learned from watching Dena was to carry a weapon. During the night, I'd found a 2x4 in a pile of lumber behind the filthy ladies' room at a gas station I stopped at. It was now tucked on the floor by my feet, just in case some other idiot tried to mash me while I slept.

So all I had left to worry about was cops, and I was too tired to care about them. If I got busted and went to jail, so much the better; they'd have hot food and cold showers and I'd serve a few days for vagrancy and maybe learn something about the city while I was in there.

With that thought, I drifted off into sleep. It was a short sleep, and pretty tranquil. My ghosts were apparently just as tired as I was; or else they had their own reasons for staying away.

A few hours later I woke up, stretched, yawned, slowly unkinked my legs and went across the street to the Greyhound. The bathroom wasn't bad at all—rusty fixtures, a few tiles missing from the floor, but nothing I hadn't seen in more than half the places I'd lived. Most of the women who came in looked about as disheveled as I did, either from traveling or from staying out all night doing something fun or paying the rent. I didn't much notice any of them except for two women huddled together near the stalls who were obviously waiting for me to finish my business and clear out of there.

Their vibes had scared everyone else away, but I wasn't feeling in much of a hurry. "Ladies," I turned to look right at them, "I'd love to leave you alone in here, but I stink too bad to skip getting washed up. So just go on with whatever you're doing, 'cause I'm not gonna see a thing."

The tall one, who seemed to be about my age, shrugged and took a joint from her pocket.

"What are you doing?" her friend shrilled. "Just 'cause a white girl says she's cool, you think she's really cool, you idiot?"

I ducked my head and splashed some water on my face. I wasn't going to leave, and I wasn't going to get involved.

"Shit," the first one sneered, "What's she gonna do, call the cops? *Look* at her!"

That wasn't flattering, but I couldn't protest since I wasn't listening. I washed my face with scratchy powdered soap from an old dispenser and wiped it the best I could with the back of my hand. Then I stripped off the shirt I'd slept in two nights running.

"Puh-leeze!" the same girl said to my back. "Don't you have any self-respect?"

I glanced up and caught that she was grinning at me; it was a joke. Must have been good grass to kick in that fast. I washed quickly, catching my neck, my armpits and underneath my breasts, which I dabbed at from below my bra, since I wasn't taking it off in front of these two. I was pulling my other shirt from the bag when she said, "My name's Chantelle. You want a toke?"

I looked up. She was holding the joint out to me, sort of waving it in my general direction.

"Sure." I yanked the shirt over my head, took the dope and dragged on it, hard. "Good stuff," I said, holding my breath as the smoke curl down my throat and up the back of my nose. "I'm Grace, by the way. You mind if I ask you something?"

"Long as it's not personal." She took the joint back.

"It's not." I exhaled slowly. "I'm looking for this friend of mine. A stripper."

The second one rolled her eyes. *See,* she was probably thinking, *I told you!*

"So?" Her friend passed the joint back to me.

"So where the hell do I go?"

That's when I found out that D.C. didn't have an adult district. No Combat Zone, no Tenderloin, no place you could walk from one end to the other and when you were done you'd seen all the clubs. No, they had six in S.E., seven in N.W., fourteen spread through the rest of the city.

How was I supposed to find all those places? How in hell was I supposed to find Blondell when the girls moved back and forth between clubs and no one could point up the street and say *that's where she went?*

Obviously I was going to spend a lot of time running around town from one seedy club to another. "Plus," said my new friend, "you need to watch what you're doing, 'cause those clubs all belong to the cops."

"All of them?"

"Welcome to DC, Sweetie." She reached up under her spandex shirt and scratched with a long, curved fingernail. "They got to make their money like everyone else. Just watch youself, 'cause DC cops don't get their hands on too many girls like you."

"What do you mean, like me?" I asked. Apparently I was pretty stoned, too, because watching that starburst-painted fingernail draw lazy circles on her mocha-colored midriff was about to hypnotize me.

"White and country," she explained.

I started to protest, and then I stopped because I thought maybe Chantelle was right.

If *country* meant lost and way over your head, that's just what I was.

♥

I knew there wasn't much point in trying to find Blondell in the daylight, but since I didn't have anything else to do, I gave it a shot anyway.

I might as well have saved my time. The three clubs I went to were a depressing lot, and no one in them would even say if they'd ever seen anyone who looked like Blondell.

So I went off to find some food and kill some time.

After dark, I put on lipstick, fluffed out my hair the best I could and hit four more clubs. They all sucked, and still no sign of Blondell, so I went back to the Greyhound, parked the car and sacked out for the rest of the night.

Chantelle and her friend were in the bathroom when I showed up the next morning. But now her friend had a black eye; I could see its outline around her sun glasses.

Not that I was going to mention it.

"You have any luck last night?' Chantelle asked.

"Just the luck of the draw," I said. "You ladies want a cup of coffee?" I'd bought a cup earlier at the concession stand in the station. Now I set it down on the little mottled glass shelf above the sink.

"No, but thanks. We got money to buy."

I nodded, and took the toothbrush and toothpaste out of my shoulder bag.

"Where you sleeping?" Chantelle asked.

"In my car," I mumbled. By now I had a mouth full of toothpaste and was sloshing it around with the brush.

She didn't look particularly surprised. "You want to fall by our crib to stay?"

Yeah, I want to fall right in with your pimp, I thought. I took my time brushing my teeth and then I rinsed thoroughly before meeting Chantelle's eyes in the mirror.

"Thanks," I said, "but I'm gonna stay loose 'till I find my friend. That'll be tonight, I hope."

"I hope you do, too," Chantelle said.

But I didn't find Blondell that night, and I didn't go back to the Greyhound, either. I wasn't going to show up a third time in a place where some girl, no matter how nice she seemed, had already told her pimp about me. Even parked outside, I wouldn't feel safe knowing that I might wake up with some guy's gun pointed at my head.

Instead, I drove out to the suburbs. Out to the classy developments, with their quiet streets and houses and trees.

The one I chose was called Ferndale. It was about fifteen miles out of town, with a wide entrance and stone columns on either side. The man-made hills had a nice little slope; the houses were old enough to look real but rich enough to look like a fantasy.

I knew they weren't a fantasy, though. They were real enough to the people that lived there—people as different from me as Martians.

Before this trip, I'd never known anybody who owned the place they lived in. Now I knew four of them: Mary Jo, Francisco, Joe, and Lillian. Five, if you counted Blanche's trailer. All those people knew how to get by in the world, unlike me, who mostly knew how to get high and mix drinks and strip and fuck things up.

I drove around for another ten minutes, slowly, so as not to attract attention, 'till I found a place that looked safe enough to spend the night. It was a dead-end street that only had four houses. I parked just past the last one on the left—a big, cream-colored thing that must have been meant to resemble a southern plantation house—with my car nosed almost up to the driveway. I hoped it looked like I was visiting.

When I turned off the headlights, I could see stars. That's how far out of town I was.

I lay down in the back seat. It felt like I'd been sleeping in this car forever; it felt like I should be used to it by now. Tonight, though, I was sad and restless. I tossed and turned underneath my jacket.

Maybe I wasn't tired enough to sleep. Or maybe I was scared that if I fell off, Rosie would come to me. It seemed like such a long time since I'd seen her. Almost as long as since I'd seen Joe—and that seemed like a century, even though I knew it was only a few days. *Marcus* was the one I hadn't seen in a million years, the only one I should have been thinking about instead of remembering the feel of Joe's mouth and his hands on my skin, his smell, his texture.

I lay there letting the guilt and loneliness and confusion swirl around me 'till I finally drifted off to sleep. But there were no ghosts waiting as I slept, floating through the thick, gray sludgy fog of my conscience. I couldn't see anything and couldn't hear much except a gentle, far-away lapping sound and, closer, a sound that was more felt than heard: A hollow drumbeat near my heart. Ka-BOOM. Ka-BOOM. Ka-BOOM. Ka-BOOM.

I came to, sitting bolt upright. The sky was slate gray, shot through with the first light of what was going to be a dreary day. I leaned against the back seat and sat there shivering.

When my heartbeat finally slowed, I looked down and saw that my left hand was spread across my chest. The fingers were splayed as if they held my heart in place. My right hand rested on top of my stomach, holding in the secret, the sorrow.

Oh fuck! I thought. It was real. It was happening. Oh, fuck, fuck, fuck, fuck, fuck, fuck, *fuck*!

I found Blondell that night. She was dancing in a place called Trixxx, the kind of place where you want to wash off the soles of your shoes after you leave. I wouldn't have gone in the joint if I hadn't vowed to check every club in town. Good thing I did, too, because there she was, up on a table, bare-assed naked with some dollar bills clamped between her cunt lips, swiveling her hips mechanically.

"Gracie!" she screamed when she saw me. She jumped off the table and ran across the room trailing dollar bills.

"Hey, girl," I said, as she fell into my arms. She felt even thinner than she looked. Blondell had always been skinny, but she'd lost more weight since I saw her last and that wasn't good. She looked about five years older than when she'd left San Francisco two months before. "Long time no see."

"No shit!" She started to say more, but a mean-looking white man had come up behind her. He clamped a beefy hand on her shoulder and squeezed so hard I could see it hurt.

"You got three seconds to get back on that table or you're fired," he announced.

"She just quit!" I snapped at him.

"Grace, I don't know if..."

"Come on," I told her, "grab your stuff."

"And who the fuck are you?" he growled.

Too late, I remembered about the baby. It wasn't smart to be picking fights, but I was overdue for a wisecrack. "Her mother," I said. "It's past her bedtime."

"You stupid cunts!" But he walked away, and I did my best to hide my relief. "Go on," I told Blondell, "get your things."

We were out of there five minutes later.

♥

I was worried about Blondell, and going back to her apartment didn't reassure me. It was one of those bare-bones jobs with nothing in the cupboards, nothing in the fridge, nothing in the bookcase, nothing hanging on the wall, no curtains, no towels but plenty of cigarette butts and hoochie mama clothes and beer cans strewn around the living room.

"Mary's got the lease," Blondell explained, as she locked the door behind us. She was whispering, which I guess was for Mary's benefit even though Mary didn't seem to be home.

Still, I know about *when in Rome*. I buttoned my mouth, took off my jacket and went to the bathroom to get cleaned up.

"You mind if we talk in the morning?" Blondell asked when I came out feeling half-refreshed.

"I don't mind." I figured we had the rest of our lives to catch up with each other.

And I was worn out, too, even though it wasn't all that late yet, barely three o'clock.

"You sleep in my room." Blondell nodded toward it. "Take the bed. I'll take the couch."

I shook my head. "That isn't right. We can share your bed, or I'll sleep on the floor."

"No," she said, "Mary doesn't take well to strangers. You take the bedroom. Lock yourself in."

I didn't like the sound of that one bit, and I was about to say so when the front door opened and Mary staggered in.

She was something, I could see that at one glance. Five-ten, maybe even taller. Midwestern white. Big eyes, long hair. Track marks up and down both arms that she wasn't even pretending to hide.

Blondell, I thought, *you idiot!*

"What the hell are you doing bringing some bitch I don't even know in here?" Mary barked.

"My name's Grace," I said pointedly. "I'm an old friend of hers and I got no place to stay tonight."

"Tough titty," she said, balling up her fists, which was funny since she was probably too high to find a punch much less throw one.

On the other hand, junkies are unpredictable.

"Come on, Mary," Blondell intervened. "Why don't you just let her stay one night?"

"Not on your fucking life," Mary said.

I picked up my jacket and eased toward the door. "Don't worry," I told Blondell. "I know when I'm not wanted. I'll catch you in the morning, we'll have some breakfast and hang out."

"Fuck that!" Blondell answered. "I'm going with you. Wait up while I pack my things."

That's when Mary realized she'd gone too far. "You're supposed to help me pay the rent," she shrilled.

"Kiss my black ass," Blondell said, which turned out to be the final word on the subject, since Mary turned around and stormed out of the apartment, possibly in search of a new roommate.

"Is she coming back?" I asked Blondell.

"Oh, who gives a shit!" Blondell said.

So Blondell and I made our second *fuck you* exit of the night. We'd only been together for an hour, and already it felt like the old days in San Francisco. I was desperately glad to see her, and also to have a running buddy, someone I could share decisions with. Being responsible for Anna May had weighed pretty heavily on my mind.

Our first decision was where to sleep. I told Blondell about how I'd driven out to the suburbs the night before and slept in the car. She didn't have a better idea, so we drove out to Silver Spring and found one of those pretty developments. This time I parked in a cul-de-sac where the car was partly hidden by trees. Last night I'd felt safer in plain view, but with two women sleeping in the car and only one of us white, it seemed like a smarter idea to lay low.

Blondell took the front seat, because she's small. I got in the back, but neither of us slept much. She popped open a few cans of beer—that was mostly what was in the bag she'd packed at Mary's—and we talked as if we'd seen each other yesterday, with me taking an occasional sip and her knocking back the rest of them.

"What's up with the new tattoo?" I asked. Blondell now had a big, mocha-colored Betty Boop, complete with Afro, hoop earrings and a short-short Kinte cloth dress tattooed on her back.

"It's a Black thing," she said.

"Betty *Boop* is a Black thing?"

"Sure. Didn't you ever hear of Minnie the Moocher?"

"Blondell, what are you talking about?"

"I'm talking about my new tattoo. Nobody that cool could really be white, so I asked the guy to make her Black, and it works great."

I yawned; it was getting late by anybody's standards. "What guy?"

"Smokey Nightingale, the guy who did the tattoo. He's got this place over by the Greyhound and he's so hard-core you have to slip him ten bucks through the mail slot before he'll even open the door."

So then I told her about sleeping outside the Greyhound station, and she told me about how she'd ended up crashing at Mary's, and that got me all worried again.

"Blondell," I said, "You're not using smack, are you?"

"Hell, no!" She gave me an accusing look and sputtered so hard that a little brew came out of her nose and she had a coughing fit.

"Well, it's not *that* crazy," I said when she'd calmed down. "Here I find you living with a junkie! And last thing I knew, you were snorting tons of coke."

"Hey, girl," she said, "I remember when you were tossing back speed like it was Good 'N Plenty, so watch that pot calling the kettle black stuff."

"We are both so totally fucked up," I said—wearily, because it was true.

"No shit, Sherlock," Blondell replied. "But I can't afford blow anymore, and I would never shoot smack. Like, *never.*"

"But Mary..."

Blondell hushed me. "That was all about having a roof. Trust me, I wasn't touching the girl and I wasn't touching her low-grade, horseshit, stepped-on-by-every-dealer-on-the-east-coast heroin."

Finally, I felt myself relax. Blondell didn't lie, and even if she had, I would have known it.

"You know what they say in San Francisco?"

"No." Blondell took a long swig of beer, and I took a tiny sip of mine, stretching it out to look like I was drinking more. "What do they say?"

"That you can get AIDS by using other people's needles."

"Then just be glad we don't do that shit!"

I *was* glad. I was glad about a lot of things, and most of all about having a friend to talk to again.

Of course being a friend meant listening, not just talking. I didn't want to hear about more death, but finally I made myself ask her, "You want to tell me what happened with Grannie B?"

She slumped a little in her seat. "It was tough," she said. "Really fucked up."

"Yeah?" I took another taste of beer, half-blocking it with my tongue so that only a drop or two slid down my throat. "What happened?"

That's when Blondell opened up about her grandmother's last days. Grannie B had died in Blondell's arms, and when she told me that part, I tried to block my own sadness so I could concentrate on hers. That's when I saw that Blondell was putting up a great big front, just like I'd been doing since Marcus died. Underneath that brassy energy, she was numb from losing her only family in the world.

No wonder she'd been dancing in that scumbag club and living with a vicious cow like Mary. It wasn't that strange when you thought about it. Grief either killed you, or made you dumb and reckless. God knows I was proof of that!

After Blondell was finished talking, we slept until the sun came up. Even though no one had come outside yet, we could feel the neighborhood waking around us. Pretty soon people would leave for work. It didn't feel safe to be there anymore.

We were both still two-thirds asleep, but somehow we found our way into town. I parked the car in front of a diner. We went to the ladies' room and

204 ♥ Jezra Kaye

brushed our teeth and splashed cold water on our faces. Then we went back out and took a booth and I ordered enough food to feed fourteen people.

"How come you're eating so much?" Blondell asked.

So then I had to blurt out my news, which somehow I hadn't been ready to share the night before.

"You're *pregnant?*" she shrieked in a loud, clear voice.

Every customer in that diner put down their knives and forks and spoons and turned around to stare at us.

"Shut up," I hissed.

"I can't believe you're gonna have a baby!" Her voice was lower but just as intense. Blondell was usually pretty unflappable. I hadn't thought she'd react like this.

She reached across the table, took my hand and squeezed hard enough to rattle the bones. "Did Marcus know?"

Oh, God. She thought it was Marcus's baby!

"He knew," I said. "But it's not like you think." The words blew out of me on a chill wind. My arms and neck felt freezing cold.

I signaled the waitress and asked for more coffee. And then I told Blondell the whole story: How Marcus had made me promise to get pregnant, how Dr. Weiss had told me to leave town, how it didn't feel right in San Francisco after Blondell went away.

Blondell was nodding as I talked, so I just kept going 'till I'd told her about hitching to Bakersfield and finding Marcus's sister, Mary Jo. And then I told her about the rest of my trip, about Blanche and Anna May and Lillian. I told her about tricking Francisco, and all those nights I'd been with Joe, though I tried to act like that wasn't a big deal. I even told her about Dena, the trucker who'd offered me a job and road advice.

When I was done, I realized that she hadn't spoken since that question about Marcus. It was longer than I'd ever heard Blondell be quiet.

Finally she said, "You been busy since I left."

"Yeah." I couldn't argue with that.

She pursed her lips. "The one guy was Mexican?"

"Francisco."

"And the other is white?"

I nodded.

"Well," she said, "at least you'll know where to send the bill."

"What bill?"

"The doctor bill," she said pityingly. "The hospital bill. And the bill for all those baby things. You know, the clothes, the toys, the diapers, that kind of stuff?" I must have looked sick, 'cause she added, "You're gonna need some money. You're not gonna live in the car with a baby."

Truthfully, I hadn't got that far; I'd only known for one day that I was pregnant. But now that she mentioned it, I *didn't* see me and Junior spending our lives in the backseat of a Buick.

"No," I said. "I'm not gonna live in the car forever. How about you?"

Turnaround was fair play, but Blondell looked just as defensive as I felt. "What do you mean, how about me?"

"You gonna dance in bullshit clubs forever?"

"No," she said. "'Course I'm not." But I knew from that guilty look on her face that twenty-four hours ago she would have given me a different answer.

"All right," I said. "What are we gonna do for money?"

"Damned if I know." Blondell grinned, like she was waiting for me to think of something.

"Well, look at it this way." I pushed my empty plate aside. "We got no home." I traced a big zero on the diner's paper placemat with my thumb. "No jobs." Another zero. "No prospects." Another.

The waitress came over and put our check on top of my imaginary zeros.

"I don't think I like this town," Blondell told the waitress matter-of-factly.

"Do I look like I care?" the waitress said, and walked away.

Blondell and I both counted our money. All she had, since I'd dragged her out of Trixxx before she got paid for the week, was $56 bucks. I still had $93 of the money I'd boosted from Joe and Lillian.

$149 bucks between us. $141.80, after breakfast.

It wasn't going to last forever.

"One of us has to work," I said. It echoed in my mind, eerily. I'd had this same conversation with Marcus after we both stormed out of The Tijuana.

"I will," she offered.

"Doing what?"

She shrugged. "Dancing, what else?"

"I thought you weren't going to do that forever..."

"Well, *you* can't do it," she insisted. "Not in a couple of months, anyway."

"No." I wasn't going to be responsible for keeping Blondell in that life. Not when I could see on her face how much it was taking out of her.

"We could waitress," I offered.

"Shit," she said. "Do I look like I need varicose veins?"

"Secretary?"

"*You* know how to type?"

"Factory worker? Security?"

She said, "You want to live on three bucks on hour?"

No, I didn't. That was the problem. Stripping ruined you for regular wages. They didn't pay much for what you went through; they just paid more than anyone else, unless you knew some kind of trade.

That was when I saw the answer. It was right in front of me the whole time we were talking. I'd even mentioned it to Blondell; I just hadn't listened to what I was saying.

I got up and paid the bill, not wanting to give that waitress my money. And while I was at it, I changed two dollars into dimes. Then I took them to the pay phone, and used them to call Dena Korzinowski's broker.

It took a few minutes, but eventually I got him to understand that Dena had offered me a job and I wanted it.

twenty-one

Two days into our stay in Dena's Western Star, Dena announced that she was going to teach Blondell to drive instead of me.

"Wait a second," I said. "How come?"

"Blondell can't wait to get her hands on this baby." Dena turned to Blondell and said, "Isn't that right?"

Blondell gave me an apologetic look. "Yeah," she told Dena, "you got that right."

"Your hands don't tingle for the gear shift, do they?" Dena asked me. She didn't sound unkind, just amused.

"Tingle?" I turned to Blondell. "Your hands *tingle* for the gear shift?"

Dena said, "Honey, her hands *twitch*."

I looked at Blondell's shit-eating grin and thought *damn!* "But I *like* to drive!" I said. It sounded silly.

"You like to drive those putt-putts," Dena corrected me. "Those little boxes. Those four wheel pieces of..."

"All right!" I yawned. "I get the point!"

"Face it," she said, philosophically. "You've got everything it takes except desire. You're just not made for the big rigs."

I didn't have any response to that, so I went to lie down.

Dena's truck had a sleeper with two bunks and I'd spent most of my first days onboard sacked out on the bottom one, drinking tea that I brewed with a little electric heating coil that plugged right into the cigarette lighter, and listening to the radio. Next to the bed was a small window with a curtain that I pulled back now and then to look out at where we were. But mostly I just lay there with my eyes closed, or studied the inside of Dena's home.

Her taste in décor was quite a surprise. Dena was a raw-boned woman— big and frank and not shy about taking up space—but the inside of her truck was a delicate world of lacy fabrics and tiny prints and knick-knacks in small baskets and trays that attached to the shelves so they didn't fly all over the place when Dena took a sharp curve or barreled down a steep hill. She had a palm-size china cat with a china bow tie and some finger-size cut glass perfume bottles. There were crocheted doilies on the countertop and an antique-looking rag rug on the floor.

None of it was particularly my style, but it gave my eyes someplace to rest while I lay there wondering what the hell was wrong with me. I didn't feel at home in my body. I had no sense of focus or drive. I felt clumsy, lazy, disoriented, lethargic—not from pain, as in those terrible weeks and months right after Marcus died, but from a deep sense of disconnection.

I figured that I probably had some fatal complication of pregnancy. My stomach certainly felt like it, with its endless, day-long *morning sickness*. The mention of food was enough to make me want to puke.

A month ago, I might have enjoyed the poetic justice of dying from pregnancy. But on the road with Blondell and Dena, I seemed to be less intent on dying. Brooding about it was more like an exercise. My gloomy thoughts were just part of the haze that was slowly taking over my brain.

Beneath that haze, I guessed there was fear. Here I was, a month pregnant at the most, and already I didn't recognize myself. I wanted to ask what was happening to me, but since neither Dena or Blondell had had kids, I figured that they probably wouldn't know and kept the question to myself.

Mostly I listened to the two of them talk about truck stops and log books, mileage and loads. Sometimes Dena called out on her CB. One time, she said, "Breaker, breaker, this is Polski. I'm looking for bears north of 44."

"Copy you Polski, this is King Leo." There was no way to know if the crackling voice was a few feet or a few states away. "Ten o'clock, past exit 47. Watch the curve coming off that hill."

"Way to go, King Leo." And Dena switched off. "You see?" she told Blondell, "they think I'm a dumb-ass broad who doesn't know how to drive. Men!" she said, with a snort of derision.

"They're not all bad," I mumbled from the back. Somebody had to stand up for men, and it wasn't going to be either of those two.

"They're worse than bad," Dena tossed back over her shoulder. "You don't know, 'cause you don't see them in their natural habitat, like I do."

"Their natural habitat?"

"The road," she said. "Why do you think men don't want women out here driving trucks? They don't want us to see how dumb they really are."

I fell asleep wondering what I thought about that. The women at Girl-O-Rama would have agreed, but Marcus and Francisco and Joe had stopped me looking down my nose at all men.

A few days later, Blondell's driving lessons started in earnest. The gear shift did feature heavily, along with a crash course in what sounded like another language. I slept through most of it, but once in a while I'd wake up to hear Dena's voice, gentle and strong, describing how to double-clutch; explaining that the gears weren't synced, so the tach and the speedometer and your road speed had to line up just right or the damned thing wouldn't go *into* gear; extolling the virtues of 13 gears, which were just as good as 15 or 18 if you didn't plan on hauling a flatbed—which Dena didn't, since she didn't appreciate crawling on top of a pile of logs in thirty-mile-an-hour winds and trying to secure a tarp over them with nothing to hang onto but a rope; and musing that when we got to the next Cat scales she was going to scale this sucker and if it came up the way she thought she was going to slide the tandems 'cause it sure felt like there was two or three thousand more pounds on them than on the steers.

Her voice, the rumble of the truck and the nausea all wrapped around me like a web, keeping me pinned on the bunk, a prisoner in my alien body. My time seemed to be equally divided between sleeping, drifting and wondering what the hell I was doing.

Sometimes Dena or Blondell would wake me. "Get up, Gracie, we're here!" Blondell said once, gently trying to shake me conscious.

"Fuck *here!*" I rolled onto my stomach, which had the side benefit of knocking her hand away. "I want to be *there*."

"Come on." She shook me a little harder. "You gotta eat something. Wake up!"

"I'm not sleeping," I mumbled, rolling another quarter turn so that my back was to her. When I came to again it was dark outside. We were back on the road, and someone had put a styrofoam container of food on the bed beside me.

It was still warm. I slipped the little tongue of the container out from the slot that held it closed. The lid popped up; it was bacon and eggs. I gagged on the smell and almost puked, but I was able to close the cover in time, and a few deep breaths calmed my stomach down.

"You need to feed that baby." Blondell half-turned in the passenger seat.

"I will." I put the styrofoam container on the floor and gave it a shove in her direction. "Tomorrow. I promise."

And then I rolled over and went back to sleep.

The next day, she was in my face again. "You gotta eat," she told me. We were standing inside a Flying J general store, Blondell beckoning me toward the attached cafeteria. Dena stood behind her, nodding.

"Fine," I said. "I'll drink some milk, but I gotta take it back to the truck." I don't like milk particularly, but I figured this would get them off my back.

I should have known better. If anything, they were encouraged. Two days later, at a truck stop near Knoxville, Tennessee that was more like a big enclosed flea market, Dena bought a tiny icebox. After that, they started shopping for me, buying ginger ale wherever they went, and keeping it in Dena's little refrigerator.

I had to admit, the ginger ale helped. It settled my stomach and got me through the worst of the mornings.

They also filled the box with things I didn't want—milk and OJ and lettuce and bread—and started feeding me three meals a day. Oatmeal and milk for breakfast. Tuna fish and lettuce for lunch. Hot soup and toast for dinner. If we made it to a truck stop before the restaurant closed for the night, they ate chicken or macaroni and cheese. If we didn't, they ate potato chips, but they'd warm up a can of soup for me, using the electric coil, and stand there watching 'till I drank the whole thing.

Then we'd all clean up and go to bed.

Bed was a pretty simple arrangement. The Western Star had two bunks—a single on top and a double on the bottom. The first few weeks, Dena took the top bunk and gave me and Blondell the double berth. That was generous of her, and it worked fine. She slept pretty heavily, and if I needed to get up and pee in a jar—because Dena swore she'd kick my ass if I walked around alone at night, and sometimes we had to park *far* from the bathroom—I could do it without disturbing them.

But one night, shortly after Blondell started to drive, I woke up hearing strange sounds above me: Slurping, squishing, giggling sounds with an occasional soft thump like someone had banged a knee, or maybe her head, against the walls of the sleeper.

"For Christ's sake," I grumbled loudly, "come down and take the double bed and let me get some goddamn sleep."

They came down, looking rumpled and embarrassed, but they needn't have been on my account. Just because I'd never gone the Lesbian route myself didn't mean I couldn't see the hope shining in Blondell's eyes. I yawned at them and nodded good night and dragged myself into the top bunk. My main thought was that I hoped Blondell knew what she was doing, and I hoped I wouldn't have to pee in the night and maybe step on them climbing down.

From then on, I was the odd girl out.

I don't know when I started thinking about sending a postcard to Joe Rollins. Lillian had asked me to stay in touch; by rights, I should have sent it to her. But Joe was the one I wanted to talk to. Joe was the one I thought about, lying in that top bunk every night trying to ignore the sounds of Blondell and Dena falling in love.

I thought about what I would say to him. *I'm sorry* were the only words that came to mind, and what the hell was I sorry about! Sorry that I'd stolen his money? That I'd snuck out on him while he slept? That he was screwing himself up on coke, when he had everything in the world anyone could want? Or was I just sorry that he'd gotten too close and made me run away again?

Finally, it came together in my mind. I bought a postcard at a truck stop near Tallahassee, Florida, that showed an alligator wrestling with a round-bellied tourist in a bathing suit. The card was like a private joke, since I would soon be getting fat, too, and was wrestling with my own alligators.

Dear Joe, I wrote,

I'm sorry about steaing your money and I'm sorry I didn't say goodbye. I'm on the road with some good people, my friend Blondell (who I did find in D.C.) and a woman named Dena who drives a truck. I'm doing pretty well and I hope you are too. Hugs to Lillian and Anna May.

Gracie

I looked at that for a minute. Maybe I was being superstitious, but I didn't feel right describing Dena as if she was totally separate from Blondell, so I crossed out the words *a woman named* and wrote in *Blondell's new girlfriend Dena.*

That looked better. The truck stop store was out of postcard stamps, so I paid a dollar for five regular stamps, put one on the card and dropped it in the mailbox.

As soon as I'd done it, I wanted to stick my hand in there and snatch the card back, but it was too late for that and I felt silly even thinking it. But two days later, I still felt the same—as if the card was wrong and I should take it back. Not that it was wrong, exactly, but that it wasn't right. It didn't say quite what I wanted to say, and since I was never going to speak to Joe again, I needed to get it right this last time.

So I bought another postcard in a place near Norfolk, Virginia. This one had a picture of Naval Station Norfolk and the words "We Support the Fleet."

Dear Joe,

I forgot to say I hope you're not messing up too bad with that stuff we talked about. Be careful 'cause it can really hurt you. Myself, I'm not missing it at all.

Gracie

I stuck this one in an envelope, so nobody but Joe would see it. But it still took me forever to drop the thing into a mailbox, partly because I remembered how it felt to mail the first card and partly because I knew it was none of my damn business to tell Joe Rollins how to live and whether or not to blow coke, and probably when he got this card he would be glad to forget he ever knew me. But Dena and Blondell were already waiting for me back in the truck, so finally I just stuffed it into the mailbox and hurried outside, trying to forget I'd done it.

Funny thing, though. As soon as I'd sent that note, the same niggling feeling that I was missing something just outside my reach came back to me. It was like descriptions I'd read of an itch on a missing limb: You can't scratch it, because the spot that's itching doesn't exist.

What was it I still wanted to tell Joe? It plagued me for days in a low-grade kind of way while I lay around listening to trucker radio and the murmur of Blondell and Dena telling each other their life stories.

Finally, I knew what it was. I didn't *like* what it was, and I didn't like feeling disloyal because of it, but Marcus used to say that it was better, in the long run, to be honest with yourself, whether or not you're honest with anybody else, and I knew he would want me to follow that advice.

So I bought one more postcard, a picture of a hummingbird dipping into a flower. This one was pretty, which I took to be a good sign. Pretty wasn't the big thing happening at truck stop stores; you could find patriotic, practical, religious, crude, lewd or funny merchandise, but things that were pretty were pretty hard to come by.

I wrote,

P.S. Think of me sometime. G.

I almost added *'cause I think about you,* but that wouldn't have been fair to either of us. I didn't want to tease Joe, didn't want to dangle a sense of connection that could never be more than a fantasy. I just wanted to touch some part of him, even if it was only for the few seconds it took him to read what I'd written on a postcard.

I felt sad mailing it, but not hesitant; and afterwards, there was a small sense of peace. It was peace wrapped in loneliness, wrapped in nausea, wrapped in—I guess that was regret, but it was peace anyway, and precious to me.

Not that I was unhappy in the Western Star. I liked Dena's steadfastness. I liked the weightless, drifty feel of sleeping high above 18 wheels. And I loved seeing the changes in Blondell.

Before we hit the road with Dena, I'd never seen Blondell read anything except Lotto numbers and restaurant menus. Now she tackled a stack of rule books two inches thick, and pretty soon she was spouting road regulations with the best of them. She sounded more and more like a Lady Trucker. She even looked like one—she now had a collection of baseball caps, and she and Dena had matching purple t-shirts that said, *These Wheels are Made for Rollin'*. Plus, aside from the few beers that she and Dena put back every Saturday night, Blondell was clean for the first time since I'd known her.

It wasn't just her feelings for Dena that had worked all this magic. Blondell seemed happier every day; she seemed to really *like* what she was doing. She and Dena talked about trucking all the time, in a way that made me grateful I'd lost the toss to be Dena's co-driver. Tolls and gears and the weight limits on various highways and whether they could pay for a lumper at the next warehouse weren't exactly my idea of fun. But to hear Blondell talk about it, even filling out a log sheet was exciting to her.

Me, I was starting to feel stronger. The nausea wasn't as bad anymore. Though it still came like clockwork when I first stood up each morning, it didn't last as long and it didn't make me feel like Niagara Falls had moved into the pit of my stomach. I even started wishing that Dena and Blondell would bring more food—something I was careful to keep from them, since more food would only make my jeans feel tighter than they felt already.

My brain also seemed to be popping through the fog more. These days, I usually knew what state we were in. I noticed highway signs and the names of the DJs on Dena's short-wave radio. I read the labels on cans of food. I noticed that my breasts were sore.

One morning, I couldn't stand the oatmeal-for-breakfast routine anymore. I went into the truck stop café with them and ate a few bites of bacon and eggs. Dena and Blondell's mouths both dropped open.

"Are you getting cravings?" Dena asked.

"No," I said, which wasn't quite true; I'd had to stop myself from smearing strawberry jam on the eggs. "And what if I was?"

"Don't give Dena a hard time," Blondell said. "We just want to know how you feel."

I put my fork down and waited for the usual wave of nausea to break over my head and pound me to the floor. Surely the bacon was tempting fate.

But nothing happened.

"I feel great," I told them, and went back to eating.

That night, I was lying in the top bunk, re-reading a romance novel I'd picked up outside Missoula, Montana. That was another change in me: Two months ago, I'd never have bought a Silhouette—I didn't see any point to the cheap sentiment and easy answers. But I loved this book by Linda Howard, about a woman who becomes her ex-lover's boss. Either it was better than I'd expected or I was going soft around the edges. When the two of them got back together, one page before the end of the book, I was happy for them along with being jealous.

"Gracie, come keep me company," Blondell yelled over her shoulder from the driver's seat.

"What, and sit in Dena's lap?" I yelled back.

"Very funny." Dena gave me a big grin. Then she unbuckled her seat belt, came back to the sleeper and threw herself on the bottom bunk.

"Come on," Blondell called out again, "I'm lonely."

I knew a set-up when I saw one. With a sigh, I put my book away and climbed down from the top bunk.

"Put your seatbelt on," Blondell said when I was sitting in the bucket seat to her right.

I glared at her. Seatbelts around the midsection weren't exactly a happy sensation these days.

"Come on," she said impatiently, "you're not even showing yet. It can't be *that* hard to wear the damned thing."

"What do you mean I'm not showing!" I clicked the belt on, glaring at her again. "My stomach's sticking out a mile."

Blondell rolled her expressive eyes and double-clutched as she downshifted. We were heading south through Idaho, so there was plenty of opportunity to downshift and glide, which Blondell did with the ease of an old-timer.

"How's the baby doing?"

I shrugged. "She's doing fine."

Blondell glanced over at me. We both listened to that pronoun, *she*, hanging in the air between us.

"I'm worried about you," Blondell said.

"Shit, you guys are taking better care of me than anybody ever did except…" I stopped abruptly.

Blondell nodded. "You don't talk about him anymore." She meant Marcus.

"Guess not." I didn't want to tell her I was scared to death to think about Marcus—scared to feel that terrible again, and scared that opening the door to him would open it back up to Rosie. Apparently the morning sickness had chased Rosie away for now, and I didn't want her coming back in these close quarters. How would Dena and Blondell react if I woke up screaming in the middle of the night?

"You miss him?"

"Yeah." For a second, I saw Marcus's smile, and then I thought about sending those three postcards to Joe and knew that I didn't deserve to remember how much Marcus had loved me. "I miss a lot of things."

"You taking the vitamins we bought you?"

"Damn," I said, annoyed that she'd made me want to cry, "what's with you, Blondell? You'd think I was eating garbage and sleeping in a ditch the way you're talking!"

"Don't get uppity with me, Girl! Am I this baby's godmother or not?"

Blondell, a godmother? That would be one for the record books. "Of course you are, if you want to be."

"I want to be. And since I'm the godmother, I get to nag you, don't I?"

Well, turnaround is fair play. "If you get to nag, I get to nag, too. Are you taking vitamins? Seems to me you're not getting much sleep lately, either!"

Blondell flashed me a toothy grin. "Hush up," she said. "That's private business."

Which made me feel like smiling, because Blondell's business with Dena was anything but private; she was wearing her heart on her sleeve. These days, Blondell looked her true age again, which she claimed was 37, though I guessed it was more like 45. Most of the dye had grown out of her hair, which was now a soft brown instead of butter yellow, and she'd gained enough weight so that she didn't look like she'd blow away in a small downdraft.

"So what are you going to do next?" she asked, while I was still sitting there smiling to myself, and I realized this is where the set-up had been going all along.

It scared me more than I'd expected. "What do you mean, *what am I going to do next?* Are you guys throwing me out of here?"

"No," she said quickly, "of course we're not. I just wondered what you're gonna do when the baby comes."

"Sell her," I answered, equally fast.

It took Blondell a few beats to smile. Of course, I was kidding her. Sort of.

I knew you couldn't raise a baby in the back of someone else's truck—*how the hell did you raise a baby anyway?*—but I hadn't been in a big rush to think about the implications.

"I guess I'll go somewhere," I said, with a feeling in my gut that I wished I could blame on morning sickness. "Get a job. Find someplace to live." It didn't sound particularly appealing.

"You probably want to get some help," Blondell said, matter-of-factly enough that I knew she'd been thinking this over for a while.

"Help? From who?"

"I don't know," Blondell said. "Dena and I'd be glad to help out, but once the kid begins to crawl, it's gonna be a little tight in here."

"Damn, Blondell, you sound like you own the place."

She gave me a bashful grin. "Dena and I've been talking about becoming partners. We need to put in someplace so I can go to driving school for a few days and get my license. But she says I've already got some equity in the truck."

"Equity? What do you mean?"

"It's like I own a little bit more every time I drive it, 'cause she couldn't make this much money if I wasn't sharing the work."

"Damn," I said. "Aren't the two of you something!"

"Yeah." She winked at me. "We are."

"I guess four would really be a crowd."

She said, "You're getting bored with us anyway. Pretty soon we'll be driving you crazy, talking about the best route to Galveston."

"As a matter of fact…" I tried to give her a game smile.

"Don't worry about it," Blondell said. I was surprised she could read me that well with both eyes firmly on the road. "You got a home here as long as you want it."

"*Home, home on the range,*" I sang out, hoping that I sounded flip.

Blondell sang back, "*Rollin', rollin', rollin' on the river.*"

And then we both stared out the front window.

I couldn't believe how hot it was in Wagon Wheel.

Had it been like this when I was here before? I remembered being staggered by the heat last May, the first day Blanche drove me through the Mojave Desert. But this August air felt like desiccated fire; I was sure it was scorching the inside of my lungs.

Dena and Blondell dropped me off in front of the Gaslight. It felt strange when they pulled the Western Star over on the two-lane road that ran past the casino. There wasn't much traffic for mid-day, and it was quiet outside the truck. Something about the place felt abandoned.

"Are you sure this is okay?" Blondell looked skeptical..

"Yeah," I said, which sounded like the lie it was.

Dena shook her head no. "Forget it, Gracie. We're not leaving you by the side of the road in front of some place that's deserted. We'll bring you back here the next time we pass through."

"It's not deserted," I said, more forcefully. "That's the Gaslight, everybody hangs out there."

Blondell and Dena both stared suspiciously at the low-slung, weather-beaten building, and the parking lot in front of it where only two cars were parked.

"If *everybody* hangs out there," Dena scoffed, "*everybody* must be two people."

We trudged across asphalt that was soft from the heat to find out what was going on. When we got to the Gaslight's front door, I saw that a piece of white paper had been taped to it, with big block letters that said,

GONE TO BURY HOMER. BACK ABOUT 2:00.

Below that, in a different color ink, somebody else had scrawled,

HOLD YOUR WATER TILL WE GET BACK!

"How 'bout that." I shook me head. "Homer was the cook here. He couldn't cook worth a damn, but half the town'll probably starve without him. Blanche will."

The mention of Blanche must have reassured them; they'd both heard my stories about her. Plus, Dena and Blondell felt better about leaving me now that they realized other people would be coming back.

Still, they wanted to wait with me, which was ridiculous. Dena'd gone two hundred miles off her route to drop me off and they had a shipment to deliver, to say nothing of the fact that I was going to lose my nerve if we didn't get this over with fast.

I finally persuaded them to hit the road.

"You be good," Blondell said, hugging me tightly.

"Girl, you've changed so much." I was hanging onto her just as hard as she was hanging on to me. "Be happy."

"We will be," Dena said, taking me into her arms when Blondell and I let go. She gave me a gentle squeeze. "We want to give you something for the baby."

I said, "You already gave me water and a sandwich and fifty bucks. You don't have to do any more."

"Take it," Dena said, handing over a box that contained the ugliest doll I'd ever seen. "This is gonna be a collector's item."

I looked at the big-headed thing doubtfully. "That is one ugly baby. What kind of name is Cabbage Patch Kid?"

Dena shrugged. "My broker said that people are fighting over these things in the toy stores."

That sounded like b.s. to me, but since Dena had boosted the doll from her load, I took it with a grateful smile. I was superstitious enough to feel that what they were hauling on my last trip must mean something: For months now, we'd been carrying desk chairs and ice cream and lawn mowers and ball bearings and even, one time, a tanker of canola oil, but we'd never carried toys before.

I stood by the side of the road, watching 'till they'd pulled away, and then I trudged back across the parking lot with just my doll, my shoulder bag, my bottle of water, my $50 and my tuna fish sandwich, which I looked forward to eating.

It hadn't gotten any cooler in the half hour since we'd first arrived. I sat down on the squat front step, shaded from direct sun by the Gaslight's frayed canopy, and drank the water and ate my lunch. Then I got up, trudged around the back of the Gaslight, found a secluded place to pee behind a makeshift cabin right behind the casino, and wiped myself with some tissues from my shoulder bag. The last few days, I'd started feeling like I wanted to pee almost all the time and we'd had to make a few unscheduled stops for me to run into the bushes. At least the morning sickness hadn't come back, but this latest little twist of pregnancy was almost as inconvenient, in its own way, as being constantly on the verge of throwing up. Business accomplished, I went back out front, sat down on the stoop again, and read a few pages of *Catcher in the Rye*. Before, I'd been enjoying the book, but now I just couldn't concentrate. After a while, I took the Cabbage Patch doll out of its box, leaned against the door frame, using it as a pillow, and closed my eyes.

I woke up to the scratchy sound of Blanche's voice. "Look what the cat dragged in, Emily."

She didn't sound all that friendly. I opened my eyes and squinted up at Blanche and Emily. Val and Helen, the two waitresses from Finer Diner, were standing right behind them, sort of peering at me around their shoulders so that I saw four faces whose expressions varied from surprise to pleasure to, in Blanche's case, sourness. Just past them, I could see Blanche's red pick-up truck, still idling. Both the doors were thrown open, as if they'd all piled out fast when they saw someone crumpled in the Gaslight's doorway.

"Hey!" I yawned, and then I couldn't help grinning at them. However they felt about me coming back, I was plenty relieved to see them.

"Hay is for horses," Helen said. Then she broke into a big smile and stuck her hand out. "Get off the ground, Gracie. That's no place for a lady to sit."

I took her hand and levered myself up. Truth is, I was glad to have something to hold onto. Whether it was the sun, the pregnancy or the reunion scene, I felt weak.

Val nodded, a neutral greeting. Emily hugged me. Blanche walked away, a blur of color.

"I'm gonna move the truck," she huffed. "Val, you oughtta learn how to shut the door behind you when you get out of a vehicle."

"Your door's open, too," Val pointed out. Val had a big, hard-looking belly that hadn't been there last time I'd seen her.

"You're pregnant!" I forced a little cheerfulness, in spite of not being sure of my welcome. I hadn't been Val's favorite person the last time I was in town. "Bet your little girl's happy she's gonna get a brother or sister."

She smiled at me and nodded, glad that I'd mentioned her young daughter. Val was young herself, and scrawny, but what she lacked in looks she made up for in loyalty, as I'd learned when she snubbed me for being mean to...

No. I stopped that memory cold. I wasn't going to think about Francisco yet.

Emily rested her birdlike hand on my forearm. "You look wonderful, Grace."

I glanced over Emily's head at Blanche, who was trudging reluctantly back toward our happy little group. She'd parked her truck right next to the exit, presumably poised for a quick getaway.

Well, I wasn't going to trip on that. Not when other people were glad to see me. "Thanks, Emily. You look pretty wonderful yourself." And then there was no time to say more because Blanche was walking up to us, and a long line of cars started pulling into the parking lot.

Helen took a key from her pocket and squeezed by me to open the Gaslight's front door. "Come in," she said. "Sit down and stay awhile."

Val nudged me through the front door and before I knew it I was sitting in Finer Diner, surrounded by about twenty people who were drinking beer and talking about what a rotten cook that sonofabitch Homer had been and how much they were going to miss him and wasn't it a nice funeral.

Time passed. More people came, and some left, but the scene stayed pretty constant. I did my best to fall in with the general atmosphere, but it was hard. For one thing, I wasn't drinking. For another, I didn't really belong there. I'd been gone from Wagon Wheel for months, and I hadn't exactly been a long-term resident when I left. Plus, even though nobody mentioned it, it felt strange to have Blanche avoiding me so obviously. She stayed on the other side of the Gaslight, in the room where the slot machines were, and whenever I glanced over that way, she made sure her head was turned so she didn't have to notice me.

I couldn't believe Blanche was that angry. Yes, she'd been steamed when I left town, even though I didn't do anything to her, not really. And even if I had, you'd have thought she'd be over it by now. *I'd* thought she would be over it by now.

I'd also expected to stay with her, which made her anger worse than just awkward.

Where the hell was I going to sleep tonight? Maybe Blanche would come around, 'though that didn't seem likely. Maybe I could crash with Emily, 'though for some reason I wasn't in a hurry to ask. It was easier to float, to figure on faith that something would turn up than to squarely face how alone I was. So I sat there at the lunch counter sipping a cup of lukewarm coffee that Val or Helen refilled now and then.

The conversation ebbed and flowed. Every so often I went to the bathroom. In between, I talked to people; and all the while, I was wondering whether I should ride things out here or get back on the road.

Finally, I got up and walked over to where Blanche was playing her favorite slot machine, the one with Ronald Reagan's picture above it. No one was at the machine to her right, so I sat down beside her and tried to look casual.

"Hey," I said, thinking *wow, that was brilliant!*

She spared me a glance, probably thinking the same thing. "Hey, yourself," she mumbled, turning back to stare at the three reels of colored fruit that were spinning in front of her.

After a few seconds, the reels slowed down until, with a mechanical crunching sound, three symbols jolted onto the pay line: Two cherries and something that looked like a dead peach.

No coins dropped into the tray.

Blanche frowned. She scooped two quarters from a plastic cup on the floor by her left foot and fed the machine.

"Didn't expect to see you back here," she said without looking my way.

"Me, neither."

She tugged the lever ferociously. It made the flesh on her right arm jiggle, made it look like the hula girl was doing a Hawaiian dance. "You just passing through?" she asked, her eyes fixed on the reels as they began to gather momentum again.

"I don't know what I'm doing." I was pissed off enough at her that I couldn't help adding, "One place is about the same as another."

Blanche stiffened, but she didn't take her eyes off the reels 'till they finally came to a jerky halt: One cherry. One dead peach. A wormy-looking apple.

She turned to face me squarely. "You're bad luck," she scowled.

I said, "Are you just figuring that out now?"

We glared at each other for a long, tense heartbeat, and then I thought I saw a tiny crack appear in the thick layer of make-up base and powder that Blanche considered her more restrained daytime look.

I chose to believe it was the hint of a smile. "Come on, Blanche!" I wasn't above cajoling her a little, though I sure wasn't going to apologize. "How long are you gonna stay pissed off at me?"

"That's my decision," she said, haughtily.

"Okay." I stood up, hovering for a minute. "If you decide to get over it, I'll buy you a cup of coffee." And I went back over to the Finer Diner side.

Helen came up behind me, holding the coffee pot out like a weapon. "Problem?" she asked, looking pointedly past me in Blanche's direction.

"Nothing except Blanche is so damned stubborn," I said.

"Hmph." She unbent enough to pour some coffee into my cup. "You know the expression *it takes one to know one?*"

"Helen," I said, "don't you start, too!"

"I don't want any trouble, Grace."

"Me, neither." It was only the truth.

"Then don't go picking a fight with Blanche."

"I won't," I promised. "But I'm not gonna kiss her ass, either."

Helen walked away, shaking her head, and I plunked down on my stool at the counter and thought that it was a damn shame that the only person in this place who was likely to offer me a bed for the night hated me.

I sat there brooding for what felt like another hour. After a while, my stomach started growling. It was frustrating that, for once, I had money to pay for food but there was no one in the kitchen to make some.

Mid-afternoon wore into late afternoon. Valerie left to go home to her daughter. Emily came and sat beside me. Blanche stayed over on the slot machine side for a long time, and then she left. Helen was pouring up a storm behind the bar, and soon I was the only person in the place who was sober enough to notice that dinner time had come and gone. Everyone else seemed perfectly happy talking and playing the one-armed bandit. Whenever a tourist walked in, they were given a drink and an earful about Homer by way of explaining why the kitchen was closed.

Well, that was all fine for the rest of them, but I was supposed to be eating for two. Dena and Blondell had totally spoiled me with all those three-square-meals-a-day.

"Doesn't *anybody* in here cook?" I whispered to Emily at one point. Emily, who *did* know how to cook, was still sitting beside me but she didn't look like she'd be upright for long. She shrugged me off, in an un-Emily-like way, and went back to speaking with the woman on her right, who wanted to know how she grew such pretty roses.

"I water 'em," Emily said. Then she hiccupped.

There went my last hope, drunk as a skunk. Forget about asking to stay with her—I couldn't ask Emily for a cup of tea, the shape she was in.

Well, if I was going to sleep on the ground tonight, at least I could do it on a full stomach. I eased off my stool and slipped into the kitchen.

Standing alone in Homer's domain, I let my eyes take it all in, slowly.

First thing I noticed, it was greasy as hell. Good thing my morning sickness was gone, or I probably would have thrown up just from looking at the sludge caked on Homer's gas griddle.

Not that it was unsanitary. Lillian and Anna May had introduced me to the fact that kitchen sludge, while gross, wasn't dangerous. Particularly in an industrial kitchen, where the high heat killed off most germs.

If I wanted to act like a squeamish girl, I would have to find a better excuse.

With a sigh, I put on the long apron that was hanging from a hook beside the stove. It was one of those old-fashioned jobs with a bib that goes around your neck. It wasn't particularly clean either, and normally I would have passed it by, but with what I was about to do, I didn't want to ruin a good set of clothes.

Homer's spatula was in the sink, where he must have left it before he died. I used it to scrape the griddle clean, shoveling piles of charred food scrap and burned bits of god knows what straight into a big trash can. Then I turned the gas on, high, and heated that sucker 'till it sizzled.

You'd have thought that, by now, someone would have noticed all the activity coming from the kitchen. It wasn't like I was being silent, but no one came to investigate. They were probably too drunk to care.

I went back to the sink and washed my hands with a bar of yellow soap that I hoped wasn't made from lye. Then I started taking inventory.

Finer Diner had a big refrigerator/freezer combo and another stand-alone freezer, which made sense since we were out in the middle of the Mojave Desert. You couldn't just run down the street to the store if you ran out of something halfway through the lunch rush.

The fridge and the freezer weren't quite bare, but they weren't exactly bursting with food. The refrigerator had four dozen eggs, some bread, a block of hard cheese with mold growing on it, and two gallons of milk that had turned. The freezer had four blocks of hamburger the size of my head and three big, industrial bags of uncooked French fries. There was palm oil in a big drum, but I wasn't going near the fryer without someone to explain it to me, so I took out the cheese, scraped the mold off the edges, and started breaking eggs into a bowl.

"Look at you!" It was Helen's voice. "You know how to cook?"

"Not really." Our eyes met over the pass-through that separated the kitchen from the restaurant. "Do you know how to work the fryer?"

"No," she said. "But I'll bet there's instructions. Homer wouldn't throw them away."

As it turned out, there were instructions, yellowed and taped on the splintery wooden wall. They were easy to understand, and it turned out that—if you ignored the fact that you were basically dealing with five gallons of boiling oil—working the fryer wasn't that hard. Before too long I was pushing big platters of French fries and scrambled eggs with cheese onto the pass-through.

"Hey, Gracie," someone called out, "you making any coffee back there?"

"Gimme two eggs over easy," someone else blurted.

"Honey, if you burn the place down there's gonna be hell to pay."

"You sure are prettier than Homer, Miss Grace."

Even though I had my back turned, everybody seemed to have something to say to me. Finally, I came to the kitchen door. I stuck my head out and said, pretty loudly, "Why don't you all go back to drinkin' and leave me alone to clean up in here!"

To my great surprise, they all did.

By then I was tired of being on my feet, but I ate my dinner standing up in preference to leaving the kitchen's privacy. The eggs weren't bad. The fries were filling. Some juice and a side of toast would have been nice. Fresh fruit would have been near to heaven, but I was grateful for what I had.

I wondered where Homer bought supplies.

After I had finished eating, I went back to doing inventory, this time looking at the equipment. Besides the refrigerator, freezer, grill and fryer, there was a stove, an industrial coffeemaker, a toaster big enough for ten slices, something that looked like a sandwich press, an ancient electric Mixmaster and lots of little odds and ends. I was just starting to go through the kitchen drawers when I heard a familiar voice behind me.

"Have I missed the dinner hour?"

I whirled around so fast I almost lost my balance.

He was leaning on the doorframe. His arms were crossed over his chest. His face was carefully neutral.

I hated to think what *my* face was giving away.

"Hey, Francisco." I tried to slow my heartbeat down. What had I thought, that we wouldn't cross paths? I should have been glad that it was happening right away.

Francisco looked a little careworn—good, but older than I remembered. Still, I felt a fondness for him stir inside me, along with a warm flash of embarrassment at the memories that came with it.

"I can make you some eggs," I offered, quickly shutting the drawer I'd been searching when I remembered the last drawer I'd searched near Francisco. "How about a cheese omelet?"

"Thanks." He hadn't moved an inch, and didn't look like he was planning to.

I took out a smaller bowl and cracked the last few eggs into it—the ones I'd kept aside, not knowing at the time why I did it. "How's things going?" I asked over my shoulder, whisking the eggs together with salt and pepper and a dash of water, since there was no milk.

"Things are going fine," he said. "How's the traveling?"

We sounded like a soap opera, stiff characters reciting stiff lines. "I've been out to Wyoming," I told him, pouring the eggs onto the grill. "And Washington D.C., and other places."

"I'm glad you're getting to see the world." But he didn't sound particularly glad. He sounded like he was being very careful.

I scooped his eggs onto a plate. Everything happens fast on a grill, and now I didn't have an excuse to keep my back turned. "I'm sorry we don't have any toast." I handed him the plate and a fork. "And people finished all the French fries."

"No problem." He still hadn't moved, and he looked a little disoriented. I wondered if the plate of eggs would slide from his hand and crash to the floor.

"Do you want a cup of coffee with that?"

"No," he said, "this'll do just fine. Would you like to sit down and join me for a while?"

Part of me did and part of me didn't, but mostly what I thought was that I couldn't afford to even *think* about getting friendly with this man. If he was really the father of my baby, getting friendly would make it a lot worse for both of us. So I shook my head, hoping that my sadness wasn't peeking through the cool, calm and collected surface. "No thanks, Francisco. But I hope you enjoy your dinner."

Francisco nodded—his old world politeness never seemed to abandon him—and took his breakfast out of the kitchen. He sat at a table I couldn't see, but I could still feel his presence, and I sensed it when he got up to leave.

Helen was over in the casino, so I went out to collect Francisco's plate. There was a dollar bill sitting beside it, wrapped around a piece of paper with his name and a telephone number on it. I put the dollar in my pocket, walked back to the kitchen, crumpled up the paper with his number and threw it away.

Around midnight, Helen came up to me. By then, she'd shooed out the last of the customers and was getting ready to lock the place up. "Nice work, Gracie," she said. "You're hired."

Her words didn't make much sense to me, perhaps because I was tired enough to drop.

"The job," she explained. "The cooking job. We're short one cook, in case you hadn't noticed."

"I don't know how to cook," I reminded her.

"You just did," she pointed out.

"Big deal. I scrambled some eggs."

Helen said, "Gracie, you fed fifty people. Get some sleep and be back here at six AM sharp."

"Get some sleep *where?*" I sounded gruff, but in truth I was too tired to care anymore where I slept that night. At that point, lying down on the floor at her feet would have been just fine with me.

But Helen reached past me and took a small key off the rusty nail where it had been hanging. "Homer had that little place out back. It comes with the job, so it's yours now. You get all your meals for free, and you can use the washing machine, but don't go crazy—water isn't cheap."

I stared at the key she'd put in my hand. Apparently, I'd taken the job.

"This key opens your cabin, and the kitchen door. Don't be late tomorrow," she said. "Six o'clock comes around real fast."

twenty-three

My first night of sleep in the cabin didn't last until 6:00am. At about 5:30, I heard something that sounded like a car crash and then someone blasted a foghorn right outside the door of Homer's cabin.

I rolled over and tried to ignore it. You wouldn't have thought I'd have been so eager to spend more time in a dead man's bed, but I'd been exhausted the night before, and Homer's bed was surprisingly comfortable.

Still, the second blast of that foghorn sound had me up and staggering from the bed to the window. I peeked outside and saw a tractor-trailer with a cab even bigger than Dena's parked beside the Gaslight. A man was busily unloading boxes.

I pulled my clothes on, struggling a little to snap my jeans around a waist that was getting thicker, and hurried outside to see what the commotion was.

"Where's Homer?" the man asked.

"Dead." I gave his truck the once over. It had a lot more chrome than Dena's, too. The effect was garish, and I wasn't too happy to catch my reflection in the side panel. I needed a haircut, and plenty more.

"Well, you can sign for this stuff," he said.

"What stuff?"

He gestured impatiently toward the boxes, most of which looked like he'd thrown them off the truck. "That stuff," he said, shoving a clipboard at me. "Write your name and print underneath."

"How come?" I yawned. It was too damned early.

"To show that you accept delivery. Come on, Lady, just sign so I can go! I gotta get to Bullhead City before six."

I scribbled my name and handed him the clipboard. Seconds later, he was pulling out and I was staring at about twenty-five boxes of... *food?*

I went back inside Homer's cottage and got the key Helen had given me the night before. I opened the Gaslight's kitchen door and started moving the boxes inside.

Helen showed up a few minutes later. "I knew you'd be on time," she said.

I didn't bother telling her about the truck. She could see from what I was doing that he'd been there and gone. "Helen," I said, "you talk just like you own the place."

"I do." Cigarette dangling from her lips, she picked up a box. "What'd you think?"

I'd stopped working so that I could stand there, staring. She still looked like a waitress to me. "I thought maybe you were the manager. You *own* Finer Diner?"

"I own the whole Gaslight."

She started hauling boxes, so I picked up another one and quickly followed her into the kitchen. "Shit, if you *own* all of this, why aren't you off lying on the beach?"

"'Cause I'm trying to keep it."

Well, that made a certain cock-eyed sense. Lillian was still working sometimes, and she was plenty older than Helen. Come to think of it, I didn't know anyone who'd ever stopped working, really. Even if you were a lazy slug, just surviving was work enough for anybody.

I put down the box I was carrying near the stove and went outside for another one. They were all different sizes and weights—some you could tell were just paper goods, and others felt like they were packed with bricks. Between Helen and me, we got it all inside pretty fast, and then she said, "Put up the coffee, would you, Grace? People start showing up soon and if they don't get their coffee, they're not too nice."

By the time I had the coffee perking, Helen had started emptying out boxes. Together, we put all the food away, with her showing me where things went and me checking out what she had bought.

Breakfast was a madhouse. Making one dish for fifty people was nothing compared to making a dozen different dishes for them. I spent half the time growling and half the time sweating and by ten-thirty, when Helen told me to go take a break, I was sure I'd never look at food again. I poured myself that glass of orange juice I'd wanted so badly the night before and took it back to Homer's cabin. Sitting on his only chair, an uninviting straight-backed thing, I put my feet up on his table and started to cry.

That shocked me so bad I bolted right up out of my seat. I was *crying* over breakfast, I thought, stalking angrily around the small cabin. Crying because my feet hurt and I'd scraped my knuckles and singed a few hairs on my left arm. Crying because I'd thrown out two batches of pancake batter before I got it right. Crying because...

All right, I was crying because of Marcus.

I sat back down on that chair with a thud and felt the wind blow through my chest.

Marcus was supposed to do the cooking. Marcus was supposed to take care of people. Marcus was supposed to have lived to see thirty-five, lived to see his baby, lived to...

And just that fast, the wall I'd built in my mind these past months came crashing down. A flood of memories and despair washed through me: Marcus and me, our bodies tangled. Marcus talking. Marcus laughing. Marcus whirling me on the dance floor in the basement of San Sebastãio, my red dress floating above my knees, his hand anchoring the small of my back. Marcus breaking orange slices into a pot of black bean soup, the juice running sweet over his strong fingers.

Marcus would have loved Finer Diner. In his whole life, he'd never had a break like this job.

I sat there sobbing, trying to choke the sound back. The last thing I wanted was somebody to hear me.

After a while, the tears ran dry, but my shoulders wouldn't stop heaving. I could feel the empty spot behind my ribs where my heart would have been if it still worked. My hand was sitting just below it, on the secret I was carrying.

Marcus's daughter. Marcusette.

It didn't matter if I wanted her or not. She was a weight I couldn't put down, a promise my soul wouldn't survive breaking.

I'll take care of her, I told Marcus, fiercely. *I won't let her die like Rosie did.*

My hand fell away from my belly and rose wearily to massage the back of my neck. The whole thing was totally out of my control, as Marcus had intended from the start.

For his sake, I would have this baby and I would guard her with my life.

But first, I had to go back to work.

I dragged myself up out of the chair and into the cabin's small bathroom. Its splintered wood walls looked just like the kitchen's, and the mirror was too yellowed and cracked to give more than a poor reflection. But it was good enough to show a woman on a thin tether, a woman who didn't look too sure that she was strong enough to make it through the day. Her stark eyes searched mine, as if she was waiting for me to offer help.

"There is no help, you fool," I said out loud. Rosie had told me that once, in a dream; or maybe she'd said that there was no comfort. *Either way, you've gotta pull yourself together.* Wearily, I brushed my teeth, washed my face and dragged a comb through my hair. Then I straightened my shoulders and walked slowly back to my new job.

Emily was waiting at the counter.

"Sit down a second." She patted the next stool. I was glad to see that she didn't look too worse for the wear of last night's drinking. Emily was so bent and frail, it was easy to forget she was tough as iron. Everyone was tough out in the desert. They would have left by now if they weren't.

"Are you OK?" she peered at me.

"Yeah, why?" I growled, going on the offensive.

"Nothing." She met my eye. "It's not my business anyway. I brought you this book," she said, putting her hand on the thick hardcover sitting on the counter.

I could read the spine. *The Joy of Cooking.*

"Emily…" I didn't feel good about growling at her a moment before.

"I've been using this for 30 years," she said. "It'll get you through just about anything."

I picked the book up and thumbed through it, curious in spite of my embarrassment. Along with the endless recipes, there was a chapter on canning foods and a chapter on different cuts of meat and a chapter on mixed drinks to serve at a party.

Some of the recipes were splattered with food stains. I knew those would be Emily's favorites.

"Don't you need this?" I asked, confused.

Emily shook her head vehemently. "I've been tired of cooking for twenty years. It's no fun when you're on your own. Now that poor old Homer's gone, I guess I'll be coming in here to eat."

"Well, thanks, Emily," I said soberly. "I'll try to live up to this."

"Now don't go getting unctuous on me," she said. "Just take it and learn what you want to know."

"Unctuous?" Modesty aside, it wasn't too often that people used words I didn't know.

"Creepy. Oily. Grovelly," she said. When I stared at her, she added, "I used to be a high school teacher. Everyone in here used to be something."

"Yeah, me too." I picked up the book and rose to my feet. Then I surprised myself by leaning over to kiss her weathered cheek. "Thanks, Emily."

"You're welcome. I hope you enjoy it."

I just had time to get in the kitchen and put my apron on before Finer Diner opened for lunch. Emily sat at the counter a while, then came to the kitchen door and waved goodbye before she left.

Lunch was even crazier than breakfast. Helen's menu ran heavily to beef, which basically meant hamburger and steak, but you could also order pork chops or bacon. A few people wanted casseroles that I would have had to prep the night before, and two of them wanted seafood, which was stupid in Nevada, but I gave them what we had in the freezer. That was fine as far as it went, but one woman ordered a veggie burger and Valerie didn't know what that was. Ten minutes after we'd finished the lunch rush, Helen was showing me how to prep for dinner.

We closed for good a little after nine that night. By Helen's count, I'd cooked fifty-three breakfasts, seventy-eight lunches and forty-seven dinners. Back at the cabin, I barely got my clothes off before my head hit the pillow and I conked out.

The next morning, it all started again.

My first thought, when the alarm clock shrilled, was that it was wonderful being too tired to dream. The last two nights, I'd slept like someone with amnesia, or maybe someone in a coma.

My second thought was that I hoped little Marcusette appreciated what I was doing for her. And just like that, I was hearing, *You little stuck-up bitch, you better show some gratitude or I'll tan your hide and lock you in that closet!*

I wrenched myself free of my mother's voice and pushed my still-sore feet out of bed. My legs followed reluctantly, and soon my whole aching body was upright. Trudging into the bathroom, I thought, *I might not know how to raise a kid, but I sure know lots of things to not do.*

Today, Helen didn't have to tell me to put the coffee on first thing.

"You okay?" she asked. "You look a little tired."

Haunted was more like it, but I sure wasn't going to say that to my boss. "Now I know why Homer was such a pain in the butt," I told her, half-joking.

But she surprised me with a serious reply. "This job isn't for everybody," she said. "The hours are long, the pay is shit. It's good for a person who has no life. That's why you won't last too long."

"Thanks a lot!" I said, indignantly.

"Don't worry." She gave me a grin. "You'll *think* you been here forever by the time you quit."

The next few days went by in a blur of meat and potatoes, eggs and vegetables, moments snatched to read the cookbook or swill some coffee and, sometimes, even sit down. I thought about Helen's words a lot, and they worked like a dare, as she'd probably hoped they would. I was damned if I was going to cave in to something new and complicated, damned if I was going to let people say that I couldn't handle a little hard work.

I'd been used to long days bartending, but this was different, this level of concentration. Turn around for the wrong two seconds and something burned. Mix the wrong two things and they were ruined. Touch the wrong thing—the stove, the fryer—well, I tried not to think about that, but it wasn't ever too far from my mind.

Each night I went back to Homer's cabin and wrestled with an unsettling mix of exhaustion and over-stimulation, loneliness and over-exposure to people. For years I'd had Marcus to help me cope with coming down after a hard night's work, and for the last two months I'd had Dena and Blondell watching over me like mother hens. Now I had nobody to talk me down, or even just to talk to, period.

The only good thing I could say about my otherwise extreme state of mind was that I hadn't heard from Rosie. I lay down every night in the silence of Homer's cabin, dreading a visit. When night after night she didn't come, I didn't know what to make of it.

Was she staying out of my way on purpose, as she'd stayed away while I was getting pregnant? Was she saving up for a big attack when she thought I'd make a better target?

The other person staying out of my way, for reasons I could imagine all too well, was Blanche. She hadn't stepped foot in the diner since that first day—I knew, because I was there all the time—and I wondered if she was living on snack cakes, or those nuts they served on the casino side.

Finally, on my fifth afternoon on the job, she walked in with Francisco. She was clearly on a mission, and Francisco seemed embarrassed, which is how I knew she'd dragged him along.

You had to admire Blanche's timing. At 2:30 in the afternoon, not only was the place almost empty, but Val and Helen were both off somewhere, which meant I would have to wait on her.

I picked up a pencil and one of those little pads and walked resolutely out of the kitchen. It felt like I was crossing a prison yard under the watchful eye of tower guards who'd be happy to shoot me for one false move.

The two of them made an odd-looking couple: Blanche, the proverbial painted lady, had crinkly skin and a teenager's temper. Francisco, younger and broodingly handsome, looked like he'd lived a thousand years.

"Howdy," I said to both of them, ignoring the glare Blanche angled up at me. Obviously she'd decided that my version of an olive branch, thrown out that first night over in the casino, either hadn't happened or didn't count.

"Hello, Grace," Francisco said quietly. He smiled in a way that was nicely gauged to express approval without any demands. "How's the new job working out?"

"I'm doing my best." I gave him a tepid smile "What would you two like to eat?"

"Two orders of huevos rancheros, please."

"I haven't learned to cook that yet," I told Francisco with genuine regret. I would have liked to be done taking his order and halfway back to the kitchen by now. Then Blanche rolled her eyes, which pissed me off. "But I'm willing to try," I added quickly, "if you don't mind waiting while I check my cookbook."

Francisco gave me that gentle smile, the one that made him all the more dangerous. "Go ahead and try," he said. "Blanche and I, we're not in a hurry."

I almost ran back to the kitchen, praying the recipe was really in *Joy*. I was damned if I was going to fail in front of Blanche, and as it turned out, I didn't have to. Huevos rancheros was nothing but poached eggs with homemade salsa. I didn't have some of the ingredients they listed, like powdered cumin and red pimiento, but I had onions and jalapeno and salt and pepper and fresh tomatoes. I chopped them up fine and simmered them all in a cast iron skillet until the tomatoes juiced into mush. Then I cracked four eggs on top of the mixture and covered them to poach while I toasted bread.

If a few pots got slammed around in the process, that was no one's business but mine.

"You learn fast," Francisco said when I brought out two heaping plates of food.

Of course that reminded me of the other things that I'd learned fast around Francisco: How to trick him into having sex with me. How to sabotage a condom.

Remembering that night, I had to stop myself from rubbing the hard lower part of my belly—the place where cells were slowly dividing and starting to take on a form that might be half his.

No! I thought. *This is Marcus's baby!*

But Francisco could make plenty of trouble. He was stable, educated, well-to-do. If he wanted to fight me for custody of Marcusette, I wouldn't have a prayer of winning.

"Enjoy your lunch," I managed to mumble, before I turned and fled back to the kitchen. It didn't help my state of mind that Blanche hadn't said a word to me.

Alone again in my new domain, I started prepping for the dinner rush. I cut up onions and peppers, shaped a new batch of hamburger patties, poured more oil in the fryer to heat and checked my stores of bread and vegetables.

Throughout it all, I kept my back turned resolutely toward the door. But still, I could feel it, or maybe hear, when Blanche and Francisco got up to leave.

Eventually, Val and Helen came back. Val started gathering the ketchup bottles and salt shakers at one table to refill. Helen walked around the room, as she did before every meal, emptying ashtrays and picking up stray plates and cups, getting ready for the next batch of diners.

I held my breath when she walked into the kitchen. "You forgot your tip," she said, setting a pile of dirty dishes carefully down in the sink.

"The cook doesn't get tipped," I pointed out.

And then I knew I'd made a mistake. "Whoever waits on the table gets the tip," she said, sounding a little too curious. "Didn't you wait on a table while I was gone?"

"Yeah," I mumbled, leaning over the green pepper I was seeding, as if scraping that pesky little thing took all my concentration.

Fortunately, Helen decided to drop it. "This is yours, then," she said, putting two worn-looking dollar bills on my cutting board.

The rest of the week passed without any drama. Emily stopped by every morning. She always ate oatmeal for breakfast, no matter how hot it was outside, and she always had some little suggestion to make things easier for me in the kitchen.

Helen gave me good advice, too. "Homer used to do this," she'd say, or "Homer did it like that." Frankly, I doubted that Homer had done any of the things she said, but her advice was good—things like cooking food three-quarters through so it was ready to finish off fast when people ordered it. And some things I figured out myself, like working the grill in smaller sections—meats near the front right, eggs near the front left, and a big pile of hashed potatoes steadily browning all across the back.

Val was actually warming to me. Of course, we were thrown together at work and she got to see that I wasn't that bad, but the real reason we were getting to be buddies was that I asked lots of questions about her pregnancy: What she was eating, how she felt, whether the baby was moving yet, things like that. She seemed happy to answer them—she didn't know I was studying on her—but I couldn't ask the things I most wanted to know, like when was I going to start showing, or how long before I stopped having to pee so much?

Blanche had made herself noticeably scarce, but Francisco stopped by the diner every day, and every day I was nice but aloof. I didn't enjoy being stand-offish, but I was truly scared of what I might say in a moment of exhausted, unguarded conversation. *I'm pregnant and it might be yours* came to mind as one particularly sobering example, so I had to make sure that we didn't talk.

By Saturday night, when we closed up, I was really glad to learn that I had Sunday morning off. Helen taped a handwritten note to the front door that said:

WE OPEN AT NOON ON SUNDAY.
STAY IN BED OR GO TO CHURCH, WE DON'T CARE WHAT YOU DO
BUT YOU CAN'T DO IT HERE.

Obediently, I stayed in bed and figured that Helen had done the same. But when I finally got up around ten o'clock and picked my way over to Finer diner, she was already sitting at the counter, sipping fresh coffee and paying a stack of bills.

"Smells good," I said reaching for a cup.

She nodded, distracted by the bookkeeping. "It's not bad. You know we don't open 'till noon today, right?"

"I wanted to get ready for the rush."

I poured my coffee and was about to head for the kitchen to prep for the thundering hoards when she said, "Wait a second," and held out an envelope. "Don't spend it all on the slot machines."

Inside were five $20 bills.

"I thought you said the pay was shit!" I blurted out, ungraciously. In San Francisco, I'd made a hundred bucks a night. Now it seemed like a small fortune.

"Well, hell, if that's too much, give it back."

"Not on your life!" I snatched the envelope out of Helen's reach and, grinning, tucked it into the back pocket of my jeans.

The next week, when she handed me the same amount, I felt like a truly rich woman. No bills to pay and two weeks' salary in my pocket. I asked Helen if I could borrow a stamp.

Back in the cabin, I took out a pen and wrote,

Dear Lillian,

I hope you're well and that Anna May and Joe are, too. You said to write when I got someplace. I'm actually more in the middle of nowhere, but I have a job, so I wanted to send some of the money I owe you.

Would you believe I'm working as a cook? Anna May will love that, I bet.

Would you please split this money with Joe? I hope he isn't too mad that I stole that cash from his wallet, but I wouldn't have done it if I'd known another way to get where I was going.

Well, that's all for now. Unless I get fired, I'll send more money next week.

Gracie

I folded a $20 bill in the letter, stuck it in the envelope and licked it shut. I wrote Lillian's name and address on the front. And then I stared at the envelope, wondering whether or not to add a return address.

I was still wondering when someone knocked on the door. I went to open it, and there was Francisco, looking like a man who had his hat in his hand, even though he wasn't carrying one.

He said, "Hello, Grace. Do you mind if I come in?"

I did mind, but it wasn't fair to say so after I'd kept him at arm's length for the last ten days. I felt bad enough about Francisco without slamming the door in his face.

Still, I stepped aside cautiously, and said, "I have to be at work real soon."

"I won't be long." He walked into the cabin and looked around with frank curiosity. I remembered being like that in his house—wanting to take in every sight, every texture, wanting to find a clue to the man. But his place had truly been a home. This cabin was just a temporary shelter; I hadn't changed it in any way.

"Sit down," I said, motioning to the only chair. I sat down on the edge of the bed, suddenly noticing how stuffy my home was. The air still reeked of cooking oil and Homer's long-gone cigarettes. I got up to open a window and sat down again.

He waited quietly until I'd stopped fidgeting. "Grace," he began with such grim determination that I realized he was struggling. The idea of Francisco struggling with anything was sobering in the extreme.

"I promised myself," he finally went on, "that I wouldn't bring up what happened between us. Not when you so obviously didn't want me to talk about it."

I might have almost stopped him right then, and blurted out something—who knows what—but I kept my mouth resolutely shut. It was all I could do to look at Francisco, and then I had to look away before he got the wrong idea, or the right one.

He said, "I've thought a lot about it, though. Whatever that night meant to you, you made me think about what I wanted. You made me want to live again."

God, what was I going to say to this man? Anything designed to keep him away would be cruel to the point of being criminal. But he would take anything nice as encouragement, and I couldn't afford to have him in my life. I couldn't afford for him to figure out the claim he might have on Marcus's baby.

I took a deep, guilt-ridden breath. "Francisco…" I started.

He held up his hand. "I'm not trying to pressure you. You've made it very clear where you stand. But I'm finding that it's hard—much harder than I thought it would be—to know that you don't even want to be friends. It's hard because you're the one who woke me up again, after I'd been sleeping for a long time. So I didn't come by to hassle you. I just want to know if you think there's any chance, as time goes on, that you might change your mind."

God, I respected the way he said that. So calm and clear that he might have been asking if it was too late to order the breakfast special. But I remembered him sobbing in my arms. I remembered his grief pouring into me. That wasn't the start of a casual friendship, and I couldn't let him think that it was.

Still, I owed him more than he knew. "You woke me up, too, Francisco." I made myself look him in the eye. "I'm grateful, and I always will be. But you're not what I need in my life right now, and I don't want to lead you on. So, no, I'm not going to change my mind."

He took it well. There was nothing else for him to do, with me copying that calm, clear tone of voice he'd taught me only a moment ago. He flinched a little when I said it, and then he smoothed out his face and stood up tall and gave me a smile that was sad but still warm, still fond, still okay.

"Thanks." He reached out and touched my cheek—a gesture with more than a hint of longing. A gesture that would have hurt, if I'd let it. He wasn't the only one who was lonely. "I appreciate you telling me the truth," he said, "even though I wish it was different."

I wished it was different, too, but I knew better than to tell him that. I wished I'd treated him more fairly. Wished that things were different for us. I didn't have any idea what I needed; I just knew Francisco wasn't it.

"You're a really good person," I said. And even though it felt like I was wishing him terrible pain in the future, I added what I knew he wanted. "I hope you find someone to love."

"You, too," he answered.

He let himself out.

twenty-four

When Blanche walked into Finer Diner two weeks later, everyone stopped to stare at me. I happened to be sitting at the counter, taking advantage of a momentary lull, and I couldn't even pretend to not notice her—not with the way everyone else in the place was gawking, waiting to see what was going to happen next.

I guess they figured she was there to throw it in my face about Francisco leaving town the day before. He'd driven over the Arizona line to Kingman on Saturday and come back with one of those little U-Haul trailers hitched to the back of his car. Then he'd packed everything he owned into it. It turned out Francisco had an engineering job lined up at the mine in Boron, California. He was going to rent his house to some college professor who wanted a quiet place to write.

No one was more surprised than me—and certainly no one was more relieved—that Francisco thought the grass was greener across the state line. But he didn't seem to hold that against me; he hugged me the same way he hugged everyone else when he came around Finer Diner to say goodbye.

"Take care of yourself, Gracie," he whispered in my hair. His arms were tight around me, but not constricting, as he lingered over letting me go.

"You, too, Francisco." I gave him a small, sad peck on the cheek.

And then he was gone and, I hoped, forgotten.

But now here was Blanche, not twelve hours later, looking like a crazy woman who hadn't slept. Her make-up was too heavy, her hair all scraggly, her clothes the ones she'd worn yesterday.

I'd figured Blanche would get around to picking a fight with me about Francisco. But I hadn't expected her to do it so fast, and I hadn't expected her to do it so loud that even folks across in the adjoining casino could hear.

"I hope you're satisfied!" she screamed, the words careening upward, like they might crack or fly away.

"Satisfied about what?" I bit back. It was a snarl. A slap. The sound of pure contempt. As much as I'd loved Blanche before, I hated her now and I didn't mind showing it.

Of course that only made her angrier. Hadn't that been my whole point? "You're probably happy he's gone!"

Helen stepped out from behind the counter.

"Blanche…" she started.

Blanche just waved her away.

"You were just too good for him, weren't you?" she shrilled at me. "You're too good for all of us! You think because you're young and pretty, you can sit back and laugh at the people who're trying to help you."

"Listen, you…"

Helen grabbed the coffee pot with a grip that reminded you it could be a weapon. "Grace," she said, "get back in the kitchen!"

I was walking away by then, but I heard Helen's voice loud and clear behind me, saying, "Blanche, you sit down and order something or else you get the hell out of my restaurant!"

"You're going to *excuse* what she did?"

"I didn't say that," Helen replied. I couldn't believe I'd heard her right! What the hell was I supposed to have done, anyway? "All I'm saying," Helen went on, "is that this is a place of business and if you're in here, you need to have some business to do."

"Well, that's just fine," Blanche told Helen angrily. "You tell your little cook to get me some steak and eggs over easy, and I'll have a Bloody Mary from the bar so I can celebrate this town losing the best man who ever lived here, thanks to her."

My hands were shaking as I cooked Blanche's order. How dare she hold me responsible for Francisco! He was a grown man, in his forties. If he wanted to pick up and move away from his hometown just because some girl said she wouldn't go out with him, how the hell was that my fault?

I slammed her eggs up on the pass-through. Then I stalked out the kitchen door and went to my cabin to kick something and slam around until I calmed down.

But before any calming down had happened, the cabin door flew open behind me.

I rushed over and tried to push it shut, but Blanche was strong and fast for her age. She got one foot over the threshold and shoved the door hard enough that I had to either step back, or knock her down to keep her out.

"That's just like you, running from a fight!" She strode into the center of the room like it was a big stage, and flung her extravagant arms out. The flesh jiggled, her tattoos shimmied—all of her was vibrating with righteous anger. "You don't care how bad you hurt people!"

I said, "You're not talking about Francisco."

"You were supposed to keep him in town," she snarled, "not humiliate him into leaving."

That was the first I'd heard of her little plan. It kicked up both my guilt and my temper. "We spent one night together," I shot back, "ONE goddamn night, and it was *your idea*!"

"Worst idea I ever had! If I'd known you were a using little bitch…"

"Using?! *You* were using *me* to try and keep him around."

"Yeah, well I was a dumb-ass fool. You're not good enough to kiss his feet!"

"You bitch." I'd had enough of her shit. "You were just too scared to fuck him yourself!"

She flinched, and then she slapped me hard enough to spin my head halfway 'round. I twisted it back and flexed my jaw, testing the muscles, glowering at her.

"You know it's true," I spat out through the pain. "You wouldn't have hit me if it wasn't."

Her eyes glittered with the same malice I felt. "And you know what *I* said is true, or you wouldn't have pushed me into hitting you."

She walked out the door and I slammed it shut behind her. Then I staggered to the chair and sat there, dazed, taking careful stock.

My neck hurt bad. My face felt like she might have left a welt on it. I cradled my bruised cheek in my right hand and sat there thinking that I wasn't half as smart as I figured. I'd never noticed that Blanche was left-handed. I'd never thought she would be so bitter. I'd never guessed how she felt about Francisco.

And here was a thought: If Blanche hated me this much now, there was surely worse to come. Already, I'd stopped zipping my jeans and was closing them with a safety pin. It was only a matter of time 'till Blanche realized that I wasn't getting fat for no reason, and maybe started wondering why I'd been so hell-bent to avoid Francisco.

Well, she can wonder all she wants! I thought. Nobody knew who my baby's father was—not even me, though I had a powerful intuition. And nobody's half-baked, hostile suspicions were going to stop me from spending the next six months in Wagon Wheel with a good job, free meals, a place to sleep and friends of a sort. *Fuck you,* I hissed at Blanche in my mind. *I'm not going anywhere to make you comfortable.*

I dragged myself back over to Finer Diner, where Helen looked at me cautiously. "Put some ice on that cheek," was all she said, and then she went over to work in the bar. No one else would meet my eye, and I wondered how much everyone had heard. The cabin wasn't exactly soundproof, and Blanche and I had been pretty loud.

For the next few days, I did my best to ignore the disapproval I felt swirling all around me. Helen talked to me in short sentences. Emily was nowhere to be seen. Valerie tried to act normal, but you could see she was conflicted and upset. Even the people in town that I didn't know well appeared to be giving me a wider berth. They lowered their voices when I walked by.

Well, I wasn't going to let their attitude bug me. I had what I wanted, no mistake. And I needed to protect Marcusette. I wasn't going to leave here just because Blanche had turned some people against me, blaming me for something that wasn't my fault. So I held my tongue and ignored the looks and tried to treat people like everything was fine.

That lasted about a week, until Val and I were setting up lunch one day and I blurted out, "Are people *still* pissed at me about that thing with Blanche?"

She shook her head. "Naw. They know she started it."

"Then why's everybody still mad at me?"

Valerie stopped what she was doing, which was filling ketchup bottles, and turned to look straight at me and said, "Francisco was somebody we counted on, that's why." The way she said it, more than her actual words, told me she'd rehearsed this in her mind.

"Somebody you counted on for *what*?" I didn't mean to sound dumb or surly: For all that he was dark and middle-aged, I knew that Francisco had been Wagon Wheel's fair-haired boy, while I was just some trash girl from nowhere who'd supposedly driven him out of town. What I didn't understand was why people were taking it so *personally*.

"We counted on him for being there, I guess." She patted her round belly absently. Val was getting big enough that I wasn't sure how much longer she'd be working, and then I really would be talking to Homer's cook stove for lack of human company. "Francisco was a really nice guy. There wasn't a person in town he didn't help out, one time or another. And he knew how to make a woman feel special just by smiling at you or by how he said your name. I guess we looked to him for that."

I said, "Val, I didn't *do* anything to him!" I hadn't planned to defend myself, but I was sick of all the rumors. "He asked me if I thought we could maybe get together and I said no, which is the truth. What was I supposed to do, string him along? I didn't think he'd *go away.* "

"Thing is," Valerie said, looking suddenly older than her age, which I figured was twenty-three, tops, "he was so lonely after his wife died. And then he met you, and when you came back to town, he must have thought you were his big chance. You know how that is, right? It doesn't hurt when you don't want anything, but when you start wanting stuff, it hurts real bad."

Marcus had once said something similar: *"You ever notice how one minute you're solid as a rock, got everything covered, and then when you let your guard down, that's when the feelings hit you?"*

"No. I never noticed that," I'd told him.

And he'd said, "Well, maybe you never let your guard down."

With an effort, I pushed Marcus's voice away, willing myself back to Finer Diner.

Valerie was looking at me funny. "Gracie, you all right?"

"Yeah," I lied. My head was fuzzy. I felt like I was truly seeing Valerie for the first time. "You just surprised me, that's all. You don't usually talk like that."

She looked embarrassed. "Like what?"

"All philosophical."

"Well, hell," Val said, pointing to the tray of bright red bottles she'd been filling, "how philosophical can you get about ketchup?"

I thought about what she'd said all day and in the end I decided that Valerie was on to something. Francisco hadn't really known me—not any better than I'd known him—so it stood to reason that it couldn't have been *me*, my rejection, that had flung him out of Wagon Wheel and into a new, improved life in California. I was just the one who'd made him hope for something better. I was just the wake-up call, the bell that had sounded on the day he was listening.

Understanding that, I stopped feeling guilty—at least for his leaving. I had more patience for the people who were mad at me, knowing I wasn't the real source of their problem. I even stopped brooding over how I would get back at Blanche. Not that I would have *done* anything to get back at her, I knew that would only have made matters worse, but it was easier now not to fantasize about all the nasty things I could have done.

I kept my head high and kept plodding along. And gradually, I felt the tension around me, the silent accusations, begin to fade.

When Emily finally came back one morning for a bowl of oatmeal and some talk about recipes, I took the first deep breath I'd drawn in weeks. And the day she brought me some beef bones to simmer with parsley for a brown stock, I knew things would eventually be all right.

The one person I didn't try to win back, the one person I knew wasn't going to budge no matter who else got over what they thought I'd done, was Blanche. She didn't speak and she didn't acknowledge me, but sometimes when she came in to eat—which she did once a day now, though never again when Val and Helen were out—sometimes I'd catch her peeking at me like she was trying to figure something out, or like she was waiting for me to speak.

Well, I wasn't planning to speak to her, so she could wait 'till hell froze over.

Meanwhile, the lack of people to talk to had given me more time to think about myself. 'Till now, I'd barely noticed my *condition*—I'd noticed the nausea, the morning sickness, the bouts of weariness and wild emotion, but I'd noticed them like you notice the flu. I hadn't thought much about being *pregnant*.

Now, in what I assumed was month four, I felt like I'd crossed a subtle divide. There was a reason my body had gone haywire; somebody else was sharing it with me. Much as part of me didn't want to face that, the signs were getting stronger every day. Even though I didn't look pregnant yet, my stomach was hard and beginning to swell. My breasts were sore, my legs and feet thicker. Once in a while, lying in bed, I'd feel a little fizz of movement—nothing you could put your finger on, just a little tadpole sensation—a streak, a twinge, a harbinger. I'd always moved easily, had good balance. Now my back felt pulled-upon. My arms and legs were out of whack. I felt like Blondell had looked when she was learning how to park Dena's truck: Not sure where the perimeter was, and a little afraid to find out.

On the plus side, I was incredibly grateful that my bladder had settled down. There are just some moments when you can't leave a short-order kitchen to go and pee. Feeling less pressure in that direction made it easier to do my job. And now that the morning sickness was gone, too, this was an easy time physically.

I desperately needed new clothes, though. My t-shirts had stains that wouldn't come out, no matter how often I washed them. Those endless hours on my feet had blown out the cushioning in my sneakers. My underwear was way too tight. I needed those polyester pregnant pants.

After we closed up one night, I spoke to Helen about shopping. She had warmed back up a lot since the day after my yelling match with Blanche. I wouldn't have said we were back to normal, but I didn't have to tiptoe around her anymore.

"Maybe you should ask Val," she said, when I asked her to recommend an inexpensive place for clothes. "She knows where to get maternity things."

"Whoa!" I sat down heavily at the counter. I hadn't told her I was pregnant! "Helen, what are you talking about?"

Helen took a Salem out of the pack she always carried in her apron pocket. She never actually smoked unless we were closed for the night or she was paying bills, but sometimes when she'd pat that pocket you could see how bad she wanted to.

She lit the cigarette, inhaling with her whole body. "Maternity clothes," she said matter-of-factly. "That's what you're looking for, right?"

I didn't say anything—*couldn't* say anything.

"Back when Val first said you were pregnant, we all thought she was nuts, I'll tell you."

God, I was an idiot! I hadn't been near a mirror in months. But just because I was in denial didn't mean the whole town of Wagon Wheel was, too. "When did Valerie say that?" I ventured. "When did she say she thought I was pregnant?"

"That first day you came back here."

"But I wasn't showing then!"

Helen shrugged. "She said she could tell. Something about the way you moved when you got up from the front step after Homer's funeral." Helen too another drag and carefully exhaled away from me. "I guess that's what got Francisco's hopes up, 'cause you sure weren't giving him the time of day. But he always wanted children so bad that maybe he thought, with you being alone and pregnant, you might want a man to help out."

"Oh, my God." I dropped my head into my hands and closed my eyes, fighting humiliation. All those scenes with Blanche and Francisco. I'd been so sure of my little secret, and now it turned out they'd probably both known.

"It's all right, Grace," Helen said. "You've got a right to your privacy."

"I don't... I'm really sorry, Helen. I'm sorry for all the trouble I brought."

She said, "You got nothing to apologize for. You work hard. You mind your own business."

We sat there in silence while she finished her smoke. "Talk to Val," Helen finally said. "Maybe she'll take you to the store."

I didn't do it right away, though. It took me days to get over the feeling I was wearing a big sign that said STUPID GIRL. I felt like, if I said anything to Valerie, it would prove that people had been right about me.

But later that week, my safety pin broke and I had to start holding my jeans up with string. So finally, I spoke to Valerie, who just said sure, if I could kick in for gas money she'd take me shopping, she needed a couple of things herself.

That's how, early the next Sunday morning, Valerie, her toddler Stephanie and I got into Val's old car and drove toward a department store that Val liked over the line in Kingman. I was happy to get out of Wagon Wheel and "see the sights," though Valerie told me that mostly what there was to see was more desert.

Valerie was wrong, though. To my shock, the first thing we came to when we crossed the state line into Arizona was a big lake.

"That water's down from Lake Mead," Valerie explained. "They boat on it and everything. It's just like mountain stream water—so cold you think you're going to freeze your ass, but it's so hot here no one minds."

She parked the car at a scenic vista, and we got out and walked to the end of a lot that looked down over the shoreline. A dirt path with stone steps wound down to the shore. Below us, hundreds of people were spread out.

Valerie held Stephanie in her arms. I stood beside them and stared down at all that blue. It was the first open water I'd seen since Marcus and I walked on the beach in Bolinas more than a million lifetimes ago. That day had been gentle, quiet, private. This place was a madhouse, with crowds of people in bathing suits and t-shirts gathered all along the shoreline, swimming, playing frisbee, blasting their radios, cooking food on portable grills.

"It's Columbus Day weekend," Valerie explained, as if I was a visitor from another planet. "People are hunkered down for three days of fun."

I pictured a calendar in my mind, with a big star in the middle of October. Marcus had been dead six months. His baby would come near the end of winter.

"Mommy, ride!" said little Stephanie, staring at the water with a longing that stirred in me.

"We can't ride, Baby," her young mother said. "We don't have a boat to go on."

"Swim!" Stephanie wriggled, desperate to jump in.

Valerie just looked embarrassed. "I don't know how to swim," she told me. "Never had any call for it, living in the desert."

I eyed Stephanie warily. I knew how to swim, a little. But if I volunteered to take Stephanie in the water, it would mean having close contact with her—something I'd carefully avoided in the car. "And we don't have bathing suits," Valerie added. Maybe she'd seen my uncertain glance.

That was going to be my way out. I would shrug and say, *yeah, we don't have bathing suits.* I didn't need to get close to a two-year-old. I didn't need to put myself through the pain of touching her, talking to her, seeing her as a real person and not a grubby extension of Valerie. I really didn't need that.

Or did I? Something burned behind my eyelids, something that wasn't from the glaring sun, wasn't from exhaustion, wasn't going to go away. In less than five months, I would have my own child—a child who would want to be touched and talked to. A child who would deserve to be loved. Not a house for my ghosts to inhabit. Not a chance to make restitution. A small, strong person who would squirm and want and demand and give, like Stephanie.

Suddenly, I couldn't believe what I'd done! How was I going to raise a child when I could barely look at Valerie's daughter?

"Grace?" Valerie's voice was tentative. Her hand on my forearm was light as a bird's wing. "Are you OK?"

No, no, I'm not OK! I've done terrible things, and I'm about to do another one.

"I'm just tired." I studied my sneakers. "You know we work too hard."

"You got that straight," Valerie seconded.

Over Stephanie's wailed objections, we walked back to the battered car. The seats were painfully hot on our skin after just a few minutes without AC. The air was stale and burning hot, compared to the clean-smelling breeze off the lake.

Valerie rolled her window down. "Let's go shop," she said with forced cheerfulness.

"Sure thing." I sat with my eyes closed, feeling the killer sun on my face, feeling sick about what was going to happen next. There was money burning a hole in my pocket—everything I'd earned that month, minus the $20 I sent Lillian each week—and I knew that, after I'd bought some shirts and a sweatshirt and pregnant pants and waitress shoes, I would buy cheap bathing suits for all three of us. I would buy them because Valerie couldn't, because she was a friend, because of Stephanie. And then we would drive back to this lot and park the car and walk down the path and the three of us would wade into Lake Mead together. There was no way to resist that blue allure. And there would be no way to resist the moment when Stephanie jumped into my arms and I walked out with her, deeper than Val would dare to go. I could already imagine the weight of her body wriggling against me, an accusation. She would squirm and kick and giggle and grab me, squealing with delight. Muscles would bunch in those pudgy arms and legs that were real, that were strong, that were alive with feeling—even though I wasn't and might never be again.

twenty-five

Early in November, I put my last payment to Lillian and Joe in an envelope. That was the end of what I owed them, and it would have been the end, period, except that after I'd sealed the letter and tossed it into the wire basket that Helen used for outgoing mail, something made me take it out again.

Lillian, I scrawled on the back of the envelope,

I'm settled for a while in a good town, Wagon Wheel. I just wanted you to know I'm doing OK. Please hug Anna May for me and tell Joe I said hey. Goodbye and good luck. Your friend,

Gracie

It was scary to write even that much, but I wanted Lillian to know I was safe. And truthfully, I wanted Joe to think about me, because I thought about him every day. Thinking about Joe was most of what kept me going through a pretty lonely time, and if this note was the last contact I was ever going to have with him and Lillian, I wanted them to remember me, remember that I was alive out here, somewhere.

Alive, of course, was a qualified description. After that day at the lake with Stephanie, I'd gone into a long, long numbness. My early pregnancy in Dena's truck, with its constant nausea, constant grief and constant mothering from Dena and Blondell, had yielded to the isolation and routine of my new life in Wagon Wheel: work, sleep, work, sleep, work, feel guilty, work, sleep.

Not that it bothered me; aside from the loneliness and regret, I didn't have any particular complaints. I was eating good food, sleeping in a real bed, not in much pain most of the time. I was surrounded by pretty nice people, people I could chat with easily. If there was no one I could really talk to, like I did with Joe or Blondell, it was still more than I'd expected to have again; still more than I deserved.

Things were easy physically, too. My skin broke out, my hair was greasy, sometimes I felt tired enough to sleep standing up. But mostly that was no big deal, and the weariness was a blessing of sorts. Sometimes I wanted to sit down and cry, but since I didn't have time, I toughed it out and the feeling always passed, eventually. Everything in that second trimester passed eventually, except for the low-grade, constant sensation that I was making a terrible mistake.

Toward the beginning of month six, in late November, my belly suddenly popped out. It was hard to believe that, just six weeks earlier, I'd thought it was possible that people didn't know. Now I was half-waddling, half-dragging my bulk around the kitchen. The polyester pants whose waistband had been gigantic on Columbus Day were beginning to feel a little snug, and when I peeked over my looming stomach, I could barely see the toes of my sturdy Clark Wallabie waitress shoes.

People who didn't know me started asking when the baby was due. People who knew me started asking when I was going to get a wheelbarrow to haul my belly around. The joking was a tremendous relief, because it meant that everyone (except, of course, Blanche) had forgiven me for that business with Francisco. Maybe they couldn't hold a grudge against a woman with a baby on the way. Or maybe they were just nice people and couldn't hold a grudge for too long, period.

Either way, I was grateful for their tolerance, because I had my hands full emotionally: After weeks of hide-and-seek on the road, after months of quiet in Wagon Wheel, Rosie had come back with a vengeance to haunt the edges of my dreams.

How she'd changed in the months we were apart! It almost seemed like she was growing up. Could the dead grow up that way, or was it that our relationship had shifted? Gone were the blatant, angry gestures: the scalding vats of chemicals, the storms that stripped my skin away, the endless, frightening Gothic horrors that woke me screaming, bathed in sweat. Gone were the rites over Marcus's corpse, the doomsday pronouncements, the scathing pity. And gone was her baby image. I could feel her thinking, taste her breath and sense the chill of her intent—but I couldn't see her, or speak to her. She hovered just outside my sight. She didn't answer when I called.

I didn't know what this new Rosie wanted. I didn't know what she was capable of. Would she try to drive me mad? Would she kill the baby, or make me do it? Her contempt—or perhaps that was mine—was just as caustic as ever. But now I could feel a showdown coming. I'd never been more scared in my life.

Helen thought the job was making me tired. Valerie said it was just pregnancy. Emily begged me to eat more meat, and even said I should go see a doctor. They didn't know that I barely half-slept, on guard all night against Rosie's vengeance.

In mid-December, Valerie had a little boy. Stephanie made Val name him Gus; or maybe Stephie was trying to say something altogether different and Val just heard it as "Gus" and liked the sound of it. Stephanie wasn't a big talker, and when she did say something we mostly had to guess what it was, but she always managed to get her point across. Val had been hoping for a Christmas baby, but she and her husband were just as happy to get a healthy one on December 17th. Helen gave her two weeks of leave, which Valerie seemed to mostly spend sleeping. When we opened up on New Years Day, she was there with Gus and an old egg crate. She lined it with a stack of newspapers and put a warm fuzzy blanket on top, set the whole thing on the counter, put Gus in it and went back to work. Every few minutes one of us would come by and chuck him on the chin, make a face, tell him a silly story. Even I did it, to my surprise, since I didn't really see Gus as a person. To me he was more a collection of sounds and smells, a little pink thing lying in a crate that had "Our Chickens Eat Corn" stamped on both sides. I could go for days without thinking that Marcusette was due in ten weeks. I could look at Gus for hours without remembering that Rosie had started out like him.

The worst thing about little Gus being born was the baby shower that Helen gave Valerie. Two days after Val came back to work, Helen closed the diner early so that we could celebrate.

Every woman in Wagon Wheel came, and all of us brought whatever present fit our budgets and imaginations. Helen gave Valerie a gift certificate to the department store in Kingman. Emily gave her two dozen jars of baby food she'd made herself. I gave Val a fancy bottle of bubble bath I'd sneaked into my cart that day she took me shopping.

Blanche, to my surprise, gave her a little blue blanket for baby Gus. It was handmade, from thin, soft-looking yarn, and scalloped around the edges in a dainty kind of pattern that made me think of both Mary Jo's and Dena's taste in home decorating.

"This is beautiful, Blanche," Valerie gushed, and she smiled and wrapped Gus right up in it. "I didn't know you could knit like that."

Blanche gave her a crooked grin. "I have my secrets, like everyone else," she said. I thought she was talking about me.

After all the presents were given out, Helen poured everyone a glass of wine and I cut up a big chocolate sheet cake with Gus's name written in vanilla frosting. People took their plates and drifted off, and suddenly I was standing at the food table—alone, except for Blanche.

"Nice blanket," I said. My voice sounded rusty. Blanche and I hadn't said a word to each other since our encounter in my cabin. I don't know what prompted me to speak now, except for my sense that we couldn't go on like this forever.

She nodded, acknowledging the compliment without looking directly at me. That's why I didn't see it coming; if she'd looked at me, I would have read it in her eyes. "Is that Francisco's baby you're carrying?" she asked, reaching past me for another piece of cake.

My stomach dropped. I didn't know what to do. For months after coming back to town, I'd waited for someone to ask me that question. But now that so much time had passed, I guess I'd figured I was safe.

Having no idea what to say, I said the first thing that came to my mind: "No."

Blanche gave me a disgusted look. "You must think you're the only person in the world who can count," she said, and walked away.

A few days later, a letter came. It was addressed to "The Gang at Finer Diner," and Helen read it out loud at lunchtime. She made people stop playing their slots so that folks in the casino could hear it, too.

Dear Friends, the letter began,

I hope this finds everybody well. You are a fine group of people, and I appreciate that even more after settling down in a new place.

To my relief, Boron is a lot like Wagon Wheel, though it's bigger and better irrigated and doesn't have any slot machines.

I snuck a look around the room, and wasn't surprised to see a lot of people smiling. I wanted to crawl under the table, dreading what else Francisco might say.

The mine I'm working in is where they get the mineral that's used in 20 Mule Team Borax, the laundry powder the President used to advertise. The mining company's expanding right now, which is why they needed new engineers.

I think I'm going to like it here, but I hope you won't all forget me. I'm sending you my new address in case any of you are ever out this way, or want to write. Come visit me, and I'll show you the sights in a big town of 2000 people. There's even a giant picture window up at the mine's Visitor Center's where you can look right into the excavation.

Until I see you, be well, everyone. You're in my heart and my memories,

Francisco

That was it, except that Helen announced he'd sent his address and phone number. I looked around again and thought I saw a lot of people avoiding my eyes. Not Blanche, though. Her eyes were boring through me, probably to see if I showed a guilty reaction.

That was a tough day for me, but not much tougher than many of the others. By now, being pregnant was challenging again. I didn't recognize the violence of my own moods. Sometimes it was hard to breathe with Marcusette pushing up against my lungs. My bladder felt constantly ready to explode. My lower back ached from holding up that big belly. Valerie said I should lie down sometimes, but I couldn't do that in the kitchen, so I started squatting down between orders, wrapping my arms around my bent knees and tucking my head down for a change of position. That worked well, but it was hard to get up again, with all the front-loaded extra weight, and one time, when Helen came into the kitchen too fast, I couldn't get out of her way and she almost fell over me.

"What are you doing on the floor?" she growled, a tray of dirty glasses teetering on her arm where she'd come to a dead halt, two inches behind me.

"Stretching," I mumbled, trying to figure out how to get up off the floor without knocking into her.

She took a breath, then stepped around me. "How can you be stretching when you're all curled up like a rattlesnake?" She set her tray down next to the sink.

I uncoiled myself with a sigh and, taking the hand she offered, rose shakily to my feet. "My back's the part that's getting stretched. It hurts," I added, sulking a little.

She gave me a look that was half sympathy, half sternness. "Don't you go having that baby in my kitchen."

"I won't," I promised, picking up my spatula and shooing her away from my stove. Just where and how I was going to have this baby was a subject I'd been trying to avoid, and I didn't see any need to tell her about the sharp twinge of pain from my womb that had driven me into this particular stretch. "I'm not due for weeks and weeks yet."

"Good," she said. "I need that time to find someone to replace you."

I ignored that, knowing full well that Helen wouldn't have anyone to replace me when Marcusette came. An hour after she was born, Helen would probably be hassling me to strap the baby on my back and get ready for the dinner rush.

One day, another letter arrived. This one was addressed to me personally, or rather addressed to:

GRACIE
WAGON WHEEL, NEVADA

"I guess this is for you," Helen said, handing it over as she sorted through the day's mail.

I put it in my apron pocket and went about my business, trying to pretend it wasn't there. Trying to pretend I wasn't scared of what Lillian Rollins had to say to me, even though I'd basically asked for it.

The rest of that day seemed to last forever, but finally we got the last customers fed, the kitchen cleaned, the place closed for the night. I went back to the cabin and locked the door behind me before sitting down on my chair. Normally, this would have been my laundry night, but laundry was going to have to wait.

Gracie,

It was great to hear that you're doing well. I hope you don't mind me tracking you down. It turns out there's only one place called Wagon Wheel in the whole country, and I felt that if you truly didn't want to be found, you wouldn't have told me the name of the town.

Anna May sends her love. You would be proud of how she's doing. She studies every day to be ready to start high school in September and I think she's going to do well. I have to confess that when I first met Anna May, I thought she would be a slow learner. Now I'm seeing that what I (and maybe you) took to be a low intellect was actually the result of trauma and isolation. I don't know if she'll ever fit in with people her own age—she's been through too much to relate to young girls—but her reading and writing are getting better, and I think she'll be able to graduate eventually. She's very drawn to learning, and she talks about you a lot and how smart you are and how much she wants to be like you.

Joe has been having a difficult time. Shortly after you left, Fred Coombs arrested him for possession of cocaine. I know that sounds cruel, but Fred is a true friend to Joe. You probably knew that Joe was using cocaine, and Fred apparently knew for a while before he decided that things were out of control and he had to step in. Joe was able to plea-bargain for probation and community service, but he had to resign as sheriff, and that was very hard for him. He went out to a rehab clinic near San Francisco (that's where you're from, isn't it?) and decided to stay out there and try to pull himself back together. I sent him your postcards, and I think he was glad to hear from you. Joe likes you a lot, but then you know that. I'm not trying to pry into your business, but I'm enclosing his current address and phone number. If you ever want to be in touch with him and he's moved on from there, give me a call. I hope I'll always know where to find him.

I have to say that it's lonely here without him. If it wasn't for Anna May, I'm not sure what I would do. I'm grateful to you for bringing her into my life, Grace. I probably wouldn't say this if you weren't so far away, but I feel that, with her, I have a chance to redeem some of the mistakes I made with Joe's mother. Back then, I was so busy proving myself—there wasn't much middle ground for a woman in my younger days—but she was the one to suffer for it, and now Joe is suffering, too.

So, as you can see, it's a complicated story, but one that benefited from your influence. Gracie, I hope and feel confident that you're building a life you can look back on with pride, and I hope you'll stay in touch with us.

With warmest regards,
Your good friend Lillian

I almost wanted to cry, reading that. I could picture Lillian at her desk in that room with all the leather-bound books, feeling guilty because she hadn't known that Joe was strung out and needed help.

I could have told her how useless that guilt was. Joe hadn't wanted to listen to me, and he wouldn't have listened to Lillian, either. No one could make an addict turn, though sometimes you could throw up a wall that stopped them, like Fred had done when he busted Joe.

Part of me wanted to write and say that, but what was the point of dragging things out? And what if I was wrong about Francisco; what if *Joe* was Marcusette's father? Wouldn't it be better for everyone if Joe and Lillian never knew that he had a kid with a murderer who couldn't love and couldn't sleep and would never feel safe walking on this earth?

No, they didn't need the burden of my life.

After Lillian's letter, it was all downhill. I ached with loneliness, with fear, with pregnancy. My nerves were delicate, my mind disordered. People's voices were too loud. Their orders sounded like a foreign language. I couldn't stand straight, couldn't sit, couldn't walk; I was desperate to jump out of my skin. I dragged myself through every day hoping that it would all end soon, and sat through each night like a crazed vigilante, ready to fire if Rosie showed herself.

It was early February, and cold at night. I wouldn't have thought it, with the sun still burning so fierce all day, but at dusk the temperature dropped fifty degrees and there was nothing to block the wind that came through every crack between the boards in the cabin. I lived in the sweatshirt I'd bought in Kingman, and huddled under my jacket all night, and still it wasn't enough. All the energy my body made was going to Marcusette.

The temperature was particularly frightening because so many of my old dreams had been cold. Cold was something that sucked you in, that snaked through you, that you drowned in like bleach. Each morning I'd get up half-dead and rush to the kitchen in Finer Diner to turn on the stove and drink hot water 'till I had to pee so bad it streamed out like a pressurized hose. I turned on all the gas jets and cranked the oven up, and when Helen objected, I told her that I needed to thaw out my hands. Finally one day she went into her storage boxes and found two extra blankets for me.

With the end so near now, Marcusette was trying to bust out—or else, she was learning karate. She had a tough little foot (unless that was her butt) that she'd smack up against the front of my womb 'till it pushed far enough out for me to feel it. Sometimes I'd catch myself thinking that it was no wonder she was big and strong, given that her father had been solid as a brick wall. But then I'd remember that Marcus wasn't really her father, and then I'd have to watch myself so I didn't start crying on someone's stuffed pork chops.

More than any time since Blondell had almost kicked my door down back in San Francisco, I felt completely alone in the world. I was far from the only woman who'd ever struggled through the last few weeks of pregnancy, but didn't most of them have someone to talk to? A partner, or at least a friend?

I had none of those things, not really. Emily liked me, Valerie appreciated my companionship, Helen valued my work at the diner. That was about the extent of it. Six months spent alone in the kitchen hadn't produced any new friendships, though I'd met a lot of nice people. Making friends hadn't been my strong suit at the best of times, and now that I needed one, needed one badly, I'd woven such a thick web of *keep out* signs, it wouldn't have been easy to let someone through, even if someone had been trying to reach me.

Still, I was grateful for what I had. A job. A roof. Warm clothes, good food. People around me, even if they weren't too close. Nobody trying to use or oppress me. I thought of what Anna May had been through, and knew I was a lucky woman. I'd had love, and I'd had friendship, even if I never had either again. And whatever else the last year had brought, I'd seen a lot of pretty country.

Late in February, a package arrived from Francisco, once again addressed to *The Gang at Finer Diner.* Helen took me aside near closing time and asked if I wanted to see the letter that came with it before she read it out loud to everyone.

"No," I told her, my stomach tightening. "It doesn't matter to me what he said."

"Suit yourself."

She banged a big spoon on the counter until everybody in the place quieted down.

"We got a letter from Francisco," she announced loudly. "I'm gonna read it, so everyone settle down, and if you don't know Francisco you can settle down anyway."

It always surprised me that people were so quick to fall in line when given a direct order, but I guess in this case they were curious, too. Blanche and a handful of other folks who'd been in the casino wandered over and everyone in the diner hushed up. Most people also stopped whatever they were doing, but I had a few orders left to fill. Fortunately—if you wanted to look at it that way—Helen's voice was loud, so I could keep working quietly and still hear what Francisco had to say.

Dear Friends,

> *I hope this finds everybody well and happy. I am settling nicely into my new home. Boron is a lovely town, with lots of greenery, as well as good schools, many churches, and friendly people (more on that in a minute).*

> *My new job is varied and interesting. When I wrote last time, I told you about Borax. But borates, which are what we mine, are important in the manufacture of everything from gold to ceramics to paint, fertilizer, make-up, adhesives—it's a very long list of things, so I'll just say that this mine has been in operation for over 100 years now, and if we manage it correctly, it might last another 100.*

> *With this letter, I'm including some samples of calcium-sodium borate, which they give out free as a souvenir when you come to the Visitor's Center. You'll have to come in person to get the whole explanation, but trust me, this is not what it looks like coming out of the ground!*

> *I'm also enclosing a few other presents, too. Valerie, I know that you must have had your baby by now. I hope that he or she is doing fine and that Stephanie is enjoying being the "grown-up" one. This book,* **Goodnight Moon,** *is for you to read to her, although I'll bet she'll be reading to you one of these days, and the diaper bag is for your baby.*

> *Blanche, I am sending you a sample of the cigarettes that some of the Mojave Indians around here smoke. They're mostly tobacco,*

but they have a few other natural things, and they don't have the chemicals in regular cigarettes. I'm told they taste pretty good, and if you like them, I'll send you a big supply. (Or you can drive out some time and pick it up!)

Well now for my big news. You may think this is a little precipitous (hasty), since I've only lived here four months, but last week I got married.

There was a loud gasp from more than one person in the diner, followed by the sound of me cursing in pain. I'd jolted the spatula I was holding and flipped some hot grease back onto my left forearm.

"Grace, are you all right?" Helen called out.

By then I was at the sink, running cold water over my arm. "Yeah, I just got a little burn." The water wasn't cold like it should be to stop a burn from blistering. I turned it off and went to the stand-alone freezer for ice.

"Well, why don't you come out here?" Helen called. "I can't read with you wreckin' the joint…"

Reluctantly, I came out of the kitchen with an ice-filled towel pressed on my arm, and sat down at a table near Helen where Valerie and two local men—Ralph and Bunchie, brothers who lived at Paradise Mobile Homes, near Blanche—were sitting. I tried not to notice where Blanche was, but of course that was useless; her energy was like a beacon, pointing me to the last table on the left where she sat next to Emily and another woman I'd met but only half-remembered.

My wife's name is Sarah Jane Winslow, Helen continued reading. *She was the first person I met out here—she's a high school English teacher, but she gives tours at the Visitor's Center on Saturday mornings, and that's where they did my new employee orientation. She's a widow (her first husband was a foreman at the mine who died three years ago) and she has two beautiful children, Damian, who's 7, in the second grade, and LizAnn, who's 5 and just started kindergarten this year. LizAnn and Damian are both solid, outgoing kids, in spite of losing their father*

*at such young ages. I guess that says more than anything else about
the kind of person and mother Sarah Jane is, so you can see why
I'm so happy. I feel blessed to have found this wonderful family,
and I'm enclosing a picture of the four of us, in case you're curious
to see what they look like.*

There was more—a conventional goodbye—but I'd stopped listening. Helen had passed a photograph to Valerie, who smiled as she studied it, then handed it to Ralph, who handed it to Bunchie, who handed it to...

I glanced down at Bunchie's weathered hand. He might as well have been passing me a stick of dynamite as the cheerful image that winked up at me before I could turn my head away: Francisco had his arm around a small blond woman in her mid-to-late 30s. Each of them was holding one of their healthy-looking, tow-headed children. Everybody in the picture was smiling.

I handed it to Valerie, stood up and walked back to the kitchen, ignoring the buzz of voices behind me.

Helen came in a minute later, carrying her first aid kit.

"Give me your arm," she said, reaching for it.

"Go away, I'm working," I snarled.

Helen sighed, which wasn't like her. "Don't be such an ass, Gracie. Give me your arm and let me disinfect it."

Since she was the boss, I stuck my arm out. She splashed some burning liquid on it, followed by an antibiotic cream, and covered it with an oversized Band-Aid.

"Don't take it personally," she said.

I said, "Helen, get the fuck out of my kitchen."

After she'd gone, I slammed around a little. It was late, and no one was ordering. By rights, I should have been closing up, but I wanted to hide out in private and lick my wounds 'till Finer Diner was totally empty.

I couldn't believe how humiliated I felt. Damn Francisco, to make me *burn* myself. How could he have done such a thing? Sweet, slow-moving, conservative Francisco—how could he have married some woman he barely knew, with kids to boot? It was way too much for me to understand.

And how was I ever going to show my face again, after being so publicly kicked aside?

Of course, I knew that was stupid thinking. Francisco's life was nothing to me. And how did I think things should have been different? Was I supposed to have married him? Was he supposed to have stayed single forever? Would I feel better if this had happened, say, when Marcusette was two years old?

This entire line of thought was stupid, just like the frustrated tears I was blinking back. I'd done the right thing, the only thing I could do. I didn't love the guy, I didn't want the guy, I didn't belong with the guy and I'd told him so. Where was the crime, the error in that?

But oh, it hurt that he'd found Miss Perfect. High school teacher. Exemplary mother. Blond and petite and smart and well-educated. Stable and loving, the right age, the right style. She probably even owned a house.

All I would have brought Francisco was an unwanted baby, a minimum wage job, a murky past and a bad attitude. Was it any surprise that he'd done better?

Of course, technically, *I'd* turned *him* down, which was completely typical of me. I didn't know something good when I saw it; my principle skill was fucking things up. Yes, I was fast on my feet in a crisis—but as far as building a life, a future, you couldn't do worse, as Francisco had realized.

Come to think of it, maybe he wasn't the only one. Maybe it wasn't an accident that I didn't have one friend left in the world. Blondell had gone off with her lover, as any sensible person would have done. Blanche had completely stopped talking to me, and Emily and Helen just went through the motions. Valerie and I were friends-of-convenience, and that was the end of my list of relationships.

Even when somebody wanted to be my friend, I always screwed them up eventually. I hadn't been able to save Marcus, I hadn't been there for Joe when he needed me. Who the hell was my presence on earth helping? Exactly what the hell was I here for?

Disgusted, I turned off all the lights, locked up Finer Diner and dragged myself back to the cabin, where I threw my aching body on the bed. I wanted to close my eyes and sleep forever. I wanted the damned baby to stop kicking. Wasn't she supposed to have stopped by now? What did she think I was, a punching bag? Probably she wanted to get her licks in now. If I ended up killing her, like I'd killed Rosie, at least she'd have given me a few good punches.

Well, fuck that, I lay there thinking. *I never wanted a baby in the first place. All of this was Marcus's idea—a bad idea I'd been too grief-stricken to see through. Now we were all going to suffer for my stupidity, which was the usual way of things.*

God, what a mess I'd made of my life. I'd been fucked up from the day I was born, and having this baby was going to be like tying up the whole poisonous package with a big, floppy bow. Imagine the head case I'd turn her into—and that was the best way that things could turn out.

My stomach twanged, as if the baby was listening. *Yeah, I'm talking about you*, I snapped. *I didn't ask for you to get conceived, and I don't give a shit what happens to you.* Then I started crying like a crazy woman. The tears were like rainwater, washing me away. I couldn't stop the acid words, the feelings that scraped inside me like ground glass.

I must have cried myself into a stupor or fallen into exhausted sleep, 'cause the next thing I knew, Rosie was sitting beside me on the edge of the bed, all grown-up. *So this is your moment*, I thought. *Of course.*

Poised and beautiful, she grabbed my shoulder and shook me 'till I looked straight up at her. Then she kicked me in the stomach, hard.

"Snap out of it!" she sneered.

I wanted to curl up with pain, but my body wouldn't move. That's how I knew that I was either sleeping or dead.

"Snap out of what?" I spat. I'd never felt such hatred toward her. Of course, she'd never kicked me before.

"That's right," Rosie said. "Go ahead and blame me. It's my fault that you killed me when I was three years old. It's my fault that you're so pathetic. It's my fault that you can't get your head out of your butt long enough to do one decent thing with your life. It's *my* fault, 'cause I'm a big, bad three-year-old and you're just a sniveling piece of shit who can't get it together and can't figure out why."

If I hadn't cried every tear in my whole body, I would have been sobbing for mercy by then. Rosie had never attacked me directly. She'd stuck by me, comforted me, kept me company in dark times. Even these last months, as she'd waited just outside my dreams, she hadn't done anything more than threaten me.

Why was she turning on me now?

"Because I can read the future," she said. "You're probably going to kill this baby and if you don't, she'll wish you had. Every single day of her life, she's going to curse you for being her mother. She's going to curse you just like I do."

I screamed and woke up on my hands and knees like a dog, shivering, my eyes screwed shut, my head low, my mouth open to vomit up the life inside me. I knew that, if I looked down, I would see the baby lying blue and dead between my legs, as Rosie had lain on the floor that last time. But when I forced myself to open my eyes, there was no blood, no vomit, no dead baby, only a gush of milky water sloshing down my thighs to puddle on the dirty carpet.

That's when the first contraction kicked in.

Nothing I'd read or heard about had prepared me for how this really felt. I'd thought there would be some mild little warm-up, and then a few annoying twinges. This was like having my guts hosed with pain; like being snatched up by a giant pair of pliers.

"Get ready to die," I heard Rosie say, calmly. "You're going to suffer, and you deserve it."

Oh, no, I thought, collapsing back onto the bed in a pool of sweat and straining nerves. There was no point in living through this anguish, just to destroy another child's life. If Rosie could read the future—and why not?—this baby would never thank me for anything. She would never grow up to be happy. She would never escape the past.

The contraction was getting worse. If I'd had a doctor, I would have called her, and now I wondered why I didn't have one.

Because you fuck everything up, I thought. *You never meant to go through with this.*

My guts were twisted, and now it felt like the pliers were dipped in fire. I wasn't going to make it. I wasn't *supposed* to make it. I'd run for a long time from my punishment, but now the road had begun to unravel. The idea filled me with a strange peace. I'd always known it would come to this. Now I didn't have to fight it anymore.

When the pain finally died down, I stood up and pulled on my jacket against the early morning chill. I was dazed but lucid, filled with acceptance. This was how it must be to freeze to death—the cold that finally, inevitably, turned into a warm embrace. I put one foot in front of the other, wondering when the next contraction would come, and walked over to the little bathroom sink that had just enough room beneath it for one bottle.

When had I acquired that bottle? How long had this been living in the back of my mind? I took a glass from the medicine cabinet and stumbled back to the table and chair. *It's all right, Marcusette,* I thought. *We'll both be finished with this soon.*

I poured myself a glass of bleach and took a breath, preparing to drink it.

The smell engulfed me as I raised it to my lips. Clean and cutting, bitter and vile. How had Rosie endured that smell long enough to sip from the cup of death? How she must have wanted to please me! How I must have egged her on.

I was sobbing again, my body shaking. *Marcusette, I'm sorry,* I thought. *I'm sorry I can't be what you need.* My tears were falling into the glass, into the gray fog of a thousand dreams. My lips were closing on the rim. It would be like jumping off a roof. It would be like falling into grace. It would be like...

Another jolt of screaming pain ripped through me; the kind of pain you never dare to contemplate in waking life. And suddenly I knew, beyond the shadow of a doubt or prayer, that I couldn't go through with this, whether I deserved it or not. I couldn't steal Marcusette's life as she was literally clawing her way into the world.

I couldn't destroy her because I felt guilty.

And now the other voices came; ghost voices, dancing in a ring around me.

"You're my hero, Gracie-Grace," half-lisped in Anna May's childish voice.

Lillian saying, *"I think you're a good girl."*

Marcus's sister Mary Jo. *"He looked happy enough that time I saw you."*

And Marcus. *"I want you to have a baby."*

Remembering, I felt something rip apart inside—my heart, sliced open by light and memories, skittering to find some new place to stand. My stomach heaved and this time I *did* vomit, onto my hand that was holding the glass.

I jumped up and flung it all away, the glass, the bleach, the vomit, the past. I was staggering to the bathroom sink, half-sobbing, half-moaning in pain when the door of my little cabin flew open. I could hear someone walk in behind me.

Blanche found me sitting on the toilet, shaking like a rabid dog, water and puke and a few drops of bleach staining my jacket, my hair matted with sweat and tears, my eyes swollen with desperation.

"Jesus," she said, "you need a keeper."

"Come to gloat?" I couldn't look up at her.

"No, to apologize," she said, her scratched-up voice daring me to make something of it.

"No need," I murmured, drifting toward unconsciousness.

She ran hot water over my washcloth and wiped my face, then down my front. I was too exhausted, mentally and physically, to even think about slapping her hand away.

"Maybe not," she finished swiping at me, "but I probably should have stayed out of your business. You two seem to know what you're doing."

She meant Francisco. I nodded weakly. My eyes were rolling back in my head; my link to this world was getting tenuous. *It would be funny if I died now,* I thought, *right after deciding I don't want to.*

"Aren't you dramatic," Blanche said. Was that fear in her voice, beneath the phony disdain? "Wake up and get your shoes on, Gracie."

"Shoes…" My tongue felt like sludge. I didn't know if she'd heard me.

"Never mind, you can wear your slippers. But *hurry* up and get on your feet. I'm damned if I'm gonna carry you out of here."

"Carry…?"

"We're going to the hospital. *Now!*"

twenty-seven

When they first put Marcusette in my arms, all I could think was that she wasn't much bigger than a good-sized chicken. All 20 inches of her were curled into a tight ball and wrapped in a pink baby blanket that balanced easily on one of my hands. She lay against my still-heaving chest, her eyes screwed shut to keep out the overhead fluorescent lights. But even without seeing her eyes, I knew what I was looking at.

I read once that, before the continents settled into their current form, people walked from Asia to North America, bringing those broad, low cheekbones that showed up next in Native Americans and then—when Conquistadores enslaved the Indians—got spread throughout Central America. In silent tribute to Francisco, I reached out and gently traced my daughter's extraordinary cheekbones. They were soft and smooth and covered with a down so delicate it might have been fairy's breath. And the rest of her was just as beautiful: Her skin was pale, almost translucent, but you could see the faint brown undertone that was probably going to darken as she aged. Her head was covered with soft black silk. Her little rosebud mouth looked crinkly. I touched it with a shaking finger.

Maybe you've never had a kid. If not, you probably don't know how it changes you, how it picks you up out of your life and plops you down in another place, Planet Baby, a place where only two things matter: loving your child and keeping her safe.

I thought a lot about my mother in the days after Marcusette was born. I'd thought I understood about heroin, understood how powerful it was. But I didn't, not really, until I realized how thoroughly it had blocked my mother from feeling the love that I felt now. Heroin was obviously stronger than love. I was grateful it had never tempted me, and grateful beyond words for Marcus and the legacy of love he'd left me.

Marcusette and I went back to Wagon Wheel and, a few days later, as I'd predicted, she made her debut in Finer Diner. Helen didn't quite beg me to come back to work, but she stopped by my cabin several times each day and I could tell she was more than a little freaked out by the "No Food Today" sign on the diner's front door. So as soon as I felt like my insides had healed, we put another egg box next to Gus's and set up a nursery on the counter.

"It's only temporary," I told Helen. "You're going to have to replace me soon."

She said, "You can go whenever you want, but please teach somebody else to cook first."

Well, I owed her at least that much—she'd given me the best job I ever had—so the next day I started teaching Valerie, under the theory that you can always get someone to carry a plate but how many people can run a kitchen? Valerie took to it pretty well, especially with Emily adding suggestions, and every day the babies would come to work with us and sit up there on the counter together and coo and cry and let us take turns feeding them and playing with them and flipping burgers, and it was so much fun I knew that if I didn't get out of Wagon Wheel soon I was going to spend the rest of my life there.

Even so, Marcusette was three months old by the time I got it together to leave. It took me that long to save up enough to buy a cheap car, and it would have taken longer except that one day, in a fit of impatience, I walked over to the casino and put three quarters in Blanche's favorite slot machine. It was a triple-pay-off machine, which is why it cost triple, and no one in the place was more surprised than me when I won the damned thing. It played some corny carousel-type song, the lights on top of it flashed on and off, and so many quarters poured into my hands that they spilled over onto the flour like silver rain and I had to go to the kitchen to get an empty cooking oil can and rinse it out to collect them. When I came back out, Blanche was standing over my haul like a guard dog just waiting for someone to tease it.

"Beginner's luck," she sniffed at me.

"Karma," I said. We both smiled.

After that I had enough to pick up a second-hand jalopy and even buy some more clothes for Marcusette. People figured I'd leave any day, and still I found myself holding back, dawdling.

The last day, I went over to Emily's house and gave her a hug and a box of chocolates. Then I went by Finer Diner and gave Val my *Joy of Cooking*. "I think it belongs here," I said. "It brought me good luck, and it'll do the same for you. Plus, you can see what people liked best by looking for where the grease stains are." Valerie hugged me and, and so did Helen. They gave me a big bag with food for the road—fried chicken and sodas and even some fruit. They both kissed Marcusette and asked me to write.

Then I went by Paradise Mobile Homes to say my toughest goodbye, to Blanche. I could have driven with my eyes closed; the last few weeks, I'd spent lots of time there, getting two amazing tattoos.

Yes, I'd said I never would get tattooed. Yes, I'm a coward when it comes to pain. Yes, the thought of Blanche with a needle had still given me a couple of qualms. But the idea of getting tattooed had come to me pretty soon after Marcusette was born, and finally it had grown too big for me to pretend it wasn't important.

Maybe it started that first time I held Marcusette, and realized I wasn't alone anymore. Or maybe it was the first time she stayed up all night crying and I cried along with her, letting go of Rosie.

Rosie was gone from my dreams forever. I knew that with total certainty, the same way I knew that Marcus was resting easier now. She was in my heart, deep in my mind, but I knew that I would never see her or hear her childish voice again. The space she'd filled in my imagination was open and tender to the touch. Not empty—never empty—but open to the life ahead. And still...

"I have no remembrance of Rosie," I told Blanche over a cup of tea one day, as Marcusette slept in a nest of blankets on the couch. Blanche and I had started fresh after she rushed me to the hospital. Clearly, her having saved me and Marcusette more than made up for what had gone before, and in time, I told her everything—my crime, my penance, my promise to Marcus. She understood now about the glass of bleach. She even understood about Francisco.

"What makes you think you're going to forget her?"

"I don't mean that *I* would forget her. But there's no picture of her, no words. There isn't even much of a grave. It's like she never existed, except to me."

"You could tattoo her name on your heart."

I shook my head, feeling sad but not devastated. "That's what Marcus did for me. It would always make me think of his death."

She poured more tea for both of us. "Marcus tattooed your name on his heart? You never told me that."

"Yeah. It was his second tattoo."

"What was the first one?"

I didn't feel she was prying. With Blanche, it was professional interest. "A dragon that came up his arm. It was beautiful, I used to love to touch it."

"Was it a sleeve?" Blanche asked me.

I knew from the time I'd stayed with her that she meant, did it cover his whole upper arm? "No, it sort of wrapped around his bicep and then around his back and over his shoulder. The head came back down toward his chest." I could picture it so vividly. Why wasn't it killing me to remember these things?

Blanche pointed to the flash, the drawings that took up most of her living room walls. "Do you see anything like it over there?"

I went over and looked closely. There were evil dragons, smirking dragons, drunk-looking dragons, fire-breathing dragons. "No," I said, "these are more like cartoons. His dragon was... dignified."

Blanche went to the shelf and got down a book that she brought to the table. "Like this?" She rifled through it, found the page.

"Yes." I thought about crying, but that moment had already passed. "More like that."

"He probably had a Japanese design." She bent her head and read from the text. *"The Japanese dragon can live in both air and water. It is thought to be both wise and benevolent, with a fluid, graceful power that is the ultimate resolution of yin and yang."*

She looked at me. "The power of male and female. Kind and wise and fiercely protective."

Now I did cry. The tears spilled over my hands like rain. "God, I miss him. He was just like that. He would have loved Marcusette so much."

Blanche just let me cry it out. After a long while, I sniffed the tears back and dried my face with the back of my hand.

"Think about it, Grace," she said. "It might turn out to be just what you need."

I did think about it, for weeks after that, and spent lots of time looking through Blanche's books. She'd been right about the dragons. If I wanted to commemorate Marcus, that was surely the way to go. But nowhere did I see a picture that reminded me in any way of Rosie. And Rosie was the one I couldn't move on without laying to rest.

By now, everyone knew what I was considering. "Just draw something," Helen said in her usual, no-nonsense way.

"I can't draw," I pointed out.

"Blanche can. You just need to get her started."

I thought about it, late that night, curled up in my cabin with Marcusette tucked under my arm. I listened to her baby breathing and thought about what a blessing she was. Rosie would have been the same way; an angel, too good for the life she was born into.

I fell asleep thinking about that, and the next morning I knew what to do. Blanche sketched out a picture of a tiny heart with angel wings. The heart was torn, but not broken. Silver tears dripped from its wound.

"That's it," I said. "That, and a dragon."

Blanche looked at her handiwork and nodded. "Put it over your heart," she said. "That way your heart and hers will be close together."

We started that day. I sat half-naked in Blanche's chair while she sterilized the needle in her autoclave. "This is going to hurt," she said, and I didn't have any doubt about it. Turns out *hurt* didn't begin to cover it. It felt like being ripped up with a can opener at a thousand pounds pressure.

I didn't scream—I couldn't, not with Marcusette lying ten feet away, snoozing to the white noise whine of Blanche's needle—but I must have turned ghost-pale.

"Chicken," Blanche sneered.

"Oh, fuck you!" I said.

"This is the worst," she told me conversationally. "Lots of nerve endings on your breast. You won't even feel it when we do the dragon on your leg."

By that time I figured she was right. I wouldn't feel the dragon because I wasn't going to have the guts to do it. But when she finished the angel heart, just about an hour later, I was so moved by how beautiful it was that I almost forgot how it had felt.

"I think you were right about not doing her name," Blanche said. "This way has more class. It's subtle."

And then we both starting laughing, because the one thing you could never accuse Blanche of was *subtle*. But that's just what she'd created for me. I felt like she really did understand.

The dragon was another piece of business entirely. It took days to get Blanche's sketch just right, choose the colors, plan how it would lay. As for the tattooing itself, she probably spent forty hours on it, divided up over fifteen days. I knew she wasn't charging me full price, and still it came to plenty of money, but I didn't care. I wanted it right.

"So, when are you gonna leave?" she asked, the day she put on the dragon's whiskers. It was hard for either of us to admit she was finished.

I thought about the last time I'd left Wagon Wheel. Blanche had been so mad at me it had taken a year and almost dying to get our friendship back on track. "Before I answer, you'll have to promise to not be pissed at me when I come back."

She lit up a cigarette, like she always did at the end of a session, if I'd left Marcusette with Val. "When's that gonna be?" she asked me.

"I don't know. I haven't left yet."

"Oh, fuck that." She made a face and stubbed out her smoke in the overflowing ashtray. "You don't come back, I'm coming to visit *you*. Give those San Francisco folks something they can really gawk at."

It didn't take me long to pack. Marcusette owned more clothes than I did, and all of them fit together in a pillowcase. Mine, I shoveled into a bundle and tied it up in my denim jacket. The biggest things in my '77 Valiant were a giant box of disposable diapers and the bag of food Val and Helen had packed for us.

I was shaking a little when I went to say goodbye to Blanche. Even though she'd said she was OK, I didn't want history to repeat itself. And truthfully, the last few months, we'd gotten so close it was hard to leave her.

"You come visit us," I said.

"Make sure you stay out of the sun 'til that dragon heals. Use that ointment, and whatever you do, *don't* pick the scabs."

I'd already been through this routine with the angel heart, which had healed up easily and true, so I knew she was just telling me that stuff to get out of saying goodbye.

I said, "You gonna give Marcusette a kiss?"

"Do I look like a woman who kisses babies?" she shot back.

"You look like a godmother. So suck it up and wish us luck."

"Good luck." She hugged me and Marcusette. "Tell Francisco I said hi. And if you don't bring this kid for a visit, I'll chase you to hell and back."

I said, "That's in the other direction." And then I had to get out of there.

I drove without looking back or stopping. It would have been harder if I hadn't been distracted—by fear, and by the letter burning in my pocket.

Just over the California line, I found a payphone and dialed Francisco's number. Marcusette was sleeping in the car seat everyone had given me for a going away present, tucked beside Blondell and Dena's doll that I still thought was ugly as sin. With the back seat window open, I could hear her rhythmic breathing. I hoped it meant she would sleep through this phone call.

Someone picked up on the fourth ring. "Hel-o."

Damian, I guessed. The seven-year-old.

"Hi. Can I speak to…" *your Daddy,* I'd almost said, but who knew what Sarah Jane's children called him. "Can I speak to Francisco, please?"

"He's at work," Damian said, in the voice of a little boy who's been through more than other kids. "Do you wanna speak to my Mommy?"

I thought about hanging up the phone and driving straight through to San Francisco. I might have done it a year ago, but now I knew it was out of the question.

Damian's mother picked up the phone. "Hello," she said, surprising me with what sounded like an English accent.

Well, if she was surprising me, that was nothing compared to how I was about to surprise her.

"Hello," I said. "My name is Grace, and I knew your husband in Wagon Wheel."

We stayed in Boron for almost a week. Francisco and Sarah Jane had a guest room, and she'd saved her children's' basinet, so Marcusette even got to sleep in a bed for the first time in her life. She liked it so much that, when we left, Sarah Jane gave it to us to take.

I can't say it was an easy week. Everyone was confused and emotional. I was lucky that Sarah Jane was just as Francisco had described her—calm, or maybe wise was the word. You could see she loved her new husband, and once she got it clear that we weren't going to be fighting over him, her choices were pretty simple: To love and accept his other kid, or to cop a hard-nosed attitude. There wasn't much chance she would call that one wrong.

Francisco had a more complex time. I know he felt betrayed and angry, especially when I told him the truth about how I'd gotten pregnant with Marcusette. I know I didn't have to tell him that, but I wanted to be honest from now on. Francisco had talked once about what we owed the dead, and that made me hope that eventually he would understand—and maybe, eventually, forgive.

The first few days, our conversations were mostly of the *how could you do it?* variety. But after a while he got tired of that, the way people who are happy get tired of feeling bad. He still wasn't okay with me, not in any meaningful sense, but he started talking about other things and we spent a lot of my last few nights there walking around town after he got off work, and talking about things that had happened to both of us before we met. I have to say that Francisco was a good listener. He wanted to know more about his little girl's mother.

The people in the house who took it best were Damian and little LizAnn. For all that they looked like angels in the photo, they were flesh and blood children, very real. I thought they would be jealous of the baby, but they thought she was a wonderful toy. Damian was very responsible—you could see who'd become the family's little man three years ago when his father died—and LizAnn was a five-year-old hellion, pure and simple. It scared me to death to see her with Marcusette, and finally I broke down and told Francisco why. After that, I was ready to leave. It made me feel vulnerable to have told him about Rosie, to have shared the most horrible thing in my life; and we'd been in Boron for almost a week. It was time for everyone to get back to real life.

The morning we were set to go, Francisco arranged to be late to the mine and Damian and LizAnn stayed home from school. Sarah Jane made a big pancake breakfast and then they all gave us going away presents. Hers was a carrier for Marcusette, the kind that straps around your back so you're holding the baby to your chest. Francisco gave me two hundred dollars, and Damian and LizAnn made a card telling Marcusette that they loved their baby sister. It almost made me want to cry and I would have if, like Blanche, I hadn't had a reputation to maintain. As it was, they made me swear on my heart to come back for a visit as soon as I could.

"You're sure you're okay?" Francisco asked as he strapped little Marcusette into her car seat.

"I'm sure." I watched his big hands adjusting the delicate straps that would hold her in place. I was probably more surprised than anyone to realize that I *was* all right—more all right than I'd been for a long time. Maybe more all right than I'd been ever.

"You promise to call?" he asked again, which made it the seventeenth time I'd promised.

"I'll call you every Sunday. And you've got the number where I'll be," I reminded him.

"You promise to come back soon?"

I did, and then Sarah Jane had to drag him away, saying, "Let her get on the road, Francisco. You don't want them driving after dark."

"You're right," he said, and he smiled at his wife. He opened the car door and leaned in one more time and stroked Marcusette's downy cheekbones, the same way I'd done the first time I held her in the hospital. "Goodbye, Mami." He leaned over and kissed her. "I love you, little girl. Come back soon."

"We will," I said, and then I drove away.

♥

I only stopped once, to take out Joe's letter and read it one more time, for courage.

> *Gracie, did you put a spell on me? I haven't seen you for almost a year, but I still think about you every day. Not about your body— hot as I am for it* (and there he'd drawn a smiley face)*—no, I think about your fighting spirit.*

When you and Anna May showed up in Foster, I was so caught up in her problems, and then in what was going on with us, that I didn't give much thought to how scary it must have been for you to bring her out of that situation. You didn't say much about it at the time, but from things Anna May has told Lillian this last year, I can see that it was true heroism on your part. Anna May always said that you were her hero, and at first I thought she was being poetic, but she's not—she means exactly what she says.

I've been thinking a lot about heroism these days because I find myself so lacking in it. I know Lillian told you about Fred busting me. When we were together that week in Foster, you tried to tell me that you thought I was strung out, but I wasn't ready to hear the truth and I didn't get any more ready over time. That's why Fred had to do something so extreme—there was no other way to get through to me.

God I was so pissed at him! (I was pissed at you, too, when you up and left; it took me a long time to calm down.) I thought he was lower than a rattlesnake, but now I can see that I didn't leave him much choice. I was too far gone to understand at the time, just like I was too far gone to hear a lot of things you were trying to tell me, like for instance about my mother. You tried to make me see that she was a person, too, that maybe she had reasons for the things she did, whether I liked them or not, but I wasn't having it. I was too busy staying shut down and coked up.

Well, that all ended about six months ago. I was lucky to get a plea bargain that didn't involve my doing jail time, and lucky to get into a good rehab program, but I'll never work in law enforcement again. I don't know what kind of work I'm going to do—I've been bartending to get by (didn't you say you used to do that?)—but I'm thinking about enrolling at San Francisco State to study something that'll let me help other people not screw up the way I did.

Gracie, I don't know what's happened to you this last year, aside from the little bits that you told Lillian. For all I know you could

have settled down and gotten married, or you might have made
some other plans. I don't even know if you're going to get this letter.
But if you do get it, and if you're interested, I hope you'll come
and visit me. I won't load you up with a lot of expectations, but I
also won't lie by pretending this is a casual invitation. I've never
stopped wondering whether the way we got along last year was
unique to one place and time, or whether it could happen again.

Whether or not you come to San Francisco, whether or not that
spark gets fired up again, I hope you'll stay in touch with me,
and I hope you'll take good care of yourself. What I want most is
for you to have a good life.

You deserve it, Gracie. Trust me.

                                                              Your friend, Joe

P.S. As someone once said, think about me!

Well, I had been thinking about him, a lot. Thinking about being back in
his arms. Thinking about having him to talk to. Wondering if he would love
Marcusette. How could he not, when he seemed to love me?

It was hot on the desert road, and the Valiant's air conditioner barely cut
it. I opened the windows and turned up the radio and revved the engine and
spun my wheels. I told Marcusette to hang onto her hat, and I'm pretty sure
she gurgled back at me.

I'd never felt such total freedom, heading north with my precious
daughter. I knew the miles would melt beneath my tires. I knew the last year
would fall away. I knew, somehow, things would be better. I was going home,
and maybe I would stay.

♥ ♥ ♥

ABOUT THE AUTHOR

JEZRA KAYE is the author of a civil war romance novella, *Rebel Heart,* a poetry collection, *Kicking: Love Poems*, and two business books: *Managing the Unmanageable: How to Motivate Even the Most Unruly Employee*, which she co-authored with Anne Loehr, and *Speak Like Yourself... No, Really!* a book on communications which will be released in the fall of 2012.

Jezra is also a speaker coach, speechwriter, and President of the coaching and consulting firm *Speak Up for Success*. She lives in Brooklyn, New York, with her husband, jazz musician Jerome Harris. They have one grown daughter, Laurika Harris-Kaye.

TO ORDER THE TATTOOED HEART,
Visit www.thetattooedheart.com

3Ring Press
New York

Come From Nowhere
a novel by Ellen Greenfield

In the early hours of July 13, 1977 in New York City, seven female characters—ranging from a nine-year-old girl and her Greek immigrant mother, to a young chef losing her vision, to a brown rat—share the same subway platform. They are unaware that the next 24 hours will see them struggling to find their way home, both literally and metaphorically, when a historic blackout hits the city.

"Written with grace and perceptive intelligence, the narrative that follows is humane, mysterious, tragic, compelling and beautiful."

> —Chuck Wachtel, author of *3/03*, *The Gates*, and *Joe The Engineer*

∞

Mutually Assured Destruction
poetry by Aaron Samuels

"In his first major book effort, Aaron Samuels gives notice to the poetry world that he is a g-force to be reckoned with. Driven by his switchblade wit, and uncanny knack for melding accessible, everyday dialogue with seamless prose and honest, gut-wrenching narratives, the poems in Mutually Assured Destruction are bound to strike a chord with anyone who has ever known the singularly joyful agony of growing up on the wrong side of normal."

> —Joshua Bennett, star of the HBO series *Brave New Voices*

∞

Kicking: Love Poems
by Jezra Kaye

From the author of **The Tattooed Heart** and **Rebel Heart**, this collection of poems takes readers from the communes of 1960s San Francisco to the halls of Wall Street in 1980s New York to the wilds of contemporary, middle-aged marriage. A fresh, poignant look at the ever-changing, ever-challenging face of love.

www.ingramcontent.com/pod-product-compliance
Lightning Source LLC
Chambersburg PA
CBHW030033180626
46810CB00001B/349